Second Edition July 2023

Book design by Garrett R. Melick

ISBN 978-1-0881-2517-5 (Paperback)

Table of Contents

Welcome to the Milky Way

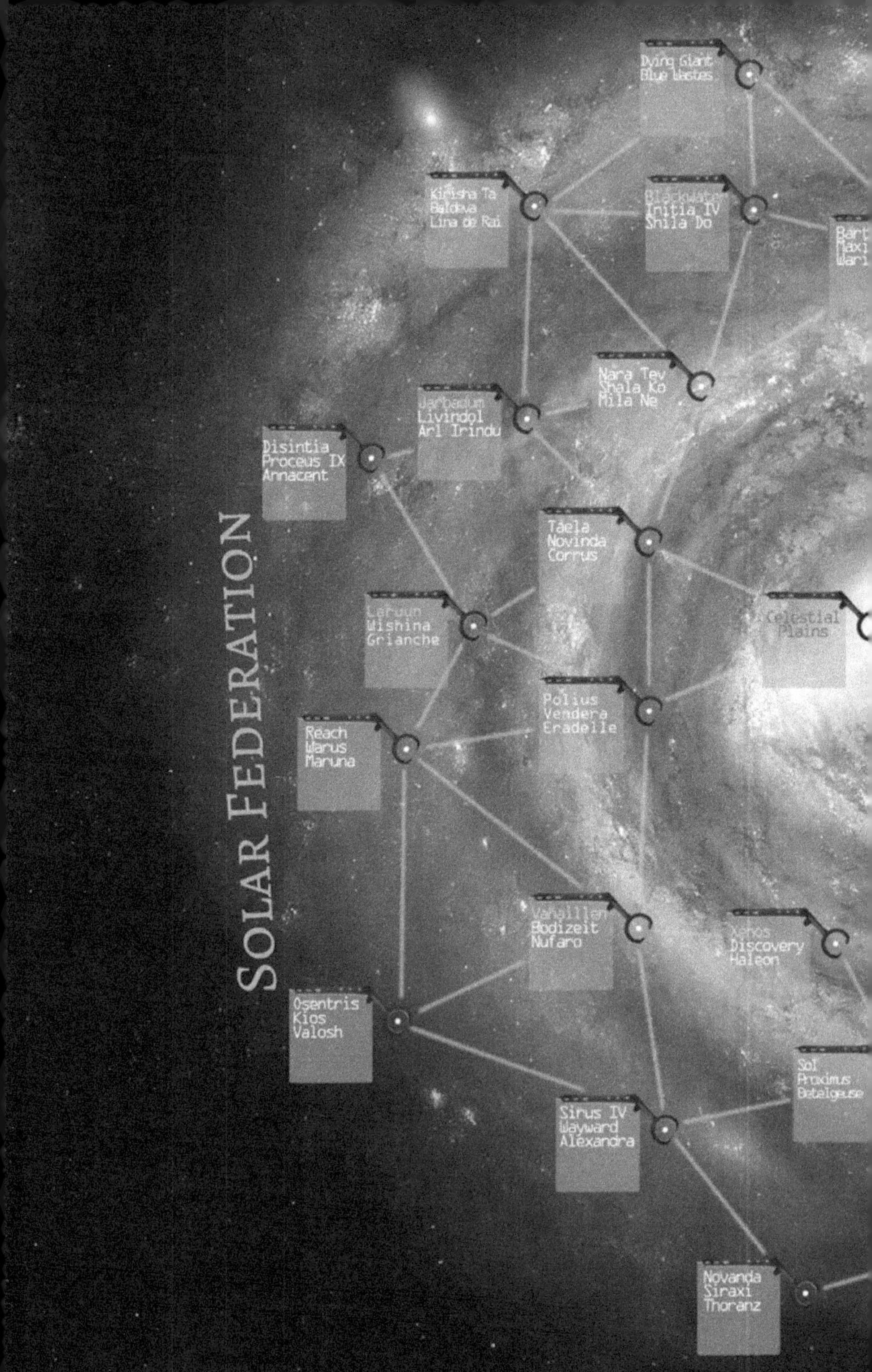

THE MILKY WAY

SOLAR FEDERATION

Dying Giant
Blue Wastes

Kirisha Ta
Baldeva
Lina de Rai

Initia IV
Shila Do

Nara Tev
Shala Ko
Mila Ne

Livindol
Arl Irindu

Disintia
Proceus IX
Annacent

Taela
Novinda
Corrus

Celestial
Plains

Wishina
Griancha

Polius
Vendera
Eradelle

Reach
Warus
Maruna

Bodizeit
Nufaro

Discovery
Haleon

Osentris
Kios
Valosh

Sol
Proximus
Betelgeuse

Sirus IV
Wayward
Alexandra

Novanda
Siraxi
Thoranz

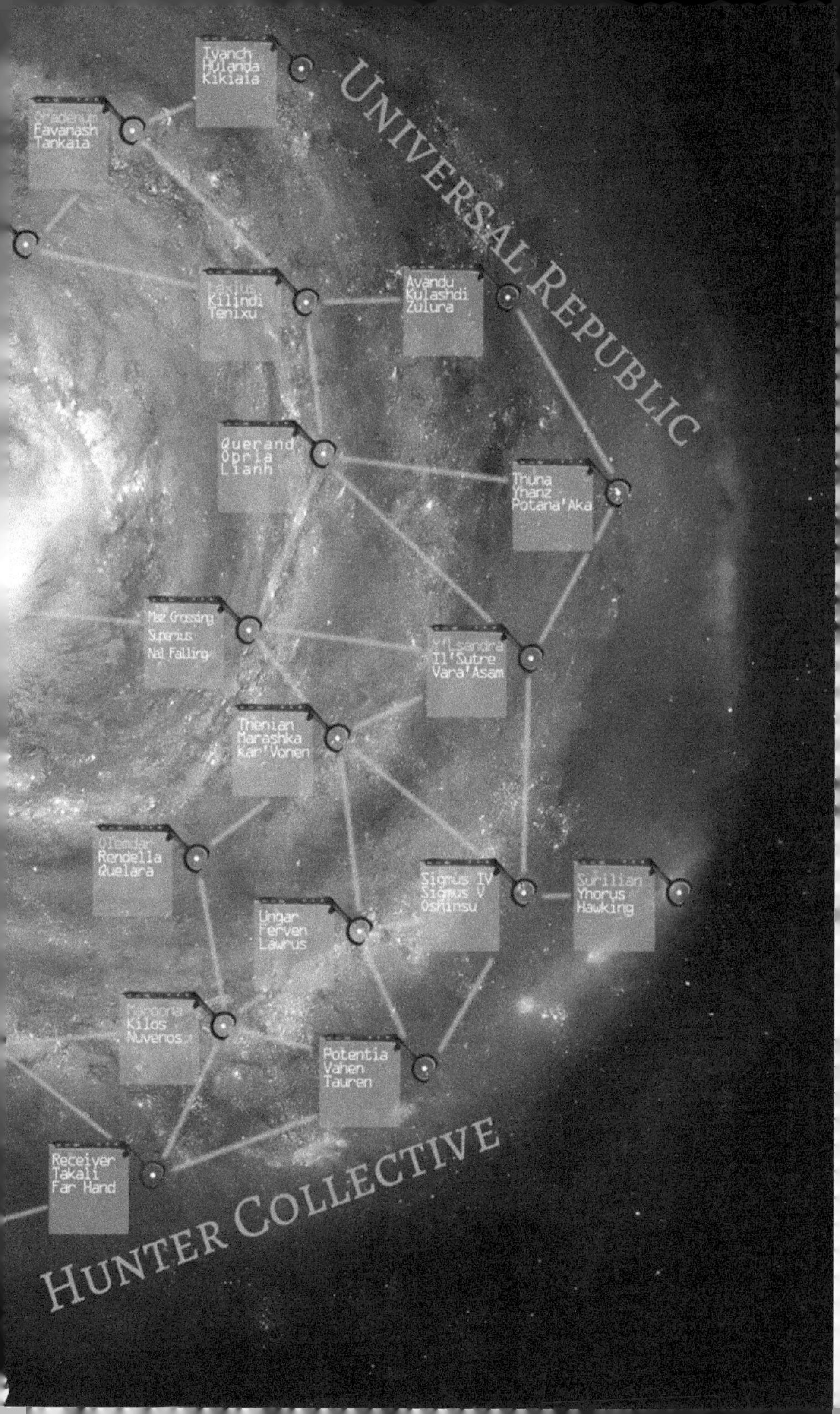

Universal Republic

Iyanch
Hulanga
Kikiaia

Eavanash
Tankaia

Kilindi
Tenixu

Avandu
Kulashdi
Zulura

Querand
Opria
Lianh

Thuna
Yhanz
Potana'Aka

Nal Falling

Il'Sutre
Vara'Asam

Thenian
Marashka
Kar'Vonen

Rendella
Quelara

Sigmus IV
Sigmus V
Oshinsu

Surilian
Yhorus
Hawking

Ungar
Ferven
Lawrus

Kilos
Nuvenos

Potentia
Vahen
Tauren

Receiver
Takali
Far Hand

Hunter Collective

Furelle:
Surillia Ra
Galactic Date 59:47:070 5027

The western lowlands of Furelle are something to be admired if ever you have the chance. The water there sparkles a type of blue you could never begin to imagine. Houses lined rivers that stretched into the woods behind our little town, and you could hardly walk ten feet without nearly being tripped by some group of kids running about. Women and men would walk the streets, exchanging talk of the galactic markets, or the newest conflict between the Federation and the Republic. In all, our life was boring, but in a good way. It was boring in all the ways that you wanted a life to be. We always knew what the next day had in store for us.

At the time, I was only 14, and I think I took some part of that for granted. Even looking back now, I can understand why. My parents were scavengers, plain and simple. Furelle was loaded with tech from its last war, so it wasn't exactly difficult to find a haul, pull out the good parts, and bring them back to sell. It wasn't exactly a glamorous job, but it put food on the table for us.

As I said, though, I always seemed to look for more. Oft, one would find the kids of Surillia Ra around the waterfront, swimming about with the turtles and other fish of the sea. You might find others along the gold and white rocky mountain paths that seemed to stretch infinitely along the coast. The one place we were not to enter alone was the forest. You would be sure to find me there, even after the multiple scoldings I'd received. You would always find the most interesting things there, though, so how could I resist?

I remember the last day I entered those woods. It was a colder day, a sharp wind blowing through our town. Blackwater, our system's star, hung low by the horizon, threatening to dip almost as soon as it had risen, casting long shadows across us all. My feet pattered along the wet ground as I ran through the town, leaving deep marks in the mud and dirt. A grin stretched across my face as water splashed up, staining the black canvas of my pants, leaving grimy prints across my legs. My destination wasn't far. A small household at the end of the block.

Stopping to catch my breath as I pulled up, I took a moment to take the home in. It was much the same as almost any home in the town. A whitish-gray portable colony house that had been put up years ago now. I didn't know when Surillia Ra had been settled, but it was long before I'd been around. Despite its similarities to all the homes around it, this one seemed to stand out. Plants imported from around the galaxy bloomed from within windows, searching their way out into the open air to find the sun. Seamless improvements had been added on, such as a fireplace and chimney that puffed smoke from its tip. I took a deep breath, knocked, and waited, tugging at my jacket, straightening my collar, trying to look the slightest bit presentable.

When the door slid open, a heavyset man stood in the way. A thick, black, caterpillar-like mustache hung over his mouth, tickling at his lip as he spoke, looking at me under bushy eyebrows.

"William." He said, his tone flat, almost disappointed, "What do you want?"

"Hello, Mr. Illani!" I said, trying to appear as chipper and innocent as possible, "I was just wondering if Maurel might be free for a few hours." He sighed, getting on one knee, his eyes meeting mine.

"Ortell..." he reached forward and straightened my collar. "You heading back out there?" He asked, eyeing the line of trees in the distance. With a smile on my face, I shook my head no, and he sighed. "Alright son, you know there's no need to lie to me." He stood up, limping back into the house. I ducked inside, bathed in an orange glow as candles lined the edges of the room, taking a seat on the plush couch just under the window. Brown furs were draped from the walls, and the room smelled of cinnamon. It was familiar, almost more than my own home at this point. Mr. Illani cupped his hands to his mouth, calling out.

"Maurel! Ortell's here to see you!" A pair of footsteps could be heard clambering down the steps. A young woman stopped at the end of the stairway, her hands locked to the rail, looking in my direction with a spark in her eyes. A toothy grin stretched across her face as she vaulted over the banister, landing softly on the carpet. She ran over and pulled me to my feet. Her dad rolled her eyes, pointing to us. "Back before sundown now, the both of you. Understood?" We gave him a nod and ran out as he let out a breath.

Outside, Maurel stopped me, turning me about.

"Right, before we do anything…" She grabbed a handful of my red hair, pulling it back. I winced for a moment as she tied it up into a ponytail. "There we go." She dusted off her hands. I rubbed the back of my head, turning back to her. Maurel and I had been friends since we were children. We'd grown up together and explored together. Hell, the first time I'd secretly gotten drunk, it'd been with her. She stood a little taller than me, with moss-green eyes and hair dark as water at night. Her olive skin seemed to glow like a fire in Furelle's sun. Her adventurous spirit was the only one in the whole town that seemed to rival my own. I straightened myself up, brushing out my coat as she eyed me.

"Okay, so," She dragged me along, beginning to walk toward the woods. "What's the new gossip?" She asked.

"Alright, get this," I began, turning to face her, walking backward. "I was out there the other day, and you'll never guess what I stumbled across." I held my hands up in front of me, my boots sloshing through the thick mix below me. Maurel tapped her chin in mock inquisitiveness.

"Leeet meee gueessss… it was another old, crusty, Furin temple?" She asked, raising an eyebrow to look at me. I pouted a little at her.

"Well, you don't have to put it that way." I huffed before turning back to the trees. "Alright, yeah, it was another temple, but this one was *different*." Maurel was silent, so I continued. "This one had *ash* in it!" I said, looking back at her. Her brow was furrowed, not seeming to put the same links together I had. "You know, *Soulless* ash. You shoot them and they burst into the stuff." I spun back around before feeling her hand tighten onto my shoulder.

"Whoa whoa, wait." I looked back up. Her face was stern. "Listen, I'm all about exploring the woods, but Soulless stuff is *dangerous.*" I scoffed.

"Well, yeah, but like," I patted my chest, "I'm a scavenger! I'm used to handling old, dangerous tech." She seemed unpersuaded. "Maurel, just think of the cool stuff we'll find in there!" I clasped my hands together. She took a moment before letting out a long, deep breath.

"Alright… alright fine. Since I can't convince you," she patted my arm as she hopped ahead of me. "The least I can do is make sure you don't get yourself in *too* much trouble." I grinned, running off after her.

Ferns and thin vines whipped past us as we hurried through the trees. There wasn't much light left in the day, so we had to be quick about it. The winter months never had many hours of daylight, and some days, the sun never came out at all. The air was frigid, and you could tell it wouldn't be very long till the snow would start to come down and the rivers would freeze over. Doing this wouldn't be possible once that happened. That's when things would get boring. We had to do this now.

I squeezed my way between two trees into a small grove, flicking on a small flashlight. Barely any light broke through the dense canopy, especially at this time of the year. Dead leaves and rocks littered the ground as I popped through, feeling the wet mulch squelch under me. Maurel looked around as I stopped.

"So… where is it?" She asked. I smiled, kneeling down, beginning to brush aside the leaves and dirt to reveal a half-rusted metal door surrounded by intricately carved stone, inlaid with shimmering purple and blue crystal. I reached for the latch, grunting as I began to pull it open.

"Got my foot caught in the hole when I was- urgh -out here the other day," I said. The door made a loud WHUMP as it hit the dirt. Birds squawked, fluttering away. A steep stairway led into the black below. Maurel pursed her lips at me, looking in.

"So *that's* how you twisted your ankle." She said.

"It was well hidden! Not my fault it was all covered in plants." She looked up at me.

"You're telling me you went in here with a twisted ankle?"

"I mean, it wasn't *that* bad, and I only went in a little bit!" She shook her head. Hesitantly, she took a step onto the stone. Once she was sure of her footing, she began to descend. I followed closely behind her, reaching my hand up over her shoulder to shine our light further in. Down and down we went until the narrow tunnel down opened into a massive chamber. Our every step echoed across the vastness of the temple; our nostrils hit with the smell of a thousand years of age. As I shined my light across the walls, we found ourselves met with statues that stood to the ceiling of alien warriors, their bodies protected by carapace and shell, but their skin scaly and reptilian underneath it. Many wielded weapons from a time long ago, wore makeshift mining gear as armor.

Maurel regarded it all with attention, gaping at the sheer size of these things. As we reached the bottom, we looked up to them. It almost felt as if their eyes bore holes through us. I swallowed, taking a deep breath as I looked forward, searching the ground. We heard a crunch and looked down; seeing the pile of ash left across the ground, we kneeled beside it and I swiped my finger across it, leaving a line through it as my finger was stained black. Maurel slapped at my hand.

"Don't *touch* it. Who knows what it'll do to you!" She said. I shrugged.

"What's the worst it can do? It's ash!" I stood up as she muttered.

"My pa says that stuff'll turn you into one of them…" I rolled my eyes, spinning back around on my heels.

"Re*lax*, I'm fine! I'm not gonna turn into one of them creepy lil…" I gestured with my arms, faking my hands as being big swords, gently chopping at her shoulders. She laughed, pushing me off her.

"Alright, *fine,* you aren't gonna turn into one of them." She stood up and wiped off my finger. "Still probably a bad idea to touch it." I sighed.

"Fiiine. Let's just look around and see if we find anything cool." I said, moving deeper inside. As I swept my light over the ground, the beam passed over something pale and white. I jumped back briefly, bumping into Maurel. She didn't say anything, but rather steadied out my hand, pointing it at a pile of bones on the ground. I grimaced a little; seeing it lying on its side, the ribs broken in. It was a Furin, much like the ones in the statues. Red marks lined the shell on its head, almost completely faded with time. It had some sort of primitive rifle clutched in its hands. Instinctively, I began to reach for it.

"The dead should be left to their lives beyond." A voice broke through the silent darkness. Maurel and I shrieked, turning about. Our light shined on a figure that towered over us like a mountain. He was a Furin, his face wrinkled and grizzled with age. Scars lined his skin, and his beady black eyes struck us like arrows. He looked to the bones behind us. "That one was married. You can tell by their marks," he said, before looking back to me, "Let those who were loved rest in their peace." Slowly, and shakily, I nodded, as did Maurel. He cleared his throat, leaning down to look at us. "What are you doing out here? Surillian kids are restricted from the forests, are they not?" Maurel spoke up.

"Sir w-we were just curious what was out here. We didn't-" he cut her off.

"So, you are here when you are not supposed to be?" He asked. We nodded, looking at the ground. The old Furin sighed. "It is dangerous here. Come. I will take you back." We nodded, following him.

He held us both at the shoulders, guiding our way to the surface. The sun had just hit the mountains in the distance. A few more minutes and it would be dark. The old Furin turned around, shutting the door to the temple, tracing a sigil over it. The handle glowed blue for a moment before fading out. He reached out, spreading dirt and leaves over it. Curiously, I tapped his shoulder. He looked up.

"Sir… what was that?" I asked. He grunted.

"Magic. I sealed the entrance so no one else can enter." He said. I tilted my head.

"I thought Furins didn't have magic?" He paused for a moment before finishing up, patting the soil.

"It can always be learned." He said, a somber tone in his voice as he looked at the entrance to the temple. "Let us go." He turned, guiding us. As we moved closer and closer to the town, something felt off. A scent lingered in the air, something like… burning. He seemed to smell it too. Looking up at him, I could see a worried look on his face.

It was when we broke through the tree line that our worries were confirmed. A fire from the depths of hell spread over the town, erupting it in a blaze of orange, and that's when I saw it. A ship hung low over the water, black as pitch, with sharp square edges and an eerie purple glow. The worst part was its engines, roaring with an ungodly howl. Soulless.

The Furin stood in shock for a moment, enough time to break free from his grasp. I felt him try to grab at me again as he shouted.

"Child, wait!" I heard him grunt as Maurel broke free as well. She sprinted after me as I ran into the town. She grabbed me, dragging me under a building as a pale figure jumped down. We watched as a woman was dragged down into the dirt. A look of horror flashed over her face in one moment, before a bone-like blade was driven through her chest. We watched it sink deeper into her, getting a clearer view of her attacker. A grotesque form, skin dry and pale, muscles pulsating as it leaned down, its head drawing closer to hers. It was featureless, save for an arcane symbol etched into it. We saw the black pit in its chest seem to suck the very life from her as we watched her very being change, seeming to match that of her attacker. I looked on in horror before scrambling back. Maurel stood beside me on the other side.

"Soulless… but," I started, looking to her, "Weren't they only in the Republic territory? What are they doing here? Where are the Celestials? The Federation?" She put a finger to my lips.

"William! We don't have time for questions; we *need* to get out." I took a deep breath, my body shaking as I nodded. She looked around, pointing. "There, shuttles. We need to get out now!" She grabbed my shirt, pulling me along. The streets were filled with these creatures, dragging people from homes and slaughtering them. In the distance, we could hear the sound of weapons firing, holding off the Soulless from the shuttles. We passed by an alley looking out onto the main road. I turned to look and immediately knew I shouldn't have. Maurel stopped too, as we watched her father dragged out. A skinnier one, this one with long razor-sharp claws, had its hand wrapped around his throat. He struggled, punching and kicking, and then he looked at us. He yelled for us to move, but I couldn't. He screamed and waved, but I watched as the other hand plunged into his chest. Blood spewed from his lips as time seemed to move again. I grabbed Maurel. I could only assume what happened to my family, and part of me didn't want to know.

I pulled us past the last rows of buildings, seeing the lines of gunmen firing past us. I caught a whiff of ash as a bullet whizzed past, hitting something directly behind us. Ducking past the soldiers, we entered the mob of hysterical townspeople. Maurel was still in shock, her eyes wide, her breathing ragged. I couldn't say I was much better. I coughed, realizing now how much my lungs burned from the smoke. We felt the ground shake as a building exploded, sending us to the ground. One of the shuttles attempted to take off, but the shockwave sent it back into the water. The fire was spreading fast, and the Soulless were approaching. The soldiers were screaming at us to get on the shuttles, to get out. Maurel composed herself enough to get up and pull me on.

The shuttle rumbled as the doors closed, the only light being through a small window on the side. I pressed myself to it, my knuckles white as I gripped the sill, staring out as we lifted off. My chest tightened as I saw the smoke rising from the town, blotting out the sky. Tears welled in my eyes as Maurel put her hands on my shoulder. As we exited the atmosphere, I continued to watch, seeing one Soulless ship after another begin to pour into the system. The Celestials, our so-called protectors, were nowhere to be found. I think some part of me died that day. I stepped back out of Maurel's arms, gripping the rail on the ceiling. I looked first at the ground, and then to the pilot.

"Where will we go?" I asked. The pilot kept their eyes forward.

"To Draenica." They said. It sounded like they were trying to hold on to some hope that everything would be okay, but you could hear the cracks in it. "We… we hope they'll take us." I nodded, looking back out at Furelle, my home, in flames. "Hey kid," I looked back to them, "you'll be okay… right?" I sighed, and then I began to just sob, tears rolling down my cheeks as I curled up. Maurel beside me, but in the end, broke down as well.

After what felt like hours, I just… couldn't cry anymore. There was nothing left. Maurel had fallen asleep. The others in the shuttle weren't looking much better. Many were injured or burned. Solemnly, I stood up, looking out the front of the ship to the new planet. Draenica, they'd called it. Our sister planet; one spot over in the system. I could only hope that what lay there was better than where we'd come at this point. I didn't have much more to hold on to.

Minutes later, we'd gotten clearance to land in a port just outside one of the cities. Everyone was woken, each of us told to stand and be ready to be received. Maurel and I stood close. As the doors opened, we were greeted by the dull brown, hot, rocky landscape. We looked to each other, linked arms, and stepped out into our new lives.

5028

By Garrett R. Melick

DRAENICA: THE ASHLANDS

GALACTIC DATE 00:08:380 5028

The next ten years passed by in what felt like a flash. The Second Soulless Celestial War had raged on the entirety of that decade, and a new Galactic year was ushered in. A lot of us from Furelle had spread to the stars in search of new homes. Maurel had gone her own way in life, while I'd chosen to stay on Draenica. It wasn't *too* bad once you got used to it. The constant volcanic activity was manageable if you had the right gear, and the Draens were generally kind people, with… a few exceptions.

The Draen are a more bird-like people. Wings, feathers, horns, and such. They had these big ol' eyes, all one color and not a pupil to be seen. You'd typically only see two types of Draen, each with their own coloration. The Frev'n were black from head to toe, with green eyes and a sharp set of munchers. They were the good ones, as I'd come to find out. I was afraid of them when I first landed, but they were good to me and Maurel growing up. The other kind were the Oc'r. Opposing their brethren; they spouted white features with a set of bright orange eyes. They were the ones you needed to watch out for. Some of the most cold-hearted people I've met, they are. I don't want to generalize, though. There are good and bad on both sides.

But like I said, it's definitely not the worst place to live, even if that's what a lot of people would like to have you believe. If it had been up to me back then, I probably would have tried to live out the rest of my life there. Fate had other plans for me.

My speeder zipped over ashy dunes, a high whir blaring from its engine. I tipped back as I hit the peak of the dune, soaring off over the ground. As I touched back down, a burst of ash and dust erupted, spraying into the air. I wiped my goggles clean, leaning forward and regaining control. Twisting and turning, I made my way through the Ashlands, a hazardous environment stretching between the settlements. Draens had adapted environmental shields from other races to protect their homes from the constant volcanic activity on the planet. Not many people chose to brave the Ashlands if they didn't have to. If they did, they usually did so in the comfort of a ship or car. I didn't have that luxury. Not a lot of money to be made here as a Terran. Oc'r made sure of that after being forced to loan out their home to aliens. Can see their side, but it's easy to be bitter on the short end of the stick.

Either way, I had something out here I needed to get my hands on. It wasn't easy to see through the storm, but I could just barely make out the flashing red light of a crashed ship. Three days was our rule as scrappers. Once that had passed and no one had come to claim it, it was free game. I'd usually come out the first day to scope and assist anyone who might have been on board. This one had been a Solar Federation dropship, likely trying to escape from the battle on Furelle. Didn't get a chance to ask the crew. Dead by the time I'd gotten there. I buried them beside the ship.

As I pulled up, I set my foot down beside a fallen set of sticks I'd used to mark the graves. Sighing, I down, the wind whipping over my cowl. I grabbed one of the sticks, thrusting it back into the ground upright. I made sure to twist and dig it in, hoping it wouldn't fall over again, before doing the same to the one beside it. I paused, hearing another speeder pull up beside mine. Someone else stepped off, walking toward me.

"You always get this sentimental?" A thin, smooth voice asked from behind me. I grunted as I got to my feet, turning to face a dark Draen lady. She was lanky, covered in similar gear as mine. The wind pulled at her cloak, much of her face obscured by either her hood or the mask she wore to breathe out here.

"The dead deserve to lie in peace respectfully," I said, nodding toward the ship. "You gonna help me out with this, Tara?" I could sense a sly smile underneath that mask of hers.

"Why else would I be out here, Ortell? You know that where you scrap, I'm there to reap the benefits." I rolled my eyes, beginning to trudge toward the wreck.

"Of course you do," I said, matter-of-factly. "we're roommates. You get all your info from me." I paused, pulling out a plasma cutter. "Thought you said you were taking the day off." She shrugged, leaning against the wing.

"Was going to. Got bored. Don't like the Shack when it's empty. So I decided to follow you." I pulled my gloves off to climb the hull, hauling myself to the top of the ship, setting myself down beside the core. Looking down to where she was leaning, I tossed a tool bag.

"Here. Make yourself useful and start getting those engines taken apart while I work on the main drive core." Tara let out a less-than-subtle groan, pulling out a few tools. "Hey, you wanna get a cut of the pay, you gotta do the work too," I said, adjusting my goggles, starting to cut away at the plating around the core.

"What's so special about this ship that you wanted to get here so early, anyway?" She called up to me.

"This is an older ship." I explained, "The Federation recently swapped over to newer parts. A lot of it is incompatible with current ships." I finished making my cut, the paneling falling through, making a nice hole into the center of the core. "Our main crashes here are all Feds. New parts are worthless, but…" I dropped down, reaching into the center of the engine, cutting a few parts, adjusting a few hoses, before pulling out a large canister, and hoisting it up onto the hull. "People are willing to pay a good chunk for these older parts." I dragged myself out, nabbing the casing. I slid to the ash below, shoving the end of the part into the ground. Tara plucked away at the engines behind me, nodding.

"Alright, that makes sense but," she struggled for a moment with a bolt, swearing as her hand slipped and smacked the metal, "Fuck…" She wiggled out her hand, looking over to me, "but why do *we* have to be up so early? We're the only real scrappers in this area, anyway." I moved back to the wing, wrapping a wrench around one of the other bolts.

"Guess you could say it builds character," I grunted against the rusted metal before the head snapped clean off. "Damnit. Toss me the drill, will you?" I reached up as she threw it my way, getting to work.

"Character, huh? Thought just being out here'd do that to ya."

"Well," I began drilling through the metal, intent on just grinding out the whole screw at this point, "shops open early in the day as well, and their rates are better in the morning than later on."

"Then we just sell *tomorrow*." She groaned, flopping back on the plating. I pushed the drill through, leaning back against the hull.

"Selling tomorrow means no food today." I said, tapping the wrench against my head. "Anyway, I don't think either of us wants to be lugging this stuff around for the next day." I leaned forward again, working on the next section.

"Alright, fine, you win." I looked up at her, grinning under my mask.

"Didn't know it was a competition," I responded. She huffed at me.

"It wasn't!" She said, sitting up on her knees. "Maybe I just like to complain!" I shot her a look as we continued at our work.

A few hours later, we'd pulled what we wanted from the ship. We honestly could have grabbed more, but it wouldn't have been worth the time and effort. In no time at all, we were speeding back toward our home. Tara led the way, ducking between the dunes, kicking up ash in her wake. Overhead, we heard the low rumble of thunder as lightning crackled through the thick black clouds. They billowed up from nearby cracks in the earth, coating the sky in their thick ash. I felt my bike tug to the sides as strong winds picked up. I reached up to my ear, tapping my radio.

"Storm's worse than we thought," I said. When Tara responded, it was crackly, barely audible.

"We're almost back. We should get through the gates before the worst of it hits!" She said. I revved my bike, pulling it into gear, pushing up beside her. Ahead of us, we were just able to make out the outline of our city's shields, crackling a dull white-blue. Underneath, the black stone buildings rose high into the air. Red cloth stretched from wall to wall, offering shade to the people below. Towers lined the walls, one larger than the others in the center, each contributing to the shield. As we drew closer, we saw the guard house come into view at the city entrance. A single dim light illuminated the dusted windows. Approaching, the two of us stopped, now under some amount of shelter as we passed through the shield in front of the station. An Oc'r man sat idly by, sipping some thick liquid. He slurped as he gulped it down, turning to look at us. The white feathers on his body seemed preened to a tee, nary an imperfection on them. He looked us up and down.

"Have fun out in the dirt, Ash Crawlers?" He said with a heavy voice. Hmph. 'Ash crawlers', he called us. Typical slang for anyone who spent time out in the Ashlands. Usually used by the Oc'r for people less fortunate than them. He let out a thin chuckle as we grimaced at him. "A'right, a'right in ya go before the storm gets any worse." He shoved his head in the direction of the gate. I grabbed my bike, leading it inside, Tara beside me.

"Jerkwad…" I muttered as soon as we were out of earshot.

"Tell me about it," she said, rolling her eyes. Once we were safely inside, the two of us pulled back our masks and cowls, strapped our goggles to our foreheads, and took a deep breath of nice clean air. Anything beat being out there, but it was where the best money was made, and it was a job I knew. I looked at the sun, and then at my watch.

"Still got an hour before the stalls open. Guess you were right about getting up so early." I said, looking at her. She locked into me with half-opened green eyes. Dark bags formed underneath them. If looks could kill, I'd have been dead four times over. I patted her on the shoulder. "Come on, let's grab a quick bite. I think we both skipped breakfast."

"Of all the roommates, I had to choose you, didn't I?" She asked, "Remind me how I ended up like this?"

"Well," I began, "if I remember correctly, you wanted a roommate who could help pull in a decent amount of credits and," I turned, walking backward to face her, "I *believe* I offered to help if you were willing to put in the hard work."

"I also believe you begged me to help you find a place to stay." She said, a half-smile on her face. I went flush.

"Listen, I *wasn't* in a great place financially at the time!"

"Oh-ho, and yet you were planning on helping *me* with *my* financial situation?" She asked.

"I mean, it worked, didn't it? We're not exactly rolling in creds, but we can afford to live comfortably, relatively speaking." We pulled up to our usual haunt, a cafe near the center of town. Ordering our usual, we sat down, continuing our conversation.

"I want more than that, though," she said. "I want more than this. Than this *place*." She gestured to the whole of the city. "I'm sick of being stuck here in Zor Kunda." I was about to speak when I was cut off. Someone out in the square was shouting. Didn't sound distressed, but it sure was loud. I leaned over in my chair, looking out. A small Dervan woman, skin purple, eyes glowing an eerie pink, hair tied up in a tight bun behind a face that stretched back like a mask, stood there, holding what looked like a data pad.

"Join the Celestials! Fight back the Soulless horde! Protect your home and your planet! Fight for the people you love!" They shouted. I scoffed, rolling my eyes as I turned back to Tara. She raised an eyebrow at me as our drinks were set down.

"Not gonna lie, thought you might be the type of person to be all over that offer," she said. I took a sip of my tea. Warm, hot, just a touch bitter. It felt nice sliding down my throat, heating me up.

"Could say the same about you, with that talk of wanting to leave the world." I sat back in my chair. "Hate to say it, but the only way someone gets off this rock is by enlisting…" I looked off to the table behind her. Two Oc'r sat there, reading. A man and a woman. I noticed the scars first, then the earpiece. "Or through the slave trade… Come on, let's go." She furrowed her brow at me, but nodded. We stood up, walking away as the two eyed us. She seemed to notice them too as we grabbed our bikes.

"Were they scoping us?" She asked.

"Think so. Might have been that gate guard." I said, "We should be on our toes." She unfurled her talons slightly. I gently put a few fingers against the back of her hand. "Don't. They likely won't follow us if we stay in crowded places."

"You know a lot about this Ortell," she said, eyeing me. My brow furrowed as I looked down at her, my eyes cold.

"Furellian refugees were easy pickings for the slavers. The first couple of years, we did a lot of dodging about. It wasn't easy to not get caught." I pursed my lips, remembering seeing people I'd known from my town being caught and rounded up. I felt her hand grip my sleeve as we walked.

"I understand how you feel."

"I know." I said, "A lot of Frev'n had it far worse than I did." She flinched at the thought, but I didn't want to press her. She took a moment, the two of us quiet as we walked, until she checked her watch.

"Hey…" she said, "Stalls are open, time to go?" I got ahold of my bearings, nodding.

"Right. Yeah. Let's go."

Only made a total 500 creds. Not an insane amount, but it was workable. Our bikes light, and our stomachs grumbling for real food, we headed home. The Shack, as we called it, wasn't anything special. As with many of the homes toward the edge of town, it was somewhat shoddily put together. Corrugated metal for the walls, somewhat half-assed panels from old ships for the roof, reinforced with wood and glass. It… wasn't much. I was hard-pressed to even say it was home, but it *was* a place to sleep. Frev'n kids ran up and down the busy, trash-ridden streets, playing to their heart's content. As we pulled up to our door, we chained our bikes to the side of our home, beginning to open the door when I felt someone pull at my pants. Looking down, I saw one of the kids. He'd been around a few times before.

"Mr. Ortell?" He asked. I nodded for Tara to head on in and get some rest. She happily squeezed herself past me and right through. I kneeled down to the kid whose arms were outstretched to me, lifting him up and onto my shoulders.

"Alright Aki, what's the news?" I asked, beginning to walk back through the slum. He crossed his arms on my head, leaning down.

"They say the storm's supposed to get *real* strong tonight. Some o' the older folk are worried it'll knock out the weather shield!" He said.

"Ah, don't worry about that. Those things were built real strong." I waved at some of my neighbors as we passed. "Anything else?"

"Hmmm, oh! I heard a rumor that the Soulless were getting closer." My blood ran cold for a moment, but I kept moving. "Everything alright Mr. Ortell?"

"Yeah, I'm fine. I'm sure we'll be okay, bud. They've been too preoccupied with Furelle to worry about us all that much." He tapped his chin.

"Hmm… I guess so." I raised an eyebrow.

"Oh? You *guess* so?" I teased. He giggled. "Oh well, I *guess* the sky is blue, and I *guess* we can breathe air." I picked him up from my shoulders as he laughed, swooping him dramatically through the air, before setting him down in front of his home. His mother stood there waiting for me. She smiled weakly at me, giving me a little wave as I leaned against her wall. She cleared her throat, gesturing to my leaning, and I stood back up off it, putting my hands up. She looked down at Aki as he ran to her, gripping her leg.

"Thank you, William. He always gets so excited when you get back in from work." I adjusted my hair, brushing it from my face.

"It's alright Mrs. Inarak. I enjoy the extra stroll." She put a frail hand on my shoulder.

"May the gods bless your heart." She looked back into her house. "Say, do you think you could help fix up my roof in the next few days?" She asked.

"I'll… try. I've got a few other things penciled in to fix up, but I'll try to get it done as soon as possible." She pulled me into a hug.

"I don't know what we'd do without you, dear." I smiled, patting her back. She let go, pulling Aki back inside as I made my way back home.

Ducking into the main room, I found Tara passed out on the couch. It amazed me how quickly she could fall asleep sometimes. I sighed, pulling up a chair to our table. My computer had a small flashing light. Someone had messaged me. Tiredly, I swiped it open. It was from Maurel, telling me she could call whenever I got back from whatever I was doing. I rubbed some of the tiredness from my eyes, swiping to call. It rang for a few seconds before she appeared, wearing her full Federation uniform.

"Well, well, look at the sleepyhead," she said, putting her chin in her hand.

"Morning details. You know how it is." I responded.

"I do, as I *still* do them." She sat back, folding her arms. "You're looking tired, William. Are you sure you're getting enough sleep? Drinking water?" I nodded along as she went off on me, until she paused, "Taking time for yourself?" I glared down at her. "And there it is." She sat forward in her chair, looking me in the eye.

"These people need help. A lot of them are sick, or can barely lift a hammer to fix things." She reached out, touching the screen. I could almost feel her fingers on my face.

"I get you want to be there for them, but you're going to drive yourself crazy. You really want to do some good? Maybe you should reconsider enlisting." I didn't respond, leaning back in my chair. She sighed. "William you… listen. I know it's hard, but you have to let go of that grudge. It's not healthy." I let out a breath.

"I'm good, really," I said, smiling for her. "Listen, the soldier's life is for you, not for me." She shook her head.

"Man, there really is *no* persuading you, is there?" She looked back up at me. "Well, just… take care of yourself, okay?" I gave her a thumbs up.

"That I can do." She nodded, only slightly content, but decided to drop it. "What's new with you guys, anyway?"

"Hoo boy, where do I start? Soulless aren't letting up anywhere, and it's been tough being in space for so long. Hoping to go planetside at our next stop, though, which is nice."

"Oh? Where you stopping?"

"We're in the Maz Crossing right now." My brow furrowed.

"Why's the Supernova even out that far? There's nothing out there, and it's pretty deep in Republic territory." She glanced to either side of her.

"It's also a connection point for the Soulless. Apparently, we're studying some tech they left behind on a moon here. Supposed to be top secret stuff buuut," she gave me a wink, "I think my adopted little brother can hear about it." I scratched my chin.

"Sounds dangerous, and fun."

"And, as I said, secret. We're supposed to cut all contact for the next month." I raised my eyebrows.

"Wow, that's a while." She shrugged.

"I've seen worse, but we were each given a last call to make. Just wanted to let you know, and tell you that you'd better still be alive when I get back." She stopped for a moment, before continuing, "Oh, and don't do something stupid. We still get the news out here."

"I'll do my best," I said. She gave me a little nod, before leaning back. Someone in the background called out to her.

"Oop looks like I'm out of time. See you in a month!" I gave her a wave.

"See you in a month!" She reached forward, the call cutting off. I let out a deep breath, getting to my feet, dragging myself over to my bed. I felt exhausted, even with how early it was. I could probably use a nap. I lay down, stretching my legs out. It felt like my whole spine decompressed as I sat there, shutting my eyes. Before I knew it, I was drifting off to sleep.

I awoke with a start, the hairs on my arms standing on end. I sat up, looking out. Night. I must have slept through the day. Guess I *had* been working myself too much. Tara was still asleep, but that feeling, I couldn't explain it. It felt like static running over my body, drawing me out. I moved quickly to the door, looking outside. A streak of red crossed the sky, tumbling toward the ground outside of the city. I couldn't see the ship through the storm, but as I watched that streaking flame, I could feel that static feeling pull me even harder.

I weighed my options. I knew the person in there would need help, but this was one of the worst storms we'd seen in years. Even with the shields, you could hear the howl of the wind whipping outside. I pursed my lips, heading back inside. No. If I didn't go out there, no one would. I marched back to my bed, grabbing my jacket, my hood, my mask, and goggles, pulling them around my neck. As I began to walk back to the door, Tara stirred. She looked up at me with dreary eyes, her brows furrowing as she saw me.

"Where the hells do you think you're going?" She asked.

"Ship crashed." I said, my eyes locked on the door. Tara got up, grabbing my shoulder with a firm hand.

"Hell no. That storm will rip you to shreds if you head out there." She said, "You don't even know what you'll find or if they're alive." I shook her hand off me.

"If you don't like the risk, then don't come. I'm going out." I said. She recoiled, an offended look striking her face. She recomposed herself, pursing her lips as she grabbed her gear.

"Fuck that." She pulled her goggles up. "I still need a roommate at the end of this." She strapped her mask on. "Let's go." The two of us rushed out of the door, undoing our bikes, kicking them into gear. We maneuvered our way through the streets and toward the gates. I kept my eyes on the streak as we lined ourselves up with the gate. We kicked our bikes into full speed, blasting out past the shields. The wind buffeted us as soon as we were out past the safety of the city. I squinted, ash managing to push its way into my goggles. The storm blew my hood back as we turned, following after the ship. It crested toward the horizon, falling quickly. Tara and I ducked our heads as thunder and lightning roared overhead, striking the open ground.

I could feel the wind trying to push me to one side, forcing my bike to correct, trying to squeeze any last bit of juice it might have. In the distance, we saw the red streak reach the ground, erupting in a bright orange flash. We both shot each other worried looks, heading off deeper into the storm. Black clouds loomed overhead as we drove, constantly fighting the harsh terrain and winds, but eventually, we *did* make it.

Flames illuminated the ground as we ducked down into the crater, temporarily safe from the storm. The ship was small, the size of a fighter at most. As I looked it over, I saw that symbol on the side of the hull. Celestials. I gritted my teeth for a moment but knew I couldn't let whoever was in there just burn. That feeling of static had grown even more as we approached. I got to the cockpit, tilting my head back to Tara.

"Still sealed! Not sure how after a crash like that, but give me a hand!" I called.

"Right! On it!" She hopped to me, crowbar in hand. We dug it in under the seal, pulling it up. With a loud 'Fshhhh,' the cockpit slid open, revealing a Furin man. I reached to help him, but quickly realized I knew him. Grizzled, old, this was the one whom I'd met on Furelle those years ago. The one who brought me back to the village. He was scraped up and unconscious. Still, that feeling of static grew stronger as we looked at him. That's when I heard a faint sound, like something skittering nearby. I saw a brief flash shoot through the air and braced myself. I rolled as a Soulless tackled me to my back, swiftly kicking it off me. It landed in the ash nearby, skidding to its feet. Tara backed into me, a tremble in her voice.

"Uh… William…" I looked back, seeing two more of them, each with long clawed hands, stalking around us. I got to my feet, backing toward the ship as she drew her pistol. I looked around briefly for a weapon, seeing a sword on the old Furin man. Instinctively, I grabbed it. As soon as my fingers wrapped around its red wooden handle, I felt a surge of energy overwhelm me. That static feeling was gone, and ho boy, I felt… *powerful.* As the Soulless circled us, I held out the sword, readying myself. I'd been in my fair share of street fights, but I had no idea what to expect here.

Two of them lept at the same time. Tara raised her gun, ducking just under one, firing, only to have a second Soulless hit her. I took the full brunt of another. As it raised its claws against me, I knew where it was going to strike. I shifted the sword over my chest, its claws striking the metal, rebounding off. I twisted the blade, making a cut upward. It cut clean through the thing's neck, lopping it off. The beast faded into ash, blown away quickly by the wind. I got to my feet, seeing the Soulless on Tara about to thrust its hand through her. I reached out a hand as if it were instinct. Blue lights ran up my arm, coalescing at my fingertips. A shard of magic formed from the palm of my hand, drawing out that energy from my fingers as it flew. Streaking through the air, it struck the Soulless, knocking it off her, but not killing it. Tara got up, backing up beside me.

"What in the gods' names was that?" She asked. I looked back at the Furin, then to my hand, and back to her. Maybe that old man was right, maybe anyone *could* learn magic.

"If I could tell you, I certainly would." There were still two more, though. One limped, the other was still fine. They jumped at us again. I ducked, attempting to make a slice at it, only to feel the sharp claws of the creature dig at my back. It pulled me down as I felt hot blood dripping down my body. Stinging, searing pain ripped through me like a hot iron pressed to my skin. I was slammed into the ground, the air knocked from my body. As I moved to roll, I felt it grab my leg, tossing me into the edge of the crater. My vision blurred as I hit the ground, looking over to Tara. She wasn't fairing much better, and she had the injured one. I tried to sit up, only to feel the claws of the beast pin my throat into the ash. Its face drew close to mine as it pulled its other hand back. I threw my arms up, waiting for the strike, but it never came. I felt the hand around my neck go limp first, and when I opened my eyes, I found the creature stumbling back. A translucent blue wall had formed in front of me. I had no idea what was happening, but I wasn't about to look a gift horse in the mouth.

I got up, picking up the sword again, approaching the Soulless as it backed away. I was bleeding, in pain, but still holding myself up. It stood to its full height, attempting to slash at me. I deflected the attack with the sword, cutting through its fingers. It fell back as I approached, my face drowned in light and shadow from the fire as I brought the sword down on it. It, too, dispersed into ash. Just one left. Tara danced around the thing, just trying to stay out of the way of its claws. She'd managed to get a few good shots in. Its shoulder was badly burned, and it continued to limp. It was still quick, though. I stepped in as it attempted to slash at her, trying to block the attack. Instead, it grabbed the blade, pulling it away from me. In the blink of an eye, it had my neck tight in its grasp, lifting me high into the air. I could barely breathe as it pushed me into the storm, the wind and ash cutting at my face, drops of blood forming on my skin. I grunted and struggled to no avail when I heard a gunshot below me. The hand disappeared into ash as I was dropped, landing on the ground.

Tara and I breathed hard, trying to catch our breaths. It felt like the tips of my fingers were burning, and I barely had strength in my arms. Was this how it felt to cast magic? Hazily, I stood up, grabbing the sword. It rang as I pulled it from the ground, moving back toward the cockpit.

"William, what the hell do you think you're doing?" Tara asked. I reached the side, gripping it tight, trying to hold myself up, feeling my vision blur.

"I just... I need to..." I reached for the Furin, before collapsing to the ground, my vision fading to black.

DRAENICA: ZOR KUNDA

GALACTIC DATE 00:08:383 5028

Morning light struck my face, making me scrunch my eyes and nose. As I dragged myself to sit up, I became painfully aware of the splitting pain in my head. I groaned, lying back down in my bed, holding my fingers to my temples. Wait… my bed. I sat up again, looking around. I was back home in the Shack. Was everything from the night before a dream? The Soulless, the Celestial, was any of it real?

As I sat up, I felt pain shoot through my body from my back. I took in a sharp breath, recalling the sensation of those claws digging into me, and the burning feeling they left behind. Opening my shirt, I found bandages wrapped around my torso. I closed my shirt, took some deep breaths, and pulled myself to my feet. As I moved to take a step forward, I felt my foot bump something. The sword I'd used last night clattered to the ground. I felt something like a shock pass through me. I recoiled, feeling my hairs stand on end again, just like the night before. Cautiously, I kneeled down, my hand wrapping around the red wood of its hilt. The metal of its guard and pommel were gold, inlaid with silver. The blade stood tall, its metal shadowy and gray.

As I gently cradled the sword, I became aware of something else in our home. A smell, and a sound. Sizzling echoed across the walls as the aroma of breakfast wafted through the air. I turned the corner into the living room, seeing Tara sitting at our table, and the old Furin man standing over our stove, tapping away at something akin to bacon frying in a pan. Tara looked up to me, as she took a sip from a mug, seeming to look for anything that might be wrong. I looked between them before I spoke.

"So… it really wasn't a dream, then?" I asked. The Furin put up a finger, moving some slices of bacon to a plate, before sliding a plate of food to the table. There was an assortment of different meats and pastries across it. He gestured to a chair across from them.

"Sit, eat. You need to rebuild your strength… William." The way he said my name was… the best way I could describe it was pointed. He furled his fingers and closed his eyes. I pursed my lips.

"Now hold on, I have some questions-"

"And they will be answered. First, eat." I looked at Tara, but she just shrugged. I groaned, but I couldn't deny that I was hungry. I reached forward and grabbed a few things from the platter, pulling them to a plate near me. Tara spoke up as soon as I had food in my mouth.

"I had to pull you both back after you passed out." She said, "I thought… you might have died to one of those things." I looked down at the table. "I told you it was a terrible idea to go out there. We could both be dead out there now if-" The Furin raised a hand to her.

"William was reckless, yes, as he has always been." She pursed her lips. "But had it not been for his instincts, I would likely not have survived," he eyed the sword, then her again, "nor would much of the planet." She looked at the sword.

"You're saying that old dusty thing is…" she began.

"A powerful relic, handed down to me by a sister-in-arms when she passed." He said. I stopped eating it, lifting the blade from the table. Unlike the night before, I didn't get that rush of power when I held it.

"Last night, when we found you, I was able to use magic when I held it. I'd never cast a spell in my life, yet it seemed to come to me like instinct." I said. The old Furin lowered his head, a shadow cast over his eyes as he sighed.

"Yes… you certainly did, didn't you?" Tara leaned forward, eying him.

"Alright, you aren't telling us everything. What exactly is going on with him?" She demanded. I'd never seen her so riled up, but then again, I could only imagine the night she'd had. I reached out to put a hand on her shoulder, but she smacked it away. "No! You almost died," she screamed, pointing to me. She turned her gaze to the Furin, poking a finger at his chest, "You crash land with Soulless on your ship and some sword that makes William spew blue stuff from his hands, and I had to jury rig a sled to my speeder just to get you both back here in the middle of one of the worst storms we've seen out here!" Her face was flushed blue with frustration and anger as she slammed a palm into the table. "We deserve the truth from the beginning." She lowered herself to her seat, folding her arms over her chest, the feathers in her wings puffed up and frazzled. The Furin sat up, glancing between both of us before he stood. Even now, after I'd grown, he still towered over me.

"Alright. If you must know, my name is Xenrus Arturi, a Celestial soldier, and holder of the sword William now bears." He began, "It has been my job for centuries to look after the blade, and to keep it out of Soulless hands."

"So, you came here because they found you?" I asked.

"Yes… and no," he said, his eyes turned to me. "It is not a coincidence that we meet a second time, Mr. Ortell." I cocked my head at him.

"What are you saying?" He sighed, shaking his head.

"That sword is, in a way, sentient. It…" he paused, looking for words, "It chooses the one who is to wield it." My brow furrowed. Is that what happened last night? He continued. "I've known from the moment you were born that it was you. Great energy surged within it and drew me to your village." I looked at him in disbelief.

"What… what exactly does this mean?" I asked.

"That blade was once wielded by a great man. The one who ended this war for 500 years." He said, "A temporary victory over the Soulless. A short-lived one." He sat back down, grunting as he slowly moved back into the chair. "That sword carries with it power and duty." He nodded to the sword. "Pick it up, read the inscription on the blade." I hesitantly did as I was told, turning the sword over. Surely, a patch of metal appeared lighter than the rest. It read…

"Isngr." A wave of blue energy burst from the weapon, flowing over each of us. A tingle ran up my spine. Tara looked at me wide-eyed. The Furin just smiled for a moment, before it faded.

"As I thought. It has bonded to you. I tried to keep it away till you were older, hoped that maybe you wouldn't have to fight in this war." I frowned.

"Fight?" I asked, putting the sword back down. "Now hold on, I can't do that! I don't know if you've noticed, but I'm not exactly a soldier. Not to mention, I don't exactly hold Celestials in the highest of regards." He looked at me again, his eyes delicate and gentle.

"You really do hate us, then?" He asked.

"Where were you when Furelle burned? When the Republic collapsed to the Soulless? I almost lost a second home, had the Federation not stepped in. Do you know how many people have died waiting for you to come?!" I was standing now, my knuckles white against the table. He kept his eyes locked on me.

"I cannot answer in a way to satisfy you. We are, many of us, not the people we used to be. Many of us didn't live to see this war, and we are short of numbers. You saw the woman in the square, begging for people to enlist? Her name is Olivia Sterling. Lost her old crew early on. She's had to resort to this to try to find a new one. It is…" He shook his head, crossing his arms on the table, "We are not in a good state. I cannot, in a right mind, tell you we did all we could to save your home. Had I more courage, I may have stayed to repel those who took your town." He looked up again. "What I can say is that we need good people if we want to make it better."

"You're still forgetting the part where he's got no fighting skills whatsoever." Tara chimed in, "No offense, of course."

"Oh, none taken. You're absolutely right." A grin cracked on Xenrus' scaly face.

"That didn't seem to be the case last night." He said, "Magic seemed to come intuitively. Fighting will come to you in time." He stood up, beginning to walk to the door. "I cannot force you to make a decision, but I urge you to consider." He took one more look at me. "Somehow, you're just like the boy I met all those years ago. Headstrong, reckless… yet I trust you'll make the best decision for you." He nodded, continuing to walk.

"Wait! Where are you going?" I asked.

"To fix my ship, of course. My job with Isngr is over, but a war will not win itself." He smiled at me, waving as he shut the door behind him. We both let out deep breaths, as if we'd been holding them in the entire time. She looked over at me as I watched out the window.

"You… aren't considering it, are you?" She asked. I groaned, throwing my head into my hands.

"Honestly, I have no idea." I said, "I've… blamed them for so long." Her head tilted slightly as she scooted her chair closer to mine, taking another swig from her mug.

"Ortell, you've always been one of the most hard-headed, stubborn people I've met." She started, "I don't believe in this galactic duty thing he's spouting, but I've seen how you treat people here."

"You're saying I should join?" I asked. Her lips scrunched to the side as she looked into my eyes, leaning back against her chair.

"I'm saying that you've always done what you thought would help people, and I also know that as much as you've been fooling yourself, this isn't exactly extravagant living. You have a chance to have a one-way ticket out of this hellhole."

"Well, what would happen to you if I left?"

"I mean…" She sulked forward, cupping her mug in both hands. "I've got nowhere to go anyway," she perked up a touch, a smile striking her face, "plus with your skills, you're going to need someone to look after you." I chuckled, pausing to look between her and the sword. Finally, I grabbed Isngr.

"Alright… Let's do it." Her face lit up.

"Really?!" I smiled as I got to my feet. She hopped up, her eyes having fires in them.

"I mean, you always said you wanted to see what's out there. If what Xenrus said is true, maybe we can make even a little bit of difference." She bared her teeth in excitement, jumping in front of me, stuffing clothes into a bag.

"You have no idea how long I've waited for this!" she said. I shook my head, moving to pack my things.

A little while later, we were out in the square, bags in hand. We'd decided to pack relatively light, one bag each. Mine was stuffed full, but looking at Tara's, it seemed like not much had been brought. We'd each said our goodbyes to the small community we'd grown into, and now we stood here. The small Dervan woman stood in the square again, calling out to anyone who would listen. I took a deep breath.

"You sure about this?" I asked.

"As long as you are," Tara responded. "You gave me a place to live and a chance to survive. The least I can do to repay the favor is make sure you survive the trip out." I nodded.

"Right. Let's do this then." We began our approach, the woman keeping a smile on her face as she ushered out to different people with no response. As we drew closer, she slowed down, looking up at us from her soapbox, stopping as we pulled up in front of her.

"Olivia Sterling, right?" I asked. She closed her mouth, standing up straight as she adjusted her jacket. It was blue with what I assumed was an officer's patch sewn onto the shoulder. Her hair was tied up into a tight bun, but with two loose tendrils dangling over her ears. She nodded.

"Aye, that's me. You two looking to enlist?" She asked. You could tell she was forcing herself to be formal. Tara and I gave each other a quick glance before nodding. She let out a heavy breath, slumping forward. "Oh, thank the gods. You have no idea how long I've been out here looking for anyone." Ah yeah, there it was. She straightened herself up again, clearing her throat. "Right, erm, you may address me as Captain Sterling. May I have your names?" She asked.

"William Ortell," I responded. I watched as she jotted it down before she looked back up.

"Tara Verikov," Tara said. Sterling's lips pursed as she wrote it, before snapping the holodevice shut.

"Alright. Follow me, while I show you to the ship," she said.

"Hold on, is there anyone else?" I asked. I watched as her eyes went wide and she let out a nervous laugh.

"Well… if I told you that you two were the only two who enlisted, would you… not join?" Hoo boy.

"Let's… just go see the ship." She let out a sigh of relief as she brought us through the city. As she did, she went over a list of regulations and things to remember, half of which I haven't retained to this day. We made our way to the far end of Zor Kunda, to the spaceport. As our feet clicked over the pavement, I looked at her.

"So, which ship is ours?" I asked. She looked up at me with a light in her eye.

"Oh, you'll know when you see her," she said. I furrowed my brow. She gestured ahead of us. "Hanger 15." I looked up.

Seeing the Blue Sparrow for the first time is something I could only hope to experience again. She was a ship unlike any other I'd seen. She was long, sleek, regal. Its dark blue hull was highlighted by streaks of white, and shimmering blue and gold lights around its exterior. Cannons lined its wings, ready at a whim. Six thrusters, two in the aft and one at its bow, held it aloft where it stood. You could sense that this ship knew its greatness. The Blue Sparrow, SPC-57. That name, from that moment, was etched into my mind. Sterling saw the look I gave the ship, nodding at it.

"Impressive, isn't she?" She asked. Tara and I nodded. This thing had to be one of the most advanced ships in the fleet. "I'll give you the details on board." She said, bringing us around the back of the ship. We made our way up a ramp, first through the cargo hold, and up to a hallway. White walls decorated the interior as the low hum of the Sparrow's engines echoed about like a warm, inviting purr. "For now, we don't exactly have time for a grand tour. Orders are to get everyone back to meet with the Gods." She said the last part so nonchalantly that we had to do a double-take.

"I'm sorry," Tara asked, "the who?" Sterling stopped, looking back at us.

"The Gods. They wanted to meet with the recruits." We nodded. Right… the Gods. THE GODS. I'd known the Celestials were led by Gods, but I'd always thought that they only had time to meet with the top-tier people, not low-lifes like us. I silently and slowly nodded. Sterling waved a hand at us.

"Ah, you'll get used to it. Come on, set your bags down. We need to get this show on the road!" We obeyed, leaving our bags in the hall as we followed Sterling to the helm. "Right. Have either of you piloted a ship before?" I shook my head, but Tara raised her hand with a modicum of caution.

"I've piloted a ship… once?"

"Fantastic, you'll be on helm. You, the… Orville fellow."

"Ortell."

"Right, Ortell. What can you do?" I pursed my lips.

"Well… I'm good at taking old ships apart." I said.

"Great, then you can put them back together then. For now, you're on engineering." That sounded like a terrible idea. "Don't worry, I'll teach you what you need to know once we're in warp. For now, let's go." We found ourselves in the helm next. Two sets of stairs curved around the side of the room, leading to a lower floor. Sets of chairs were lined up at terminals below. A small section of the upper floor jutted out over the lower one. Sterling strutted up to the chair in the center of the platform, standing in front of it. "Alright, piloting is the center console. William, the engines are on the console to the left of me. Get them powered up." I nodded, standing in front of the computer.

Numbers and diagnostics flashed in front of me. I tried to take in all the information as best as I could and made a guess. Seeing a slider to the right of the screen, I put my hand to it, pulling it up. The ship roared to life as Sterling gave me a thumbs up.

"See? You're a natural. Alright, take us out Ms. Verikov!" I saw Tara fiddle with the controls as we lifted off, pulling out from the hangar. The ship jolted as Tara apologized, quickly fixing something on the controls, steadying us. Once we were clear, she pulled forward on the throttles, the Sparrow gracefully taking off. I stepped away from the computer, putting my hands on the rail as I looked out into space all around us. The lights dimmed, leaving us with only our running lights. The last time I'd been out here, I'd been watching my planet burn. I could only hope to prevent other kids from seeing the same thing. I sucked in the air through my nose, letting it out long and slow. Off in the distance, you could barely make out a little green speck. Furelle. I hoped I could go back one day. From there, we looked to Sterling.

"Alright Cap'," I said, "What's our heading?" She kept her gaze forward. It was fierce, ready. I may question her judgment at times, but I in no way could question her conviction. Despite everything, that stare filled me with a sense of hope in the choice I'd made.

"Sol System." She said, "The Celestial base on Titan. We've got a week's journey ahead of us. It'll give you time to settle in." She said. "Are you both ready?" We both affirmed, and she nodded back at us. "Warp core to full power, Mr. Ortell." I turned to the computer, swapping out components. She was right. Once you knew where one thing was, the rest came easy… at least here. I pulled our main engines down, powering up our central core. The low whir grew in intensity as the engine grew to full power. A loud 'whum whum' echoed throughout the ship, and I looked as Sterling's ears perked up at the sound. "Perfect." She said. "Ms. Verikov, plot a course. Once ready, the mark is yours."

"Yes, ma'am," she responded, sweeping over the controls. I'd never seen her work like this. You could see the gears turning in her head as she pulled up maps and charts, doing the work of two people as she set a course across the galaxy. The Sol system was on the far end of the Milky Way. It would be a long journey there, but as Sterling said, we'd have time to settle in at least. I heard a ping and looked down, seeing Tara push a map off to her side. "Course set. Hitting warp in 3… 2… 1…" She punched the throttle. Space seemed to stretch around us, a light appearing in the black ahead of us. I braced myself as, with a rapturous boom, the Sparrow took off into the depths of space, and my journey finally began.

THE BLUE SPARROW: TRANSIT TO TITAN

GALACTIC DATE 00:08:389 5028

To say the next few days aboard the Sparrow were grueling would be an understatement. We were worked practically to the bone while Sterling had us learning everything we could about the ship. I can't say I exactly blame her, though. Seeing the Sparrow's complexity, we'd need a crew that would know her inside and out. Tarah was made to train with me while she wasn't on watch, but I got the worst of it. Thankfully, the work wasn't unlike what I was used to, though there was nary a day I wouldn't come out of the underbelly of the engine covered in grease.

We were three days in, at least it felt like it. I wasn't really used to using Galactic Time yet. Olivia had taught me about it when we were talking about shifts. 500 ticks to a second, 60 seconds to a minute, 60 minutes in a galactic year. Each "day" in our time was three galactic ticks. I could barely wrap my head around it. I think the worst part was that each day in space still used 24-hour time, but was calibrated to work with Galactic Time. From what Sterling said, I wouldn't need to know much past ticks and seconds anyway, unless I looked far back in history. Thankfully for our sanity, there wasn't too much work at the moment. Four hours on shift, eight hours off. That said, for at least the first day, it was nearly a full day of training to get us up to speed.

On the third day, I'd been down under the core for an hour or so. It was coming close to the end of my shift, but we'd met with some turbulence, and Sterling wanted to check on our fuel arrays. I was squeezed down underneath the cold metal grates, tools in hand, as I reset some of the canisters. I felt one click and pushed with my shoulder, shoving it back into place with a hiss. Letting out a breath, I turned, lying on my back, wiping the sweat and grime from my brow. My shoulder and neck were so sore from being down here, and there was barely any room to move. I heard footsteps clack on the grates overhead, and soon I saw Sterling's face leaning down to look at me.

"How are the arrays looking, Ortell?" She asked, cocking an eyebrow at me, "Lying around on the job, are we?" I took a long, deep breath and rolled back to my side.

"Not at all Cap'. One canister left is all." I grunted as I picked up one more of the large pieces, keeping my eyes on getting it aligned. "Aren't you on watch now, too? What are you-" I pushed, "doing down here?" The canister clicked and hissed as I forced it back into place. She kneeled down, inspecting it closely through the floor.

"Not bad... and yes, I am on watch. Watching *you* currently, Mr. Ortell." I rolled my eyes, reaching between the canisters to an interface behind them. The entire time we'd been on board, Tara and I had done the heavy work around the ship. I think I'd nary seen her lift a finger. "Should I also remind you, Mr. Ortell, that you are to refer to me as 'Captain,' not 'Cap?'" I flipped a few switches, fuel beginning to run through our starboard lines again.

"You can remind me all you want." I remarked, "I'm not exactly a fan of regulation, though. Gets in the way." I rolled to my back, seeing her look at me with a stern look. We glared at each other for a moment, before she softened up and smirked.

"Alright then, Mr. Ortell." She strode past me, wiping a finger across one of the pieces of the core, grimacing, and wiping grease on her coat. I furrowed my brow in her direction, trying to get any sort of read on her. She turned on her heels and walked back to me, popping one of the grates open over me, offering a hand. "William, correct?" She asked. I took her by the wrist, and she hauled me to my feet. She was surprisingly strong for her size.

"That's right," I responded. She dusted off my shirt and straightened up my collar.

"It's Captain, or Ma'am, if you'd please." Her tone had softened as well as she brushed out my hair. I opened my mouth to protest, but she put up a finger. "This ship, the Sparrow, is one of, if not the best ship in the Celestial fleet. It is beyond a privilege to serve on her. I will not be having my crew running about looking and speaking like a rowdy, ragged mass of monkeys. Am I making myself clear, William?" I sighed, nodding.

"Yes."

"Yes, whom?"

"Yes... ma'am." She nodded, content.

"Alright. Thank you." She patted my shoulder. "Good work. Get some rest. I'll see you in a tick for your next watch." I bit my tongue and nodded. There was so much more I wanted to say to her. Frustration and embarrassment burned in my throat, but... she was right, and I knew it. Sterling looked up at me for a moment longer before clearing her throat. "Right, well, it's a few minutes past my watch. I should return to the helm," she said before speeding back off through the ship. I shook my head, climbing back up to the white walls of the main deck, covered in grease and grime. Welp, watch was over. Time to head back to the room and relax for a while. Groggily, I sulked my way toward my quarters. I'd chosen the one farthest back. I found I liked the sound of the engine when I slept. It made this soft, low hum while we were in warp. You could barely hear it through the walls, but there was just enough for it to be comforting.

I pressed my hand to the pad by the door. It slid aside in one smooth motion, and I stepped inside. The cabins were all the same. A set of lockers and bunked beds to the aft wall, and a bathroom to the right. There was space to decorate a little, but it felt like this place had been stripped bare of personal belongings. It just felt... empty. Olivia had said the ship was one of the best in the fleet, right? Then where was her crew? I tapped my finger to my chin, walking to the window on the far side of the room, staring out into space. There was a tap at the door. I turned to look, seeing Tara waiting there.

"You mind if I come in?" She asked.

"Not at all." I said, "What's on your mind?" She stepped through the door, flipping on the lights. I noticed she was carrying her bag and looked back up at her with a confused expression. She saw my look and spoke.

"I… have issues with sleeping alone. I was wondering if I could take the top bunk."

"Why not room with the captain?" I asked. She pursed her lips, looking at me as if I already knew. "Right, yeah… that's fair."

"I've gotten used to sleeping around you. I'll stay out of your hair, and-"

"Don't worry. Top bunk's yours. I shared a small shack with you for the past half a year. I think I can survive rooming with you on a ship." I said, hopping down onto my bed. I sprung up before landing back down again, putting my hands behind my head. She nodded, shoving her stuff into the locker next to mine.

"Thank you. It really means a lot." She kneeled down, hopping up to the top bunk in one smooth motion. She was almost catlike in her nimbleness. I guess with the feathers, it would be more… sphinxlike? Either way, I nestled into my bed, closing my eyes, letting my thoughts stir. I could feel myself drifting off into a nap when Tara's words snapped me awake.

"Hey, William?" I opened an eye to the voice above me.

"Yeah, what's up?"

"Thanks." I furrowed my brow.

"What for?" I asked.

"For everything on Draenica. I… didn't want to mention it then, but you really got me out of a bad situation." She said.

"I'm not sure I follow." I saw the black shape of her body pounce down from the top bunk. She still wore those red, padded, scrapping clothes. I honestly wasn't sure she had anything else. She sat on the edge of my bed, locking her eyes to mine as she put her head in her hand.

"Before I reached out… before I even came to the city, I…" She bit her lower lip before sighing. "You know what? Here." She pulled down the back of her collar, revealing a symbol scarred into her skin, the mark of a slave. I immediately sat up.

"You were an escaped slave? I had no idea." I said. She nodded, pulling the collar back up. "So those slavers in the market the other day? Were they after…?" She shook her head.

"That I don't know, but it was only a matter of time. Us Frev'n had to look after each other during the escapes. It makes it hard to…" I could see tears welling in her eyes. She took a deep breath, wiping her eyes, regaining her composure. "Anyway, it made it hard to sleep alone and… well, I trust you, so… thanks." She stood up, slithering back up to the top bunk. I looked down, then up to the bunk above me, putting a hand behind my head and another on my chest.

"Yeah, I…" I paused, trying to find some words to comfort her. "Yeah… anytime." I rolled onto my back, thinking. It was going to be a long trip to Titan.

SOL SYSTEM: TITAN

GALACTIC DATE 00:08:405 5028

Seven days, the journey took us. I would hesitate to call it a pleasant ride. The Sparrow was never meant to be operated with only three people, at least that's my assumption. Sterling would step in to help us on occasion, but usually just left us to take care of the duties around the ship. To say it was a relief when we heard the warp approach alarms is an understatement.

I was lying in bed, off my watch, when I heard them. A low groan that rang over the length of the ship. My head tilted upward, and I felt my whole body perk up. As quick as I was to lie down the hour before, I was on my feet, running out the door toward the helm. Sterling was already standing ready at the captain's chair. She looked at me with a knowing smile as I rushed in.

"Someone's excited." She said.

"Are we here?" I asked. Sterling checked her watch before looking back at me.

"Would seem that we just about are, Mr. Ortell. Hope you had a good rest. Get on engines. Ms. Verikov, is everything ready at the helm?" I looked down to Tara. She pushed aside a hologram, nervously fiddling with the controls.

"Just about. Switching the ship over to manual control... now." The ship lurched briefly. She corrected, bringing the Sparrow back on track. I looked to Tara nervously, but she seemed unfazed, her gaze as steely as ever. With a nod to herself, Sterling looked to me.

"Alright, Mr. Ortell. Bring primary engines online." I instinctively turned back to my console, tweaking the settings. The warp core's hum quieted as our engines began to draw power. She looked back at Tara once more. "Alright, now Ms. Verikov, easy with the steering. She can be a bit touchy when she drops out of warp." I watched as Tara furrowed her brow. We could see the lights of the stars begin to slow around us, a light appearing at the end of our tunnel. "Brace yourselves," Sterling ordered. I was thankful she did. I grabbed onto the rail just in time as the ship slammed to a stop.

Tara lost hold of the controls, the Sparrow spiraling as she struggled to regain a hold of the ship. Calmly, Sterling walked down the stairs to her, ignoring the disorienting display in front of us. Stars seemed to be spinning wildly, the planet moving in and out of view. Sterling reached out a hand to the controls, slowing the ship, stabilizing it. I felt like my stomach had been twisted in knots, and it took all my effort to just hold in my breakfast. Tara sat back up, her palms shaking.

"I'm sorry, Captain." Sterling patted her shoulder.

"Told you, she's touchy." She gestured for Tara to move. She stood up standing aside, folding her arms as Sterling sat down. "I'll bring her in."

"What should I do?" Tara asked.

"Just watch for today. We'll figure out something you're better suited to later." Tara looked down, stepping aside. I narrowed my eyes. Tara seemed perfectly capable on navigation, and while she was an excellent driver, piloting was an entirely different ballgame. She looked shaken up over the ordeal, too. Honestly, had that been me, I couldn't say I'd have fared any better. I watched Sterling's hands as she began to pilot us toward the moon. Even in her hands, the ship didn't look fully in control. Her movements were minute, but the Sparrow felt like she had a mind of her own. We'd need a *very* skilled pilot to handle her.

I was snapped out of my thoughts by Sterling speaking. She pulled up a radio, opening a call to someone on the surface. There was no face to the person who answered, and the voice was jumbled but understandable.

"Ship callsign and Identification." They demanded. Sterling looked at us as if to tell us to remember this. She cleared her throat.

"Titan ground control, this is the Blue Sparrow SpC-57. Callsign Charlie Alpha Juliet 1999." She said. I'd never heard someone call in like that. When I was brought to Draenica, they just dropped us off at the nearest camp and left. I guess it was important for them to know exactly who we were.

"Copy that Blue Sparrow. State your purpose." Sterling leaned to the side in the chair, scratching at her cheek.

"Flying in with new recruits. Requesting a docking bay and welcome party." She said. Welcome party? That sounded pleasant. There was a moment of pause before the voice returned.

"Very well. You're clear to land. Docking procedures forwarded to your navigation system. Welcome home." Sterling smiled a little as she dipped the Sparrow down, pressing forward on the throttles. The ship shook, flames appearing around its edges as we pushed through the atmosphere. We held on once again, waiting for the flames to disperse. When they did, we were met with the full view of Titan.

Towers stretched across the surface of the planet. Mist poured out from their peaks, dispersing across the brown land. I began walking down from where I was stationed. In the distance, deep in the mountains, white buildings stood, watching over the starts of green fields on the surface below them. I could hardly believe what I was seeing. Tara stared on in awe with me, her jaw hanging open.

"What is all this?" I asked.

"This," she said, "is Titan. The Celestial's base of operations. Work began on its terraformation within the past couple of years." She looked on with a sense of longing in her glowing pink eyes. "When we started, it was nothing but red rocks. To see things actually growing around here is…"

"Incredible…" I finished for her. She nodded and pointed to the mass of buildings in the mountain.

"That's where we're heading. You two had better get yourselves ready. The Gods will want to meet you immediately. I'll get us docked and settled in." The two of us stepped off, heading back to our quarters. Stepping inside, the two of us couldn't help looking out the window in disbelief.

"Titan…" she said. She smiled, laughing. "I can't believe it!" She pressed herself against the glass, looking at the rows of crops passing us by.

"With Earth gone," I said, looking out with her, "I never thought I'd see anyone back in the Sol System." She stood up straighter, clearing her throat.

"Of course, it only makes sense. It's the perfect place to hide," she said. She picked up my sword, tossing it to me. "Right in plain sight." I caught Isngr, swinging it over my shoulder. I felt something tickle my neck and looked up, seeing a blue piece of cloth tied through the pommel. I furrowed my brow. I hadn't noticed it before. "Something wrong?" She asked.

"Oh, no… nothing. Sorry." She raised an eyebrow, getting closer to me, standing only inches away.

"That so? Seemed like something was on your mind." I tilted my head back at her.

"Like I said, it's nothing *important*. Just didn't notice the little…" I batted the cloth with my finger. She crossed her arms, squinting at it.

"Weird. I don't remember that being there." She said.

"Well… if you don't remember it, and I don't, then how did it get there?" I asked. Tara shrugged, lightly punching my shoulder as she walked past me toward the locker, unzipping her bag, pulling out a fresher set of clothes.

"William, you have a magical sword that an old man said made you special. I don't know if either of us are in a position to question how pieces of ribbon mysteriously end up in places."

"I suppose you're right," I said, looking outside once more as she began to change. "Well, you're about to set foot outside Draenica for…"

"First time!" She said, tapping the side of her horn.

"For the first time. Hard to imagine that everyone here has probably been all around the galaxy." I said.

"You've never been off-planet yourself, right?" She asked, walking up from behind me, tapping my arm. I turned. She wore another set of scrapping gear, but at least it was clean. I guess I was right about her not having much else.

"Not since before we lost Furelle," I said. She put a wing over my shoulder, turning me back to the door.

"Well, then, it's a new experience for both of us. We succeed here and it's a whole new life." I smiled at the thought. She dropped her wing as we walked back out to the helm. Just ahead of us, we saw the side of the mountain, open ports dotted across its surface. Sterling navigated the ship into the nearest one. The ship came to a stop with a soft huff. I moved over toward the engineering station. Sterling looked up at me, gesturing for me to go ahead. I pulled the power levels down. The hum of the ship died out as the engines powered off. Sterling stood up, dusting off her hands.

"Alright, you two. You look as ready as you'll ever be… if a bit grimy, but I don't think I've met a perfectly clean Celestial yet. It'll have to do." She walked up past us. "Follow me. There's someone you need to meet before we head up to the big guys." We hurried after her, passing through the ship, down into the cargo hold. The rear door had opened and a cold fresh wind blew past us from the world outside. Cool air. I think I'd forgotten what it felt like.

The voices of people echoed across the stone walls of the hangar. I backed down onto the pavement, taking it all in. In the distance, you could see a red-stained sky, the Sun barely on the horizon, while Saturn sat proudly in the sky above. Sterling tapped my shoulder, giving me a wink.

"New world, huh? What do you think, Mr. Ortell? Suit your liking?" I nodded slowly as she asked, keeping my hands on the strap running across my chest.

"Yeah, you could definitely say something like that," I said, walking out toward the edge of the hangar, getting on one knee. Sterling joined me, resting her chin on the back of her wrist.

"Well, take in the sights while you can. We have a lot of work to do," she said. Another voice cut in. It was nasally but dignified.

"Well, now, Ms. Sterling, I see you've brought some fresh new faces with you this time around." I looked up to see another Dervan man. His skin was fairer than Sterling's. His light blonde hair was combed to the side, overlapping with his three horns. He looked to me with piercing eyes, a data pad in hand. He cleared his throat, saluting me.

"Up now, son. I see Ms. Sterling has yet to teach you much in the form of regulation. You there, Draen lady. You join him, please." The man waited as I got to my feet, pulling my hand up to salute him. Tara hurried to my side, doing the same. "Hmm... Wrist is bent, elbow needs to be pulled out to the side more, but... it'll do for now." He dropped his hand, and I followed suit. "My name is Cardenian Hal. Head Quartermaster and Intelligence Specialist, though most just call me Hal." I was quiet as he looked up at me expectantly. "Well, come on now, son, spit it out."

"Oh, sorry. William Ortell." He nodded.

"And I'm Tara Verikov."

"Very well. Two new names for the roster. Sterling, do you mind if I steal your recruits for a little?" Hal asked. Sterling shrugged.

"Sure, give them the grand tour." She said. "You two, I'll be waiting to brief you with the Gods. Make sure *he* doesn't dawdle too much." She gave Hal a little smirk, gesturing to him with two fingers pointing from her eyes to him. He only let out a small smile in return before looking back at us.

"Alright. Follow me if you please." He began to walk us through the halls of the base. Passing out of the hangar, we found ourselves in an elevator. With the push of a button, we were sent up. "Nice to meet you two, by the way, I forgot to say, and welcome to the Celestial base." He said.

"Where are we going exactly?" Tara asked.

"Well, first, to your on-base quarters. Every crew gets their own, of course." Tara and I raised eyebrows at each other. "From there, I will show you the facilities, recreational areas, and lastly, the industrial quarters." I leaned back against the wall, folding my arms over my chest.

"Other than the industrial sections, it sounds more like this place is a resort than a headquarters," I said. Hal looked back up at me.

"I wouldn't take it for granted. While on-base living is nice, for the vast majority of your missions, you will be in space or on other planets. Most crews rarely even stop in anymore. That said, even living here has its issues."

"Such as?" I asked.

"Local wildlife burrowing through the civilian sectors below ground, atmospheric breaches, Soulless sweeping the Systems." He answered.

"Hold on, backpedal. You have civilians on base?"

"Of course we do. People come from around the galaxy, and some bring their families who have nowhere else to stay. Here we provide them free living and protection." The elevator stopped, the doors sliding open. Light poured in from a glass ceiling, reflecting off the white-tiled floors. Celestials all moved about through the large atrium, some stopping to check in with others, while many moved along, seeming to have a place to be. "Come now, we have much to do." Hal's voice cut through my thoughts, pulling me back to reality. I hadn't realized how far ahead of me he'd walked. I ran to catch up, following as he took us through the base.

It was easy to get caught up in it all. The rooms were the epitome of comfort, and there was a bar with just about anything you could imagine. Swimming, library, you name it, they had it. I almost wished I could live here, but as we made our way back through the walkways with windows looking out to the skies, it was hard not to think about where I'd come from. Tara looked to me, our footsteps quiet on the rug floors.

"You thinking about home?" She asked.

"Sort of." I admitted, "You?"

"Sort of." She started, "Well… I can say that I'm happy we aren't there." I shifted my mouth to the side.

"I miss the people, and the simplicity," I said. Hal looked back at me as if he was about to say something, but I continued. "More than anything, though, I'm thinking of Furelle." Tara's gaze fell.

"Never pinned you as a Furellian kid," Hal commented.

"Grew up there before the Soulless took over," I said, a shiver riding up my back at the memory. "We… never had a chance."

"I'm sorry. I wish we could have done more." He said.

"I heard about some of the shortcomings," I responded. Hal shifted, his gaze drifting to the floor.

"We weren't prepared. Most of the forces we could muster up to fight back were older war vets, and there wasn't nearly enough to stop the sheer numbers they threw at us." I looked down.

"You were… there?" I asked, confused.

"We weren't many, but we were there." He patted my arm. "I'm sorry we couldn't do more." I was quiet in response. He sighed and began to turn.

"We'll take it back," I said. He raised an eyebrow in my direction.

"Excuse me?"

"We'll take it back, one way or another, and I plan on being on the front of that push." Tara shook her head, grabbing me by my arm.

"Maybe wait till you're a bit more experienced before making bold claims like that," Tara said. Hal smiled at me, giving me a nod.

"Alright now, son, I think you two are ready to meet the Gods. Best to do it before the nightfall. Please follow me."

"What happens at nightfall?" Tara asked.

"Eight-day night. Systems have been having issues and some of them have a tendency to glitch out and go dark when we switch to our nighttime mode." He gave me a wink. "Wouldn't want to get stuck in the elevator up, now, would we?" I shuddered at the thought.

"Right, let's get a move-on then, why don't we?" I said. He nodded, leading the way.

Sterling stood by the entrance to the lift, her foot tapping impatiently. She perked up as she saw us heading her way, jogging over to us. She folded her arms, looking at Hal with stern eyes.

"Took your time. It's almost night." She said with a hint of scorn in her voice. Hal folded his hands behind his back, a smug smile stretched across his face.

"You asked for a welcome package, and I gave it to them, Olivia. I don't know what you have to be so angry about." He leaned forward, his hands tucked together. Sterling was red in the face, pointing a finger at him. She opened her mouth to say something, but quickly closed it, realizing she had nothing to say. She looked back at us.

"Alright let's… let's go on up. They're waiting." We were ushered onto the lift. Sterling put her palm on a pad on the wall, the doors shutting. The ride was silent, and I could practically feel my heart pounding in my chest. Looking at Sterling, she seemed nervous too. From what I'd heard, this was more of a formality than anything. She shouldn't have any reason to worry… should she? I began to doubt myself. Maybe she didn't think we were good enough, or worse. Who knows what these gods would do if they *didn't* approve of you? I began to tap the tips of my fingers together as a distraction, trying to keep how nervous I was to myself.

It felt like the ride up took years. Each moment that passed felt like a moment too long. Just when I was beginning to think it would never end, the doors slid open. Sunset light blinded us, casting a silhouette over two figures. The far end of the room overlooked the entirety of the base, and there they stood, their feet inches from the glass, hands tucked behind their backs. Sterling swallowed as they turned to look in our direction. My heart fell into my chest as they looked at us. The one on the left seemed to almost double my height, wearing shining armor adorned with carvings and silver inlays. The sun gleamed off the golden plate. A sword sat at his side, the jagged edge putting a fear in my heart. Any features of him were hidden below the metal and the shimmering gleam from within.

The figure to the right stood at height with the other, a cloak flowing over their frame. It was white as the purest snow. The sunlight sparkled off the surface of it and her gloved hand. They stood with one hand tucked behind their back, a mask of wood covering their face. As with the other, light flowed from within their clothes, making discerning any of their features impossible. It was without question. We stood in the presence of gods.

Sterling stepped out first, gesturing for us to join her. The Gods looked down at her, and then at us, then back to her. Sterling steeled her face, saluting to them.

"Sir, Ma'am, I'm here to present you with the crew I've assembled," she said. The two gods looked to each other, then back at us. Without a word, they walked past Sterling, standing directly in front of Tara and me. Their forms shrunk as they walk, seeming to float across the ground. They inspected Tara first, looking her up and down, checking her wings, her arms, before moving to me. It felt like their eyes pierced my very being. The entire time, I stood as still as I could, stayed as silent as possible. I heard the armored one mutter something before nodding to the other. The two walked in front of Sterling, growing once more in size. The robed one looked at her. When she spoke, her voice was like silk in the wind.

"Sterling, if I remember correctly, this was your final chance to fetch a passable crew, correct?" She asked. Sterling nodded.

"That is correct, ma'am." Last chance? How long had Sterling been at this exactly, and what did they mean by a 'passable crew?' The armored one spoke now, his voice like rocks breaking under a hammer. With every word, it felt like the room shook.

"Sterling, it is clear your conviction is strong," he began, "however, *this*?" He gestured to us. "You've brought along nothing but pathetic whelps with no experience. You expect us to sign off on a crew of civilians?" My brow furrowed, a deep pit of anger starting to bubble in my stomach. The Goddess spoke.

"Sterling, this is a failure and lack of judgment we cannot tolerate." She rubbed her forehead in disappointment. "The Blue

Sparrow is to be put on lockdown and grounded, and you stripped of your rank as a Celestial. Your last mission is to bring these two home." She looked up from Sterling to us. "They have no place here." That pit of anger overflowed, and I stepped forward. Sterling tried to grab at my arm to stop me, but I marched past her and right up to the goddess.

"How *dare* you?" I started, "I gave up my life, my *home,* because of your failures. I leave my planet, the people I love behind to join your cause and all you have to say is to '*go home?*'" There was a pain in my throat as the frustration and anger at these gods welled up even more. "*No*. I refuse!" I shouted, "One of your own people convinced me to come here because of *this,*" I drew Isngr, pointing it at the goddess' mask, "and you tell me to *go home?*" I felt cold metal against the back of my neck, looking over to see the God with his sword drawn. The woman put a hand up, lowering the blade of my sword, before speaking.

"Clearly, the sword made a mistake," she said, "and if it does that, it's of no use to us, anyway."

"Much as you are." The God said, "Go. Home." I grimaced, my eyes narrowing at them. I sheathed Isngr, turned on my heels, and stormed out. Tara and Sterling followed me out, sulking as they dragged themselves into the lift. Sterling couldn't make eye contact with us as the door closed.

"Sorry..." she said, "I should never have dragged you two into this." My brow furrowed.

"You're just going to take this lying down?" I asked. She and Tara both looked at me.

"What exactly do you expect us to do?" Sterling asked, "The Sparrow's on lockdown."

"Then we... I don't know we could..." I struggled to find my thoughts, the door sliding open to the bottom floor, "We could steal it!" Tara gave me a look that could kill but thought it over for a moment.

"You know… you might just be right." She said, a smile starting to form. A voice cut in from behind us.

"Do you three mind if I inquire as to what it is we are stealing?" We turned, seeing Hal. He must have been waiting just outside of the lift for us. We straightened out, saluting him.

"Oh, we weren't planning to steal anything!" I said. He smirked.

"I see. A lack of regulation, *and* terrible liars." His face turned hard as he looked at Sterling. "They turned them down too?" He asked. She nodded solemnly. "And here I thought your will indomitable, yet your new crew are the ones coming up with the plan to steal your ship back."

"You seem to forget that the Gods both shot down the proposal to make them my crew to begin with," she said, defeated. He cocked his head to the side.

"Is that so?" Hal looked to me. "You, William. Are you willing to serve Ms. Sterling here in combat and war?" I nodded.

"Of course."

"And you Tara?" He asked.

"I wouldn't be here if I wasn't." Hal nodded.

"There you have it." Sterling looked at us with a gleam in her eyes.

"You… really mean it." She said. She took a few deep breaths, straightening herself out. "Right, well, Mr. Ortell, this was your idea, correct?" She asked, "Do you have a plan of action?" Tara spoke up before me.

"I actually had an idea about that." She said. Hal raised an eyebrow. "It might include you, Hal, if you're willing." He shrugged.

"I am but a simple quartermaster at your command." He responded.

"Good. Well, nightfall should be in less than an hour, correct?" She asked. Sterling and Hal nodded. "Great. They likely have grav locks in place on the Sparrow. When I had to escape the slave trade on Draenica, we needed to learn to deactivate them. They're standard for grounding ships. Well, when things go fuzzy during the shift is our perfect chance. Hal, can you get to the flight controls?"

"Not normally, but I'm sure I could finagle something during the outage. We don't often have people stationed up in there, but if there is, I can improvise." He cracked his knuckles and neck, "Been all too long since I was in a good tussle." Tara gave him a nod.

"Good. We'll need you in there to disable the security on the locks. Once you do, me, William, and the Captain can manually undo the binds on the Sparrow, and we'll be home free." I scratched my chin.

"Are you sure this will work?" I asked. Hal chimed in.

"There's a good deal of confusion during the switch to our night systems. The distraction will serve you well." Sterling nodded in approval, a curled finger at her lip.

"It's risky, but William's right. We aren't about to stand here and let them tell us who we're meant to be." Hal gave us all a warm smile.

"And here they thought you weren't the perfect crew." He folded his arms, shaking his head, "I will be waiting by the flight controls. When everything's ready, I'll give you the all-clear to disengage the Sparrow." We agreed, beginning to make our way respectively to our positions. Looking at Sterling, who had been a mess only moments before, I saw a fire in her eyes, and it was mirrored in Tara.

Not to mention, I'd never seen Tara plan like that. It was like wizardry how quickly she pulled together that idea. Looking at her now, I could almost see the cogs in her mind turning faster than ever. I'd never questioned how she'd managed to escape as a slave. On Draenica, her work ethic left much to be desired. Seeing her out here made it all make so much more sense.

The three of us stepped onto the elevator down to the hangar. The door slid shut behind us. The ride was quiet, but through a window in front of us, we could see the sun just beginning to dip below the horizon. It wouldn't be long now. Every beam that passed in front of us as we lowered seemed to make the sun lower and lower in the sky until finally we were there. The doors opened to the hangar. Blue lines of energy held the Sparrow to the cold concrete. People stood all around but hadn't seemed to pay us much mind yet. As we drew closer, however, we heard a voice approaching.

"Hold on there!" A young Terran man was walking up to us, a clipboard in his hand. We slowly turned to look at him. His brow was furrowed as he tapped his datapad. "The Blue Sparrow's on lockdown. No one's authorized to take it out."

"Oh, well, we were told by the Gods that we had a mission on…" I began. Tara followed up.

"On Furelle!" She said, trying her best to smile. The man's brow furrowed further, confusion and suspicion mounting.

"Furelle?" He asked, scrolling through the data pad. "We have nothing on that in our database." He looked back up at us. "Who are you three exactly? I need to see some ID." I fumbled over my words for a moment, before the sky faded into black stars. The lights shut off as we were illuminated by just the tethers to the Sparrow. I knew we were out of time.

"I'm *really* sorry for this, buddy," I said, drawing a fist back. I struck him across the chin, knocking him to the floor. If anyone had seen that, they'd be on us, and fast. This was all on Hal now. Tension rose as we ran to the tethers, waiting for them to open. We could hear the elevator in action. I looked at the datapad. The bastard had set off an alarm. We didn't have much time left. I looked up at the flight controls, worried. Had Hal been caught?

My worries were alleviated when the clamps on the tethers snapped open. We were still good, but we didn't have much time. I watched as Tara pulled back a lever on her tether; the beam flickering out. Olivia followed suit. I reached down, grabbing mine to disengage, and pulled. It wouldn't budge. Try as I might, the damned thing was rusted in place. I looked up, seeing the door to the elevator open, a small platoon swarming out. Time was up. I pulled Isngr from my back.

"Hope this works…" I muttered, thrusting the blade deep into the machine. Sparks flew and burst out as the blue energy dispersed. We were in the clear. "Everyone on, now!" I shouted, ducking up through the cargo hold. A blaster bolt struck the ground beside. Were they really trying to kill us?! I dipped between the crates, a bolt hitting a box beside me as Tara flew in, gripping the ceiling. Sterling ran in, the bolts striking her, but a thin veil around her seemed to be blocking them. I noticed the small contraption on her hip, a kinetic shield. She spun around the corner, slamming a button on the wall. The door began to raise up. She gestured to me.

"Ortell, Verikov, to the helm now. Plot us a course out of here."

"Right." We said in unison. Tara glided down from the ceiling as I pulled myself back to the stairway, the two of us sprinting up out of the cargo bay. Past the rows of rooms we moved and out into the helm. I turned the corner, working the controls. Power to the engines, warp core online. I turned to her, giving her a thumbs up.

"We're good." I looked up. The doors to the hangar were beginning to close. "Alright Tara, up to you. Get us out of here!" She nodded, the ship lifting off. The whir of the engine gathering energy filled the ship. The doors were closing fast, though. There was no way we were going to make it through. Sterling dashed into the helm, seeing the heavy doors.

"Shit. We'll never squeeze through that at this rate. Half power to weapons, Mr. Ortell. If they won't *let* us out, we'll just have to do it with force."

"Can do Captain." I adjusted energy from our core to the weapons systems. Sterling hopped over the railing to the front console, furiously working the controls. We heard the Sparrow's cannons come to life. A barrage of six shots fired, leaving a massive hole in the steel barrier, more than large enough for us. She nodded to Tara.

"Take us out Verikov, double time!" She commanded. Tara slammed the throttles forward, the ship blasting off with a boom. The Celestial base disappeared behind us quickly, as Tara pulled us up toward the atmosphere. We took a moment to breathe, only to feel the ship rock. Something had hit us. Tara brought up our radar, looking to Sterling.

"Six ships behind us, Captain." Sterling swore.

"Shit." She said, "We need to be anywhere but here. Plot a course to any nearby star system!" The ship rocked again. I looked at the engineering panel. Our shields were holding, but they couldn't take much of a beating. Tara pulled up navigation, her mind racing. She plotted a course around multiple stars before centering on one.

"Got it. William, full power to the Core!" I nodded, redirecting everything back to our warp core. With a groan, it woke. I looked back at her.

"She's ready. Get us out!" I yelled. Tara pushed forward on the warp throttles, space beginning to stretch, a blue and white light forming around the edges of the ship. With a crack, we disappeared into deep space, free at last.

We came to a stop around a red star. The three of us were exhausted and out of breath from the ordeal, and had no idea where to go from here. When Sterling gave the order for us to rest, I was more than happy to oblige, going to nap in my quarters. It took some time with my racing heart, but just flopping onto my bed felt good. The adrenaline slowly subsided, followed by the realization of what we'd just done. We'd stolen a *Celestial* ship. On the one hand, I should have been terrified of the consequences. Instead, I felt… exhilarated. I took some deep breaths, calming myself down.

The tiredness set in soon enough. I closed my eyes, put my hands behind my head, and let myself drift off to some much-needed sleep.

Proxima Centauri: The Blue Sparrow

Galactic Date 00:08:407 5028

Waking up, I felt like I was lying on cold stone. Grimacing, I sat up, still dazed. How long had I been out? As I set my hands down to prop myself up, it registered to me that this wasn't my bed. Cold, hard stone. I opened my eyes, squinting as I got my bearings. Stars stretched out in all directions around me. I rubbed my eyes, squinting as I brought myself to my feet. I looked down, seeing that I stood on a ledge of rock. Between the cracks of that rock was a faint blue light. I backed away from the ledge, bumping into a wall. I stopped, turning to see an endless expanse of mountains and floating stone walkways. They snaked toward a tower in the distance, a blue beam of light piercing the heavens from its peak.

Turning once more, I looked out at the expanse of stars. I felt like I should be afraid. I had no idea where I was, or where the Sparrow was. How had I gotten here? Yet, despite these questions, I felt somewhat at ease here, like I was safe. Looking along the path, I felt like I should follow it. It was like a string was being pulled to guide me. I took my first steps, the sound of my feet tapping against the stones echoing all around me.

I found myself at a collapsed section of the path. Across, I could see a tunnel leading deeper in. I stopped, looking down and then back up. That's when a figure caught my eye. White robes flowed across her body, a mask and that white glow. It was the Goddess from before. I took a step back, reaching behind me, putting a hand on Isngr, not saying anything. She stood there just watching me. When it was clear I wouldn't talk or move, she did.

"Bring it back." She said. I figured she was talking about the ship we had just stolen.

"Not a chance." I said back. She shook her head, lowering it to her hand.

"I only wish to save you grief and pain. I commend your determination, William, but that is not going to be enough." I stood up straighter, removing my hand from Isngr.

"Try me." I said. She just sighed.

"Fine. You want to prove yourself so badly? Make it to this side without falling and we might be able to talk." She said.

"And if I don't?" I asked.

"Then you won't need to worry about waking up, anyway." She watched me for a few moments before turning, seeming to glide away around the corner. My blood went cold as I realized the gravity of the situation I'd put myself in. The gap had to be at least fifty feet. Jumping that would be fruitless. I approached the edge, peering over it. Long way down… endless way down. Would I really just die if I fell? Honestly, I didn't want to find out, but I also wasn't about to just let them shortchange me like this.

The wall wasn't a great climbing surface either, at least not for someone of my level. They were almost smooth. Maybe for someone with some more rock climbing experience, but I was just a scrapper. I paced back and forth on the trail, my brow furrowed in thought. I had to get there, but how? Jumping was death, climbing was death. Maybe magic? I drew Isngr from its sheath. I'd made a shield once, right? Maybe I could do that again.

I took some deep breaths, thrusting my hands forward like I'd done before, and… nothing. I tried crossing them, wiggling my fingers. Nothing. Nothing. Nothing. I groaned in frustration. What good was this stupid sword if I couldn't do anything with it? I chucked it at the wall, only for its blade to sink into the stone with a churnk. I stopped, walking over to Isngr, pulling it from the wall with ease. I dusted the blade off, looking back at the wall. An idea began to form in my mind.

Wielding the sword in one hand, I thrust it into the wall above me. I hopped up, hanging from it. It held fast. With my free hand, I reached up, holding it in the groove I'd made with the last stab. It would just barely be deep and wide enough that I could get a grip. I found surface with my feet, drawing my sword back out, thrusting to the side, shifting to the next hole. That was it. Just fifty feet to go.

I began the process. Stab, shift, grab. Stab, shift, grab. I could feel the sweat beginning to drip from my brow already. My arms were growing sore from the strain of holding my entire body up. I looked to the side. I'd barely gone anywhere. At this rate, I didn't know how long I'd be able to hold on. I took a deep breath, pushing myself further. Stab, shift, grab. Stab, shift, grab. Just a little further each time. My core was on fire. My arms felt like someone was stabbing them with a thousand needles. I needed to hold on just a little longer.

I stabbed at the wall, but Isngr slipped. I felt my body begin to fall. The world seemed to move in slow motion. I reached for the wall as I began to plummet, managing to thrust Isngr back in. I caught my breath, bracing my feet against the wall, looking back up. I'd fallen so far now. My breathing was shaky. I had to get myself under control. I'd almost gotten to the other side. I just needed to get to the top again, and I'd be there. I gritted my teeth, a yell escaping my chest as I drew Isngr out, thrusting my body upward. I stabbed into the wall again, and again and again, each time going higher and higher. I ignored the fire growing in my every muscle as I reached further and further. One more, I told myself over and over again. I took in one more deep breath, thrusting myself up one last time, my hand grabbing the ledge of the path. With all of my strength, I dragged my body up.

I hacked and coughed as I sat there, slumped over. Looking back, I looked at the distance I'd crossed. My chest rose and fell as I tried to catch my breath. My entire body burned and felt so weak. It felt like I'd just used every last ounce of my strength. Still, I had a goddess to talk to. I pulled Isngr from the ground, bracing myself against the wall to get to my feet. I leaned against the sword as I walked forward and into the tunnel.

Around the corner, I strode, finding her sitting in a chair on the far side of a stone table. She looked up at me, sipping something under the mask she wore. I swore that for a brief moment, I could almost see a smile. I stood up taller, placing Isngr back in its sheath.

"I passed your damned test." I said. She tilted her head and nodded.

"You did. It seems I may have judged you too harshly, William," she gestured to the chair across the table from her. I was grateful to sit down, hunching over the table. She reached forward, tipping my head up to look at her, "but be wary. What you seek out is no game. It is a life full of danger. You will be put through hell and back. Are you sure this is what you wish?" She asked.

"If I were afraid of that, I would have turned around at that gap." She nodded again.

"You…" She looked at the sword on my back. "You remind me much of the prior owner of that sword. Headstrong, disobedient, stubborn." I narrowed my eyes at her. "In your case, those may be the best qualities you could have," she continued. "You will need them for the journey ahead."

"So you don't want me to bring the Sparrow back?" She shook her head.

"While I am… unhappy with your stealing our best ship… no. You do not need to bring her back. That said, we do need to sort out a few things." She stood, reaching behind her. "A drink?" I stared at her with a level of angst. She shrugged. "More for me, I suppose." She pulled a bottle from within the stone. It seemed to just form within her hand. She brought it back to the table, pouring it into her cup.

"What exactly is this that we need to sort out?" I asked.

"Well, first, introductions. I know your name, William, yet it seems you have yet to learn mine." She said. "You've likely heard mentions of me and my brother. My name is Cleva. My brother, who you also met, is Solvemos." I nodded. I had heard the names, yet somehow hadn't pieced together that these were them. Once she was satisfied, she continued. "Next, a direction." She said.

"While you need not feel obligated to listen, as you have yet to do so thus far anyway, I'd make the suggestion to head to Xenova."

"And why is that?" I asked, folding my arms.

"I have an agent of mine searching for something of importance in the Grand Archives. She could use the assistance."

"So we're your librarians now?" I asked.

"Don't be so hasty to judge your task before you've even begun." She said. "Again, the choice is yours, but I don't see you having many other avenues." I pursed my lips.

"I'll… bring it up with Sterling." I could sense a smile.

"I'm glad to hear it. I look forward to meeting here with you again." She said.

"Wait, where exactly is here?" I asked, "And how do I get back?" She stood up, walking to where I sat.

"Where you are, I will divulge in my next visit. As to how you get here, just trust that I will do my part," she said, tapping my forehead. "Now it's time you wake up." I felt myself tip backward, feeling as if I had fallen through the ground into a void. My vision went hazy as I tumbled and…

I shot up in my bed, gasping for air. I sat there for a while, letting my body rest, catching my breath as I leaned back against the wall. Was that just a dream? If so, why were my arms so sore? No. It felt too real, too vivid to just be a dream. I wiped sweat from my face and brushed the hair from my eyes as I got up. The room was bathed in a red glow, and looking outside, I remembered why.

We'd been in orbit around a red dwarf. Out of curiosity, I dragged my finger down the glass of the window, bringing a holographic screen down, showing a map of the galaxy. We hadn't gone far. Proxima Centauri, just one system over. Nothing remotely habitable was nearby. No wonder we hadn't been tracked down yet. I dragged the screen back up and looked to the top bunk of the beds. It was still made. Tara hadn't come back in to sleep. I must not have been out for too long then.

I picked up my shirt, giving it a sniff. I grimaced a little. Probably could use a wash. I tossed it in my laundry, heading to my locker. Sterling had stocked them with these Celestial military uniforms. I hadn't touched them, but I was out of clean clothes. I pulled one set out off its hanger. It was sheer black, trimmed with a light gray. The sleeves were rolled back and clipped into place. The shoulders had pads on the outside. These were lined with a black rubber, and the armor itself was a sort of light gray plastic. Blacks and grays, blacks and grays. Couldn't say it didn't appeal to me. I slipped it on, buttoning up the front. It was a slim fit. I moved to the bathroom, looking myself up and down in the mirror. It was slick. Something about it just seemed to click with me. It felt… right. I adjusted the shoulder pad and brushed the shirt off.

Turning on my heels, I left my room, looking up and down the hall. No one in the helm. Galley was empty too. I started to make my way aft. As I began to pass a fork in the halls, I heard Sterling and Tara talking the next room over. I stopped for a moment, listening in.

"We don't exactly have any heading now, do we?" Tara said. "William and I don't have the training to go to the front lines."

"Well, we need to think of something," Sterling said, "We can't exactly hide forever. Even if we do, we need to get food. We're practically outlaws at this point." I decided I should probably step in. I turned, heading down the hall. The two of them sat around a large circular table, a galaxy map projected over it. They looked up at me as I approached.

"Hey William," Tara said, "You sleep well?" I cracked my neck to the side, sitting down beside her.

"Sort of…" I began.

"Sort of?" She asked.

"Yeah just… Captain, does Cleva have the power to talk to you in your sleep?" I asked. I wanted to make sure what I'd seen was reality. Sterling put a knuckle to her chin.

"She does… Why? Did she contact you?" She asked. I nodded. "What… did she say?"

"Well," I began, "she started by telling me to bring the ship back," I said, recalling the memories of what came after vividly. "When I refused, she gave me a test, saying it was pass or die." Olivia let out a relieved sigh.

"Well, given that you're still with us, I assume…" she started, and I nodded.

"I, thankfully, passed. She's giving us a chance to prove ourselves." Everyone in the room let out a relieved groan. Sterling looked at Tara.

"Alright, so an outlaw's life is off the table. Did she give you any orders?" Sterling asked.

"Not an order, just a suggestion. She said she had an agent on Xenova who might need help in the Grand Archives."

"Great, then we head there!" She said, starting to get up.

"Hold on, Captain. Real quick," I started. She sat back down, gesturing for me to continue. I nodded. "we've done well so far on our own, but the Sparrow's a large ship with a lot going on. We need to find a crew. An actual engineer, a dedicated pilot, science, medical. We are going to need people." Tara nodded in taciturn agreement. Sterling tapped her knuckle to her chin again, thinking.

"I… might know some people willing to help, now that we've gotten a start." She said.

"They weren't willing before?" I asked. She shrugged.

"Not a lot of people are willing to take a gamble on starting a crew," she replied. I could see the logic behind it. Starting a new crew would mean uprooting your whole life. Just look at me and Tara, and without the guarantee that it would stay together, that's a big risk to take. Sterling looked to the two of us. "Alright, here's the plan. You two will investigate the archives. I'll go and see if I can't locate a few old friends of mine to drag along with us. There aren't many, but it'll be a start." I sighed. A start was really all we could hope for.

"Right." Tara said, "Xenova then. We head out immediately? See if we can't get there as early as possible?" Sterling nodded.

"To Xenova. Ortell, Verikov, you have your heading. Get us there in one piece." She said.

"Aye, Captain." I said back, the two of us getting up and heading to the helm. The two of us got to our places. I charged the core, and Tara got to planning our route. I looked to her as she worked out the math.

"Excited?" I asked. She looked up at me with a smirk.

"Of course. New planet, new sights," she said. "Warp core up to speed?" She asked.

"Heard Xenova was a moon covered in cities. I'm eager to see it up close." I said, tapping my foot as I waited for the gauge. "Alright, we're good." She nodded, pushing the throttle forward. We shot off into the depths of space, aimed for the Great City of Xenova.

XENOVA:
THE GRAND ARCHIVES
GALACTIC DATE 00:08:410 5028

W*hump.* The Sparrow slammed to a halt as it dropped out of warp. I rocked into the sudden change in velocity, gripping the rail to my side. Every time we dropped out of warp, it felt like there was a twist in my stomach that made it churn. I'd never get used to that feeling. I swallowed the bile that caught up in my throat, standing up straighter, if still a touch dizzy. I looked out of the helm to the cloud-coated Xenova. The gray storms surrounding the moon spiraled and swirled in an endless dance. Sterling stepped forward, leaning against the rail by the captain's chair.

"Alright," she began, "Verikov, Ortell, are you two ready?" She asked. I gripped the strap on Isngr's sheath, nodding affirmatively. "Good. Word of warning," she said, looking at me, "keep that sword sheathed. You'll probably run into Soulless down there. We're on neutral ground here. They shouldn't hurt you, you shouldn't hurt them. If they strike first, defend yourself, but we don't need a political shitshow."

"Right, don't hit unless we're hit first," I said. Sterling sighed.

"Preferably don't hit at all, but I suppose that's about as close as we're getting." She looked to where Tara sat, gesturing to her, "I'll take up the helm, drop you two by the archives." As Tara moved aside, she looked down at Sterling.

"Where will you be heading?" She asked.

"Like I said, meeting a few friends." As I adjusted the power on the engines, warming up our mains, I leaned over the railing.

"Where exactly do you know these guys from, anyway?"

"They're… people I've worked with in the past. Most of them either lost their crews or who've worked jobs with me before, but settled down."

"And you think they'll join us just like that?" Tara asked. Sterling shrugged.

"Can't really say. I'm sure many of them will walk out, but if we can even get a few people-"

"Then that'd lighten the load on the lot of us." I said.

"Exactly." She adjusted in her seat, pulling up the piloting hud. "Engines warmed up Mr. Ortell?"

"All looks good here, Captain." I said. She nodded, easing us down toward Xenova.

We cruised lower and lower. Ships flew in and out past us. Surrounding the planet were destroyers, dreadnaughts, and carriers. I thought the Sparrow was big, but we were dwarfed in the shadow of the behemoths around us. Federation ships floated on one side, their signature axe-head shapes recognizable even from where we flew. Republic ships that looked like arrows against the night sky were interspersed. Then, black as pitch, you could barely see them. Soulless. The sharp edges of the block-shaped ships made them akin to war hammers. Seeing them here felt like a nail through my heart.

I flashed back to that scene on Furelle, seeing them there. Those cursed ships overhead as Surillia Ra burned. That nail in my heart? Those ships were the hammers driving it through. I felt a warmth at my back, almost as if the sword were trying to comfort me. To some extent, it worked. I looked back out at those ships, nearly impossible to see in the darkness of space. It wouldn't be hard for them to sneak right up on you. Narrowing my eyes to see them, I counted. One, two, three... four. There were only Four. One was substantially larger than the others.

"Sterling, that ship out there. What is it?" I asked, pointing out the largest of the Soulless vessels. She looked out, pulling the throttle back, furrowing her brow.

"That's... concerning." She said.

"What is it?" I repeated.

"That's a Command Ship." Tara looked over from the ship to Sterling.

"What's so special about it?" She asked. Sterling exhaled, raising her eyebrows.

"Where to begin on that?" She said, "Well, among the Soulless are soldiers, some specialists, a lot of the monsters you see running about, your typical military affair, but that," she shoved a finger at the ship, "belongs to one of the Ten Commanders." I didn't know who they were, but how she said it sent a chill up my spine. Her words were coated with ice, laced with what I could only describe as fear. When we didn't respond, her eyes narrowed, and she continued. "Commanders aren't your average Soulless. The power they wield, the devastation they could cause. They are *not* a trifling matter. If they're after something here, it can only mean trouble." I wandered down from my station, leaning against the wall, eying that ship. I guessed I could only *hope* that we didn't run into whoever this Commander was. Going by what Sterling had said earlier, trouble was the last thing we needed here.

"I see." I said, "So we keep our eyes open. Hopefully, avoid any confrontations." Sterling nodded, pushing us forward again.

"That's absolutely correct, Mr. Ortell." The ship rumbled as we ducked in under the cloud layer. As we straightened out just below the clouds, the Sparrow was pelted by rain. Above us, black and gray storm clouds brewed, spewing water over us. I noticed the shields on the ship were activating with ripples as the droplets hit us. Below us, a blue shield surrounded the moon. Towers shot up through the shield and into the cloud cover.

Sterling dipped us down once more, sending us through the barrier. The city came into view in all its glory. The multi-level moon stretched seemingly infinite in all directions. Looking down, you could see cars moving about, flowing like water between the buildings. Those towers stretched down below the city, and up through the shield. As I looked, I realized that they were *creating* the shield. I remember having learned about this.

Xenova's rain was acidic to the point where, for most races, it was deadly. To Xenovans, this rain kept their skin from drying out, but they wanted to ensure their homeworld could unite the galaxy. They developed the Universal Weather System to funnel the rain to the seas under the city. However, they could not survive. That's when a race known as the Faraxians stepped in to help.

You see, not much is known about the Faraxians. Throughout history, they appear and disappear, always seeming to show up where they're needed the most. Temples belonging to them dotted Furelle and other planets throughout the Milky Way. The feats of engineering they accomplished seemed to surpass anything we'd come close to making. Hell, they'd been the ones who'd propelled us into the age of warp technology. Yet they were secretive. Wherever they went, they always did their damndest not to leave a scrap of their technology behind. Whenever pieces of their past were scrounged up, it could either mean leaps and bounds forward or the worst trouble you could imagine. There was little in between. Yet, despite all this, they hadn't been seen by a single living soul since the first Soulless-Celestial War hundreds of years ago. No one knew where they'd gone.

Either way, they had stepped in to help and had assisted in creating the environmental suits that the Xenovans wear to survive. Xenova relies on the Universal Weather System, and even I could figure out that even one of those towers breaking without warning could be devastating to a lot of people.

The city was dark from the clouds, shrouded in constant gloom. Lights and signs of neon illuminated the many alleyways and nooks about the "streets" if you could call them that. Sterling pulled us up over the peaks of the buildings, turning as she did. Ahead of us, we could see a dip in the cityscape. She slowed us down as we stopped overhead, setting us down. She turned to both of us.

"You're all set. Give me a call when you're ready for a pickup." Sterling said. Tara and I grabbed our stuff, heading down through the cargo hold. Off the ramp, we felt the cold brisk air hit us. A cutting wind blew through the hallways of the city. Standing out here, it made you feel minuscule. The buildings stretched endlessly above you. Ships flew past, docking and departing, cars rushing through the air with a squealing whir. The noise was unlike anything I'd experienced. A cacophony of sound everywhere. Already I missed the quiet of the Sparrow.

Tara and I turned to look back at the buildings behind us. We'd landed on one of many platforms leading to a short but wide structure. Its stark white exterior contrasted the surrounding neighborhood's deeper grays. Blue lights adorned its angular faces, plants surrounded its edges. Above a set of double doors was an engraved sign. The Xenovan Grand Archives.

The Sparrow's rear bay doors climbed back up, sealing shut behind us. The deafening roar of the engines filled the air as she rose up. Our hair and coats whipped as we watched her lift and fly off into the distance. We watched for a while before Tara turned to me, then to the archives. She put her hands on her hips, stretching her wings out, cracking her back.

"Fiiiinally!" she said, twisting her torso, stretching her arms across her chest one after the other, "Feels good to get out!"

"It's barely been a couple of days," I said, nudging her with a smile. "You sure you can stand being on a ship for weeks on end?" I joked.

"Titan didn't count." She said, squatting before pulling herself back up. "Too stuffy. No *real* air." I turned, walking backwards past her, beginning to make my way toward the Archive. She followed after.

"No real air, huh?" I asked, "What's that supposed to mean?"

"You know. Air that isn't filtered or recycled in some way. Real *outside* air!" I put my hands behind my head, toying with my ponytail between my fingers.

"I suppose you're not wrong." I said, spinning to turn around, "Guess I just haven't really noticed."

"Didn't you grow up in a forest?" She asked.

"*By* a forest," I said, smirking back at her. "I wasn't just running around the forest like some little wild child." I thought it over for a moment. "I mean… I guess I was, but not in *that* way." I smiled, thinking back to those times. I thought back to Maurel. If only she could see me now. I'd have to fill her in once she was off of her current duty.

"Either way, I thought you would have preferred the outdoors." She said.

"Certainly enjoy the quiet of it more than this." I said, "That said, I don't mind being on the Sparrow. It's somewhat comforting, actually." Tara raised an eyebrow, jogging to catch up with me.

"How do you figure that?"

"Well, it's like the Shack was, except, you know, comfortable." I said. She thought about it.

"I… see your point."

"It doesn't feel that way to you?" I asked.

"Not all the time. Don't get me wrong, it feels right being there, but it's not *home,* you know?" I nodded, thinking about it.

"Yeah. Yeah, I definitely get what you're saying." We stopped as we watched the door to the archive swing open. A person I could only describe as fishlike stepped out, gripping a data pad. A Quan'en. They had what looked like four fins on their head, making it almost look like the bud of a flower. A set of whiskers drooped from their dull orange skin. They quickly hid the data pad in a compartment on the armor they were wearing. A second person exited the archive. Another Draen, like Tara. However, something struck me as odd about her. I couldn't put my finger on what it was, though. She approached the Quan'en, pointing at her. We could hear the yelling that ensued as we got closer.

It sounded like whoever this Draen was, she knew that this Quan'en had that datapad, and she demanded it from them. The Quan'en denied her, and we saw the Draen reach for a sword at her side. She paused though as she looked back. Seeing us, she let go, saying something else, before straightening herself. She puffed her chest forward, beginning to walk out toward the docks. We eyed her as she came closer to us until she was right beside us. I shifted my gaze, looking ahead, only to feel an icy hand stop my shoulder. Sharp claws dug at my skin, enough to hurt, but not enough to pierce.

"Hey." she said, not looking at me. "That sword of yours. Does it have a name?" She asked. Her voice made my blood run cold. It was soft, soothing, alarmingly so, but you could feel the hatred that breathed from it, the rage that quietly erupted from it. I pursed my lips and steadied my breathing.

"Can't say it does." I lied. I felt the claws dig in further.

"I see. Well, that's good." She said, her lips drawing closer to my ear. My whole body shivered as she spoke. "I *do* hope I don't find you in my way in the future." She released my shoulder, and I felt like I could breathe again. I looked back as she walked off down the docks. A Soulless shuttle dipped from the sky, and she stepped on, disappearing into the crowd of ships and cars. I almost jumped when Tara touched my other shoulder, the warmth catching me off guard.

"Hey." She said. Her piercing eyes gazed into me. "Are you okay?" She asked.

"Yeah." I said, still shaken, "I was just… caught off guard." She tightened her lips and looked out to the dock.

"She didn't have wings." It immediately struck me as she said it. She was right. That was what had looked off. I'd seen it before on some other Draen. It happened rarely, but it had never been something I picked up on. Tara looked distant. She snapped back to reality, looking at me. "Let's go. I have a feeling I know who we're supposed to be meeting," she said, looking at the Quan'en.

"You may just be right about that." I said, leading the way. We approached the Quan'en as they collected themselves. They looked up at us.

"You." They said. Their voice was somehow both soft and gruff. We stopped.

"You know us?" I asked.

"Cleva told me you'd be coming the other night. She let me know who I was looking for." They stretched a hand out to me. I took it. They grasped me firmly, shaking. "Arneli Tauren. Gunnery expert and a researcher of the Furin Era Faraxians."

"Quite the range," Tara commented, shaking her hand.

"You must be Tara." She said, "In war, it pays to be versatile." She let go, stepping back. "Good to finally meet you two, though there was supposed to be a third…" I jutted a thumb over my shoulder.

"That'd be Captain Sterling. She's… off recruiting." I said. Arneli huffed, crossing her arms.

"I see… well, at least I have you two," she said.

"We saw you were carrying a datapad. That woman seemed to be after it," I said.

"That *woman* was a Soulless Commander," she said. It felt like the world went quiet, a certain direness setting in, "and she was after this." She pulled out the datapad, handing it to me. It seemed to be a long archive of old writings, almost unreadable.

"What… is it?" I asked.

"As of right now? I'm unsure. That Commander seemed overly keen on it, though."

"And anything a Commander's interested in is something we are as well." Tara said. Arneli looked past us to the docks the woman had left on.

"I thought I'd kept it from them successfully, but she seemed so calm." I remembered how she'd stopped me, the vindication in her voice, the calmness of it. Arneli was right, something was wrong. I turned back to her.

"So we keep this," I said, holding up the datapad, "out of their hands as long as we can then." I smiled, about to put the pad away, when something caught my eye. A glimmer on the glass of the pad. It shined in my eyes as I turned it from side to side. In the reflection, I could see it. Something, someone, on a nearby roof. My eyes widened, as I turned as if on instinct to draw Isngr, letting go of the datapad.

I felt the impact before I could hear the shot fired. I pulled my blade up, a barrier forming in front of me. A shot struck the barrier, and I felt the force of it hit my whole body as it bounced off to the ground below. Arneli and Tara caught me as I skidded back. The glimmer was gone. Whoever had taken the shot had left with it. So much for neutral ground. Tara moved to grab the datapad from the ground as I got my bearings. I eyed the rooftop, ready for another attack.

Tara never could have seen it coming. A foot shooting out from the shadows, striking her across the face. She was sent flying backwards as a hand cloaked in black and purple grabbed the datapad. The sniper was just a distraction. I got back to my feet, helping Tara up as the figure snatched the data, sprinting off. The three of us looked to one another. We had to get that data back.

"Arneli, they're heading through the alley. I'll follow, you flank. Tara, you're on air," I directed, taking off in a sprint after them. I could feel Tara's hand reaching out to try and stop me, but

I was already off. The thief ducked and dodged around bins and cans, shoving them over to try and slow me down. I vaulted and jumped, kicking up off walls to avoid them. I could see the thief attach the pad to their arm as they ran. A bar appeared, slowly filling. They were uploading the data. I looked up. The Command ship. I dug deep, sprinting harder.

I could feel the burn in my lungs. I wasn't used to this, but adrenaline had taken over. The thief jumped over a fence. I drew my blade, slashing clean through it. Above, I could see Tara soaring through the air. Ahead, the alley opened back up to the streets. We broke from the shadows into the open daylight. He snaked his way through the crowds and out onto a catwalk. I shoved my way through, pushing people out of my way, stopping at the edge of the catwalk. The thief stood there and turned back to me. Their face was covered, couldn't make out anything about them. What I could see was the static forming at the edges of his knuckles. He cracked his neck from side to side, putting up his fists, urging me to get closer.

I twirled my sword, about to step forward, when Tara landed on the other edge of the catwalk. I remembered what Sterling had said. Right. Avoid a political shitstorm if possible. I put away my sword, putting up my fists. Arneli broke through the crowds, standing beside me. The thief looked between all three of us.

"Looks like he's cornered," she said. I could see the thief take in a deep breath.

"I have a sneaking suspicion that he has us right where he wants us." We began to run at him. Tara reached him first, swiping at him with her claws. He raised his arm, pushing her aside, landing a kick directly on her chest. I saw the air leave her body as she recoiled, off balance. Arneli tried to catch him off guard, but in the blink of an eye, his attention had turned. On one foot, he landed the kick, but before he could even return to the ground, his fist struck her shoulder. Arneli grunted, but fought past it, slamming her other shoulder into the thief. They were knocked back, but gracefully flipped back to their feet. They placed one hand behind their back, taunting us to come closer once more. Arneli pressed a hand to her shoulder, resetting it with a crunch as I rushed past. Tara called out to me as I began my approach.

"William! He's too fast!" Thanks. I already knew that. Then she called once more. "You need to keep your distance somehow!" Keep my distance? How was I-

It was too late. I was already too close, I realized. I swung, but he caught it, thrusting a fist into my gut. I could feel the surge of electricity burst through my core as my body tensed up. The thief grappled me, twisting me into a lock. I had to think fast, else I'd be a goner. I lifted my body as he wrapped his elbow around my throat, kicking off the railing beside us. The thief lost their balance, tumbling over the other edge, but I was in tow. I saw Arneli and Tara running to grab at me just before I went over, but they weren't fast enough.

Air whipped past us as we fell. I tried to jab an elbow back, but the thief shifted his body, shoving me below him. Another catwalk was just below us. Before I had time to react, I slammed into it; the thief releasing me, backing off. I coughed, my body feeling like… well, like I'd just fallen down a catwalk. I was surprised I was still even in one piece at all. At the same time, I wasn't one to look a gift horse in the mouth. Even if I wasn't injured, that didn't change the fact that I was in a lot of pain. I could feel my energy wearing thin. I grabbed the rail, dragging myself to my feet. I drew Isngr once again. To hell with not getting in trouble. *I* needed to not die.

Tara was right. I had to keep my distance from this guy, and I wasn't going to be able to do that if I was fighting him head-on. I had to use the magic I'd used on Draenica, but I had no idea how I'd done it. So far, it'd all been reactionary. Guess there was no time to learn like the present. The thief thrust their knuckles together, sparks dancing from the energized gloves. Right. Don't want to get hit by those again. I could already feel the burn where he'd hit me.

The thief made a dash at me and I tried to back away, stepping out of the way of his swings and kicks. He lashed out with an ungodly speed. I felt the wind hit my face, his fists only inches away. I brought up Isngr defensively as he punched, his fist connecting with the metal. I felt the shock of it hit my hand immediately, and I felt my fist clench over the blade. I grimaced as he pulled back, drawing my hand away, blood pouring down the tips of my fingers. They still were twitching from the electricity. The pain was red hot, and I could feel that adrenaline from earlier wearing thin. It was now or never. I dug deep for something, *anything*, and pushed my hand forward.

I felt the rush of energy flow past me before I realized what had happened. A beam of magic arched from within me, firing from the tips of my bloodied fingers, striking the thief. They were launched back, put off balance. This was my opening. I pulled from that reserve in me again, launching another barrage of thin blue wisps at the thief. They dodged some, but before they could react, they were hit again. They flipped through the air, landing on their side on the far edge of the catwalk. They dragged themselves up, looking intently into my eyes, before taking off down the alleyway behind them.

I gathered myself, pushing myself to run after them again. How did they have so much energy? I could tell I was slowing down. Despite my best efforts, I could see them starting to put distance between us. They stopped, though, when a tall silhouette stepped out in front of them at the far edge of the alley. Weakened and taken by surprise, they were knocked to the ground. I heard a gunshot ring across the metal walls. I slowed down as I approached, gasping for breath by the time I was able to stop. A single shot. Right through their head. I looked up at the figure standing in front of me. I stood barely at his chest he was so tall. He looked down at me with two large, round, black eyes. Tendrils drooped from his carapaced mouth. The shells surrounding the rest of his body were a dull brown. I'd heard of them but never seen one. He was an Actillion.

Scourge of the Milky Way, they called them. A violent race. If you believed what the stories said, you'd have heard they'd destroyed their own homeworld. Made it inhospitable through nuclear warfare. My heart stopped as I saw him in front of me. He reached out to me.

"You are unwell." He said, kneeling down. He pulled a machine from his belt as he eased me against the wall. I had no energy left to fight back. Arneli and Tara fluttered down from above. Arneli was quickly beside the man.

"William!" she said, before looking to the man. "Rex. Thank the gods. How is he?" Tara kneeled down beside me. Rex, I think his name was, placed the machine on my chest, carefully moving it across my body.

"Multiple small fractures, but he is quickly healing. Magic, very likely to do with passive regeneration," He said, standing up. Multiple fractures? I… didn't feel bad, and what was this about 'passive regeneration?' Tara helped me stand up. He turned to me. "That you can stand at all in your condition is impressive." He said, turning to Arneli. "Forgive my lateness. I had matters to attend to." He pulled out a set of translators. She eyed them.

"Guess none of us *can* read Faraxian," she said, turning to us. "William, Tara. Meet my partner in crime, Rex." He placed a hand over his chest, bowing to us. I supposed my misgivings had been misplaced.

"Rek'shav Na'and." He said, "But there are many who refer to me as Rex. If it is easier, you may as well." I caught my breath, and Tara eased off me, looking at Rex.

"You're a doctor, right? Not many would be carrying around that type of equipment," she asked. Rex nodded.

"Astute. Correct. I am a medical practitioner."

"Rex here's patched me up more times than I can count," Arneli said. I looked him and her up and down before moving over to the thief. The datapad was still embedded in their glove. I pulled it out. Arneli reached out for it, and I handed it over. She scrolled through. "Looks like they managed to upload a copy somewhere, but at least we still have the original." She said.

"That's good," I said, "but if the Soulless have what's there, then we need to figure out what they were after." I looked between the two of them, straightening myself out. My body was sore all over, and I was shaky, but I pulled myself together enough to talk. "Listen, we could really use people like you on the Sparrow. We're in need of crew and if we're after the same thing…" Arneli put a hand up.

"Say no more," she said, punching my shoulder gently. "I've seen how you fight, kid. I like your spunk." Rex nodded.

"We have wandered much of our career. We'd discussed joining a larger crew prior." He said, "I sense recklessness in you as well. You will need a medical practitioner." Tara smirked at me.

"Yeah, reckless sure is the word for it." I rolled my eyes, looking between them. Tara and I outstretched our hands.

"Well then," I began as they clasped their palms to ours. "Welcome to the Blue Sparrow."

Sterling called us in when she was ready, and the four of us called a cab out to the docks she'd listed. We'd had some time for food and recuperation, and already I was feeling better. I could see what Rex was talking about with regeneration, but how? Was it the sword? What was I talking about? Of course it was. Everything so far had been caused by this thing. I had to be grateful, though. Even if it had forced me out of a relatively okay life, as I looked out at the buildings passing us, I figured this was better. Tara nudged me.

"Hey." She said, "You think Sterling actually *found* anyone?"

"I mean," I started, "how long was she out there till she found us? I wouldn't get our hopes up too much." Tara shrugged, staring out the front of the taxi.

"Huh, I wouldn't count her out yet." I sat up, looking out, seeing the Sparrow, with four people standing outside of it. The taxi landed, the doors opening on either side. Arneli paid the driver as we stepped out. Surely enough, there stood Sterling waiting for us.

"You find what we were looking for?" She asked. I gestured to Arneli.

"Datapad from the archives. Had a run in with a Commander, but we got a few crew members." I said. She folded her arms, smiling up at me.

"Well, look at you two," she said. "Impressive."

"And it looks like you found a few people yourself," I commented. She gestured with her head for us to follow.

"Alright, Ortell, Verikov. Meet your new Yeoman, Iraka D'jaan." She waved a hand at an Olari man. He had snake-like features and golden eyes that seemed to stare through you. He was thin as a twig, towering over me. I understood how Sterling felt around us now. He reached out a hand, and I shook it.

"Nice to meet you. I look forward to getting to know you more in-depth." His voice was level, smooth, and calm. Despite almost being monotone, it conveyed every emotion you needed. I smiled, cocking my head slightly.

"As with you Mr. Djaan."

"Just Iraka if you'd please." I nodded.

"Will do, Iraka." He stepped back, and Sterling spoke up again.

"Next, Chief Engineer, Gatha Kori," she said. I looked down at the woman in front of me. She was half my height at most, with a set of dragonfly-like wings stretching from her forearms. She had deep red skin, with blue stripes along her head. A Kinth. She put her hands on her hips, looking up at me, giving me a wave.

"Nice to be back in the action. Been too long since I served on a ship," she said.

"You were in the military before this?" Tara asked.

"Hunter's collective. Did some work in the private militaries," she said, waving that off. "That's how I met Sterling. I owed her a few favors, anyway." Sterling cleared her throat.

"Right, right," she said nervously, "before we divulge any more of my history, this is our new Science Officer, Natasha Krugoff." She was a Furin, red markings adorning the shell that crested along her head. Her gaze was distant, and she was quiet. I felt like I'd heard the name before, but couldn't place it. I looked between all of them. They all seemed to be veterans of some sort. I wondered how Sterling had gathered them all up. I guess I short-changed her a little. Hands on her hips, she looked at the crew we'd assembled.

"Well," she said, "we aren't many, but we're enough." She took in a deep breath. "We have a direction, right?" She asked, looking at me.

"Arneli. You have the data, right?" I asked. She nodded, pulling out the datapad.

"I do."

"How quickly do you think you can gleam something from it?" I asked. Arneli bit her lower lip.

"I don't know. It could be a day or two to sort through and get an understanding of the Faraxian carvings." Iraka raised a hand as Arneli spoke.

"If it's about Faraxians, I may be able to assist," he said. "I have some experience in their texts." Sterling nodded.

"Okay. We head into orbit. You two, see what you can get from those files. If the Soulless want it so badly, then we should do our best to get it first," she said. "Everyone. On board. We take off at once."

We funneled our way through the ship's halls. Already, she felt so much more alive. Gatha took up the station where I normally stood, Iraka to one side of Sterling, me at the other, somewhat unsure what to do now that my job was taken. Natasha took computers to one side, Arneli at the gunnery station, and Rex stood at the entrance, arms folded behind his back. It was a skeleton of one, but it was a crew. Sterling gave the word, and we lifted off, ready to plan our next move.

The Blue Sparrow:
Xenova Orbit
Galactic Date 00:08:415 5028

The following day felt like an eternity of waiting. I feel like I spent the majority of it pacing about in my room. That woman, the Commander, everything about her just struck a chord in me. My mind flashed back to her icy claws digging into the skin of my shoulder. I reached back, feeling the thin holes that had been torn into my shirt. Yet she'd been careful not to leave a mark on me personally. I remember the feeling of my chest tightening as she drew closer to my ear. Some part of me wished never to see her again. Another part of me hoped I would.

As I got lost in my thoughts, I heard a knock at the door to my quarters. I quickly pulled my hair back, tying it up in a ponytail before turning.

"Come in," I said. The door slid open to the dim room. Iraka stepped in, looking about the place.

"Quite dark in here." He commented.

"I like it that way," I said. "The light from Warp is calming."

"Mmm." He gestured to look out the window. I turned, leaning on the sill.

"Any reason you're here? Thought you were working with Arneli."

"I was," he started, folding his arms across the sill, leaning forward beside me, "but she was just finishing up. Anyway, I wanted to check in on you."

"Check in on me?"

"I'm the yeoman. It is my job to keep up to date with everything happening, and," he put a hand on my shoulder, enveloping the tear in my shirt, "to make sure everyone on board is mentally sane." Despite his reptilian appearance, his touch was warm and comforting. "You're a long way from home, aren't you?" He asked.

"First time, actually. Draenica, and Furelle before that." His silence spoke volumes.

"Did you lose anyone?" He asked.

"A lot of people. Parents, friends…" I turned, facing him, "but that was then. This is now."

"You can't pretend that it doesn't matter to you, William," he said.

"And why's that?" I asked, folding my arms over my chest. He stood up, patting my shoulder again.

"Because if not for them, why would you be here?" I went silent, looking into the ground. Iraka began to stride toward the door again, "That sword you have," he said, "It's a lot to live up to. If you ever need to let it all out, I've got an open ear." I nodded, quiet. He returned the gesture, tapping his hand at the door frame, before looking back at me. “Right. Arneli wanted me to let everyone know to meet at the war room.”

“I’ll be right there.” Iraka took his leave, the door sliding shut behind him. I finally let out a breath, staring back out the window. Was Iraka right? Why exactly *was* I doing all of this? I thought I’d let go of all the people on Furelle. I reflected on the topic. No… I couldn’t have. Why else would I have held a grudge against the Celestials for so long? I looked down at Isngr, my face contorted into a frown. I’d say I left to do all of this because of the sword, but now I wasn’t so sure. I needed to clear my head.

I made my way into the head, flipping the tap on, staring at myself in the mirror as I leaned over the sink. I could see the beads of sweat on my brow, could feel the tiredness starting in my eyes. I splashed water up into my face, feeling its sharp coolness. The sudden shift in temperature shocked me awake. I gasped as I drew my head back, staring at myself. Right. Arneli had some findings. It was time to meet with the crew.

I threw on a new shirt, laying the torn one across my bed, heading out into the hallways. From the sounds of everyone’s voices, it sounded like they’d already started gathering. I kicked off into a jog, heading back down the hallways. I turned right, then halted by the war room. The crew was gathered around the circular table. Most of them were here. Arneli, Sterling, Tara, Gatha. Notably, Iraka, Rex, and Natasha had yet to arrive. Sterling looked up at me as I walked in.

“William.” She said. I nodded, sliding into the seat by Arneli.

“Where’s everyone else?” I asked.

“Rex won’t be joining us. He’s setting up the medical bay for use.” Arneli said. “As for the other two…”

"Sorry, we're a touch late!" Iraka said with a cheer as he strode through the door, Natasha at his heels. She gave me a silent look with those pitch-black eyes. Iraka took a seat, and without a word, Natasha pinned herself down to the end of the couch surrounding the table.

"Right, we're all here." Sterling said, "Ms. Tauren, you said you found something?" Arneli nodded, swiping up the documents to a hologram before us.

"Iraka and I have been working at the scriptures here. Most of it," she swiped away a large chunk of the photos and documents, "was useless. Either too degraded or had little substance."

"Okay…" Sterling said, "but did you find anything useful?" Arneli eyed her for a moment before pulling over one of the images.

"There were a few texts that seemed to be from the same location." She pointed to some scripts that were cut off along the edge. "It was hard to make out, but they seemed to be talking here about a weapon of some kind. We couldn't make out much more than that, but it's the only suspect we have on what that Commander would have been after." I leaned forward, eyeing the text.

"Is there any clue on where that is?" Tara asked. "We know there's something important there, but we can't figure out anything else without an idea of where to look." Arneli pulled at her collar.

"We don't…" Sterling put her head in her hand.

"Fantastic. So we-" I began to tune them out, arguing ensuing in the background as I pulled the image closer. I'd… seen this before. Where though? My brow furrowed as I zoomed in, going over all the details. Oh, gods damn it, it was right *there*. Right on the tip of my tongue; why couldn't I remember? I looked at the brown stone, the plants, the leaves coming in from the ceiling, the weapons held by the scientists, the… no… the soldiers. Furin soldiers. Shit, that was it! I pushed the image back as they argued.

"I know where this is." I said. The room went silent, the group of them looking at me. Sterling urged me on with her hand. "This is on Furelle. It's a… temple just inland of a coastal colony, Surillia Ra." They were quiet for a moment longer before Arneli spoke again.

"You're… sure of that?" She asked.

"It's where I grew up. I was in there when the Soulless first attacked Furelle. I recognize these." I said, pointing to the weapons the Furins were using. "There were skeletons down there holding them, and a lot of ash." The group looked at each other, nodding, taciturn. Iraka patted my shoulder, leaning over.

"Good eye." He whispered, before sitting upright, jotting something in the ship's logs. Sterling nodded.

"Right. Furelle then." She said, "Are we all in agreement?" The group each affirmed in their own ways before she put a hand up. "Very well. Mr. Ortell, you know this place the best by the sound of it. You'll have to lead us in." A dry, harsh voice cut in. It sounded like sandpaper that had lost its grit.

"This is going to be dangerous," Natasha said. It was the first words we'd heard from her. "Ma'am, we are flying after a Commander, and into an active war zone." She looked at me and Tara. "Are you sure this is safe for everyone present?" Arneli caught her meaning and leaned forward.

"I've seen these two in action. They may not stand up to a Commander, but you can be sure they'll hold their own in battle." She said, putting a hand on my arm. Natasha's face dipped, shadows masking her eyes.

"That won't be enough…" Sterling put a hand up as Natasha spoke again.

"It will have to be. Mr. Ortell is Isngr's wielder, and he has express orders from Cleva to be here." There were some murmurs among the crew. I don't think they all knew. I sighed, crossing my arms as I leaned forward. "The fact of the matter is, we have a heading, even if dangerous. Our new mission is to investigate this 'weapon' and, if need be, stop the Commander from obtaining it." She looked for any sign of disagreement among the group. Seeing none, she spoke again. "Begin preparations for warp. Iraka, send the logs of this meeting to Titan. Dismissed." Everyone began to funnel out of the war room, but Sterling stopped me. "Just a minute. I wanted to talk to you alone." Everyone else vacated as I leaned against the wall. Once we were the last two, I looked back down at Sterling.

"Everything alright Captain?" I asked. Sterling sighed, rubbing at the bridge of her nose.

"Yeah, yeah, just…" She took a moment and gestured to the seat. I slid back into the table. "Listen, in the past, I've made some… mistakes as a leader. I need someone honest, and who I feel I can trust to keep me in check. A first mate." She looked at me, her glowing eyes piercing me, reading me.

"You're…"

"I'm asking you to be my Number One." I felt my mind stop working for a moment. First mate? Really? Me? There were so many questions spinning through my mind as I tried to comprehend this.

"I'm sorry… Captain, I'm… not sure that I'm exactly the best choice for that. You could have anyone else. Iraka seems smart, or maybe even Natasha. She has the experience and-" She cut me off with a hand.

"It's unorthodox, I know. Arneli told me of your actions on Xenova though. She was impressed, I'm impressed. You took initiative of the situation and led everyone." She sighed. "You can say no. I don't expect you to take on all of this responsibility on your first month off-world. I'll tell you now. It *will* be tough. You might need to make some hard calls, but if you want it, I think you'll be capable." She slid a patch my way. It had a mark at the top of it, a white bar under it, and two stars. I looked up at her shoulder, seeing the same patch with three stars. She was right, it would be a lot of responsibility. I reached out, my hand hovering over the patch. If I accepted this, there was *really* no turning back. Then again, I'd stolen a ship and fought someone on the catwalks of a city over an acid ocean. It would be hard to get much more dangerous than that. Still, was I ready for this? I looked up at Sterling, her expression steely, locked to mine. I closed my eyes, let out a breath, and took the patch. I pulled it close to me, looking at it. Sterling got up, walking to my side.

"It's the Celestial's Mark," she said, referencing the symbol at the top of the patch. "The diamond in its center represents our soul and spirit. The mark that coils around it is our body." She looked up at me, adjusting my collar again. "We must stay strong in both." We heard the core hum as it drew in power. Sterling cleared her throat as I looked out into the hall.

"To our stations, then?" She nodded, stepping back, pointing at the patch.

"I'll, uh… help get those sewn to your uniforms. For now, though…" She pinned a matching set of symbols to the breast of my shirt, patting it. "There." She said, giving it an affirming nod before turning on her heels and striding away. I looked one more time to the patch in my palm and gripped it firmly. Time to get a move on.

I hopped to my feet, running up to the helm. Everyone was working hard at their stations, the ship turning slowly to face its heading. I took up a position behind Sterling. She looked up at me, a beam across her face.

"You ready?" She asked. I leaned forward, hands on the rails.

"More than ready." I said. She waved her hand forward.

"Would you like to do the honors?" She asked. I nodded as she stepped aside. I moved forward, hands folded behind my back. Everyone looked up at me, confused at first. They saw the pins. Some looked concerned, but others gave a smile in my direction, turning back to their work. I was nervous. I could feel the fluttering in my stomach as I attempted to recollect myself. Sterling put a hand on my arm, mouthing that I'll do okay. I nodded, looking back over the crew.

"Gatha, what's the status on the core?" I asked. She gave a thumbs up in my direction.

"Aye, all good here." She said, "Core's juiced up and ready to run when you are." I nodded.

"Tara, do we have a course set?" She looked back at me, pushing the navigation computer aside.

"That we do." She said. "Gotta say the new duds look good on you." I bent forward, leaning on my elbow.

"Now, don't butter me up too much," I said, looking out to the empty blackness ahead of us. "Next stop, Furelle." I said under my breath. I looked down at Tara again. "Take us out." She nodded, pushing the throttles forward. We jolted as the ship launched itself out into space. I stepped back, taking a breath, looking to Sterling. "How'd I do?" I asked quietly. She gave me a wink and a thumbs up, stepping in to take my place.

"Alright everyone. Initial diagnostics, then we follow the watch schedule. Let's fall out." Most of the people left the helm,

Sterling sitting at her chair. I leaned forward, watching as everyone did work… except me. Sterling looked up at me. "Need something to do, Mr. Ortell?" She asked.

"What exactly… do I do?" I asked. She sat up, leaning her elbows on her knees.

"Well, you still have other duties outside of being my number one," she said, looking back down the hall. Right, I guess even now I would still be in engineering. I tossed her a salute.

"Right. I'm on it." I said, heading back down the hall. I could hear a thin buzzing from the engine room as I approached. Ducking in past the doorway, I could see why. Above me was Gatha. The wings on her arms fluttered as she ran tests around the top of the core. As I entered, she put a finger up to me.

"One minute!" She yelled over the core. "Just running this test real quick." Her voice was thick with an accent I couldn't quite place. I stood there awkwardly as her brows furrowed at her instruments. "Ah, blasted things!" She smacked the side of it with her palm. I winced, hearing the small machine squeal. She shook it and looked again. "Ah fuck it all." She strapped the tool to her belt, fluttering down.

"Everything okay?" I asked as she shoved past me.

"No, it ain't." She said, crawling down underneath the plates. I remembered being down there days before. Her small size made it look easy. She was able to kneel and fit in. "Damned thing's drawing too much fuel and putting out too much power." She struggled to reach back behind the fuel canisters to the cut-off switch.

"Yeah, she tends to do that," I said, hopping down in beside her, reaching back to flip the switch off. She folded her arms to look at me.

"Oh, look at us with the long arms," she said. "Well, Mr. First Mate, what exactly can this little engineer do for you?" She asked, twisting a few of the canisters loose to reset them.

"Nothing really. I've been working down here since I joined. I'm just here to help out."

"That so?" She said, moving her way down the line. "Alright then, you can help. Your long arms will be useful." She grunted, pushing a canister back into place. "Just to be clear, though. This here," she gestured to the engine room, "is my domain. You got that?" I leaned on my elbow, nodding. "Good. Sterling's told me already you're new meat, not a lot of experience. You want to work in my engine room, you learn fast and you work hard." She looked at me, setting the canisters. "Looks like you have the learning down. Good." I didn't look up as I kept at it. "Right," she ducked in front of me, her eyes inches from mine. I jumped back. "I hope you're ready for a long few days, kiddo. We've got a lot of work to do to get this here engine really ship shape, and if you're going to be my little engineer trainee, then I'm going to be working you till you drop." She grabbed one of the tools from her belt. "So, you ready to get her purring?" She asked, throwing it to me. I caught the tool, a grin on my face.

"Let's get started."

Blackwater System: Furelle

Galactic Date 00:08:431 5028

The Sparrow sat above Furelle. The broken planet, people called it. Not hard to understand why. I looked out at my old home, held together by a machine at its core. The initial destruction of Furelle was the Soulless' handiwork. They'd cracked the planet into pieces to make an example, much as they'd done with Earth before it. Who would have expected the ever-mysterious Faraxians to step in and piece it back together? This had all been long before I'd been born. Now, you could barely see the cracks in the planet's crust. Most of what remained as a reminder were fragments of rock jutting from the ground as if it'd been struck by hundreds of meteors made of itself.

My eyes couldn't help but drift to the hundreds of ships dotting the skies. We'd dimmed the lights in the helm, and an eerie silence had befallen the ship. Engines off, core off. Quiet. The darkness of the helm only helped to exacerbate the uneasiness. My eyes drifted over Surillia Ra, my home. The Soulless had swarmed it. It'd be hard for us to get close enough to get into the temple. Sterling looked up at me.

"Hmm..." She hummed. Our next move was uncertain. We'd have to find the nearest outpost and move from there. Sterling sat forward, crossing her fingers together. She looked to Natasha.

"Ms. Krugoff. Open a secure channel with the SFS Vigilance." She turned back to the computers, rapidly typing in commands. A hologram of an Olari woman appeared in front of me and Sterling. She turned, looking at us.

"CNS Blue Sparrow. We're reading you."

"Reading you as well, SFS Vigilance." Sterling said.

"We don't have you on our arrivals, Sparrow. What's your business here?" The woman asked.

"We're on a new mission, not here for the siege. There's a temple on the Surillian Coast. It's a time sensitive matter." The woman on the other side pursed her lips.

"You picked quite a time to show up, Sparrow. Surillia's currently being heavily contested." She turned, typing something into a nearby console. "There *should* be an opening in one of the nearby camps for landing. I'd be careful, though. A Soulless Commander was spotted in the area." We looked between each other, that silence even more deafening than before. Sterling kept a calm, cool expression, scratching at her chin.

"Understood. Send us the coordinates and let them know of our arrival, if you will." The woman on the other end saluted, and Sterling swiped the hologram aside. We looked out over Surillia

Coast, my eyes focusing on the small, yet unmistakable dot in the distance. It was the same Command Ship we'd seen on Xenova. Natasha leaned back, folding her arms over her chest, before looking over at the two of us.

"Our chances of success aren't looking too high here." She said. The crew was silent, deep in thought, as we waited for the orders to come in from the Federation. No one wanted to say it, but she was right. Tara eventually broke the silence.

"We still have the advantage." She said.

"Oh? How do you figure?" Iraka asked.

"Well, the Soulless know of the planet, sure, but they're going to have to scour the area to find that temple." She said, looking up at me. "We have a living, breathing map." Iraka raised his brow.

"You may just be right about that. Arneli, you're a strategic mind as well. Any thoughts?" Arneli leaned over her console, tapping her fingers together. When she turned, the whiskers on her face whipped along with her.

"That all depends. With a war waging for the past decade, who knows how much that forest has changed?" I pursed my lips as she said this.

"That's true." I said, "I might be able to get us directly there, or it might take some doing. Either way, we know we need to get there before the Soulless do." There was a quiet agreement among us. I wasn't a fan of all this waiting. I paced back and forth, tapping my finger on my chin. Every second we wasted up here was a second the Soulless were using to find that temple. I felt a small hand tug at my arm, looking down to see Gatha.

"Hells kid, you're gonna make me anxious you keep pacin' like that." She whispered, fluttering up on top of the chair by the engineering computer.

"Can't help it." I said, "A touch nervous."

"Ah, it'll be fine." She said, "You run into any Soulless down there and you just put the beatin's their way, y'hear?" I chuckled as she boxed against my arm.

"Ah, I'm just antsy is all." She folded her arms, staring up into my eyes. The wrinkles in her skin were all the more clear, highlighted by the light from outside.

"Antsy, eh? Well, a little advice from lil ol' me to you." She said, "Ya gotta learn to respect these quiet moments." She gave me a tap at my side again, spinning the chair around to the computers. I sighed, leaning back against the wall. Maybe she was right. I could only assume that once we were on the ground, we wouldn't have much time to rest for a while. A voice cut my thoughts short, however.

"Captain, they've sent us the clearance." Natasha said in her droll, bitter voice. Sterling clapped her hands together.

"*Finally*. Bring them up on the flight plan. Ms. Verikov, set a bearing and follow through." She spat out the orders in quick succession as I watched from my dark corner of the room. I kicked myself up, only to feel Iraka's warm hand on my shoulder.

"Ah, William. Before we head down, Rex wanted me to ask you to stop by the medical bay for a moment." I furrowed my brow.

"Did he say why?" I asked. Iraka shrugged.

"Didn't ask. Just said he wanted to have a moment to check in with you on a few things before you headed out." I nodded.

"Fair enough. Thank you Iraka." Iraka returned my nod, returning to his position near Sterling. I looked out over the crew for a moment longer before making my way aft. The bright lights of the hallways nearly blinded me. I had to squint, my eyes watering up as I got used to the sudden change. I felt my way to the medical bay. First set of doors, right in the middle of the ship.

I slid my hand over the panel to its side, the door opening. The smell of sterile chemicals hit me almost immediately. My nose wrinkled. It sure as hell *smelled* like a doctor's office, that's for sure. As for the look of it, I could say it looked a lot better than most of the hospitals I'd been in. Then again, given where I lived, that wasn't saying much.

As I stepped in, Rex looked over his shoulder at me. He slid a microscope back, standing from a squeaky, black rolling chair, pushing it back under a table with his foot. He cleared his throat, straightened out his coat, and began walking toward me.

"Ortell. I'm grateful to hear you received my message from Iraka. Come in. Please take a seat, if you will." I moved past him to where he aimed his hands, hopping up onto a medical bed. I always felt like these things were way too high. My feet dangled off the side like limp noodles as he walked over to me, pressing a stethoscope to my chest.

"I did. What exactly is this for, doc?" I asked. He moved the stethoscope to the other side, the metal cool against my skin.

"I have two reasons for my call. The first being that you have yet to be checked up, unlike the rest of the crew."

"Ah, regular checkup. Right." He moved around to the back of me.

"Yes. Breathe in slowly, please." I obliged. "As well as this, I am aware that you are inexperienced with how magic affects your body. Is that correct?" I furrowed my brow, letting out the breath.

"Didn't know it *did,* to be honest with you." Rex wrapped the stethoscope back around his neck.

"You are… new to magic, are you not?" I nodded, and he grumbled. "Then there are some things you must know to protect yourself." Protect myself? What exactly is he talking about? "The sword you wield is a relic, as I'm sure you've been told. It allows you to tap into a well of magical potential your body has yet to develop on its own. You have seen this already, on Xenova for example." I thought back to when I'd first picked up Isngr. It felt like a surge of power had hit me. That magic I was casting was... this thing?

"Alright. So the sword gives me magic. That's a good thing, right?"

"Yes, but no." He kneeled down, his eyes meeting mine. "As with working your muscles, your body normally needs time to exercise its strength. As you are right now, you could not lift 200 kilograms without severely injuring yourself, I would assume."

"I couldn't lift it period to be honest with you, doc."

"Imagine that sword allowed your body to lift that 200 kilograms, but your muscles didn't have the power to truly hold it. They would tear themselves apart, but you *could* still do it." He stood back to his full, towering height. "William. When you use magic, it is the same concept. You have access to a great potential of magic, but your body cannot withstand it all." I think I was understanding what he was saying. I thought back to how sore and tired I was on Xenova after only a few spells. It felt like I was about to pass out, and back on Draenica, I *did* black out. I remember how much my hand burned after I'd fought the Soulless.

"So... what happens if I use too much magic?"

"Your muscles will begin to tear. Bones fractured. Internal bleeding. You've shown a decent strength so far, but I would refrain from pushing yourself too much for now. While your body is partially maintained by your sword's magic, it cannot nullify the damage to your body from that amount of exertion." Rex looked off, seeming to stare into the distance. "We have yet to develop a full understanding of just how much power you were gifted. You have yet the understanding *yourself* to wield most of it. I would be thankful of that for now. Hopefully, your body will strengthen as you learn." I looked down at my hands, flexing my fingers. Was there really that much power in me? Enough that I could destroy myself? The thought shocked me to my core… but he was right. Even now, I didn't have a clue about what I was doing. I'd barely managed small projectiles on command, maybe a wall here or there, but I couldn't really *control* it per se. Rex tilted my chin up, examining me further.

"So keep the magic reasonable, and… anything else?" I asked.

"Train. Your body will not strengthen unless it is being worked." He wrote something out on a data pad. "As you said, though, keep it reasonable." He tapped the top of the pad. "You're cleared. Body is stable, not that it was any surprise." I hopped up from the bed, but he stopped as I moved to leave. "I want you back in here after the mission. We need to gauge where your body is afterwards." I nodded to him, and he let me go.

As I walked out, I felt the ship shift under me. I found myself careening into the nearby wall, grabbing at the rails for balance. What the hell was going on? The ship settled out as I looked in at the helm. A red light flared up from the engineering console by Gatha as she swore, spewing curse after curse in various tongues at the thing. She stormed off past me, muttering under her breath as I walked in. Looking out, we'd made it to Furelle in one piece, but that didn't explain the commotion. Everyone seemed tossed about, Tara nervously recalibrating everything as we settled down. Sterling had her head in her hand, rubbing her temple. I stepped up to her side.

"Did I miss something?" I asked.

"One of the port side engines went out." She said, rubbing her eyes. She sat up, looking at me. "I was planning on helping lead the ground team, but it looks like we're going to be busy with repairs." I glanced over at the engineering console. It looked like one of the parts had failed. Hope there was a replacement nearby or that could be trouble. "You'll have to lead a team out to the temple." My eyes shot back to her.

"Me?" I asked.

"You're the first mate. Think of it as a training mission. A... very high stakes training mission." She smiled, slapping my arm. "I believe wholeheartedly in your abilities, Mr. Ortell. Just let me know who you need." I looked over the available people. Gatha would be busy, Natasha too. We needed technical people to stay behind to work on the ship. Iraka wasn't an option as he wasn't combat personnel. Arneli was a soldier through and through, so she was an obvious pick, and Tara would make for some decent backup. I gave Sterling a nod.

"Tara, Arneli. You're with me." I said. The two of them looked up at me and got to their feet, moving up to the upper level. I looked back to Sterling, and she gave me a thumbs up.

"You'll do great." She whispered. I took a long, deep breath, shaking out my nerves.

"Right. We'll be back before you know it." I gestured to Arneli and Tara, leading the way. Tara looked up to me, skipping up beside me.

"So, William, what's the plan?" She asked.

"Hmm. Good question. We can't just run out into the forests." I said. Arneli spoke up.

"There's bound to be other Celestial crews here. It might be a good idea to figure out what the situation is before we proceed." She said as we passed down into the cargo hold.

"I agree." I said, squeezing past the crates of supplies. "Let's get an idea of what we're dealing with. Try to find someone who seems to know what they're doing." We walked down the ramp and out into the forest clearing. The first thing that hit me was the smell. Dense redwoods and the aroma of pine floated in the air. It felt so familiar, so much like home, yet another smell twisted it. Ash and burning mixed its way into the fray, distorting that familiar scent. I was reminded, brutally, that this wasn't home any longer, despite everything. Still, there was *some* familiarity. That wind on my face; that cool coastal breeze. It felt odd, to be fully honest. I was back, but it didn't feel right.

I shook myself out of my dazed mind, looking about. Federation troops mingled throughout the camp, moving food, crates of weapons, and tents through the clearing. Multiple ships, some Federation, some Celestial, lined the outskirts of the camp. Looking up, I could see the broken engine sparking and fizzing. I couldn't be stuck thinking about that all day, though. We had a mission to take care of. I stopped a passerby, tapping his shoulder as he strode beside me. He was a young Terran man, looked barely old enough to be fighting. His black hair curled around his freckled face, and he looked up at me with soft brown eyes. Given his getup, though, a loosely fit green button up jacket and greased up jeans, he certainly didn't look like he was a Federation troop. Another Celestial perhaps?

"Oh, I'm sorry, can I help you?" He asked. His voice was thick with a New Irish accent. Must have been from Terra Nova. "I didn't mean to impose. I was just admiring your ship, was all." He stammered, clearly nervous. "Oh, I'm Lux by the way!" He held out a hand. I gave him a cocked smile, shaking it.

"Not imposing at all, Lux. I'm William Ortell. This is Tara Verikov and Arneli Tauren. We're just looking for someone who knows what the situation's like here."

"Oh! Right!" He said, "You'll be wanting to talk to Jewls." He looked up at the Sparrow again, then back to me. "Right, I can take you to her, if you'd like." He seemed all over the place. I wondered how someone so young could have gotten mixed up in all of this. Then again, I was younger than him when Furelle had been hit. I looked back to Arneli and Tara, each of them giving me affirming looks. I turned back to Lux.

"Alright. Show us to Jewls." He nodded, leading us forward quietly. As he took us across the camp, I found myself unable to deal with the quietness of the situation, looking once more to Lux. "I noticed you seemed interested in the Sparrow." I said. His eyes lit up almost immediately.

"Yes! She's a marvel, by the looks of it! I've never seen anything like her!" He said, a certain energy vibrating through him. "I've heard tales of the Blue Sparrow from other Celestials about how it always seems to stay leagues ahead of other ships in its engineering. It's an absolute legend!"

"You seem very into ships." Tara commented.

"Of course! I built my own, after all." He pointed out to a ship toward the end of the line. It was certainly crude, but it looked better than some hand built ships I'd seen. "I… had help of course, but I've been flying since I was a kid, and the Olympus has seen me through it all." Olympus, huh? Must have been his ship. Had to admit, the kid had something about him that just struck me. A young Celestial, built his own ship, flying since who knew when? I thought back to other Celestials and wondered just how far behind the curve I was. "I like to look at other ships to see how I can upgrade the Olympus, at least when I have the funds."

"Well, maybe if Gatha's feeling nice, she'll let you check out the engine room. Might get an idea or two." His eyes went even wider than before.

"You really mean that?"

"Really do." I said, as we approached a tent. Lux stopped. "Well, this the place?"

"That it is." He said, pulling the flap aside, "Good luck." His last words hit me like a dagger in the side. Before I had time to think about it, through the slit of the tent I walked, seeing her. She was unmistakable. She had dark skin and slicked back, shimmering silver hair, parts of it sticking up in the front. Black markings adorned her face, a diamond on her forehead, two lines on her cheeks, each with a set of three dots below them. She wore an ornamented white and gold jacket, a decorated pauldron lashed to it on her right shoulder. By far, the part that stuck out to me the most, though, were her eyes. As she looked up from the map on her table, they felt like they saw through me. There were no noticeable pupils. The iris just… glowed a glaring blue. Her eyes darted to the sword on my back, then to my face, seeming to inspect every inch of me.

"Hi, you're Jewls, right?" I asked. She strode from the table to me. Her hands were on her hips as she looked at me with a hard, expressionless face. She squinted, looking at me, her gaze shifting from first my left, to my right.

"You're bonded to it." She said. Her voice was calm, deep, serene, yet it did not bring me any peace. I cocked my head in question. "Isngr. You are not just a carrier, are you?" She asked. I understood, drawing my sword, resting the blade on my hand. She drew fingers over it.

"I am." I said.

"Your aura told me everything I needed to know," she said. Her eyes, that glow, was that what it was? I wondered if she could really "see" at all. Her eyes locked to mine, "but the potential for magic is worthless if its user doesn't understand it." She dropped her hand as the two of us paced around each other, both of us sizing the other up.

"Can't say I've been trained. You can see auras?" I asked.

"I can do far more than that." She said, holding a hand to her side. A golden ornate staff flashed into existence within her palm. I took a step back, both of us halting in our pacing. Her eyes narrowed. "Unskilled, untrained. You lack discipline. What is your name?" I narrowed my eyes back to her, subtly pointing my shoulder toward her.

"William Ortell, and you must be Jewls." I responded. Her head tilted back, and I could practically feel the animosity in the room thicken.

"Jewls Reynar." She clarified. "Tell me, William, how much have you learned in ways of magic?" she asked.

"Haven't exactly had much time to learn. A spell or two on the journey." I said, keeping my voice steady.

"Pathetic." She spat. I recoiled.

"Excuse me?"

"It's pathetic." She repeated. "That Isngr would choose someone with no skills to make use of its power." I narrowed my eyes further, leaning in closer. We shot daggers at each other.

"You think it's so pathetic? Try me." Tara pushed the two of us apart.

"Alright, we aren't here for a dick measuring contest." Tara locked eyes with me with a look that said, 'You're better than this.' I sighed, straightening up, Jewls doing the same.

"Fine. What exactly do you need, William?" She said, striding back to the table. I leaned over it, seeing a map of the coast and the forest. I could see Surillia Ra, the coastal waypoints where Soulless and Celestials had set up camp.

"We're after a temple nearby." I said, scanning over the details of the surrounding area. "If Surillia Ra is here, then the entrance should be somewhere around… here." I circled a small area on the map. It wasn't more than a mile or two outside of the town. Jewls looked over at me from the map.

"What's so important about this that you need to get in there? The Soulless have been crawling all the way up and down the coast." She said, scanning my eyes.

"We know a Soulless Commander is after it. We have reason to suspect it contains information on some sort of weapon." I said. Jewls sighed, rubbing the bridge of her nose, thinking.

"Alright… alright." She groaned under her breath, leaning over the table once more. I joined her, the two of us staring at the pieces on the board. It looked like there were three groups of our troops out there, each focusing on trying to punch through the line. She was right. The Soulless were sitting over a potential gold mine, and they didn't even realize it. Tara looked over the pieces with us.

"Do you think we might be able to draw them south?" She asked. Jewls tapped at her jaw in thought, looking everything over.

"Possibly. All we need is to get through the North edge of their line."

"Preferably unseen." I added.

"Definitely unseen." She agreed. "They'd have forces on us within minutes if they caught us." She seemed to mull something over, her brows furrowing. "We might draw their attention here." She gestured to the center group. "If we pull the north squad south, it *could* draw their attention in."

"What's the downside?" I asked.

"Downside is that we have no clue if it will actually work." She stood up straighter, peering at me through those harsh eyes. You could see the touches of a grimace on her face any time she looked at me, yet still she attempted to keep her composure. “If what you say is true, however, then we have little time that can be wasted on planning.” She stopped, as if she wanted to say more. I watched her intently, looking for any crack or sign on what she was going to hit me with next. Finally, she let her shoulders relax. “I will be coming with you.”

“Excuse me?” I asked.

“You want to prove to me you aren’t a pathetic excuse for a Celestial? Then prove me wrong. I’m coming with you. This is too vital to leave to just your group. This is not up for debate.” I looked to Arneli and Tara for their input. Arneli shrugged.

“We could always use the extra firepower.” She said. I sighed, turning back to Jewls.

“Fine.” I said through gritted teeth. She nodded, content.

“I’ll have someone call in the plans and go gear up. Meet me by the Northern gate, if you would.” She said, flexing her fingers as if it were a taunt. Silently, I turned on my heels, leading the way out. The two followed me as I stormed from the tent, throwing the flap out of my way. Lux stood outside, waiting for all of us. Seeing me, you could tell his fears had already been confirmed. He hopped and jogged to me to keep up.

“Ah she… wasn’t gentle was she?” He asked.

“Who the hell does she think she is?” I said, seething, “Pathetic? Really? I’m *sorry* I haven’t had years to practice!” I threw my hands in the air.

“Oh, she was especially harsh.” He shook his head. “I am *so* sorry for her behavior. She’s… always been like this.” I stopped, turning to Lux.

“What’s her deal?” He halted, almost skidding to a stop in front of me.

"She's..." he sighed, "listen, Jewls is harsh. She has... strong beliefs, but she's smart, and she's strong." Tara cocked her head as she looked at him.

"You seem like you know her quite well." She said. Lux sighed, rubbing his forehead.

"Yeah, she and I make up the Olympus crew." He began, "She saved me and she needed a pilot. She's always been a bit of a loner, so the small crew kind of fit." I looked back at the tent.

"A loner, huh?" I said, "I think I can understand why."

"She's not awful if you get to know her and earn her respect. Like I said, she's always a touch prickly at the start, but... Ah, listen, I know it's not easy, but just give her a shot if you can." I pressed my finger to my chin with a sigh, nodding in acceptance. A thought came to mind as I continued to walk.

"So, what did you do to get her to respect you, then?" I asked.

"Oh! I uh... well... not much, honestly." I raised an eyebrow. "She respects me as a pilot, but..." He eyed the tent as we walked away from it, "not so much as a Celestial."

"Hmm." I said, looking down at him, "So you're an expert pilot then?" I asked. He looked away, scratching at the back of his neck.

"Oh, well, I wouldn't want to brag, buuut," he paused for effect, "I *am* one of the best pilots in the fleet." He puffed out his chest proudly.

"Oh ho, is that so?" I asked.

"It's true! I've been flying since I could barely stand! I promise you'll find almost no better pilot."

"Oh, I'm not doubting you." I looked to the Sparrow, and thought of Tara. We *needed* a dedicated pilot, and I mean no disrespect to Tara when I say that her piloting wasn't incredible. I've said before, but I know I couldn't do better. Ah, I was sure it wouldn't hurt to ask. "How would you like to pilot the Sparrow?" I asked. You could practically see his heart flutter, but quickly, it settled out.

"I… I really would want to, but…" He looked at the tent.

"No, it's alright, I understand." He nodded at this.

"Sorry again. I'd love to, but I wouldn't forgive myself for just ditching her." I patted his back as we approached the gate.

"No need to be sorry. You've got a good heart on you, and you should follow it." He nodded.

"I'll do my best." He said with a beam. He checked his watch. "Oh gods, I need to be on my way. Some of the ships' nav systems need calibrating. Wish you three luck!" We all waved as he darted off into the distance. He seemed a good kid. The contrast between him and Jewls was unbelievably stark. I couldn't imagine the two of them cramped into that small ship for so long. I shook my head, the three of us turning to look out into the dark denseness of the woods. The long shadows of the short day stretched across the mulch and dried leaves. It reminded me almost too much of the day they'd attacked. That cold winter wind blew between the trunks of the forest trees, whipping at my hair. We looked back as we heard the crunching of leaves underfoot. Jewls strutted toward us, a bag lashed over her shoulder. She looked to us as she stood by the edge of the gate.

"Orders have been sent out." She said, "If we want to make it there before they can see us, we'll want to leave now." I nodded, looking out over the canopy of trees above us. Long ago, that canopy meant comfort and exploration. The shadows they cast now, though, drove a deep fear into my heart. Jewls' glowing eyes watched my face with deep interest. "You aren't having second thoughts, are you, William?" I shored up my resolve, looking out into the darkness of the forest before me.

"No. Let's go." She nodded, the four of us taking our first steps past the gate of the camp, the shadowy claws of the trees wrapping around us, drawing us into the unknown.

FURELLE:
SURILLIA COAST
GALACTIC DATE 00:08:432 5028

The denseness of the forest both impeded us and aided us. While on the one hand we would have to move far slower, on the other, it made it much more difficult to see us. The four of us traveled with our bodies close to the ground, creeping between the thin gaps of the trees. Ferns and vines grasped at our boots as we dug our way into the Soulless infested territory. Already we could hear the sounds of the gunfire shifting in the distance as the different teams began making their way south. It would hopefully only be a matter of time before the Soulless moved with them, giving us a clear shot to the temple. I could only hope I remembered where it was.

My calves stung from the constant crouching, and I could feel my breathing shake and tremble as we moved. I could tell Tara was just as unused to this as I was. She had her wings tucked in, and her ears tilted back, almost like a cat as she kept herself close to the ground. Still, her arms shook as she crawled. My eyes scanned the treeline above us, squinting, observing. I listened out for that odd skittering I'd heard from those Soulless on Draenica, but it was eerily quiet. Birds tweeted, wind blew, and miles out you could hear fighting, but the area around us just seemed too empty.

The part that worried me the most, though, was Jewls. Her eyes could be a problem. They'd stick out like a firefly in the night. I turned my head, looking back at her. It surprised me to see, however, that her eyes were dull and pale now. No longer did they glow that blazing blue-white, but almost appeared as if she were completely, normally, blind. One would think little of it if they hadn't seen her as we had. Her eyes flicked to me, pointing forward as if to tell me to 'keep my eyes on the road' as it were. I grumbled, turning to look ahead of me.

I despised taking orders. Burned me up good it did. Sterling was one thing. I'd known what I was signing up for. Jewls I already wasn't fond of. To have her telling me what to do… I could barely stand it. Still, I recognized some amount of necessity in it. As much as I hated to admit it, Jewls knew a lot more about this than I did. Plus, if she really *could* see auras, or whatever they were, she'd be able to spot things long before any of us could. My eyes darted up to the branches above me again, looking for anything shifting, moving. Nothing so far. We'd been traveling for the past hour, at least. Tara put a hand out, the four of us stopping. She looked back, propping herself against a tree. The rest of us quickly sunk below the line of grass and ferns, concealing ourselves from view.

"Something wrong?" I asked.

"Not yet." She said, "If I'm correct, though, we should be approaching the section the Soulless had been patrolling." Jewls frowned.

"If our plan worked, we shouldn't need to worry." She said.

"*If* our plan worked. Tara, are you suggesting something?" I asked, looking up to her.

"Well, if they decided to leave troops behind, we need to be weary." She began. I'd heard that tone before. She was leading into something, a breakthrough of some sort, but Jewls cut her off.

"We don't exactly have time to be overly cautious. If our plan worked, the troops will only be able to handle that number for so long." She emphasized, beginning to rise. I put a hand on her back, pushing her back to the ground.

"Just listen for gods' sake." I said. She furrowed her brow, squinting as she slapped my hand from her.

"Don't you dare give me orders." She spat.

"I'll damn well give orders to listen to my crew if the situation calls for it." I spat back. Her eyes burned as she glared at me, her face contorted in disgust. She shoved my arm back, standing back up, continuing to move further. I groaned. "Fuck's sake." I muttered, getting up slowly, turning to Tara. "You had something you wanted to say?" Tara looked alarmed, not seeming to want to make nary a sound. She reached out at Jewls, but had her hand pushed away. Her eyes shifted from me to the surrounding area. I followed her gaze, and that's when I saw what she had seen. Burns in the trees. Blaster shots, magic bolts, artillery fire. It was still smoking… still fresh. I moved to grab Jewls again. A solitary *crack* echoed through the trees as a branch broke under her foot.

We froze, hearing birds flutter from trees around us. Time ground to a halt as we opened our eyes and ears. Burns on the bases of the trees, claw marks toward the top. I took in a sharp, frigid breath through my nose, feeling my heart pound in my chest. Arneli reached behind her, pulling a rifle from her back, checking the distant ranges through her scope. Tara instinctively drew her pistol. In through the nose, out through the mouth, my breath went. Nothing at first. We took a step forward, cautious in our movement. Nothing again. Another step forward. I caught the brief movement of Tara's ear. She'd heard something. I listened and heard it too. A thin whistle in the air, growing louder by the second. Jewls eyes widened as she heard it too.

"Artillery! Get down!" Arneli and Tara dove back as the two of us drew weapons, thrusting our hands forward. When I say I felt the force of that shell through my whole body, I would be understating. I could feel my body strain under the impact, my heels digging into the dirt as an eruption of flame and steel burst forth on the other side of that blue barrier. Jewls held herself firm against the strike, but it was obvious that, had we not both been there, we wouldn't have survived that. The blue light from us flickered out as smoke and dirt rained down around us. Coughing, I turned, helping Tara and Arneli up. As she got to her feet, Tara's ears perked up again. Her eyes met with mine.

"They're coming." She said. I listened out, hearing it too. It was faint, but getting closer. Skittering. I tapped at Jewls shoulder, hopping into action.

"Alright, folks, no time to dawdle anymore." I said. Jewls' eyes met mine. She'd heard it too. She nodded.

"Correct on that. We've been spotted." Her brows furrowed, looking to me, "Lead the way Ortell." She ordered. I pursed my lips, gesturing for everyone to follow, breaking off into a run. I looked over everything around us, trying to get a sense of my bearings. The forests had changed a great deal since my time here. I could recognize small things, little landmarks like a stone pile here, or a clearing with an odd tree there, but none of that got me close to figuring out where this damned temple was. As the four of us darted between the trees, we could hear that skittering growing closer and closer. If I couldn't find this place fast, we'd be overrun for sure.

Another whistle sounded in the skies above. We didn't have time to react before the ground beside us exploded. Dirt and fire burst forth as the shell crashed into the ground. We were thrown off balance. I flipped through the air, crashing hard into the ground. I rolled, stopped by a tree smacking into my side. Dazed, I could only sit there for a moment, but I knew I couldn't lie there forever. I coughed, sitting up. My ears rung as I tried to see through the smoke all around me. I gritted my teeth, spitting out the grime from my mouth. Shoving Isngr into the ground, I pulled myself to my feet. My legs wobbled, but I felt a set of arms catch me, setting me upright. I looked over to see Jewls' glowing eyes through the haze. The two of us nodded to each other as she let me go. I stood up fully, seeing Arneli and Tara's forms approach us. I grabbed them by the shoulders, coughing from the smoke. My lungs burned something fierce. I shoved the cloth of my sleeve into my mouth, glancing around us. I gestured forward, pushing us out into the fresh air of the forest. We hacked and gasped, dragging ourselves free. I listened again once we were clear, taking in gulps of air. They were close.

One more time I looked around me. This place, I recognized it. A clearing here, a bush with orange flowers there, fungus coated trunks of trees. I stumbled forward, sheathing Isngr. Tara looked around us as I pulled myself into a grove. The trees bent in around us, enshrouding us in their gloom. She looked to me next as I fell again to my knees, placing my hand on the dead leaves.

"This is it, isn't it?" She asked. I nodded, brushing the leaves aside.

"Yeah. Yeah, I think it is." I said, pulling away at plants and dead brush. Jewls watched me for a moment, before sweeping her staff across the ground. A rush of wind blew the dirt away, revealing the singular hatch in the ground. A blue sigil spun across its surface, holding it closed. I got up from my knees, approaching it. My fingers drew lines over the sigil before reaching down the handle, pulling at it. It wouldn't budge.

"It's not just going to open." Jewls said, whacking the back of my head with her stick. I yelped, rubbing the spot where she'd hit me. "Use your head." I grunted, standing back up.

"Well then, *you* open it." I spat back at her. Jewls huffed, leaning down and holding her hand over the sigil. She closed her eyes, taking a deep breath. A flow of blue energy shifted from her to the hatch. I could see her hand tremble as she concentrated before she whipped it away. The sigil remained. "Damn it all, it's stuck fast." I didn't know magic *could* be stuck. Jewls groaned. "Fantastic. Any ideas now?" She asked me, vindication thick in her voice.

"Shit, you think I know? I told you my experience with magic." She grabbed me by the collar of my shirt, dragging me to her.

"You must know something of this place, or you would not care about it so much. Search your mind for something, Ortell." I tore her hand from me, tossing it down. We didn't say anything. I turned, my brain kicking into gear. I could hear the Soulless moving closer by the second, and our only escape was into that hatch.

Alright Ortell, time to think. We have a magic sealed hatch leading into an old Furin-Faraxian temple. Place was a playground for me as a child, right? Wasn't sealed when I was here. Or was it?

I thought back to almost a decade before. *Right*, Xenrus had sealed it when he'd caught Maurel and me in there. Alright, we had who made it, now how to open it. Jewls had described it as "stuck tight" almost like it was a door itself. What if it needed a key? If Xenrus wanted to make a "key" of some sort, what would he have used? The answer, as I thought about it, seemed all too obvious. I stepped forward, pulling out Isngr once more. Jewls watched me intently as I approached the seal. I turned the blade over, pointing its tip toward the ground, thrusting it through the center of the spell. Runes across the sigil lit up, the magic flowing into the blade of the sword. I drew it back out, looking to Jewls with renewed confidence.

"Should be open." I said. She rolled her eyes, kneeling down. She pulled the hatch open. The musty smell of old, wet stone burst free of the temple, hitting all four of us. It was a familiar scent, one of my childhood. I took a shaky breath, remembering back to my youth here on Furelle. My mind flashed back to Xenrus bringing me and Maurel back to Surillia Ra, to seeing the Soulless invading, the people impaled on the blades of their arms. I felt a hand touch my shoulder, snapping me from my trance. Tara leaned down, looking into my eyes.

"Hey. You doing okay, Ortell?" She asked, her voice quiet and soft. I nodded, regaining ahold of myself.

"Yeah… Yeah, thanks." She gave me a nod, the two of us standing back up. "Alright. Plan is: we get in, figure out what this weapon is, grab it if we can and if it's *there*, and then get out as fast as possible." I looked down into the darkness below. The hollow sound of air flowing through the temple's depths echoed across the stone walls and out to us.

"You'll need this," Arneli said, tossing me a light. I caught it, shining it into the stairway spiraling deep into the ground. She strode up beside me, whistling as she looked inside. "Wow. Deep."

"Thank you, very insightful." I teased.

"I mean, it is!" She pointed her rifle inside. "It's a deep hole in the ground!" She took a step on the stone, feeling it before moving back. "Wet too. We should watch our step. I'm sure slipping would not be fun." I thought back to my sprained ankle from the first time I'd been there.

"Right. Walk slowly. I'll lead the way down." I said, taking my first steps into the temple. With my hand along the railing, I began my descent. Jewls shut the hatch behind us, shifting leaves and dirt over it with a flick of her wrist. Our breathing seemed to stop as I shined the light out into the cavernous hall. I'd almost forgotten the glory of it. The giant statues' gazes fixed on each other, yet somehow it felt as if they watched us. As we continued to move downward, I shifted the light to the wall closest to us, seeing a mural carved and inlaid with multi-colored tile into the stone. I'd never noticed it before. We stopped, scanning the beam over it. To the sides, Furins. Some built ships, others painted and carved stone and crystal. As we moved inward, they sat in prayer. We looked to each other, shifting our gaze to the center of the mural. A series of blue mermaid-like aliens had their hands raised, holding in their gathered palms a black orb, dots lining its edges.

"Faraxians." Arneli muttered. So that's what they looked like. I'd heard so much about them, but, lacking much in terms of ancient history lessons, I'd never really had an image in my head. They looked so regal with their crested heads, striped skin, aquatic features. You could see bits of so many races in them. There was that subtle warmth from Isngr again, almost as if it were tying to tell me something. I put my hand up, holding at its hilt, a powerful set of emotions and flashes hitting me, rushing through my mind one after another.

I saw the world through a young woman's eyes. At least I thought it was a young woman. I couldn't see it, but I just... felt it. My hand reached up to the wall, feeling the bumps and grooves in it. Looking at my hand in this... memory? It was blue, the skin bumpy and coarse. I could feel the stiffness in it from grasping a blade for hours on end. I shook it out as someone called my name. Luccia. I turned, another Molusion walking down the steps. His head held a grand crest of horns, and his frog-like eyes watched me with an indomitable intensity. At his side, I could see it. Isngr. He ushered me further into the temple, saying something about how we needed to keep moving.

I flashed back into my own mind, yet in my vision I could still see the echoes of what I could only describe as a memory. But from who? Luccia, the man had called her. I thought maybe she'd been the sword's previous user, but quickly reminded myself that the man in her memories had been the one holding it. So then, who was Luccia? As I turned my head to the side, shining my light further into the temple, I could swear I could see the faint outlines of people below. Furins, Molusions... Faraxians. I blinked, shaking my head, and they were gone. I took my hand from the sword as Tara tilted her head at me.

"You see something?" She asked. I shook my head.

"No, just... my eyes playing tricks on me is all." She furrowed her brow, not seeming to believe me. Jewls pushed past us.

"Come on. We don't have time to lollygag." She said, shoving her way down the thin stairway. We looked between us, shaking our heads before following her further in.

Our footsteps echoed across the walls as we took our first steps off the stairway, shining the light out across the temple. The inscriptions lined the top parts of the walls, stretching all the way back to its rear. Arneli had her translator out, holding it up high above her head at the wall as I shifted the light across it. I turned back to her.

"You getting anything on that?" I asked. I could see her lips purse in confusion. She shook her head, scratching her chin as we walked along the length of the room.

"Sort of. There's talk here and there of a weapon, but it almost seems incomplete, as if part of it was cut off, or they didn't have time to finish the script." Jewls groaned.

"Great, so we came here for nothing." She muttered, rubbing the bridge of her nose. "Shit. We need to get out of here before we waste any *more* time." I looked back to Arneli, who was shaking her head.

"Something the matter?" I asked.

"It just doesn't make sense. The Faraxians are one of the most detail oriented races we know of. Why would they just leave it all unfinished?" She shifted the translator over the room. I followed it with the light, continuing to walk until my foot hit something. I shifted the light down, seeing the old Furin skeletons there. The one with the red markings on its shell still laid there, weapon grasped firmly in its hand.

"We can't turn back yet," Tara chimed in. "The Soulless must know *something* about this place. Why else would a Commander be looking for it?" She asked.

"How about to pull you into a trap?" Jewls asked. "You have Isngr's wielder here, completely untrained. It's the perfect time to corner him and finish him off." I glared back at her, but put it out of my mind. What Arneli had said, they were one of the most detail oriented races. We had to be missing *something*. I pulled my hand back again, reaching for Isngr once more. As my fingers touched at it, I felt that connection again.

I was back in Luccia's memories. Around me, all assortment of races worked, rebuilding the temple. The destruction of the planet recently had sent things askew, and with the Faraxian's help, they'd put them back together. The Molusion man from before stopped me, told me there were important things he needed to attend to alone. Begrudgingly, I waited. At the far end of the room, he raised a hand, a flow of magic connecting him to the wall. A doorway formed, cracking open with a burst of light. I pulled myself back to reality. A hidden door. That was it!

I strode forward as Jewls and Tara argued, shining my light at the wall. Surely enough, I could see a faint mark engraved into it. Touching my hand to it, the stone felt warm here, inviting, almost as if it were reaching into me, pulling away at something within me. I took a few steps back, feeling my feet bump into a short pedestal on the floor. Looking down, I saw similar rune markings to the ones Xenrus had placed on the temple's entrance. As I stepped up onto it, I could sense a sudden shift in the energy within me, as if it were being forcefully pulled toward the door, but not out of me, at least not yet.

Feeling that tug, I reached a hand up, just as I'd seen the man do it, closing my eyes. It was just a magical connection. Sure, I hadn't done it *yet*, but this thing was literally *dragging* it from me. All I had to do was just let it go. I took a deep breath, focusing my mind as I had on Xenova, trying to just let something, anything, come out. I could feel a warmth crawling its way up my arm. From beneath my eyelids, I could see a blue shimmer. Opening them, I saw the tendrils of blue reaching out from me, creeping into the stonework. The cracks and grooves filled as if with water. Inch by inch, foot by foot, the magic spread, shifting into beautiful swirls and shapes across the door, until it flashed. The magic sucked itself back into me. With a crunching creak, the two sides of the giant doors began to crack open. We squinted as light poured in from outside.

We walked forward toward it as our eyes adjusted. Into view came the sight of a forest hidden below the nearby mountains. Sunlight poured in through small holes in the side of the stone above us. A path cut its way through the trees, leading to another, smaller temple at the base of the cavern. I flipped the light off, handing it back to Arneli in a daze. Jewls approached me from behind, her gaze as steely as ever.

"Not too shabby Ortell." She said. I was ready to thank her before she moved ahead of me, starting down the path. "However, opening a door alone does not make you an expert at magic." I rolled my eyes, following her down.

"What's your deal?" I asked, "Ever since I got here, all you've done is insulted and belittled me and my crew."

"Just you, actually." She corrected. I grunted, frustrated.

"Even worse." She kept walking as she spoke.

"I simply don't think you have a place among us. You clearly are untrained in any aspect that might keep you alive here." Her head turned, her eyes matching mine, glowing intensely. "Simply put. You are a liability." Her head snapped forward again. "But we're stuck with you."

"*We're* stuck with me?" I asked.

"Yes, Ortell, us. The Celestials are *stuck* with you. You wield that sword so there's not much we can say, now is there?"

"I mean, they certainly *tried*." Tara muttered.

"I heard." Jewls responded. Tara let out a small 'eep.' "You stole your ship, and Cleva just let you keep it."

"Clearly you didn't hear the whole of it, then." I responded, hopping over a break in the path.

"Oh?" she began. "Then enlighten me, oh Wise One. What exactly have I missed in this situation?"

"Well, to begin, Cleva and I met again afterwards. She told me to return the Sparrow." I said.

"I can imagine. Yet, there was something else?"

"When I refused, she put me through a test to be able to join. One that, as you can imagine, *I passed*." I said through clenched teeth. Jewls went quiet for a moment as we walked, seeming to be deep in thought.

"What was the test?" She finally asked. Tara cocked her head at the question. No one had thought to ask.

"Cross a seemingly impossible gap. If I fell, I died. Sheer wall on one side with no grips and that was it." I explained. The path led to the side of a sheer drop, only a small walkway hugging the cliff. I began to sidle across, keeping my eyes up as much as I could.

"You used that barrier magic then? Tried crossing it like a bridge?" She asked. Her tone had smoothed out slightly, turning more to genuine curiosity.

"No. At the time, I had no control over my magic. I found out Isngr could pierce the stone. I used that to climb across." I said.

"You wouldn't have died."

"Excuse me?"

"If you'd fallen. You wouldn't have died. She wanted to test just how far you'd go." She told me, "If you didn't know any magic then, and you've already come to learn this much on your own, perhaps…" she sighed, "perhaps there's *some* hope for you." She looked down ahead of us as we reached solid footing. "At least you certainly have the tenacity to bang your head against a wall till honey comes out of it." She grumbled. A small smile hit me as we walked. Maybe I had a chance to earn *some* respect yet.

We approached the second temple. It was far simpler than the one we'd come from. It was just a cube with one side missing. Sets of columns had been erected out front, but many had fallen with age. Stepping over them, we looked around us. The walls were coated with more writing. I wondered why the man hadn't wanted Luccia to see this. Looking back, I saw Arneli with her translator up, scanning over each section of the wall.

"Finding anything interesting?" I asked. From the way her eyes scanned over the text, I could already tell it was good.

"I… can't believe what I'm seeing." She said.

"Well, go on then." Jewls said, "Spit it out. Clearly, the weapon isn't here. It's an empty hall, so what is it?" Arneli paced around the room as she read it over.

"The Faraxians here; they mention that they've been seeking ways to expand their power. The war between gods gave them reason to hurry their search. They reasoned that if the war were allowed to continue that the galaxy would inevitably be sentenced to complete ruination." She paused, scrolling further, "This is where they begin writing their ideas on the weapon. Before, it was mentioned that something needed to be created to put a stop to the war. What we hadn't seen was that they had been doing studies into the gods… and how to kill them." She looked up at all of us, a silence dropping over the room. She continued. "This weapon they were building, it had something to do with being able to actually kill a god, something no one had even come close to doing."

"So… did they succeed?" I asked. She shook her head.

"No… at least not yet, according to the text." She said, continuing to pace, "Moving on, they mention a machine like that would require untold amounts of magic to operate and direct. Furelle simply didn't have that concentration they needed." She turned to the back wall, the rest of us joining her gaze. That same mural we had seen before now filled the stone from top to bottom, but now, text looped around it. Arneli took the time to translate it before looking up once more. "After deliberating with a closed circle, they decided to focus their efforts on the weapon to another planet."

"Do we have a heading?" Tara asked.

"We do." She said, pointing to the sphere in the Faraxian's hands. This one was orange, unlike the one out in the main temple. "The Ikui homeworld, Tanahen." Before I had time to respond, a clap echoed across the stone walls. We spun around, a set of silhouettes in the light of the temple entrance. The outlines were unmistakable. Long sharp claws, or blades on the arms of others. The Soulless. We'd been followed. At their lead was a single woman. I squinted and quickly felt my heart sink. The Commander. One could feel the air in the room grow frigid as she took steps toward us. Her clapping continued.

"Well done. Truly." She said, a hint of snarkness in her voice. We all glared at her. She stopped, a sharp toothed smile stretching across her face. "What? It was a good job finding this place for me."

"Hardly." I spat toward her. She cocked her head at me.

"Oh? And here I thought you went out of your way to be such a helpful rat." A glimmer of recognition rang in her eye. "Wait a minute. I recognize you. Xenova, correct?" Before I could open my mouth to speak, she was at my side, her claws digging into my shoulder again, her mouth uncomfortably close to my ear. I could feel the frost of her breath, cold as a winter's wind as she spoke. "If

I remember correctly, I asked if that sword of yours had a name, hmm?"

"Perhaps it does." I said, quickly drawing it from my back, swiping it. The blade cut clean through thin air, as, in another moment, she was where she started. It struck the ground, leaving a mark in the stone.

"Oh believe me, I know." She said, "Wielder of Isngr. How nice it is to *finally* meet you." I shook off the icy feeling in my shoulder.

"William Ortell." I corrected, "If you're going to talk to me, at least use my name." I said.

"Oh, we're doing introductions, are we?" she asked, placing a hand over her chest. "Well then, William, you may call me Koratha." As she drew her hand back, I could see a purple mist beginning to form in her palm, "Though, then again, I would hope you won't be calling me anything for long." She drew her hand forward, a sickening beam of black and violet streaking toward me. It was faster than any of us had time to react to. I tried to bring up a barrier, but by the time it had formed, the spell had passed it.

Another light shined through the room, blinding me. I stumbled back, fully expecting to feel myself hit with the force of that beam, but it never came. When my eyes adjusted, someone new stood in the way. A young Molusion woman. Her visage was faded, translucent, and her clothes tattered. Around her neck, a blue ribbon was tied. She held the beam at bay with a blade of her own, deflecting it into the wall beside her. When her head snapped down to look at me, her eyes glowed a solid gold. She reached down, dragging me to my feet.

"Eyes up, Hero. You aren't getting anywhere on your ass." She said. Koratha stared on, a fury in her eyes as I looked to this figure.

"Who… are you?" I asked. Her eyes darted to my sword.

"I think you already know." I glanced at the ribbon on her neck, then to Isngr. The cloth wasn't there anymore. Then this was... Luccia. Seeing my understanding, she nodded. She disappeared, the ribbon swirling back into its place around Isngr's pommel. Her voice echoed through my mind. "Glad to finally get in contact. I've been trying to manifest with you since you first picked up the sword. Listen, I'll explain more later, but for now, you have more pressing matters." My eyes danced back over to Koratha, who was readying another strike. "I'll be honest with ya, Hero, you don't have a chance in hell at winning this. Your best option is to survive. Fight defensively." I nodded to myself, readying Isngr.

"Right. Arneli, Tara, you keep those Soulless off us. Jewls," she looked up in my direction, "you're with me." She gave me a nod, the two of us grouping up as Tara and Arneli split off, the Soulless beginning to rush in. They fired, holding them back as best as they could. Koratha cracked her neck, a psychotic look in her eye as she stepped toward us. Jewls and I readied our weapons as she drew a black rapier from a shadowy vortex in the air.

"Make it interesting, won't you?" She asked. I thrust a hand forward in response, wisps of blue magic darting through the air toward her. She zipped across the floor, a blur. The bolts struck the Soulless behind her, and within a blink she was upon us. She slashed at me, striking me across the chest. A red gash cut its way down my torso as I stumbled back into the wall. Jewls twisted her body, driving her staff toward Koratha. She got out of the way, spinning just past the edge of the staff, thrusting a hand at Jewls. A column of black erupted under her, knocking Jewls back to the floor.

I recovered from the attack, getting back up. I swung Isngr again, my blade catching hers. She twisted her wrist, locking the two of us together. She drew in closer, her face inches from mine. I gritted my teeth as she smiled, her eyes looking deep into mine.

"You really *are* reckless, aren't you, William?" I lifted a leg, kicking her back from me. She dragged Isngr from my hand as she backed off. The blade flipped through the air, landing in the rock. I reached forward, pulling it out with a ringing *shwing*.

"Moreso, I just don't know when to quit." I said, flinging more and more bolts in her direction. As she dodged again and again, I thrust Isngr back into the ground, drawing both of my hands back. A series of darts formed around her in a sphere. Pulling my hands together, I launched them.

I winced. It felt like I'd just ripped a muscle in my arm. I could feel the searing pain shoot up from my forearm all the way through my shoulder. I'd gotten her though, right? I had to. Looking up, as the dust cleared, I saw her figure, a purple sphere around her. She dropped her arms, letting it fade away.

"Ooh, overexerting yourself there, William?" She asked, drawing her sword from the ground. I did the same, mirroring her. "Figured you were a novice, but you have to be smarter than that." My eyes darted to Jewls who was pulling herself up. I looked back to Koratha.

"What can I say? As you said, I'm reckless." She tossed me a knowing smile, pulling her hand back again. I was ready this time. I brought up the barrier early, seeing her fingers dance, a beam arcing through the air. It struck against that shield hard. Blocking that artillery strike before felt like nothing compared to this. The sheer force of it rocked my whole body. I dropped Isngr, putting both of my arms up. I felt something in my shoulder *crack* as I held fast against the beam. It drilled against that barrier, and it was taking all of my focus to not let it through.

I felt a second body stand beside me. It was Jewls. She thrust her hands forward, and I felt the pressure ease. We pushed forward, the barrier stretching across the entirety of the temple, putting a wall between us and Koratha. We stayed, our eyes locked with hers as the beam faded out. For a moment, she just watched us. There was silence. The gunfire had stopped, the magic had stopped. She just watched… and then she laughed. A deep, hearty laugh exploded from her as she keeled over. I watched her through squinted eyes, keeping my arms held up in front of me. As the laughing subsided, she straightened herself out, staring me down.

"You really *are* something else, William. You know that?" She took a deep breath. "I don't need this, nor do I have time for it. Just this *once* I'll let you live. I don't feel like dealing with this…" She gestured to the wall of a barrier, "well, this seemingly unbreakable will of yours." She strode closer to the wall. I swore I could feel the coldness dripping from her. "However, know that if I come across you again, I won't hesitate."

"You'd better not." I retorted, "I look forward to it." We grinned at each other, a spark crossing between us.

"As do I, William. As do I." She flipped her coat as she turned. "Don't disappoint me." She said, striding away, her Soulless in tow.

It felt like an hour before we finally dropped the shield. My whole body ached, and pain shot through my arms and shoulders any time I moved. Jewls glared at me as I went down.

"You used too much." She said.

"Yeah no shit." I said, "Like I said, not trained." She shook her head.

"For fuck's sake. You're going to kill yourself if this is how you plan on continuing." She snapped. "You need *training. Propper* training."

"Then why don't *you* train him?" Luccia's voice appeared beside us. Jewls' head snapped to the ghostly figure.

"You," she said, jutting a finger at her, "and what are *you* supposed to be?" Luccia reached down, helping me to my feet.

"My name is Luccia. I am a spirit bound to Isngr." She said. She looked at me, brushing dirt from my shoulder. "It was my duty to guide whoever its next wielder was to be." She looked to Jewls, "I trust fully in his ability to learn, even if he isn't yet as skilled as you. Do you?" Jewls narrowed her eyes at Luccia. She gave Jewls a soft smile before looking at me. "We will speak more on your ship. For now, it is dangerous." She disappeared into the sword again. I took some deep breaths as Tara rushed to my side to support me. I winced at the pain, looking between everyone.

"Right… let's… let's get back to camp." I said, straining to speak through the agony in my shoulder. Jewls stopped us as we began to walk.

"William." She said. I turned back to look at her. "I'm coming with you. If you would have me."

"You're coming with us?" I asked.

"I've said many times. You are in dire need of training, discipline. I would be willing to train you." The two of us eyed each other for a while until I nodded.

"Welcome aboard then." I said, "Now, back to camp." We dragged ourselves back up the path, the sun beating down on our battered bodies. While we hadn't succeeded in stopping Koratha, at least we had a destination. Next stop, Tanahen.

The Blue Sparrow: Transit to Tanahen

Galactic Date 00:08:435 5028

We'd managed to get back as the repairs to the Sparrow had neared completion. Explaining the situation to Sterling and the crew, it was obvious we needed to make it to Tanahen. After a brief period of supplying, and an earful from Rex about pushing my magic too far, we set out. Jewls had joined up with us, towing Lux along with her. The Olympus was now docked below decks in our belly hangar. Finally, we had a pilot. The kid was happy to come along with us and was even more excited to play a part in the ship. He took to her quickly, too; it seemed.

Jewls, as per usual, was another beast entirely. Her general demeanor was standoffish at best. From the minute she got on board, we hardly saw her. From what I understood, she always said she was off meditating. Meditating on what, I couldn't tell you, but I knew she wasn't there when we took off, and only showed up again when my opening watch ended. She'd approached me, telling me it was time for us to train.

WHACK. Another bolt of magic threw me from our mats, sending me tumbling across the steel floor of our cargo bay. She was brutal, unrelenting. In the brief hour we'd trained, my body was already coated in welts and bruises from where I'd been struck. I felt the coldness of a steel bar pressed against my throat. I pushed it away, staring up at her as I heaved through my breaths.

"Again." She ordered. I dragged myself to my feet, moving to the pads. It wasn't like they did any good, anyway. Any time she hit me, it had enough force behind it to blast me into a wall. Limply, I put my hands up, wincing from the dozens of hits I'd taken.

"Don't you think… it might be time for a break?" I asked, my chest trying to get more air than I could take in. She put her staff under my chin, tilting it up to look at her.

"We've only just begun, Ortell. I came to this ship to *train* you. You've demonstrated already that you have very little actual skill. Now," she unsummoned her staff, putting her hands up, "again." I pursed my lips and drew my arms back. I fired off a few bolts in her direction. She twisted her body. The bolts swirled around her, firing back in my direction. I swept my arm aside, deflecting them into the floor with a barrier. Then I felt that familiar sting as a bolt hit my side. Again, it sent me off balance. Another bolt struck me, and once more I ended up on my ass halfway across the room. My body stung so much it felt warm in every limb. I groaned as I grabbed a nearby table, pulling myself up to my feet. I could feel how sore my muscles were from casting so much, and I knew I couldn't stand much more of this.

"You know, this would probably be a *lot* more helpful if you actually taught me something, rather than just throwing me into a wall over and over again." I spat. She squinted before stomping to where I was, hoisting me up by the collar before setting me on my feet. The two of us stood at height with each other, each of us staring the other down.

"You will not *learn* if you are not under duress. It is instinct, not just something you are taught." She said through gritted teeth.

"Oh? And how would *you* know? Have you ever tried *actually* teaching someone?!" I shouted. She took a step back, but kept herself calm, collected.

"I *never* needed to be taught. I learned all that I learned because my situation called for it. You can barely even see magic, if at all. This is a basic skill. That you have not *mastered* it is concerning. Dire circumstances call for harsher training." She held her chin high. I tossed my hands up.

"Oh *fantastic*. So, what? I just get beat up over and over again till I'm a bloody pulp and I *might* figure something out?"

"That's the idea of it." Her nonchalantness only succeeded in angering me more.

"Fucking *HELL!*" I shouted, "Have you ever thought that maybe the reason people don't learn magic from you is cause you're a shit teacher?" We stared at each other, our eyes boring holes into one another. Jewls looked down, a shadow cast over her eyes as we were silent, before she finally looked back up at me with those glowing, fiery irises.

"You're fucking hopeless." She said, "Get out. We're done here."

"Glad we agree." I retorted, grabbing a towel from the wall, wiping myself off. "Fuck this. I'm heading to the engine room." I didn't look back as I dragged myself up onto the loud upper deck.

The engine roared, doing a fantastic job of drowning out my thoughts. I leaned over the console, sweat dripping from my brow onto the glass pane. Gods, I hated her. Just the thought of her burned me up now. Who the *hell* did she think she was? Calling me hopeless, thinking she was *better* than me? I pulled down the diagnostics on the warp core, seeing fluctuations in its power output. Gods damnit.

I grabbed my tools, sinking down between the grates of the floor, lining myself up with a valve leading into the base of the core. Needed to bring the port side output down to bring it in check. My throat and chest still tight with frustration, I pulled out a large wrench, lining it up with the output valve. It was stuck, as if someone had tightened it too much already. I grunted, pulling on it with the weight of my body. I struggled to draw it back; the wrench slipping. My hand slammed into the hard edge of the grate. The pulsing heat of pain rushed through my fingers, and I could feel the blood from a cut coating the back of my knuckles, mixing with the dirt and grime on my skin. In a mix of pain and rage I shouted, slamming the wrench into the pipe, before leaning over it in defeat. I breathed heavily, sitting there hunched over the output. I felt a small hand gently rest on my shoulder.

"Hey now, what'd that poor lil' warp core ever do to you now?" Gatha asked. I said nothing, my body shaking. She sighed, taking a seat on the edge of the grate. "You look like hell, kid." She picked up my hand, wiping the blood from it, tapping a clean cloth at the cuts. "You want to talk about it?" I groaned, leaning back as she worked at my hand.

"It's Jewls." I said, "She says she wants to train me, yet tells me I'm weak, hopeless. I'm sick of it." My head hung low. "I want to be more of a use, sure, but she just acts so high and mighty, like she can't do anything wrong." I felt pressure around my fingers, looking down to see Gatha wrapping a bandage around them carefully. Red soaked into the white cloth as she wrapped more layers, setting it into place. She took another deep breath, patting at my hand.

"Jewls is… rough. I was surprised when she came aboard and joined us." She said, "Jewls has been notorious among Celestials, old and new. A young prodigy in magic. At least that's what they say. She's ruthless, tough, but also powerful enough to back it up." She put a hand on my shoulder as I took a seat up on the grates beside her. "Don't let her get to you, kid. You're doing good work with us, and I'm always happy to have you here in the back with me." She gave me a warm smile, opening her arms. I smiled back, leaning into her. The hug felt warm and comforting, and seemed to just lift the anger and frustrations I'd been feeling. She patted my back, letting me go, looking up at me. "You look like you've been through hell." She commented.

"Yeah, kinda got tossed around a lot, and swinging out spells like that really took a lot out of me." I said, poking at some of the bruises along my side. Gatha shot me a worried look.

"Get some rest, kid. I'll take over in here for a while." I nodded, pulling myself to my feet. My knees were wobbly, but I managed to keep my balance.

"Thanks, I… I really needed that." Gatha gave me a quick two-finger salute.

"Anytime, kid. You've got a family here. We've all got ears open." She said, shooting me another broad smile and a wave before disappearing below the grates. I shook my head, chuckling at the sight, before limping off.

The walk to my room felt like miles. My whole body ached, and I could barely keep my eyes open. I looked down into the cargo bay as I passed, watching for a moment as Jewls cast spell after spell into a set of empty crates we'd set aside for training. As much as I hated her, I had to commend her determination. She trained more often and harder than anyone I'd known. On the one hand, I wondered what situations had led her to this point. On the other hand, I didn't particularly care. There was little, if any reasons, to excuse behavior like hers. Her eyes met mine for a brief moment, before we both snapped our heads away. I continued on my way.

I dragged myself around the corner, looking ahead into the helm. Couldn't see who was on watch at the moment. I tilted my head, trying to look around the edge of the wall. I could barely see the back of Natasha's head working at the computers, leaning back to say something to... Iraka, I think. Barely able to keep my eyes open, I turned to my door, sliding it open. I sulked inside, turning my gaze to my bed and the sword that rested by it. Luccia hadn't come back out to talk yet. I could only assume that what happened with Cleva before might happen again. I walked over to it, placing my hand on Isngr's hilt. It was almost as if I could feel her stirring in there, yet not quite ready to show herself. I sighed, letting go, flopping onto my bed. Something stirred into the shadows, catching my eye. I turned my head, seeing Tara at the edge of my bed. I rolled onto my side to look at her. She and I had had little time together with our watches. She looked over at me.

"Hey, Ortell." She whispered.

"Something wrong?" I asked.

"Oh! No! Do you, uh, mind if I lie down, though?" I scooted my body back. Tara laid in front of me, curling herself up.

"Why do I feel like there's something on your mind?" I asked.

"I was thinking about Koratha." There was a hint of sadness in her voice.

"Oh? What about her?"

"Her wings. The fact that they're gone." I could feel her body shudder through the bed, and reached out, putting a hand on her shoulder.

"It means something?" I asked.

"It's… something the Oc'r would do to particularly troublesome slaves. Ones that started fights or tried to escape. They'd have their wings removed." I was silent, in shock. I didn't know *what* to say, but she continued. "They had to stop. Something about it just… broke some people. Something in them would snap. They'd lash out uncontrollably at anyone and anything, more often than not killing their masters. Of course, they stopped it to protect *themselves*." She crossed her arms over her chest. I could see the scar on the base of her neck, that mark. It would likely never go away. She turned to face me, looking up into my eyes. "That anger consumes you." She said, her voice barely above a whisper. "I… can't imagine going through that and then being turned into a Soulless. When all you were was rage, and to have anything else pulled out." She bit her lip, squinting up at me, pulling back. "I'm sorry I'm dumping all of this on you." She said.

"No. It's alright." I sat up, leaning against my knee. "I… I hate to say it, but I get it." I said.

"Get what?" She asked, standing back up.

"Letting anger control you." I looked up at her. "How long did I let my grudge against the Celestials control me?" I asked. Tara was quiet. "All I can say is that… had I let that continue to fester, had I not had you and Maurel to reign me in, who knows where I would have ended up?" I sighed. My mind was feeling too awake now to sleep yet, and so I pushed myself up off the bed. "Come on, we could probably use a drink."

"You sure?" She asked.

"Yeah, it'll take our mind off things, at least for now." I moved by her, gesturing out the door to follow. The two of us walked a little further up the ship toward the galley. Already, ahead, I could hear voices echoing out across the halls. They erupted in laughter before quieting, voices dipping in and out of the conversation. I peaked my head in with Tara. There around a table were Lux, Arneli and Rex. They laughed again as they spoke, the three of them with food and drink in hand. I nudged us forward.

"Y'all have room for two more?" I asked, the two of us making our way toward them.

"Sure as hell do!" Arneli said, pouring us both glasses of some liquid I didn't recognize, sliding them in our direction. "Take a load off, why don't you? Look like hell." I slid in around the bench, having heard that many times already, Tara beside me. She swiped up the drink, downing it in a single gulp, slamming it back down on the table. She sat up a little straighter with a grin.

"Right. Already feeling better." She said.

"Now that's more like it!" Arneli cheered. I smiled, leaning in over the table, taking a few dignified sips of my drink.

"Hope we aren't intruding." I said.

"Oh, not at all!" Lux chimed in.

"Lux was regaling us with tale of his travels with our new companion, Jewls." Rex said, the tendrils under his face dancing at his drink. I always wondered how Actillions ate and drank. In my head, it seemed a little less unnerving. Still, I focused back on Lux.

"That so? Well, I just came from what she described as 'training', so please, *do* go on."

"Oh, sorry for you." Lux said, "But unfortunately, you missed the last of my tales. You'll just have to come back next time, I'm afraid." He said, a smirk stricken across his face.

"Oh, will I now? Well shit, guess I missed out." I said.

"Well, you're the newcomers to the table, you two. You got any stories?" Arneli asked. Tara thought on it, before something popped into her head.

"Oh right, I haven't talked about how William and I *first* met!" She exclaimed. I put my head in my hands.

"Oh, gods, you wouldn't." She nudged me.

"Oh, gods I *would*." She leaned forward. "Right, so, get this. Back on Draenica, things were trash, like straight dump levels. Finding a place isn't exactly the best situation for most of us Frev'n types. Typical rule is you reach out and try to stick together. So, I take the typical channels, try to put out a notice I'm looking for someone who can help get a few creds together to pool into a place."

"Wait," Lux said, "you mean to say you didn't even have anywhere to stay there?" He asked.

"Pretty much. Shit was brutal out there for us. We had a few community houses, but they were cramped. Either way, I put out this bulletin and wait for a few weeks, and begin to forget about it. Think I'm SOL, ya feel?" They nodded, "Weeeell, sure's enough, fate had some *different* ideas. Get a notification somewhere near a month later that someone named Ortell's got an offer in exchange for a favor. Of course I'm thinking some other Draen, probably an Oc'r, wants something out of me, but I say 'eh, fuck it, I can handle myself if shit goes sideways.' Give him a time and place to meet up." At this point, she had everyone engrossed, quietly leaning forward. "And so I head to our meeting ground and wait. A little back alley in the middle of a fuck all part of town. No one was there for a while, so I'm about to give up. Who would have thought some Terran kid would come bursting down the alleyway like a blaster bolt to grab me by the arms and ask if 'I'm Tara,' looking all cracked up. Turns out, this dumbass had stolen half a bag of food from the markets and was being chased down by almost a dozen armed guards and had nary a credit to his name. Needless to say, I was *unpleased.*" The lot of us chuckled. It had been a hard time for me then. I was lucky to have found her, that's for sure.

"Well," she continued, "I *somehow* managed to get him out of the eyes of the guards, and he was at least smart enough to hide what he looked like. At this point, I was ready to walk away entirely, but he said he had a plan, but he couldn't do it all on his own, and that he could make us a decent amount of money if I put in some hard work. I'd heard it a hundred times, but he managed to sound so confident that I heard him out. Of course, it wouldn't be William without some idea that shouldn't work, but somehow does. See, he doesn't propose buying a house, but instead, *he* insists on buying the materials to build it. Next thing I knew, we were out in the ashlands scrapping, and he was out in the slums building one of the sketchiest looking houses I've ever seen." She wrapped her wing around me, throwing her hands up with a cheer. "And thus, The Shack was born, and we were only a *little* homeless!" I laughed, unwrapping her wing from me. The others looked at me.

"And what say you, William? She miss anything?" Arneli asked. I grinned back at Tara.

"Ah, only the part where *I* built the house as she sat and watched." I poked at her nose, "Isn't that right, Ms. Verikov?"

"It's almost criminal to call it a house at *all*, Mr. Ortell." She folded her arms, looking at me. "Either way, I do believe it's *your* turn for story time." I blew out a breath, thinking about it.

"Jeez. Gotta be honest, I don't really have a lot, unless I feel like bringing the mood down." I said, leaning in over my drink, thinking inward, "Honestly, a lot of my life up until now wasn't really great. A lot of rough shit, ya know? But, I'm here now." I looked around at the interior of the Sparrow, then to them. I thought back to Gatha, gazing down at the bandages on my hand. The longer I was here, the more it really was feeling like home. "Other than getting tossed around on a few planets, stealing a ship, finding a magic sword that made me some sort of 'chosen one,' I think my stories are just beginning." I said. Arneli raised her glass.

"Gods damned cheers to that." She said. We raised our glasses with her, letting out a unified,

"Cheers." Before swinging our heads back, letting the drinks flow down our throats, bodies growing warmer with each swig. Lux sat forward again, pushing his glass out.

"Ah, I'm just glad to be here." He said, "Been traveling practically alone in a tiny space ship all this time."

"About this," Rex chimed in, "I have meant to inquire as to your origins."

"Oh, me?" Lux said, "Oh, well, I've got a bit of a checkered past. Orphaned when I could barely form a memory and was picked up on Xenova by my adopted father." He told us, "Eser Astrova. Took his last name since I didn't have one myself. Man taught me everything I know, from building ships to flying them. Better at the latter, but he and I were the ones who built the

Olympus. Haven't been back there in some time, but he and I keep in touch."

"We'll have to make a stop." I said, "We pass by Xenova enough. I'm sure we could take some time when things calm down to make a pit stop, get some shore leave."

"That'd be awesome!" He said, "He would *love* you all, I'll tell ya that."

"I look forward to a meeting with him." Rex said, quietly sipping at his drink, "It is good to keep in contact with those you love and hold close."

"What about you, Rex?" Tara asked. "Do you have anyone back home?" Rex shook his head, letting out a hearty chuckle.

"I, most unfortunately, do not. Yet, I do not mind." He looked up from his drink. "At 73, I am quite old for my species. We have not risen to the same medicinal standards allowing the longevity of many other races. Even Terrans have far surpassed us at this point. My biological family has all long since passed."

"Oh… I'm sorry to hear that." Tara said, but Rex held up a carapaced hand.

"Please, do not be. I find great comfort and fulfilment being here. Arneli is one I have cared after for many years. She keeps me centered, and my work gives me noble purpose." She waved a hand at him.

"Oh, come now, you big softie." She said.

"It is the truth!" He said, "I have much to live for, and thanks to many modern medicinal practices, I have a good amount of life in me to continue." Rex looked between me, Tara and Lux. "I would hope you all find a similar happiness." We nodded. I had no idea he was so old. You couldn't tell it by looking at him. His carapace still held its color, and you couldn't exactly see any wrinkles on him, for obvious reasons. He took a deep breath, pushing the drink away from him. “I have had much, as have we all. I would suggest water and sleep to aid in recovery.” We nodded again, Lux staying behind to put away the drinks.

Despite the soreness of my body, as Tara and I headed back to my room, it felt like all the weight on me had been lifted. We were laughing and smiling as we talked, reminiscing of our time on Draenica, in the shack, of the dumb shit we’d gotten up to together; things like ash-ball fights going horribly wrong. By the time we got back to our room, I could feel the exhaustion hitting me again. As we stepped inside, I turned back to Tara, backing toward the window as she pulled her top off, replacing it with another, cleaner one. I reached up, and she tossed me a replacement as well. I got changed as she sniffed the first one, grimacing as she tossed it in our laundry.

“Well, I’ll tell you I’m beat.” She said.

“Make that two of us.” I said, lazily rolling into my bunk. She slinked up to her own.

“Hey, William?” She began as I put my hands under my head.

“What’s up?” I asked. I saw her head drop over the edge of the top bunk, sticking her tongue out through the side of her teeth.

“We came here together, yeah? Better promise those stories you plan on making involve me too!” She said teasingly. I shot her a finger gun, closing one eye.

“Tell you what. You can count on it, Verikov, and *that’s* a promise.” She smiled, giving me a wave.

“All I needed to hear. Night, Ortell!” She popped back up the top bed squeaking above me as she settled into place. I nestled into my blankets, closing my eyes. I felt light and free. Honestly, I felt that, even with everything, I was going to really like it here.

Celestial Plains: The Dreamscape

Galactic Date 00:08:435 5028

Once more, I woke up to the harshness of stone. Despite the chill of the rock, there was a comfort to be had in it. The soreness I'd felt in my body was gone here, and I found myself propped up in the same chair I'd been in the time prior. As my vision focused, I noticed Cleva sitting across from me, and Luccia beside her. Cleva stirred a drink before raising it to her mask, the fluid seeming to pass through it somehow as she sipped. She tipped the glass away, setting it down on the table between us. Luccia was quiet as we shot each other a glance. Cleva cupped her hands together on the table in front of her, her glowing eyes watching me from behind the mask. Finally, I broke the silence.

"Am I in trouble again?" I asked. I could sense a smile from her as she let out a deep chuckle.

"Oh, no. No, you most certainly are not, William." Cleva said, "No. We are here for different reasons. Luccia was telling me a bit of what happened on Furelle. You've grown considerably in the short time you've been here. Suffice to say that my brother and I were wrong in our assumptions about you." I looked to Luccia.

"Well, I sure hope it was all good things she told you."

"I gave my honest opinion." She said, "Listen, Hero, you're alright, but you've got your work cut out for you." I rubbed the back of my neck.

"Yeah, believe me, I know." I said, "Thank you, by the way, for your help. I don't think I'd be around if you hadn't stepped in." She shrugged.

"Hey, it's what I do. We're connected now, you and me."

"Luccia here is what we call a spirit guide." Cleva cut in, "Most Celestials find themselves paired with something known as their Destiny Weapon. Each connects with it in different ways. Some have the spirits of previous owners, or people close to them, bound to the weapon." I thought back to the flashes of memories I'd had through her eyes. The other Molusion had Isngr, so she wasn't its old wielder, but perhaps someone close to them? "Isngr, as you may have guessed, is your Destiny Weapon."

"Do all of them give people power?" I asked. The two of them looked between each other before leaning forward.

"No." Cleva said, "Isngr is… a special case."

"When its previous owner, Vale, died, he trapped his magical potential in it for whoever would come after him." I nodded, looking down at the sword.

"So… I'm not using my own magic, I'm using this other guy's… Vale, was it?" She nodded. I looked solemnly at the blade.

So I was just borrowing that power after all. None of it was really my own.

"You can learn to develop your own magical abilities as well." Cleva said, "But you are on the trail of a dangerous person, and you can use all the help you can get. While it is not the ideal situation, we will train you with Isngr's help, for now."

"Right, Jewls has been trying to train me, but" I began, but Cleva put up a hand, stopping me.

"I know. Jewls' methods are not meant for someone without the fundamentals." She said, "You have much to learn, and very little time, William. Whether you like it or not, her training will be good for you, but first you must learn to master the ability to see and sense magic in the world around you."

"You make it sound easy." I joked. Luccia stood with a smile as Cleva gestured to her.

"It is, with the right levels of magic in you. With Isngr's power, it should be elementary, with the right direction." She said. I leaned forward on my elbows, looking up at Luccia. Her eyes met mine, a determined spark in them. "Luccia will be your training partner, and this," Cleva swept her hand. I felt the ground below me shift as the world spun and shook. As I recovered from the daze, I looked around me, finding myself with the others at the peak of the tower in the distance. The blinding blue light that erupted from its center cast shadows across the floors as the chairs and table sunk back into the stone, forcing me to my feet. "will be our training ground. The sanctum of the Tower of Souls. The home of the World Spirit, and the place where your magic will be strongest." I could feel a tingle running up my spine. You could practically feel the magic here. A small blue glow shifted across my fingers as I moved my hands. Luccia smiled, as she shifted her body, pointing her hand out toward me as she moved into a stance not unlike one I'd seen Jewls do when she prepared to cast.

"William, follow my movements." She ordered, her voice dropping in tone as she directed me. I nodded, looking at her stance, mimicking it as best as I could. I spread my legs, put an arm out forward, drew one back. She stood up, approaching me as Cleva watched. She lifted my arm, pressed my knees forward with her own as she guided my body. "What I am teaching you is an old form of very potent Molusion magic, the same that was taught to me by Vale. It is ill used by many of us nowadays."

"Why's that?" I asked through strained breath, holding my body up as best as I could.

"It is extremely potent. Its strain on its user's body is unmatched, but so is its potential." She let me go, walking in front of me. "Your body is durable for your experience, and Isngr's magic further bolsters that strength, but you have already seen what will happen if you push yourself too far. I must emphasize that you must take care not to overexert yourself." I nodded in response. She sighed, putting a hand on my shoulder. "Listen, Hero, I like you. I've seen what you're like with magic. You're careless. With this type of technique, you can't afford that or you will kill yourself. Do you understand?" Those last words were pointed. She searched my eyes for a response. Again, slowly, I nodded.

"Yes. I understand." I said.

"Good." She said, taking up that same stance beside me, "We'll start with seeing magic." She took a deep breath, and I followed. "Close your eyes." I obliged, following her breathing. "Good, you can feel the magic in the air here. I want you to sense how it flows, feel its movement." I focused my mind, quieting out my thoughts as I felt that tingle. It shifted across my body almost like a wave, flowing over me like water. "Do you have it?" She asked.

"I do." I responded.

"Good, now let it carry your body, step by step. Let it move you, guide your body, your arms. The casting we teach is reliant on this flow, on feeling every last motion of magic." I breathed in, feeling those waves crash over me, let it drag my body and arms with it. I felt my foot begin to lift, but Luccia was swift to pin it to the ground. "No, in one place. Do not let it drag you. You are to be a boulder in the face of the waves."

"Got it." I said, centering myself, keeping that focus. The shifting motions pulled at me. My body shifted in turn with it, but I kept myself there.

"Good. You're feeling it. Now, keep that motion, but feel that magic shift and flow throughout your body. Feel it in your mind, in your eyes." I focused inward, allowing the magic to flow through me, feeling it move about within my body. I felt her hands behind me again on my shoulders. "Now, open your eyes." My eyes blinked open, and I was astounded by the sight before me.

Swirls of blue light spun and flowed all around me in long, thick strands. It moved around me, seeming to stretch in all directions. It passed through all of us here, moving differently as it hit each person. Through Cleva, she was a veritable wellspring of magic. It seemed to make up her entire being. Through Luccia, it fumed and bellowed like an endless storm. As I looked down at my hands, I could see it swirling and crashing like an ocean through my body. Luccia shifted in front of me with a smile.

"So, how does it feel?" She asked. I could only laugh as I looked around me, taking it all in. Her smile spread wider as she looked around us. "We call it the World Spirit. It's everywhere around us, in this galaxy and beyond. We all draw on it when we cast, and give back unto it when we pass. Our spirits, when they dissipate, will all rejoin the World Spirit and rejuvenate tenfold what we took." She made sure I looked into her eyes, a sweeping cumulous of magic hidden beneath them. "Everything we are starts and ends here, Hero. Remember that."

"I will." I said. Cleva stepped forward.

"This is just the beginning." She said, "To sense magic is one thing, but to direct it is another." She looked at Luccia, who stepped back. "Assume your stance." She ordered. I lowered myself, pulling my arms out, feeling the magic flow through me. "Now, I want to see you try this on your own. Try to shift that magic flowing through you." Taking a deep breath, I nodded. I attempted to pull at one of the strands, shifting it aside. I felt my arm dragged back into the path, tossing my body to the ground. Luccia snickered behind me. I grunted, pulling myself back up to my feet. I looked back at them.

"What the hell was that?" I asked. Luccia stepped forward again.

"It was the World Spirit asserting that you will not force it to do anything." She said, "It is not something you control outright."

"So then, what am I supposed to do then?" I asked. She gestured with her head to get back into position. I did so.

"You have to guide it, gently. If you try to force it to bend, you will find yourself forced instead. As much as you try, you cannot overpower the World Spirit. Try again." She said. I once more turned, attempting to shift that flow, only to once again be flung.

Another time, I picked myself up. Again I would try, and again. Each time as I tried to shift and move the magic, it dragged me along and sent me to the ground. By the end of an hour, I was on my knees, bruised and out of breath. Luccia beside me and placed a hand on my back.

"You need a break." She said. I dragged myself up again.

"No. I can do this." I responded, a fierceness in my eyes.

"You can, but remember what I said." She stood in front of me, lowering my hand. "Here you may not affect your body back in the real world, but if you exhaust yourself here, you will feel it, the exhaustion." I relaxed my body, letting myself collapse back to my knees. I was already exhausted, but I knew that with just a little more practice, I could do it. She kneeled by me, crossing her legs and folding her arms in the center of them. "You did good. Keep practicing. You'll get there."

"You best believe next time I'll have it mastered." I gave her a halfhearted thumbs up, heaving as I sat there.

"That's what I like to hear. When you're out there, if you ever need advice, I'm always," she tapped her forehead, "right up here. Just give me a holler!" She looked up as Cleva walked over.

"I mirror Luccia's sentiments. Keep training. I will do my best to keep in touch." She kneeled down beside me.

"Time to wake up, then?" I asked. She shrugged.

"Good guess. Goodnight, William. I look forward to our next meeting." I chuckled as she tapped my forehead, and I fell back, descending into sleep.

The Blue Sparrow: Transit to Tanahen

Galactic Date 00:08:438 5028

Once I'd recovered from my training in the Dreamscape, things proceeded as usual. I dragged myself out of bed, changed my clothes, and grabbed my laundry, heading down below decks to get some cleaning done. Figured I needed to stop putting it off, and I had a few hours before my next watch. I could spare some time. Minding my business, I passed by the splitting halls, hauling my laundry bag up over my shoulder as I groggily made my way down into the cargo hold, tossing the dirty clothes into one of the many machines lining the wall. With squinty eyes and a yawn, I leaned back against a crate.

Another day. This trip was beginning to feel excruciatingly long. There was a certain tension that hung in the air across the crew. I doubt any of us signed up for this with the thought that our first mission together would pit us against a Soulless Commander. Honestly, I found it hard to believe myself. How long had it even been since I'd left home to join the Celestials? It had to have been almost a month now. I dipped my chin into my fingers, thinking of the people I'd left behind. I hoped they were alright without me.

Since I'd left, I hadn't thought about it much. I was usually the one who would help in repairing the shacks and homes while they were off working. Couldn't help it. I guess I just never really knew how to say no, or maybe I didn't want to. Maybe that's how I ended up here in this whole mess.

"Penny for your thoughts?" Iraka stepped past me, tossing a load in another washer, leaning beside me.

"Ah, just thinking of everything that came before this." I said, tucking my thumbs into my pockets. Iraka nodded, looking down and over at me.

"I see, I see. You mind if I ask you to elaborate?" I chuckled.

"No, not at all." I said, folding my arms over my chest as I watched my clothes spin within the washer. "Thinking about home. I used to help the people there a lot. Would spend hours going from one house to another fixing up leaky roofs or busted walls and electrical."

"I see. Out of the goodness of your heart?" He asked, raising an eyebrow at me.

"I mean, I wasn't gonna ask them to pay me. Hell, *we* barely got by, could hardly imagine what they were going through." My head leaned back against the metal of the crate as I sighed. "Guess I was also just thinking about what you said before. That I hadn't really let shit go. Maybe the reason I'm here is the same reason I helped them. Didn't want people to end up like me." I stared aimlessly at the walls of the cargo bay, waiting to hear a response.

When none came, I continued. "I feel like I'm in over my head, honestly."

"Maybe you are," He said. I looked from the wall to him, seeing his face turned down in thought. "Maybe we all are. Who's to say?" He looked up, watching a similar spot on the wall. "You know, I left a pretty comfortable life to join this crew."

"A comfortable life?"

"A diplomat for the Xenovan Prime Council. Free housing in Xenova's best district, the hottest, tastiest food you could eat. Yet," he turned to look at me with a twinkle in his eyes, "I'd take this over that any day."

"Why would you leave a life like that to come here?" He grunted as he pushed himself to his feet, walking closer. He put a hand on my shoulder, leaning forward.

"Because here, we give people hope. I can make a difference in both places, sure, but the problems the Council solves are domestic at best. Yes, we're in beyond our pay grade, and far beyond our experience, but that's what we always do." He lifted his hand from my shoulder. "I've seen and heard how hard you push yourself. I admire it, but I should warn you to be careful."

"Oh? How so?" I asked. Iraka sighed.

"William, you… show a lot of self-sacrificing tendencies from the reports of the people who've worked alongside you. You're determined, and you want to help people, but that can't come at the cost of yourself. You cannot help people if you're not alive to see it." He patted my shoulder as he walked past me. "Just… try to be careful. If you ever need counseling, you know my door's always open, and I have an open ear." I took a deep breath and nodded, not saying anything. Iraka took this as confirmation as he walked off.

I let my head hang, staring now at the floor. The sound of sloshing water and metal thunking hummed along the walls as the machines ran. With a sigh, I kicked myself forward and turned to walk out.

I couldn't deny what Iraka was saying, but I certainly didn't want to admit he was right. How the hell else was I supposed to make any form of difference? I wasn't strong like Jewls, or smart like Tara or Natasha. Hell, even as an engineer, I was decent at best. I'd barely amounted to anything here, so if I couldn't at least put *my* life on the line to protect the people here, what good would I be?

My feet seemed to drag aimlessly along the floor as I made my way up and past the engine room. Through the doorway, I gave a wave to Gatha as she wiped her brow of sweat. She waved back before diving back down below the decks. I shook my head with a grin as I looked up, starting to walk up toward the galley.

A noise tickled at my ears, though. It started quietly, but grew more raucous as I approached. Shouting from the helm. I sighed, rubbing my tired eyes as I walked up past the galley. As I turned the corner leading up into the helm, I was concerned to find Oliva and Natasha at each other's throats. The two were screaming loudly enough you could see the spit from their mouths as they poked at each other. I grunted as I ran forward, pushing the two of them apart.

"Fucking hells, break it up, will you?!" I shouted between them. The helm went quiet as I lowered my arms. I took a step back, folding them over my chest. Lux, Jewls, Tara were all about the place, all on watch, all looking up at us three. "What in the gods' names is going on here?" Natasha thrust a finger forward.

"A new watch list was put up, and *one guess* who wasn't on it, *again.*" She spat, "I'm getting sick of our *illustrious* captain cutting herself out of any work on this ship." I narrowed my eyes, furrowing my brow at Sterling. I knew she liked to slack off, but this? This was a whole other level. I'd noticed I'd been running double duty as OOD and engineering watches, but I had paid little attention anywhere else.

"Ortell's the one who's been leading us most of the time," Jewls piped up, "perhaps it's time for a change of command." It surprised me to hear that from Jewls, especially after our last confrontation. Her cold eyes bore holes through both of us. Even Tara watched up with a heated look. Lux sat quietly as I stepped forward again.

"Alright, alright. Just… hold your horses, everyone. There will be no change in command." I looked over at Sterling, who had nothing to say in her defense. "However, a new watch list is going to be drafted, and the Captain and I need to have some *words*," I said, "in private." I made sure to add some emphasis to the last bit. Before I ushered us out of the room, I looked down. "Jewls, you're in charge." She nodded, turning back to her post. I walked out of the helm, Sterling leading the way. We turned the corner, and she opened the door to her quarters. We stepped inside, the door closing behind us. I let out a sigh, rubbing the bridge of my nose.

"Captain…"

"I can explain." She said. I dropped my hand, looking down at her, silent. She looked up at me, and turned back, "It… it was only meant to be for a short while. I had something I was working on." She turned around, moving to her bed. As she ducked down, I looked around. The room was cluttered, filled with sewing machines, embroidery tools, thread, needles, yarn. It was an assortment of disorganized colors and pins all strewn about. The blinds on the windows had been shut tight and a set of shelves were moved to make the space feel tight and small. I picked up a ball of blue thread, looking down at her as she popped out, pulling out a set of half completed patches. She held them out to me, and I took them, looking them over.

They each looked like drafts of a design, none quite completed. A blue bird struck through the center of the patch, streaking across a hexagon, or a circle, sometimes a shield, each with varying colors of backgrounds.

"I… didn't do well by my last crew, especially when I was first mate. The people here are something else, truly. They remind me of everyone from the old crew. Everyone I lost." She sat down against the bookshelf, and I joined her. I was quiet as I held the patches.

"You… you never really talked about them." I said, my voice softer, quieter.

"They were heroes, the lot of them, let me tell you." She said, looking up at the light dangling from the ceiling. "My old captain, Yajin Harwright, was tough on us all. He pushed us all so hard, but you could tell he just wanted you to be the best you could be. He always pushed me as his first mate, and as a soldier." She choked up on her words. "Tiko was our engineer. He always knew how to make us all laugh. He made the best drinks too, and Hichani, our pilot, used to always argue with Majim. They were… they…" Tears welled up in her eyes, beginning to roll down her cheeks. She let her head fall forward, gasps and sobs racking at her chest. Her tears collected at her chin, dripping to the ground. "I lost them all… our captain gave himself up to the Soulless, and I made a bad call. My crew was slaughtered, and I was all that was left." She clutched her hair, dragging her head down. "It should have been me!" She cried. I reached over, putting an arm across her. Her body shook with each sob as we sat there.

"Hey. None of this is your fault." I said.

"It *is*, though. I gave the order. They died on *my* watch!" Her breathing started to calm as she clenched her fists. "They… they're gone… but I have a second chance with everyone here. With you." She reached out, and I handed her the patches. "We never had any symbol to call ours. We were a rag-tag group. It isn't much, but I wanted to make this for us. A patch for each of us. I almost have the design down, but it just needs a bit more tweaking."

"That's what you've been spending all this time on?" She nodded. I sighed, thinking for a moment, before speaking. "I think it's a good idea." She smiled, quiet. I continued. "However, I don't think it's good for you to spend every last second of your day in here on this." I put a hand on her shoulder. "How about I draft up the watch lists from now on? We'll make sure everyone's on there a fair amount. You included." She nodded. The two of us sat there quietly. Not a word was said between us for a while as we just sat, thinking, and the golden light's hum was all that joined us.

Eventually, Sterling reached over, pulling herself up. She cleared her throat, wiped her eyes, and undid the bun in her hair before tying it back up, straightening out the loose hairs. Once set, she dusted off her coat and looked down at me.

"Right… Thank you for hearing me out, William." Her eyes drifted for a moment. "You know, I think if I've made one right choice in my time here, it would be to have made you my number one." She held out a hand to help me up. "I can see already that you'll be an excellent captain one day." A smile spread across my face, taking her hand, letting her pull me to my feet.

"Hopefully not for a while now, Captain." She smiled back, a motherly warmth in her eyes as she straightened my collar once again. She hesitated a moment, but against her judgement, put her arms around my waist, pulling me into a tight hug.

"Don't you ever stop being you. You got that, Mr. Ortell?" She said, pressing her face into my stomach. Slowly, I put my arms back around her.

"Aye aye, Captain." I let her go, taking a step back. She opened her mouth as if to say something, but was cut off. A low warning horn echoed across the ship. Sterling and I caught each other's eyes and nodded. Touching moment or not, something was wrong.

We rushed out the door to the helm. Red emergency lights flashed across the clean white room, an offputting shadow cast over everyone's faces. Sterling's eyes were alight in the shadow, though, and as she walked in, her eyes were immediately on Natasha, who sat at her post.

"Report." she ordered, her voice sharp and focused as I walked in behind her.

"Report from trajectory computer. We're on an impact course. Coming up close too." She said. Tara was working furiously to check her course.

"Just redid my calculations. Everything should be fine. Whatever's in our way, it isn't a planet, that's for sure." She said. Sterling nodded, walking up to the podium.

"Understood. Mr. Astrova, full stop." She said.

"Aye, Captain." He responded, pulling back on the warp throttle. As the Sparrow thudded to a halt, my heart froze. A legion of Soulless ships formed a wall in front of us. At its center, dwarfing us in its shadow, was the command ship, the Wingless Angel. I stood there, paralyzed. We were completely cornered. Sterling turned to Lux.

"Get us out of here. Now." she said through a stiff jaw.

"No can do, Captain." Natasha cut in. "They have us locked out of all systems. We're sitting ducks."

"Shit…" Olivia tapped her finger to her chin. "Nat, do what you can to regain control of the ship. Throw everything you have at it." She nodded, but quickly looked back up.

"Captain. We're being hailed."

"Put them through." She said. Natasha pushed a key at her computer. The lights dimmed and in front of us, a hologram of Koratha projected itself over us. Her eyes were sharp as needles as she imposed, her hands folded neatly behind her back. She looked at Sterling first, then to me.

"I had a feeling you wouldn't listen." She said, a sharp toothed grin stretching from cheek to cheek.

"If you're hailing us, I figured you'd rather talk to our captain." I said, being as blunt as I could. Koratha's smile faded as she turned to Olivia.

"Hmm. That would be normal, would it not?" Her eyes darted back to me. "But what about this situation is normal, William? She may be your captain, but it *is* you I'm after." Olivia looked at me, her brow furrowed. She took a step back and to my side, ushering me down to her level. I kneeled.

"Keep her talking." She whispered. I nodded, standing back up as Olivia took a few steps to the side, keeping quiet.

"Alright then, Koratha. You got me." I began, "How about we work this out, then? You're after me, so why not just take me and let them go?" Koratha laughed, placing her hand over her chest as she did so.

"Oh, you flatter me, William, but why exactly would I want to take you rather than just *kill* you?" She asked. I paced, matching her stance, our eyes locked into each other.

"Simple. You know the power this sword has. With me, you could easily take hold of it for yourself."

"Don't take me for a fool. I know it's bonded to you. We couldn't take its power if we tried." She said, matching my pace.

"Maybe not, but you'd have control of the person using it." I said, "You'd have a powerful weapon, and they'd be free to go." Koratha put a finger to her chin in thought.

"Hmm… a tempting offer you've thrown my way, William. I certainly wouldn't object to having you as a chained weapon at my side." She flashed that toothy grin for but a moment, but it faded quickly. "However, I know the potential you carry." She strode forward, the hologram shrinking till it was the same height as me. She drew closer till we were practically touching. Quietly, she whispered to me, drawing a finger up under my chin. Despite her not being here, I could almost feel her icy touch. "I can tell already from our fight that you're growing fast. I admire it, truly, but it makes you a risk, William, a dangerous one." She tucked her hand back behind her once more.

"So that's a no, then?" I asked. She smiled.

"It's a shame. I liked you. You had a spark few people have. It will be a shame to watch you die." She took a step back. I looked at Natasha, who gave me a thumbs up. We were clear.

"Well, I suppose it's your lucky day, then." I responded, drawing my face in close to hers, "I will *not* be dying here." Olivia stepped forward to the podium.

"Shields to full! Arstrova, evasive maneuvers! Verikov, begin plotting a course! Any nearby system!" She shouted. The helm went into a frenzy of action around us. Koratha nodded to someone beside her as the ship lurched and ducked. The Sparrow rocked as they pelted us with bolt after bolt.

"Well then, William. I applaud you and the rest of your crew, so long as you survive." She paused and smiled. "I look forward to our next meeting." She swiped her hand to the side, her image fizzling out. I was forced to grab a rail as the ship was blasted to the side.

"Lux!" I shouted, "Get us out of these things firing arcs!"

"I'm doing the best I can!" He shouted back, "Don't know if you noticed the *entire fleet* in front of us!" Olivia looked back at me.

"Status on shields?" She ordered. I pulled myself up, turning to the computer.

"Holding, 78%, but we won't be able to take this kind of a beating for long." I said. She nodded as the Sparrow dipped down below the Soulless wall. Their battleships began to break formation, slowly turning to follow after us. Natasha turned in her seat.

"Captain. Scans indicate the Command Ship is charging its weapons." Olivia's breath caught.

"Our shields won't be able to take that. Verikov, status on a path out?" She ordered.

"I can get us a short way from here at best. I can't get us a safe route out other than that." The ship was rocked again. A burst of sparks struck my face as the screen on my computer burst. I tumbled back, Olivia catching me.

"Fuck me!" I said, wiping my face, "Plot it in, Tara. We don't have time to figure something else out!" Olivia helped me to my feet. Computer was shot. I looked to Olivia as Tara plotted our escape course. "We don't have the power to keep shields up and our warp engine. We're going to take a lot of damage getting out of this." I said. She nodded.

"Get back to engineering. I'll handle things here." She ordered, giving me a slap on the back. I darted off back down the hall. The ship was lurching back and forth, sending me into one wall after another. Alarms wailed as booms and rumbles echoed across the ship. I gripped at the rails as we tilted, the Sparrow quickly turning, pulling itself back up and over more ships.

Letting go of the rails, I made a sprint back into the engine room where Gatha was furiously working at keeping our straining engines in one piece.

"'Bout time you showed up!" She shouted over the roar of the engines. I turned the corner, looking at our shields. Twenty-five percent. We wouldn't last much longer at this rate.

"We need to get out of here!" I said, making adjustments to the power grid.

"Aye, I think I *understood* that!" She shouted back, flying down by the warp core. The core began to hum to life, slowly… too slowly. With our shields draining, there wouldn't be enough time for us to charge. We'd be shreds of scrap long before then. If only there was some way to get it to charge faster. My eyes scanned the pipes at its base. Wait, it's fuel draw. Maybe if we opened up past its recommended amount, it would gather energy faster.

"Gatha!" I called. She looked up as I slid into the gap between the grates and the core. "Get a wrench. I'm opening the fuel lines as high as they can go." Her eyes widened.

"Have you gone batshit lad?" She asked.

"You have a better idea? We're dead if we do, dead if we don't!" I said. She pursed her lips before throwing me a wrench.

"You'd damned well better be right, I'll tell you that." She said. I turned, hooking the wrench into the line valve, heaving my body against it, Gatha mirroring on the other side. The core lit up like a disco ball, flashing blue and purple.

The ship rocked and groaned again, a red warning light flashing over the halls. Shields were down. It was all on this thing. I pulled back as hard as I could until the fuel line slipped open. The light from the core was almost blinding. Gatha gave me a barely visible thumbs up as I hopped up, picking up the ship wide radio.

"Captain, core is ready. Get us *out* of here!" I said. The core groaned with excess energy, growing to life as it was engaged. We were tossed again as the Sparrow took another hit, pelted, beaten by the legion of ships behind us. Sirens blared across the ship as I was tossed to the ground, pieces of interior plating bursting from the walls as our ship bowed from the shock, lodging themselves into the deck. Consoles erupted in flames, the engines strained to keep moving. With a crack, the warp core flashed… and it was quiet.

I got to my feet, the sound of the ship's alarm being the only noise around us now. Gatha stood with me, the both of us looking around ourselves at the wreck of an engine room. Without a word, we began a slow, silent walk out toward the helm. Looking around, we'd taken a lot of damage. Lights hung flickering from the ceiling, internal plating strewn about the floors, sparks falling from broken wires. We ducked below debris and into the helm. The entire crew stood there, looking out ahead of us. Olivia looked back at us with a subtle smile before looking ahead. The ship slowed to a stop, dropping out of warp over a small, grassy planet. Olivia sighed, looking at us all.

"Do I want to know our status?" She asked.

"A wreck." I said, "Engine room's torn apart." Natasha spoke up.

"Scanners are down. Access to our main computer doesn't seem to be working either." Olivia took a deep breath.

"Good work, to everyone. Had it not been for this crew's work, none of us would have escaped that alive." She paused, looking out at the planet. "We've got our work cut out for us. The Soulless have a head start on us now, and we need time to repair. Every one will need to work double duty to get us ship shape." She looked back at me. "That includes me. I'll oversee the repairs in all areas. Lux, find us a landing zone, preferably near a colony." He nodded, pulling us forward. I strode up to the railing, leaning on it.

"You seem calm." I said. Oliva looked at me, a smile and a wink on her face.

"I'm confident." She said, "I have a good crew, and someone who keeps me in line when I fall off of it. Even if they have a head start, we'll catch right back up." She gave me a thumbs up. I grinned, nudging her with my shoulder, before looking back out at the planet.

"You may just be right about that."

Corrus System:
Ghishar
Galactic Date 00:08:459 5028

Some days had passed since we'd landed on Ghishar and escaped from Koratha. The Sparrow was an absolute mess by the time we'd touched down. Not even our life support was in one piece. That said, we'd found a nearby Olari colony and, by some sheer turn of luck, we were able to make a trade of their scrap.

The days following our landing saw a lot of hard work from all of us. Gatha and I spent a lot of time in the engine room, reworking and repairing the damaged sections of our engines and core. Days blurred together, as our muscles ached and our fingers grew sore and red from the work. Olivia even kept true to her word, joining us all in the repairs.

By the seventh day, repairs were almost complete. Natasha had joined Gatha, Olivia, and me in the engine rooms. She and I had hunkered down by one of the engineering consoles, working on rewiring it. Sweat beaded at my brow as I steadied my hands, reaching down into the void below, feeling around for any of the last loose wires. I could feel the tip of it wiggling about, seeming to avoid my fingers as I attempted to grasp it. I found traction and grabbed the wire, drawing it up into sight. Lying on my side, I searched for an open port, moving the wire up to attach it.

A warm hand touched my own as Natasha reached over. Looking at her, she shook her head, gently taking the wire and looping it back behind the panel, through a tie, and back up into the port. She then gestured for me. I reached down, grabbing another of the loose wires. She watched as I followed her movements prior, moving it through the back, into a tie, and into another new port. She silently smiled and nodded to me before continuing on another console.

I feel I'd misjudged her. She talked little, but having worked alongside her these past few days, I think it was more that she didn't need to. What she needed to say, she would in few words. She'd speak up if she needed to, but around me, she always seemed to have a quiet sort of introspection. It made the work peaceful. No talking, no conversation, but it was never *awkward*. Instead, I felt like I could focus on the work at hand when I was with her. It made it all the more rewarding.

Finally, I clipped the final wire into place. I scooted back, flipping to my stomach, and pushed myself up. Natasha followed suit, looking over her work one last time. She gave me a thumbs up, continuing in her silence. Brushing off my hands, I looked up to Gatha and Olivia, who sat welding up a piece of the hull plating.

"We're all good down here!" I called up. "Should be the last of the internals!"

"Alright!" Olivia called back. "You want to fire her up, see if she runs?" I looked at the console, then back up to her.

"Sure thing! Let's flip her on!" The two of them hopped down from their perch, Gatha with a steady flutter, and Olivia with a graceful swing to the grating beside me. Gatha reopened the fuel lines. Since we'd gotten there, we'd drained the core to cool off. When we'd opened it up, a lot of its internals had been badly burned or even melted. We were lucky we hadn't blown up when we jumped to warp.

The core's glow grew as the fuel seeped through it once more. Its low hum echoed around us. Slowly, the lights flickered on across the ship. The Sparrow sighed with relief as power came on across its halls. I looked back, seeing the consoles come to life again, rebooting one by one. As the ship returned to its former glory, I let out a sigh of relief. I couldn't help but laugh as I leaned back against the wall, looking at our hard work. Gatha studied over the console, scrolling down through line after line of diagnostics.

"Aye, core temps are normal. Dark energy flow through engines is working as expected. Life support online. Nat, how are things on your end?" She asked. Natasha looked through a separate console, responding in her soft monotone.

"Navigation is online, comms relays active. Ship wide systems are nominal." She turned to us, cracking a smile for the second time since I'd seen her. "She's all ready." Olivia clapped, looking between us all.

"Fantastic! If I'm correct, that's the last of it." She said, looking up at the engine room walls. "There's a few more panels in the helm that need to be put in place. Gatha, Nat. I could use some help with that. William," my head snapped up to meet her eyes, "Arneli and Rex were restocking our supplies with the rest of the crew. Please go assist them." I tossed her a two-finger salute, pushing myself up from where I leaned.

"Aye, Captain." I grabbed Isngr from where I had it propped along the wall, slinging it over my shoulder, feeling its familiar warmth. In my head, I heard the tickle of Luccia's voice pop into my thoughts.

"Hey, Hero, how's the ship looking?" She asked.

"Just about in one piece." I responded internally. She'd started doing this recently; speaking to me through my thoughts. It felt like the longer I was with Isngr, the stronger my connection with Luccia was.

"So we're leaving soon?"

"Just about." I responded, "We need to restock and resupply. I'm hoping we leave in the morning. Give everyone on the crew a little time to get some rest in before we head out again."

"And have you been keeping up with your training?" She asked. I rolled my shoulder, feeling the soreness in it. She'd been working me on minor techniques whenever I had a spare moment. Most of that time she had me focusing on form, with touches of magic thrown in. Correct form, holding it, working on my endurance. The way she taught magic felt more like a martial art. I suppose that isn't entirely unsurprising, in hindsight.

"More or less. The telekinesis is going… decently."

"Decently?" She asked.

"I mean, I've been able to lift some really heavy stuff just…"

"Not for long?"

"Not for long." I sighed as I ducked down into the cargo bay.

"You'll get there." She comforted, the warmth rising from the sword at my back.

"I appreciate the thought." I said, shifting between the crates. "Question for you, though."

"Go ahead."

"So, how exactly do you *exist?* Like, are you just in my head or is the sword your body? How does it feel?" I asked. There was silence, and I could tell she was thinking of how to respond.

"It's… very different from how you exist. When we aren't together, it feels more like I'm just… sleeping. Years can go by in an instant." I furrowed my brow.

"I see. How about when you're awake, then?"

"Well, in a way, I feel through you, unless I take a corporeal form."

"Why don't you?"

"It can be… straining. Anyway, you understand me just fine while I'm in here, and we can talk in private!" I nudged my shoulder back against the guard of the sword.

"Not much for conversing with other people?"

"Not much." She said back. "For a long time it was just me and Vale. It was nice, but I'm also not exactly used to talking with many people anymore, in part due to… this." I could sense she was talking about being within the sword.

"I think I understand. Speaking of, you're a ghost, yeah? How exactly did you die?" I asked.

"I don't want to talk about it." She said with a bluntness I hadn't heard from her before. The warmth from the sword was gone now.

"Alright… I understand." There was no response from Luccia. I sighed, deciding I'd give her some space for now. I moved further out, grabbing the edge of the wall as I peered out down the ramp. A warm breeze blew over vast fields and rows of trees. Green-brown grass shifted and bowed, a soft hiss emanating from the seemingly endless plains. The buzz of bugs mixed with the grass' hiss, a hollow, quiet cacophony in the air. I put my hands on my hips, looking out at the thin lines of trees across the field. The leaves had turned into a mosaic of reds, oranges and yellows, many of them strewn messily across the ground as if they were dirty clothes thrown about the floor. The sun shined above their peaks, lowering slowly, minute by minute. Already the blues of the sky had begun to shift to red. There was still sunlight left in the day, but I guessed it wouldn't be more than a few hours.

"William!" Arneli's voice called. I snapped back to attention, looking down at the small group bringing crates up into the ship. As she walked past me, carrying supplies, her head turned. "Catching a breath of fresh air?"

"Actually," I said, taking the crate from her. I grunted from the weight, struggling to hold it up. With all my might, I shoved it up onto one stack of supplies. "We just finished up the repairs." I said between heaving breaths. Arneli laughed as she punched my shoulder.

"Maybe leave the *real* heavy lifting to me, kid." I shook out my shoulder, fake boxing her.

"Ah, don't do me in like that. I can handle it!" I said. She folded her arms over her chest, tapping her foot at me. "Oh, what? You don't believe me?" She gestured to some crates at the base of the ramp. I cleared my throat, nodded and walking down to the pile resting at the ground. Arneli followed me down as I put my hands on my hips, looking down at the crates.

"Well?" She said, "Go ahead."

"Alright, alright, give me a sec." I said, looking back at the crates again. I shook out my body, bent from one side, then to the other, pulled my arm across my chest, cracked my neck, my knuckles-

"What are you doing?"

"Oh, I'm stretching!" I said.

"You're stalling."

"Am not!"

"Then pick it up!" I furrowed my brow, and bent down at my knees and gripped the sides of the crate, and hoisted... and it didn't move. Fucking hell, what was *in* this thing? Solid metal? "You look like you're struggling."

"Not at all! I've got this!" Maybe if I used magic? I knew I couldn't hold it for long, but if I just was quick, I *might* be able to make it. I focused my mind, gritted my teeth and stood, dragging the supplies up with telekinetic power. I could feel the strain on my body. It wasn't too bad. I'd carried heavier with magic, but I still knew I wouldn't be able to hold it for too long. Dramatically, I marched my way up the ramp, trying my best to make it look like I was physically carrying the crate. I breathed in, breathed out, focused myself. Up and up I pushed, feeling my magic ready to falter at any moment. It didn't hurt, but it took so much of my focus to keep a hold on it.

Just a few more steps. The end was coming into sight. I pushed myself just a little more and set the box atop one of the piles, and took a step back. I took a deep breath in and brushed my hands off, looking at my good work. Arneli walked up beside me, nodding in approval.

"Alright, alright. Not bad." I gave her a cocky smile as she said this. "But now do it *without* magic." My smile dropped as she laughed, patting my shoulder. "It's alright, but maybe stick to what you're good at and let me do what I'm good at."

"Alright. Fair enough." I put my hands up, "I'll leave the crate carrying to you."

"Good to hear." She began to walk down again, but stopped, turning back to me. "Right, Jewls wanted me to remind you, if I saw you, that you're supposed to train with her today."

"Shit, is it that time already?" I checked my watch. "Okay, right, I should get going!" I said, hopping into gear. Arneli gave me a little 'okay' gesture as I bounded off toward the woods.

I had to admit I was nervous. Jewls and I hadn't trained since we'd left Furelle. I'd come to her after we'd landed to try again. With some extra experience, I hoped that *maybe* things would go better this time. I had been surprised when she was so willing to train again after our spat the time prior. That said, I was still unsure. Even with Cleva's reassurance that we would both be better off training together, I couldn't shake the frustration I'd felt from before.

As I pushed past the line of trees, I could see her in the field. With her staff in hand, she spun it, flinging out spell after spell. Even with us mixing like vinegar and baking soda, I had to admit that she was genuinely impressive. As I emerged from the tree line, I could feel the air around me shift, a tingle running up my arms and through my spine. Before I could urge my body to react, it had already moved on its own, almost like it was instinct. A bolt of magic struck the tree behind me, and when I looked up, Jewls was still, her arm pointed at me. The serious look across her face cracked for just a moment as I stood up straighter.

"So you *have* been training." She called, "Maybe this won't be a waste of time after all."

"Think I would have called us out here just for shits and giggles?" I asked as I approached. She stretched, tilting her head at me.

"That's what you did last time." She said as I stood in front of her.

"And so I had someone else teach me." I retorted. Jewls spun her staff at her side. The engravings along its length formed into mesmerizing patterns in the air before halting. Caught by her offhand, the tip jutted toward me.

"Well then, I suppose we will see just how good of a teacher they were. Draw your weapon." I furrowed my brow.

"But, isn't that…"

"It is." I pursed my lips, reaching back, pulling Isngr from where it rested at my back. A hollow wind blew across us as, in the distance, oranges, reds and purples lit up the sky. It licked at our hair, our sleeves, whipping at the grass that stood to our knees. "I expect you not to hold back." Her eyes were as intense as always, searching every inch of my face. "I can see, from the glow in your eyes, you can sense it too, the flow of magic around us." I glanced around. The wisps were there, if fainter. I didn't say anything, but she could tell. I knew she could. A smirk crossed her face as we waited for one of us to make the first move.

In the end, it would be her. She stepped forward toward me, thrusting her staff. I deflected it to the side, but felt it swing back around, connecting with my ribs with a crack. I coughed, stumbling back. When my head snapped back up, I blocked another strike, this time from above. That tingle rode its way up my spine again. I shifted to my side, a magic-infused kick from Jewls striking the tree beside me.

I disengaged, pushing myself back. Looking at where she struck the tree, I saw it splintered, her foot having gone clean through half of the trunk. She *really* wasn't holding back, and I would have to be on my A game. As Jewls pried her foot free, I launched a volley of bolts her way. With ease, she flowed out of the way, almost moving like water. As quickly as I'd thrown out the first set, I found them rounding their way behind her. She'd twisted her arms, the bolts curving and finding their way back toward me.

I slid through the dirt, but as I heard the bolts hit the trees and ground behind me, I felt the ground well up with magic. As a reaction, I formed a barrier below me. A burst of blue shot up, cracking the earth under me, striking that barrier with an incredible power. I felt my whole body strain under the impact as it launched me into the air and into a tree. My back struck the wood with a crunch. I rolled to the ground, but felt that tingle in my body. I rolled to my back, seeing an orb of wisping magic hurled inches over my face.

Time seemed to slow as it passed me. There were slight fluctuations, the type you wouldn't see normally, but I could *feel* them. It was moving along those wisps like a pathway. It bent with the wisps, shifting and twisting like Luccia and Cleva had tried teaching me. Maybe it was just like how I aimed my magic. If I could bait her into casting toward me, maybe, just maybe, I could bend those pathways back toward her.

I rolled around behind and to the other side of the tree, thrusting Isngr into the ground. There was considerable distance between her and me now, but she was determined not to make it last. There was a fire coursing through us as she hurled her staff like a javelin toward me. It curved like the spells she cast. My brow furrowed as I shifted my weight, reaching forward as if by instinct. I caught her staff, catching a glimpse as she passed me, holding it up to block.

Her shin struck the metal of her staff, a golden-blue shockwave reverberating across the field. My heels dug into the dirt, feeling the ground crack and crater as pushed herself back, flipping through the air. Graceful as ever, she landed in the field away from me, drawing Isngr from the dirt where I'd left it. There was a brief stillness, the two of us breathing heavily, the air cold and sharp in our nostrils, burning in my lungs.

I pushed myself free of the dirt, Jewls doing the same, both of us rapidly approaching the other. Steel connected with steel, sending sparks in all directions. She drove the butt of the sword toward me. I put up my arm, letting it connect, wincing at the pain as I shoved my shoulder into her, driving her staff down toward her ankle. She slid her foot back; the staff embedding itself into the soft soil. She thrust Isngr toward me. I caught her arm, twisting it to force her to drop the blade. I caught my sword as she spun, drawing her staff up, the two of us ready once more.

I gritted my teeth as I shifted into my casting pose, Jewls mirroring me. I pushed forward as I saw the magic focusing in her palm. In what only felt like a moment, it was cresting toward me as I approached her. That's what I was looking for. I halted my approach, steadied my breath. One hand forward, one back. As that orb flew at me, I could sense that magical shift. My torso twisted, the flow turning like a stream around me. Before my eyes, the course of that spell moved behind me and around me. My fingers contorted back, that same glow emanating from their tips. As the orb shifted around me, so too did a new volley of bolts, all firing directly toward her.

Jewls eyes focussed as she spun her staff, deflecting the bolts and the orb into the ground. A cloud of dirt and dust separated us now, yet we both remained still. As it settled, Jewls stood there, her eyes as serious as ever. Then they softened, and she smiled.

“That’s enough.” She said, her staff disappearing from her hand. I heaved, trying to catch my breath. My body was sore, but… unlike before, I wasn’t hurt. “You did good. Next time, I won’t go so easy on you.” She began walking past me, landing a soft punch at my shoulder as she disappeared through the trees behind me.

I just stood there for a minute, looking out into the horizon in the distance, almost in a trance, unsure of what to say or do. Before I had a chance to snap myself out of it, a twinkle caught my ear. I looked back, seeing Luccia pacing about in the grass. She spun about, tilting her head back to breathe in the air with a grin across her face. Dramatically, she exhaled and looked in my direction.

“Not bad, Hero.” She said. I tilted my head as I sheathed Isngr.

“Done ignoring me then?” I asked. She shrugged.

“Just had to take some time to myself is all. Got a good look at that fight, though. You’re learning quick.” I adjusted my shirt.

“You think so? I’m feeling it too. Like, I’m having these moments where things just click, like I already know what to do, you know?” I said, tapping my chin as I paced through the field.

“That,” she began, strutting over to me, tapping Isngr’s pommel, “would be his doing.” How was I not surprised?

“So what, I just have whoever owned this last just feeding me information?” I asked.

“Not quite.” She stepped in front of me. “Think of it sort of like an ancestral memory. You’re slowly remembering what he knew, or I guess it’s always been in you. I’m… not entirely sure myself.” She scratched her chin, squinting at the sword on my back. “It’s like I can almost see glimpses of him in you. In a way, I guess there are just moments that his memory shines through and it just…”

"Fits like a puzzle piece…" I finished, looking out at the sunset.

"There you go! Don't get me wrong, it's still all you, just with a touch of help." She said. I frowned, my head tilting down into my hand as I looked at the grass.

"Cleva said I reminded her of him. I don't even know who 'he' is, not really." I said, reaching back and drawing Isngr, "Yet… it's odd. Every time one of you brings him up, I feel like… I knew him, somehow. Not *personally*, but just… it feels like I'm reliving it through you, almost." I said, looking to Luccia.

"I mean, you've seen through my eyes before." She put her hands over her chest, looking down at the ground. "He meant a lot to me. I'll leave it at that for now… even if I think you already knew that." Looking at the horizon again, I chuckled.

"I had a feeling." I said. I took a breath in through my nose and shoved Isngr into the dirt. Letting the wind take me, I fell back, sinking into the depths of the grass, putting my hands behind my head. I felt the grass shift beside me as Luccia laid down too, the both of us looking up at the sky.

"It's been a long time since I did this." She said.

"Watched the sky?"

"Since I lied down." She responded, closing her eyes. "Before you, it was just one holder after another, carrying me until I met the next wielder. It's… nice to just be able to rest… truly rest." As she said this, I became even more aware of the aching of my joints. My knees, my ankles, elbows. It felt like everything hurt, but laying here was nice, relaxing. I closed my eyes too, feeling the wind pass over me.

"I'm glad you can." I said.

"Glad I can lie down?" She asked.

"We all deserve it." I responded. "After all, what's life without a good nap in a field every once in a while?" As I sat there quietly, my mind drifted to the last time *I* had done this. Gods, it had to have been back on Furelle when I was a kid. There sure wasn't a chance on Draenica. Maurel and I would sleep on the fields by town on summer days. I wondered how she was doing. It had been nearly a month now since I'd left. Surely she'd be out soon, and I'd get to explain the whole mess I'd found myself in.

Simple scrapper turned first mate in an army, learning magic, being told to save the galaxy, all in such a short time. I felt Luccia put a hand on my wrist.

"Hey, Hero," I lifted my head to look at her, "I think it's time we get back." I nodded with a smile as she whisked away, turning back into her ribbon and wrapping herself on Isngr, returning its familiar warmth. I stood up, sheathing Isngr along my back, walking back to the Sparrow.

As I approached, a thin wisp of smoke became visible. My brow furrowed as I jogged forward, breaking through the woods. Carried by the air was the sound of talking and laughter. My initial fears were eased as I passed into the clearing, seeing a campfire surrounded by the crew. They were hunched over, cooking pieces of meat in a stew, Olivia's hands darting back and forth as she told stories of her adventures. As I stepped out, her eyes met mine, and she paused before waving a hand for me to join in.

I squeezed in by Tara and Arneli. Lux and Jewls sat across from us as Rex stirred the pot aimlessly, Gatha, Iraka and Nat at his side. Olivia continued, telling some story of how she and her old crew fought against a legion of pirates back during the first war. She would always get so into it when she told those stories, and it was refreshing to see the entire crew here, together, laughing and sharing tales of where they came from beforehand.

As the sun finally dipped past the edge of the land, the sky grew dark, and little twinkles of light dotted the night. The conversation had quieted out, replaced by the sound of spoons against porcelain. Tara nudged me. I looked up from my food as she pointed up into the sky. I looked up, listening to her over the sounds of crickets.

"Up there. You see those four stars?" She asked.

"Yeah, I do."

"I was doing some reading on the local culture in my free time. They call that the Protectorate. Their shield could block even the mightiest of attacks." She told me. I set my bowl down, looking up at it.

"That so?"

"I mean, it's just a local myth, but... it's admirable." She said, "I'd... like to be like that someday."

"A protector?"

"Or just... to have that power." She looked over at me with those large, shadowy green eyes. "So far, it feels like you've done a lot of the protecting. On Draenica, on Furelle..." She looked back up. "You're getting strong, but mark my words Ortell, one day it's going to be me doing the protecting." I nudged her with my shoulder, laughing as I looked up at the stars.

"Well then, Verikov, I look forward to the day you erect a shield to protect me." I said.

"Hey, for all you know, it could happen sooner than you think!" I raised an eyebrow at her, but didn't say anything, opting to stare back at the sky again. She huffed, looking up with me. We were interrupted by Olivia standing up.

"Alright, let's break down, head in. I want us up first thing and setting a route for Tanahen." There was a unanimous groan as the flames were doused and the food packed. Before I headed back inside, I looked out to the pale moon that had risen, letting its light shine over me, and then to the nearby colony. I'd needed this. A respite from the insanity my life had become. I couldn't believe I was saying it, but I was almost grateful we'd nearly been blown out of the sky.

With a skip in my step and a smile on my face, I finally returned to the Sparrow, ready for whatever Tanahen had to throw at us.

MAROONA SYSTEM: TANAHEN

GALACTIC DATE 00:08:479 5028

Rings of golden light flashed from Maroona, the whitish-yellow star that homed Tanahen. The past seven days had been quiet, relatively. At Rex's suggested, I focused on resting my body over the course of the week. With Koratha having such a large head start, it would be hard for us to tell what state the planet was going to be in. We all knew we'd have to be at our best. Thankfully, with the repairs done to the Sparrow, she was running better than ever. We could relax with the extra time not spent on upkeep. However, with the long journey to Maroona came a sense of ease mixed with an undeniable air of caution. The longer we had to wait, the more our minds raced on about the state the planet would be in.

I stood on watch as our officer on deck at the time we finally arrived in the system. The lights were low, and there was a soft hum and whir in the air, mixed with barely audible blips from the computers. With every shift of the engines, every movement of people through doors in the halls behind us, extra little touches of noise would pierce the blend. With just Gatha, Lux, and me on watch, there was a silence between us as we all focused.

My fingers tapped at the railing as I leaned over it, my brow furrowed as I peered out, scanning every inch of space in front of the ship. A dim orange dot sat far ahead of us. Tanahen. So far, I couldn't make out a blockade of any sort, but we still had time before we could really see what we were dealing with. I sighed as I continued to tap away at the railing until a sound broke the silence between us.

"Ortell." Gatha said, barely above a whisper. I looked up from where I stood to see her holding out a holopad to me. I took it without a word, the two of us nodding in silence to each other as I moved over it line by line. Looked to be scan results for the planet. Natasha must have set the ship to automatically put it out when we got close enough. My finger slid down the lines as I skimmed through it, the blue light of its pages almost blinding in the dimness of the main cabin. One particular note caught my eye. As I looked it over, though, more footsteps moved in from down the hall.

Through the entrance to the helm, the rest of the crew poured in, having gotten word that we'd arrived in the system. I looked up from the pad to see Olivia pass through the opening last. As she approached, her eyes met mine.

"William. What's our status?" She asked. I handed her the holopad, turning once more to Tanahen in the distance. Her eyes darted down to the pad, then back to me as I responded.

"Minimal Soulless presence around the planet as far as our sensors were able to pick up." I said, "However, a large amount seemed to be grouped near a set of mountains along the Fushanin Ranges."

"Perhaps," Tara began, "they didn't want to draw too much suspicion. A large force guarding the planet could draw the attention of the Federation." Arneli tapped at her chin.

"That's a possibility. It's also possible that they just gathered all their forces *there* for defense. The Commander knew we were following her, after all." She said.

"All we know is that they are likely more prepared for us than we know. Whatever we do, we should do with caution." Olivia said, her arms tucked behind her back. Since our near brush with death on our way here, she'd seemed like an almost completely different person. There was a sense of confidence in her I had yet to have seen. She looked back up at me. "Was there anything else?" I nodded, gesturing for the holopad. She handed it over to me.

"At the end here. We're picking up a distress signal near to the location the Soulless were inhabiting." Her brow furrowed.

"I'm… unfamiliar with the language." She said. Rex stepped forward, peering over her shoulder.

"It would appear to be Ikui." He said. I looked up and to him.

"Ikui? From what I'd heard, they were unversed in technology." I said. A sigh sank from Rex's carapace.

"A misconception. They are not in the stone age. However," he began, "very few ever leave the planet."

"I see. So what do they want?" I asked. The carapace around his eyes scrunched together as Olivia held the holopad up to him.

"Let me see… my Ikui is… not what it used to be." He was quiet for a few minutes as his eyes scanned back and forth over the glowing pages of the holopad, slowing as he reached its conclusion. "Hmm…"

"What is it?" Olivia asked.

"A group is asking for assistance with reaching a nearby mountain range. There appears to be some sort of issue with crossing a large stretch of open desert." He handed the pad back to Olivia. "Forgive me. I cannot make out more than that."

"It's alright, Rex. Thank you." Olivia said, tapping a finger to her chin, her eyes focused. "I suppose it couldn't hurt to do a quick pickup and drop off."

"Wouldn't take more than a few minutes, I'd assume." Lux chimed in from below. "Looking at the coordinates, the point they're looking for is at the base of the mountains we're heading to, anyway." Sterling nodded, looking around.

"Alright. Good to know." Her head darted up. "We are Celestials, after all. Let it be known that our priority is to assist those in need. Are there any objections to the brief change in plans?" She asked. The room was quiet for a few seconds before Olivia spoke once again. "Alright. Lux, make a route for the origin of that distress signal."

"Aye, Captain." He said, pushing us forward toward Tanahen.

The planet pulled closer and closer until at last it filled the entirety of our view. The rugged golden-orange terrain was even more obvious from here. It almost reminded me of when I'd first seen Titan. The difference was the oceans. They were vast and blue, stretching across the planet. Furelle's were the only ones I'd seen who matched it. Draenica's oceans were nearly non-existent in comparison.

Tara looked over the maps, plotting a series of courses before standing from her station, walking them over to Lux. She kneeled beside him as the two discussed. He would point something out and she'd correct, before handing off the pathing to him and returning to her station. Olivia sat beside me, her fingers intertwined and her legs crossed over each other as she leaned forward. As the ship began to move once more, she broke the silence, turning to Natasha.

"Open a channel with the Ikui tribe." She said, "Let's get in contact to get a better idea of what we might be dealing with here." Natasha nodded, turning back to her computer, typing something into the console. The crew waited in the dark until a figure phased into view on the projector. The slender form of a robed creature sulked into view. A hood was draped over their head and shoulders, and they had pieced together scrap to form a sort of makeshift armor over their body. The carapace on their face clicked together as a hollow glow from their eyes stared through to us. As they spoke, their voice mixed with the clicks and gurgles as they attempted to speak Common to the best of their ability.

"Welcome you we are." They said. Their voice was heavy, gravely, as if it wasn't used to being used. As they said this, they placed a hand on their chest, bowing to us. Olivia stood up, mimicking the gesture.

"We are happy to be welcomed." She said, "We received your request for aid. What exactly is your situation?" She asked.

"We are many," the Ikui began, "but our Chieftain…" they struggled to find the words, pausing as they thought. "Our Chieftain without life."

"You mean they died?" I asked. The Ikui pointed in my direction.

"Dead!" they exclaimed. "Killed by Hollows." I furrowed my brow, looking to Rex, who stood forward.

"Hollows? Are you referring to the Soulless?" He asked. The Ikui nodded.

"Soulless name for them. Hollows our name." He paused to think on what he was saying, but continued, rubbing at what I could only assume was a pain in his throat. "Give time. Translator… need." He said, walking off of the projector. I looked at Olivia and Rex, who both waited patiently. I folded my arms, leaning against the rail. After a few minutes passed, he walked back on, strapping something to his throat. He flicked a switch on its side and began speaking.

"I am sorry. Your language is… difficult." He said. You could hear the small clicks and squeaks from his natural voice, but now it was overlaid with the sound of the translator around his neck. I'd never seen something like it. It mimicked his voice perfectly, but it sounded so clear now. Olivia straightened her jacket out, putting a hand up.

"It's quite alright. Can you understand us fine?" She asked. The Ikui nodded.

"Yes. I hear and understand." They said. They placed a hand over their chest once more. "We wish to ask for an escort across the desert to meet our sister tribe to join them so we may be led once more."

"Can't you elect a new chieftain?" I asked. The Ikui shook their head.

"No no. Chieftains are biological." They explained. "We are all Scouts. No more Chieftains in our tribe." I nodded, thinking I understood. So it was more like a genetic difference then? I had some more questions, but I figured they'd be answered when we saw them in person.

"I understand." Olivia said, "We were on route to where you're headed. We would be happy to pick you up and-"

"NO." The sudden word from the Ikui startled the crew. "We do not ride in your machines of flight. We walk or we ride on those we find along the land. The skies are not for us to travel." They said. Olivia sighed, rubbing the bridge of her nose. I watched the Ikui intently, before turning my attention to Olivia.

"Shit..." she said, "we can't afford that kind of delay." She looked up to speak again, but I put a hand on her shoulder.

"We wouldn't need to spare everyone." I said, "Rex. What do you think?" The carapace around his eyes raised.

"I know a touch of their language, and now I am an expert?" I shrugged. Natasha piped up from beside us.

"The land is mostly flat. High heat could be dangerous though, but the tribe might know how to combat it best. Whoever is out there would need to be used to the heat." She mumbled, turning in her chair to face us.

"I can go then." I said to Olivia. "You can get the Sparrow to the mountains and scout out what the Soulless are up to." She gave me a concerned look.

"William..." she began, "I'm not risking sending you out alone."

"You said it yourself. It's our job to help."

"And he will not be alone." Rex chimed in, looking down at me as he stepped forward. "If you choose to guide this group, they might need medical attention, and if I know you well enough, so will you." I pursed my lips, but nodded. He returned the gesture. Olivia slowly nodded, stepping toward the projection.

"I'll be sending two of my people to meet you. They can guide you to where you need to go." She told them. The Ikui once more bowed to us before standing hunched forward. It looked like they'd been straining to stand up straight the entire time.

"We are grateful." They said, before the projection cut out. Olivia looked up to me and Rex.

"I wish you both good luck." She said, before looking to Rex. "I'm trusting you to get him back to me in one piece. Understood?"

"I will do my best." He said. She looked back at me once again.

"And you." She gently punched my arm. "Take care of yourself."

"Come on. It'll only be a couple of days. I think you can survive without me for that long." I said. "Just make sure the crew stays in one piece, yeah?" I smirked as she gave me a knowing look. She gestured with her head.

"Alright now. Prep your bags, you two." She smiled as I dashed off to pack my things. Down the halls I went, skidding to a halt as I rounded the corner into my room, grabbing some spare clothes from my locker, tossing them in a small bag, swinging it up onto the bed. From Isngr in the corner, Luccia popped out, watching me as she paced around the edge of the room.

"And our titular hero messily tosses his clothes in a pack, ready to be on his way!" She exclaimed, leaning back against the wall, "So what's the ruckus then?"

"Stretching our legs again!" I said, "Arriving at Tanahen now. You, me and Rex are going to be leading a tribe of Ikui through the desert." I said. She pursed her lips.

"And you're... excited?"

"Hell yeah I am! This is our first longer mission on our own! Or, at least, *mostly* on our own." I said, turning to her. She snickered at me.

"You really are something, aren't ya, Hero?" She asked, pacing the room. "Remind me which one Rex was, again?"

"Doctor," I said, swinging the bag around to the ground.

"Right, right. What's the situation looking like?"

"Tribe lost their chieftain, so we're guiding them to join up with a new tribe. Refused to come aboard, so I offered to help take them across the desert."

"Ew, deserts." She grimaced. I raised an eyebrow as I down to retie my boots.

"Not a fan?"

"Look at me." She said, gesturing to her froglike appearance. "I like it cold and wet. Hot and dry doesn't exactly mix."

"Can you even feel the temperature in there?"

"*That* is not the point." She stuck her chin up at me. "I can imagine it, and that's bad enough." I chuckled.

"And you say *I'm* something." I patted the knot as I finished it before standing. "Say, you keep calling me Hero. What's with that?"

"Oh, that?" She said, "It's uh… just a little nickname is all."

"A little nickname?" I asked.

"It's… a joke I used to poke at Vale, the man who used to have that sword." She said, turning to look out of the window. I folded my arms over my chest, watching her in the cabin's quiet darkness, staring out as Tanahen drew closer, the wisps of flames appearing around the edges of the glass as we pulled into the atmosphere.

"You mentioned him before." I said. She smiled.

"You two would have hated each other's guts. He was so stubborn and hardheaded. Always put himself at the center of things." She turned to me, "Always rushed in head first without a thought in the world." She walked over to me now, flicking my nose. "And that's just how you are, Hero." She gave me a wink before disappearing back into Isngr. I scrunched up, rubbing my nose as I looked over at the sword. I walked over and swung it up over my shoulder, looking back at it.

"So a term of endearment, then." I said, "And here I thought you were just buttering me up."

"Don't be so full of yourself." She thought back to me. "Keep yourself humble, Hero, or I'll do it for you!" I rolled my eyes as I picked up my bags and headed out toward the cargo bay to wait.

The heat and dryness of Tanahen was the type to hit you like a baseball bat to the face. Stepping out of the cool comforts of the Sparrow, it felt like I passed through a barrier of that heat, the warm wind whipping at my hair, dragging it in its currents. I put my hand up to my brow, looking out over the vastness of the desert surrounding us. Red soil topped with thin brush stretched around us in all directions. Tall cacti poked out from the ground, dotting the landscape. In the distance, I could barely make out the ranges of mountains we were to be walking to. The heat, I had to admit, was familiar. It wasn't much worse than on Draenica. I was relatively certain it wouldn't be too trying of a trek.

Ahead of me was the tribe of Ikui we'd spoken to. As I heard the sounds of the crew approaching behind me, I began to descend to the ground below. I hadn't noticed on the projector, but each of them had different markings painted across the carapaces of their face and skin. They were of brilliant earth tones; reds, browns, yellows, oranges. One set of markings stood out from the others. A turquoise-blue set rested on the face of the one who'd spoken to us over the projector. They looked up at me as I made my way down, placing a hand on their chest to greet me, bowing their head. I followed in the gesture.

"Welcome to Tanahen." He said, "You may call me Iravek. We spoke on your communications system. I am acting leader of the tribe."

"A pleasure to meet you, Iravek. My name is William Ortell of the Blue Sparrow. My companion, Rex," I stepped aside as Rex walked beside me, "and I will be joining you across the desert." Rex bowed as well.

"I see. What of your third?" Iravek asked. My brow furrowed as I turned, looking behind us. The crew were all waiting at the edge of the ship. "Not them." He clarified. When I turned back, I followed his gaze. It peered at the blade sticking up from my back. "Her."

"Luccia?" I asked, drawing Isngr from my back. "You mean you could… see her?" He nodded.

"The flow of magic emanates strongly around her. She was easy to spot." He gave me what I could only describe as a smile. It wasn't particularly easy to tell with the shifting carapace, but you could see it in his eyes. "Will she be joining us?"

"She'll be along for the ride. Though I don't know if she'll be coming out very often. She's not particularly fond of the desert." Iravek nodded.

"I see, I see." He looked back to his tribe, then to us. "We are finishing preparations to leave. We suggest you do the same before we begin our voyage." I nodded. Rex gestured for me to follow him as we began walking back toward the crew. As we did, he looked down at me.

"You are quite sure about this, William? You are determined, but a trek through deserts is no small task."

"I'll be fine." I said, "Didn't exactly grow up in the lap of luxury, you know."

"Hmm? I realize I am unaware of your upbringing. Enlighten me?"

"Started life on Furelle. Parents were scrappers who taught me the trade before I lost them in the Soulless attack. I spent the rest of my life on Draenica." I glanced up at him. "At least, until a month ago." Rex was quiet as we walked. After a brief moment of reflection, he spoke again.

"Forgive me. I had not realized." He said, "I will, however, warn that Tanahen has more threats than just its heat. Draenica has ill in terms of predatory creatures. Tanahen is very different." I nodded, assuring him I understood.

As we approached the crew, Gatha walked up to me, taking my hand in hers. I could see tears in her eyes and kneeled down.

"Come on, Gatha, it's only going to be a couple days."

"Aye, I know that but…" She put her arms around my neck, "Ah, I always get emotional when people go off to do things." She let me go, a smile across her face as she wiped her eyes, "Just makes me proud seeing my little engineer in training going off on his own missions." She tapped my shoulder with a few gentle punches. "I'll see you on the other side, kid." I gave her a loose salute.

"See you at the mountains." I said as she walked back inside. I could see Arneli saying goodbye to Rex in the corner as Tara walked up to me.

"Hey. You keep yourself in one piece." She said.

"You think I wouldn't?"

"I mean, you've done an… okay job at it so far. Reminder, I had to drag you back to the shack when this all started." She put a hand on my shoulder. "Wish I could come with you, but the Captain wants me on board to help scout when we get to the mountains." She grinned, "Just remember, you promised!"

"Promised our stories would continue together." We grasped each other's hands, looking into each other's eyes. "Don't worry, I've not forgotten." I let go, taking a step back. "I'll see you in the mountains, and you can count on it." She smiled, nodded, and fluttered back up inside. I began to turn when, by my surprise, Jewls stopped me. She grabbed my shoulder like a vise, turning me to face her. She eyed me harshly, but softened.

"Keep up your training. Don't overdo it." She dusted off my shoulder pad. "I expect you in peak condition when you meet with us next."

"Simple and to the point." I said, "I'll do my best." She was silent, but seemed satisfied, turning on her heels to leave. Last, Olivia waved as the others headed inside. She said little, but as the ramp closed, I glimpsed her gesture to me to fix my collar, before disappearing from sight. Rex and I backed away, the roar of the Sparrow's engines bellowing through the air, pushing up dust and sand as she took off. She lifted and turned before blasting away, soaring gracefully across the sky away from us. I waved as I watched her disappear off into the distance. The two of us turned back to the Ikui tribe now, as Iravek approached once more.

"We are ready." He said. I nodded, looking out to the mountains miles away.

"Then we get moving. We have a lot of people, and if the Soulless are nearby, we should do our best to make the best time we can." I said, picking up a sack of their supplies, slinging it over my shoulder.

"You do not have to carry our burdens, William. Your guidance is enough." Iravek tried to say, but I put up a hand.

"Don't worry about me." I said, "I just want to help however I can." Iravek gave me a worried look, but nodded.

“The trek is long. Please, do pace yourself.” He said and looked at the rest of his tribe. Everyone had picked up their things and was ready to move. We just had to give the word. Rex passed me, placing a hand on my shoulder as he did.

“I will take the rear. If anyone is in need of medical attention, I will be ready.” He said, moving back. Iravek look from me to the mountains.

“Lead the way, Mr. William. We will follow.” He said. I nodded, beginning our long trek through the desert.

Tanahen: The Broken Miles

Galactic Date 00:08:479 5028

The Broken Miles. An empty swath of desert stretching from the western coast of the continent of Schelach to its mountain ranges far in the east. Almost a two-day trip by foot. We could have made it in minutes, if not seconds, in the Sparrow. At least then I wouldn't have to be watching for venomous bugs every few steps. On Draenica nothing survived in the Ashlands anyway, but *here*?

The sun beat down on you minute after minute without respite. Mere hours in, and I was already a sopping mess of sweat and sand. The wind had picked up, carrying with it the grime of the ground all around us. It stuck to your skin, mixing like a paste across your face. At least, that's how it was for me. Rex and the

Ikui seemed completely unbothered. Then again, I wasn't entirely sure they even *did* sweat under all that carapace. Either way, I had to agree with Luccia. I *hated* deserts.

I raised my hand to wipe away the sweat from my brow, a thin layer of grime rolling off onto my arm. My shoulder and back were aching from carrying the supplies, and my legs were growing sore from the hours of trudging through cracked ground and spiny brush. I was half certain my legs were shredded from the thorns, but that I was just too numb down there to feel it. Iravek looked at me, the two of us having been at the lead of the group, his head cocking as he looked me up and down.

"I have seen very few of your kind. You do not seem well equipped for this," He said.

"Ah, I'm… I'm fine." I heaved. I adjusted the supplies on my shoulder, trudging forward. Ahead was nothing but blue skies and more empty land. There was nary a cloud in sight, even. Staring at that expanse for so long, I felt like I was going insane. The only comfort was the sight of mountains slowly rising from the horizon. Iravek nodded, turning his attention ahead of us again.

"I see." He said. I could tell he was attempting to contain some amount of amusement. As we walked forward in silence, he turned to me again.

"You are a caster of sorts, correct?" He asked.

"Yeah. You could definitely say that." I responded. "I'm a bit new to the whole thing." He nodded.

"I can tell. The World Spirit is strong in our home." He began. I cocked an eyebrow, letting him continue. "In you, however, it struggles to flow properly. You hold a tempest of power within you, but struggle to draw from the world *around* you."

"I'm not sure I exactly follow.".

"In our tribe," he explained, "we learn that, to cast spells, one must find a balance. To draw from your magic is important, but mastery over control of the World Spirit is just as important to our growth." I furrowed my brow.

"I know how to bend and shift the World Spirit." I said. Iravek put up a hand.

"Ah, this is not entirely what I mean." He thought a moment, staring off into space, before looking back to me. "I wish to teach you. As payment for your guidance." I shook my head and hand.

"Oh, there's really no need! You don't owe me a thing! We're here doing this 'cause you needed help." Iravek walked in a stunned silence. It was as if he hadn't expected being turned down. Still, he cleared his throat, put a hand over his chest, and bowed his head.

"You are truly kind. However, I insist. You are helping me and my people. If I can assist on your journey and growth, I would be honored." If he was so insistent, I wouldn't be one to turn him down. Gods knew I could use the help. I smiled, bowing my head back to him.

"I appreciate it, greatly. If you're certain, I would be happy for you to teach me what you know." He did that attempted smile at me again. It wasn't exactly unsettling. You could see the smile in his eyes, but it was almost comedic how much his face contorted. I chuckled, looking forward again. "Say, what exactly is so important about these Chieftains, anyway?"

"They lead our tribes and keep us safe." He said, "In return, we Scouts know how to forage and hunt for food. They act almost like… a queen to a colony."

"I see. So without their guidance you, what, can't really come to a consensus on things?"

"Many tribes can have hundreds of members. Ours is small. Chieftains are necessary as they make the final decisions for the tribe."

"So they have control over the entire tribe?" I asked. Iravek shook his head.

"The relationship is symbiotic. We forage and hunt. They protect and make choices for the tribe, as well as often birth many of our young. However, with their power comes danger. If a Chieftain makes bad calls, their Scouts are like to exile them. They may wander the deserts in search of another tribe, or perish in its sands." I'm not sure if it was some sort of divine comedy or providence, but as he said this, my foot hit something hard in the sand. Looking down, I found the half eaten and whittled down bones and carapace of a large Ikui. "I see they chose to perish." He said in a flat tone. I shook away the jitters I'd gotten from seeing what could be *my* fate if we got lost out here, and stepped over the skeleton.

"You said that Chieftain are… different than you?" I asked.

"Quite, but also not." He responded. "Any Ikui may be born a Chieftan or a Scout, like us. However, it is quite rare for Chieftan to be born."

"So, is there ever more than one Chieftan in a tribe?" I asked.

"Oh, often! The group we plan on meeting is a large tribe of the area. We worked out a trade of goods for a Chieftan to join with us."

"You just… trade goods for people?" I asked.

"I understand this may seem odd by your ways of life. However, here, it is our way. A Chieftain travels the land from one tribe to another. One of them may find themselves in a new tribe every few years and this is not abnormal." He looked into the sky, a thoughtfulness in his eyes. "It is our way of life. Our world is harsh and deadly. People die. We mourn, but we move on. Such is our lives." He turned his gaze to me. "Is this not true in your war as well?"

"I…" I closed my mouth as I was about to speak. I thought back to Furelle. Everyone I knew there was dead, save a select few. In their place, I'd filled in a new family. In the distance, I imagined the sight of the Sparrow. I'd surrounded myself with people who had my back and… maybe he was right. What would we do if someone died? It would be inevitable, wouldn't it? Before I could say anything else, he put up a hand.

"Do not feel the need to respond. Think on what I have said." He hunched his head forward, his feet scraping over the cracked dirt. Looking down, I could see the dirt at his feet, caked on in layers, as if it were some form of natural boots. As I was watching the ground, I noticed the light of the sun dim, and then brighten… then dim again. I glanced up, but before I could tilt my head all the way skyward, I felt myself tackled to the ground.

A gust of wind struck at the ground as a blur of black and brown feathers swooped past us. There was a scream of chirps and clicks as one of the tribespeople was lifted from the ground and tossed high into the air. I looked into the sky as a set of giant hawks soared overhead. Iravek pulled me to my feet, pulling a makeshift rifle from his back.

"Kailow Hawks!" he shouted, turning back to me. "Be ready William." I nodded, drawing Isngr from my back, twirling it in my hand. I could feel the wind rushing through the hot desert air long before I could see the hawk swooping in. Sand blinded my vision as I danced to the side. The first hawk swirled close to the ground, creating a cloud of dirt and dust. Iravek and I stepped toward each other, till we were pressed back to back. We were blind to the world outside of the cloud.

Iravek looked back at me, pressing me down low as a set of talons darted overhead. We stayed low, an eerie quiet fallen across the tribe. In the blindness of the dust, we would hear people picked off, guns firing in a direction, a scream, a flash. Our eyes met, and he took my arm. I trusted him as he dragged me out of the dust, bursting out into the open air.

A screech echoed across the vast emptiness, diving toward the two of us. They'd been prepared, waiting to hunt us the second we were free. Iravek turned, placing his rifle on my shoulder. A crack mixed with the ring of metal burst forth from his gun. I felt the shock of it hit me as I heard one bird shriek, crashing into the ground in a flutter of dirt and feathers. I turned about, seeing one of the two, its wing struck. It struggled to its feet, lowering its body. On its head was what looked like a thick place of bone. Iravek pulled back the bolt on his rifle with a click, firing again, but the bullet bounced clean off the plates. His carapace furrowed as he tapped my shoulder.

"I leave this one to you. I will assist the tribe with the other." He said. I nodded, lowering myself, my eyes focused on the hawk. It lowered its head, tucking its wings in to its sides. As it charged, I spread my legs and braced myself. I bent my arm out in front of me, a light barrier forming as I met it head on. I watched as wisps of magic collected at its feathers, as it sped faster and faster, charged by the abundance of energy around it.

Its head crashed into the shield. A spark of blue and orange cracked between us. I put all my weight back against the strength of the bird, feeling my feet struggle for grip in the dirt. I felt it pull back, keeping its head pressed firmly against my barrier, locking me in place. I was enshrouded in shadow as it spread its wings once more. Magic collected across the strands of its feathers, glowing visible even past my vision.

With a single flap, I felt the barrier shatter. There was that familiar feeling as the shock of it rang through my entire body. Its head slammed into my chest, throwing me across the brush. The thorns of the bushes around me cut and sliced at my skin, sending waves of stinging burning through me. I rolled to a stop, stabbing Isngr into the ground to pull myself to my feet. I wiped away blood from my cheek, looking up to see the hawk charging again.

I couldn't meet it in a battle of strength. It had me far outclassed, that much I knew. I could already feel my muscles burning from that one attack. Another like that might send me over the edge. Speed would have to be my ally.

My brow furrowed as the bird shook its head out, feathers laying flat across its body. The thump of its feet across the desert sands soon filled the air. I gripped Isngr in both hands, drawing the blade in close, tip pointed at the hawk. This thing was smart. I'd need to bide my time, play "chicken" if you would.

As the hawk drew closer, I spun to get out of the way. I realized too late that I'd made my move early. I felt the air shift as its wing tilted. It hit my shoulder, and I braced myself for the force of hitting the ground. Instead, I hit someone else. A set of arms caught me, setting me to my feet in one graceful motion. I looked back to see Luccia manifesting beside me. She turned her head to glance at me.

"Looked like you could use some help there, Hero." She said with a grin. I chuckled as I pulled Isngr back again.

"Thought you'd have noticed sooner."

"Wanted to make you sweat a bit, was all!" She reached to her side, pulling a spectral blade from her belt. "Well then, Hero, I *suppose* I could offer a touch of support." Our eyes met with the hawk, who scraped to a stop. Its claws dug paths through the sand with heavy crunches. It spun to face us. The two of us prepared ourselves for whatever this thing would throw at us next.

Despite its injury, the hawk kicked up from the ground, spreading its wings. The air rushed past us as it dove, magic rushing off its body. We lept to the ground as we were hit with a gust of wind. I could feel the hawk's magic hit me like a truck as I was slammed into the ground. I flipped onto my back, Luccia following suit. The hawk soared higher up, blotting out the sun. It spun and dove again. Luccia looked to me.

"Follow my lead." She said.

"Got it." I watched as Luccia sheathed her blade. She began to cast, weaving the magic around her in a spiral. I drove Isngr into the ground. The shadow was getting closer by the second. I guided the wisps of magic until they were spinning about me. Luccia's eyes were focused intently on the shadow approaching us. You could barely see the hawk as it drew closer. The sun behind its wings shone too brilliantly to look at. Still, her brows furrowed as she held her ground. The wisps were spinning about us faster, faster. Where was she going with this?

"Luccia?"

"Hold it…" she ordered. The shadow was almost upon us.

"Luccia!" I shouted. She gritted her teeth.

"Now!" She shifted her arms. The wisps trajectory shifted, following her lead. I mirrored her, feeling the magic tug and pull at my body as it rode its way along my arm. The wisps we'd been spinning firing out along the path we'd given them. This wasn't casting our bolts. This was something else. Using the very energy that had knocked me off my feet so many times before.

The wisps of magic found their mark, striking and swirling about the hawk. It struggled against the shifting current, tumbling down into the ground. There was a wave of wind as it crashed.

Dust clouds blew in all directions. I raised my arm over my face to shield myself. Through the cloud, I began to see the shimmer of blue heading for us. Luccia contorted her body, forming a manifestation of a pillar in the air, driving it down onto the hawk. It was pinned, but I could see Luccia struggling to hold it. She turned to me.

"Finish it, William!" She shouted. I pulled Isngr from the ground and charged. The hawk struggled and snapped its beak at me. I pulled away from the clack and snip of its jaws, dancing around its wings. Ducking under its strikes, I maneuvered behind it. There was my opening. I ran forward, jumping onto the bird's back, gripping the feathers at the nape of its neck.

There was an audible shatter behind me, and I felt the hawk pull free of Luccia's pillar. I gripped tighter as it whipped its body back and forth, trying to throw me from it. It spread its wings, sending us skyward with a mighty flap. My grip on Isngr faltered. I felt the blade slip from my grasp, tumbling down to the sands below. I wrapped my arms along its shoulders, my knuckles pale as I held on for dear life.

Looking down, I watched as the ground drew further and further from us. The hawk continued higher and higher, but did not struggle to remove me. Then it stopped. I felt myself grow weightless for a moment. Then the tumbling began. The hawk ceased flapping, the two of us now in a freefall. As we spiraled and twirled, I felt myself slipping. More and more, inch by inch, till finally, I couldn't hold on anymore. I was launched off of the hawk. It spun its body, smacking me with its wing as it corrected itself.

I tumbled backward through the sky. I was dazed, but pulled myself together. I was in freefall. In a few seconds, I'd be a splatter on the ground if I didn't do something. Now would be a *lovely* time for some of that ancestral knowledge.

My mind raced. A barrier would just kill me *sooner.* I needed to slow myself down. Trying to manipulate the World Spirit would just throw me around more… but I thought about it more. When I tossed it out at the hawk, I felt it drag my body with it. It would have to be enough. I spun my body, drawing in as much magic to me as I possibly could, turning to face upward at the hawk. A deep breath now, in, then out. I aimed my arm out and guided the magic away from me. The force of it dragged my body to nearly a standstill. I could feel muscles straining, a growing soreness and pain in my chest and core, could feel myself getting more and more exhausted.

The wisps found their mark once more, just as I came to a rest on the ground. I picked up my sword as Luccia ran beside me.

"Are you okay?" She asked. I rolled my shoulder, rubbing the sore muscles.

"I will be." I said, "Let's finish this." The hawk recovered above us, swooping down. I brought my arm back, forming a set of bolts, sending them skyward. They fired up as Luccia thrust a foot into the dirt. A pillar of magic erupted from under the hawk, knocking it up as my bolts curved. It was struck again and again and again, smashing into the ground. I took Isngr in both hands as Luccia rejoined with the blade, her ribbon flapping in the wind as I dashed across the desert. With one final clean motion, I brought the blade down.

The hawk was no more.

I keeled over, wheezing and coughing as Rex rushed to my side. He stabilized me, holding me upright. The tiredness and soreness in my body were becoming more and more evident by the second… and the pain. It was all throughout my chest, my back… everywhere. It felt like I'd practically shredded myself apart.

Rex laid me down, pulling out some of his tools. Iravek moved by my side as well, looking me over.

"His body has taken on a severe amount of damage." He said. Rex's carapace furrowed and buckled as he moved a scanner up and down my body.

"Multiple torn muscles. Bone fractures across your ribs and spine." He looked into my eyes. "I do not have the materials here to help with damage like this." Iravek put a hand on my chest.

"I can heal him." He said. "Enough that he may walk, but it will take time for him to fully recover." Rex sighed and stepped back, allowing Iravek to work. His hands moved over my body, a faint blue-gold glow falling over me. I gritted my teeth, feeling an intense burn through my bones and muscles. I could see a similar strain on Iravek as he moved down my body.

The pain slowly began to subside. My head was still hazy, and there was an intense soreness and stiffness throughout, but I didn't feel like I was about to die. Looking over at Iravek, he took in deep swells of breaths as he dropped his arms.

"Forgive me, William. This is all I can do for you." He said. I sat up, rubbing my head. It felt like someone had taken a hatchet to it.

"Thank you." I said.

"Seeing you in action. It was a spectacular display." He said between breaths. "You may be inexperienced, but you use what you know to a high level." He closed his eyes in a smile. "I look forward to seeing you apply what I have to teach you." I could only chuckle, lying back down for a moment, just catching my breath. There was a warmth of blood still dripping down my arms and legs from the thorns and beatings I'd taken. Rex was quickly to the task of bandaging me up. By the time he was finished, I looked half-mummy.

And as much as I wished I could lay there all day, we had a long way to go. Before long, we had the remains of the hawks rigged up on a set of sleds as food for later. Between the two of them, there would easily be more than enough for the entire tribe for the rest of our trip.

Soon, night fell. The sun dipped below the distant horizons and the skies became a dark, inky blue and black. Overhead, visible even to the naked eye, strands of blue and green magic swirled through the air, shifting in and out of sight. Stars began to light up across the sky like a million pinholes through a black blanket. There was a quiet hum and buzz of bugs in the darkness around us, muted only by the crackle of flames. The tribe sat in circles around turning spits, roasting the parts of the hawk, handing out chunks of meat between people. The cooks had carved and seasoned the different sections, saving the pieces they couldn't use for food to be used in other ways.

Beyond the light of the camp, Iravek and I sat, our legs crossed. As he breathed in, so did I, and as he breathed out, I followed. His eyes opened, looking into mine with their familiar glow.

"I will be teaching you techniques handed down to me from my father, and from my father's father. In our tribe I am what we call a Lifeweaver." Luccia manifested beside me, peering over my shoulder at Iravek.

"A Lifeweaver?" She asked. Unsurprised, he looked up at her.

"Indeed. We specialize in healing and defense." He told us. "You are Molusion yes?" Luccia nodded. "I see. Your style becomes much more obvious to me, William. I will teach you, however, another way." He moved to his feet. I stood up as well, the ground crunching under me.

"You mentioned you didn't cast in the same way."

"We do not, at least not entirely." He said, "You draw magic from yourself. In combat, this works well. However, when you heal…" he pulled a knife, drawing it upon his carapace. It cracked under the blade, a green blood dripping out, "if I were to draw from myself," he put his opposite hand over the cut. The blue glow shone from his palm. The cut closed, but when he turned his palm over, we saw that the cut had simply moved to his opposite hand, "then the healing is ineffective. Rex told me that you heal faster than most due to the latent magic you draw from your sword. This tells me that you may know this technique already, though you do not realize how to control it yet." I glanced over my shoulder at Isngr. I'd been sort of… passive, I guess, with it. It's true I'd never had to *think* about pulling magic from it. I looked back to Iravek.

"So, you're going to show me how to control it?" I asked.

"Indeed, I will." He said. He tossed the knife my way. I caught it, wiping it clean. He gestured to my palm. I took the knife to myself, and hesitated, before drawing it across. I winced at the stinging pain now, but looked back up to him. "These techniques can be tiring to your mind as well as your body, so, though you are not drawing from your own reserves, if you try to heal more than you are capable…"

"Then I hurt myself." I said. "Seems a little counter-intuitive with healing magic." Iravek shrugged.

"It's all about *control.* Especially when we heal ourselves. We must be careful that we do not damage more than we repair." He could see my understanding in my face, and continued. "You are already worn out from the day. Hence, we will not be healing more than the small cut on your hand. As you will be healing yourself often, that is what I shall teach. Focus on the pain." I looked down at the cut. Its stinging was warm, and it felt like a heat pulsed in my palm. "When you have it, you must guide the energy of the World Spirit into yourself through the wounds." I put my hand up to begin the motions, but he stopped me. "Careful. Too much energy may have the opposite effect. *Small* controlled amounts." I nodded.

I focused, shifting just my fingers as Iravek watched. Thin lines of blue magic began to make their way out of the air. My forehead wrinkled as I struggled to maintain my hold on the magic, urging it toward my palm. The tips of the threads tickled at my hand. The sting grew as the lines sewed shut the wound as if it were a medical needle closing the cut. Soon, naught was left but fresh skin.

I pulled my casting hand back, finally taking in a gasp of air, realizing I'd forgotten to breathe. Iravek approached, putting a hand on my shoulder.

"Good job, William. You have done well for your first time." I put a hand on his shoulder in turn.

"Had more than a few good teachers." I said, looking between him and Luccia. I closed my eyes just a moment, feeling the pangs of exhaustion taking over me, before taking a seat in the sand, and finally, just lying there. The two of them stood over me, looking down at me.

"Are you well, William?" Iravek asked.

"Just a little tired, is all." I said. I tried to move my arm, but the soreness from earlier, mixed with the strain from having just cast, was too much, and it flopped back down. "Though it appears moving is a bit out of the options at the moment." Iravek chuckled, crouching beside me, then laying down as well.

"Then I will lie with you." He said. Rex walked over from the campfire, holding cups of drink. Luccia returned to her ribbon as he approached. He looked initially at Isngr, before he looked down at the two of us.

"Have I come at a bad time?" He asked, sitting on the sand.

"We are just a little tired is all!" Iravek said. A low grumbling laugh emanated from Rex as he leaned over, leaving the drinks beside us.

"I suppose that is fair." He stood up. "I shall let you rest. William, Iravek." He gave us both nods before returning to the camp. The two of us laid there, watching the stars and wisps passing by overhead. Iravek turned his head to look at me.

"What do you know of spirits, William?" He asked.

"Surprisingly little, given I practically live with one." Iravek laughed, turning his gaze to the stars once more.

"They are born of particularly powerful souls, ones who have yet to finish their purpose. They act as guardians to those around them. Some attach to people, others to places or objects." He was quiet, the two of us in thought. He sighed, turning to me. "Looking at you, since we have met, William, you look like you could use that guidance. I can see the turmoil in the magic in you. Caught in a war you never asked for, pushed to the front lines without regard for what you wanted." He looked back at the stars. "Do you ever miss home?"

I could only begin to laugh. It came straight from my chest, from my throat. Quickly followed, I could feel a tightness in both as tears fell down my cheeks, welling up in the sands under me. That laughing cry wracked my whole body as I sat there, watching the stars. Gods, I missed home. I missed how everything was on Furelle. I missed exploring the forests with Maurel, scrapping in the edges of the beaches. Hell, I missed Draenica. I missed the people there I'd helped, the shack even. Right now, I even missed the Sparrow. My body ached, my mind did as well. Here I was, so excited to set out on a mission on my own, yet here I was, crying in the sand. I reached up, wiping the tears from my face.

"I'm... I'm sorry. I shouldn't be-" Iravek stopped me, holding up his hand.

"It is only natural to miss our homes wherever they were. The people, the places that make us. The past is a lovely place at times, a miserable one at others. Yet, we are never alone in walking it." He put his hands on his chest. "I admire you, truly. You have walked a long path, come quite far in so short a time. Yet, you have people behind you to help keep you standing all the while. That much is obvious." He closed his eyes. "You're lucky, you know? Few people can claim to have that support." I chuckled, wiping more tears from my face.

"Yeah. Yeah, I suppose you're right." I looked out into the distant mountains and sighed, letting my eyes close. The people I'd met along this wonderful journey filled my mind. We hadn't been together long, that was sure, but I knew I'd lay my life on the line for each and every one of them. As my breathing settled, I let myself drift off into the silence of sleep under the stars.

The next day felt just a touch cooler than the one prior. Maybe I was just getting used to it. Maybe the approaching clouds had something to do with it. Either way, we were moving, hot or cold.

As we packed up the camp, stowed and stored the leftover meats, and broke down the tents, I moved to pick up a pack of our supplies. As I began to lean down, Rex put a hand on my shoulder.

"You need to let yourself rest." He said, "No heavy loads." I huffed.

"Come on, Rex. I can handle a little extra weight." I said, pulling the bag up. A muscle in my shoulder twisted, and a sudden pain shot through my arm. I immediately dropped the bag as my arm felt limp and numb. The pain in my shoulder was excruciating. Rex propped me up and pushed his thumbs in, rubbing at the muscles in my shoulder.

"Pulled muscle. Your body is still recovering. This can be alleviated, but I must *insist* that you rest." I sighed.

"Fine." I said, "Don't enjoy feeling useless." Iravek seemed to appear from nowhere as he lifted the sack I had dropped, propping it on his hunched back.

"You are still our guide. Just because you cannot lift a bag does not change this fact." As he said this, I nodded.

"I... I guess you're right." I looked at the rest of the tribe, taking them all in. "Oh, right. I forgot to give this back." I reached behind me, pulling out the knife he'd given me. He cupped it into my hand.

"Keep it. As a reminder." I hesitated, then nodded, stowing it away under my belt. I then looked to the mountains.

"We should be there by early afternoon, by the looks of it." I said.

"I agree with your assessment," Iravek said, staring out into the distance. "We are ready to move when you are." I put my hands on my hips

"Then I guess we get moving then." The caravan began its trip across the Broken Miles once again. Cracked dirt broke, hot wind blew, and once again, grime and dirt collected all across me. The bandages on my arms, before long, had been turned a light tan-brown. I squinted as we pressed onward.

The mountains were growing larger by the hour. We were making fantastic time, but the day was heating up, and we could tell it was going to get worse. The sun pounded down on us like a blacksmith on its anvil. I'd tied my hair up higher, keeping it off my neck. I could honestly use with a touch of a shave. Should have done so before I left, but, alas, here we were. As we trudged onward, I felt Rex tap me. I looked up to him, slinking back slightly, so that I stood under his shadow.

"Something the matter?" I asked.

"The day is hot. We are moving quick. It may be pertinent for the health of the group to slow down." I turned back, looking at the tribe. Many of them looked tired, struggling to hurry. I nodded to him. I turned to Iravek, who walked beside me.

"Let's cut the pace. We have more than enough time and supplies." I said.

"I will let them know. There is an oasis along our route. We may stop and resupply."

"Understood." I said. We slowed down. I felt a little better at this pace. My legs were still sore, but it was bearable. I shoved my hands in my pockets as we walked, staring up into the blue sky, dabs of white fluff spread across it. Rex leaned down beside me.

"There is something on your mind?" He asked. My brow furrowed as I looked out at the mountains.

"Just thinking about the crew."

"Is that all?"

"Well, that and my position in it." I said, "I'm… first mate. I'm not exactly sure what I'm doing half the time. I still don't know a whole lot about all of this, let alone about the galaxy as a whole." I turned my head to him. “What would you do in my position?” His brow raised and his head tilted to the side.

“Hmm. I do not know what I would do. I am but a simple Actillion doctor. I am not one to lead crews into battle, but to repair those who return.” He said. I nodded, putting my chin in my hand.

“You know… I realize I don’t know much *about* Actillions. They always taught us that they were violent and warlike, but…” I stopped, turning back to him, “having met you, that doesn’t seem true.” Rex sighed.

“The stigma holds its roots in our history.” He said, “We were once drawn to war as it held itself as a plague to my kind.” His brow cast a shadow over his eyes as his head tilted down. “Our homeworld was ruined by nuclear fire. Clouds of radiation destroyed our soils, the very land we resided on. Y’lsandra is unlivable. The most resilient creature could not find a home in its toxic wastes.” I looked down at the ground with him.

“But… they live in the colonies now, don’t they?” I asked. He nodded again.

“Those that survived moved to the stars. Many of our kind forsook the ideals of war.”

“What about you?”

“I understand that some wars are necessary, and that pacifism can be as deadly as the nuclear winter that overtook our home. When the Soulless took the Universal Republic, it was my people who sat back and refused to act.”

“Didn’t the war start in the colonies, though?” I asked.

“It did. Our very own Natasha Krugoff was part of the crew who uncovered the Soulless rebuilding.” He said. Gods, *that’s* where I’d heard her name.

“She was on the Wayfinder crew?” I asked. He nodded.

"She lost her only friend. I knew her then, if only as acquaintances. She used to be much livelier." He was quiet. We both were. I'd heard the stories. A tale of two bounty hunters who had discovered the Soulless, halting their initial attack at the cost of one of their lives.

"Without them," I began, "we wouldn't have had a chance, would we?"

"I don't believe we would have, no," He said.

"I can see why she's so closed off now."

"I have suggested she talk with Iraka about the ordeals, but she doesn't take me up on it." I hummed back, quiet now. The sounds of the landscape overtook us as the path stretched on endlessly in front of us.

We began to see the oasis dragging itself into view, and we picked up the pace to get there as quickly as possible. The shade of trees grew closer and closer until finally we could drink in the joy of its coolness. I leaned back against the trunk of a tree. Iravek and I watched as the tribe kneeled by the cool water, sipping it through cupped hands. As I watched, I noticed one of the Ikui looking up into the sky. The low grumble and growl of a ship echoed over the empty desert. I looked back, seeing a black shape moving through the sky. I took Iravek's shoulder, dragging us into the brush by the tree. The rest of the tribe scattered under the water and plants, watching the sky.

A set of Soulless ships began to pass overhead. The ground rumbled and shook as they approached. Their largeness cast evil shadows across us all as we watched them eagerly. They didn't stop, but rather continued past us. I peaked up, watching as they made their way toward the mountains. Rex walked to our side as we stood.

"The Hollows. They make way to our destination." Iravek said.

"Reinforcements for the ones already there, more than likely." I said. "If they're calling in more troops, the crew might have trouble." I looked back at Rex.

"You suggest we move more quickly?" He asked. I nodded.

"I would have to agree. If your crew may be in trouble, then my people may also be in need of aid."

"You think the Soulless might do something to the tribe you're meeting?" I asked.

"I would rather we don't wait long enough to find out." He said. I looked at the rest of the tribe.

"Then we pack up, back to our normal pace." The tribe whipped themselves back together, and we pressed on.

The pace almost felt like it had doubled since we'd seen the ships. There was an overwhelming air of dread and tension as we marched onward. The mountains couldn't get here soon enough. Not even the sun's heat was slowing us down now. Looking back at the tribe, I could see the determination in each and every one of them.

By midday, the mountains towered over us, finally. The relief to have completed this journey was evident among everyone. I looked over at Iravek.

"You excited?" I asked.

"Anxious." He said. "I have waited for this time for many weeks now. We have struggled. It will be nice for our troubles to come to an end." I patted his back.

"Just a little longer." I said, looking ahead to the base of the mountain. I squinted, but couldn't see anyone. "How large did you say this tribe was supposed to be?" I asked.

"Very." He said. I pursed my lips.

"Something's wrong. We should be able to see them by now." I said. He grunted.

"So you noticed it too." His voice grew grim. "I had hoped my eyes were playing tricks."

"I hope mine are too, then." I said. We continued further, yet the closer we got, the more our hope seemed to dwindle. It looked as if no tribe were there to greet us. I could see the dismay crossing Iravek's face. I frowned, looking about, squinting as we approached. Then, there, at the base of the mountain, two figures. "There!" I called. Iravek's face brightened as we marched forth with renewed vigor, our journey almost at an end.

But as we pulled up, I realized we looked not at Ikui, but at a Terran and a Kinth. Gatha and Lux stood, waiting at the opening of a tunnel in the mountain's side, hidden within its shadow. My brow furrowed as the caravan stopped. Iravek, Rex and I walked up to the two of them, who watched us with folded arms.

"Lux, Gatha. What's going on? Where is everyone?" I asked. They looked to each other, then to the three of us. Lux spoke up.

"There's been complications…" he said, looking into my eyes. "With everything."

Tanahen:
Avan Triag
Galactic Date 00:08:479 5028

"Taken?!" Iravek's voice rang through the bowels of the tunnel as we all squeezed through. Gatha put up her hands.

"They were already gone by the time we got here!" She said, "Soulless took the lot of them and have them locked up or working their arses off below." I looked down at her.

"What do you mean, below?" I asked. She gestured ahead to the exit of the tunnel. I furrowed my brow, quietly waiting as we approached the end. Light blinded us as we passed through the exit. I squinted, my eyes adjusting, unable to believe what I was seeing.

It looked like the entire center of the mountain had been hollowed out. Trees and plants lined the interior, and at the center of the cavern was a city of golden stone. In the middle of it all was a tower, a small sanctum at its peak. Soulless swarmed the streets far below the path we walked. Thankfully, there was enough seclusion from the trees that we wouldn't be noticeable, but I couldn't shake that feeling of nervousness.

We pressed ourselves against the trees as we heard an all too familiar low rumble above us. Soulless ships passed through breaks in the side of the mountain, holes they probably made themselves. I pulled myself from the wall, watching them pass us by, before turning to the other two.

"Where's the rest of the crew?"

"Just up ahead." Lux said, "They sent us to wait for you while they attempted to formulate a plan." I nodded, looking ahead of us.

"Let's keep moving then. We don't have time to be standing around." The others agreed, and we continued. I could notice Iravek fidgeting nervously, but his face told a different story. One of anger, fury even. I let myself fall back to his side.

"William." He said.

"We'll get them back." I told him.

"I worry for not only them. You have done much for us. This need not be your battle." I looked him dead in his eyes.

"It's as much our battle now as it is yours." I said, "I'm not letting you deal with this alone." He opened his mouth to try and say something, but my stare insisted.

"I see." He said. "Then we are grateful for your help beyond measure." I nodded to him. The two of us pushed forward.

"I owe you for saving my life, after all."

"Hardly. You would have healed over a great amount of time." His face turned grim once more. "Though again, I worry for you. Your wounds are still open." He looked up at me with those shadowed, glowing eyes, "Promise you will not be too rash, William Ortell." I put a hand on his shoulder.

"When have you ever known me to be rash?" I could sense a look from Gatha and Rex, and sighed. "I'll do my best to be careful, but I can't promise anything."

"I suppose that is all I can ask, then." Iravek said. "Just remember the magic I taught you."

"I will." I said. Gatha gestured for me to come over. As I did, she fluttered up by me.

"Hey kiddo, you still in one piece?" She asked. There was an almost motherly concern in her voice. I rolled out one of my shoulders, rubbing at my sore muscles.

"As much in one piece as I can be, given. Ran into the local wildlife on the way here. Gave us a bit of a run for our money." She pursed her lips as she gave me a disappointed look. "Listen, it was Luccia *and* me facing one of those damned things. If I could have gone any easier on myself, I would have!" I winced at the pain in my joints. "Believe me…"

"I believe ya. I just… ah, I dunno." She rubbed the back of her neck, the wrinkles on her face growing more apparent in the light. "Listen, kid, I care about you, ya know? Won't admit it to anyone else, but I worry about you from time to time." I gave her a lighthearted smile, patting her on the back.

"Gatha, listen. I'm not going anywhere." I said, "anyway, you wouldn't let me hear the end of it if I did."

"Damn right I wouldn't!" She looked up. "I suppose Lux here'd make a good replacement engineer, though." He put up his hands.

"Oh gods, me?" He looked between us, as if he'd been barely paying attention. "Listen, I just do the piloting, that's all!"

"You built your ship, didn't you?" I asked.

"Aye, well, *yeah*, but that doesn't qualify me as an engineer!" I looked down at Gatha, both of us sharing a knowing look.

"I mean, I came on with even less experience, Lux. Maybe I should put you down for a couple of engineering watches to see how you fare?" His face went paler, though I'm not entirely sure how. A look of nervousness struck all across him.

"I-now listen we-" I cut him off.

"Don't fret it. I'm joking. You don't have to if you don't want to." He let out a relieved sigh.

"Had me worried there a moment. Captain's been sayin she wants to put me on a few other watches but isn't sure what."

"How about we try your hand at a few things next we take off? Tara can take over on piloting for the time being. We'll see what you're good at." I gave him a warm smile and a pat on his shaking shoulder before jogging ahead. Just over the edge of the ridge, the Sparrow came into sight, hidden by the tall trees around us. A small camp had been created discretely near the treeline, much of the crew looking out over the city below. I could see, from where we were, Tara plotting out movements on a scanned map as Natasha made calls to her while peering through a telescope. Olivia caught our gaze as she stood, looking over the maps with Tara, and beckoned us over.

As we approached, much of the crew gathered around. A few seemed excited to see us, like Arneli and Tara, but the others… I could see the worry on their faces. Iraka seemed especially concerned, glancing back to Iravek beside me. I put a hand up to them as we made our way to circle around the map.

"Good to see you made it back." Olivia said.

"Have some faith." I said with a smirk.

"We did." Jewls said, looking to me. "Good to see you didn't take your time getting here." I nodded, my brow furrowed as I looked down at the map. Many lines were laid out in different colors across the streets.

"Figured there might be some trouble. Didn't want to waste time." I said.

"And it's a good thing you didn't." Iraka said. "I'm not entirely sure we would have remained unseen had we stayed much longer."

"I agree." Gatha said, "The Sparrow's optical cloaking systems got us in undetected, but we're sitting ducks out here till we come up with a plan." I looked between her and the rest of the crew. I could tell tensions were high all around. They were getting impatient. Seeing the state of things below, I could understand why. I leaned forward, looking to Natasha and Tara.

"Alright. Give us the rundown. What's the sitch?" I asked. Tara stood up, placing her hand on the map as she did so. As she lifted it, a projection of the city rose from the flat hologram below. She pointed to the tower at its center.

"This looks like it's our target. Koratha was seen multiple times entering and exiting here. We think it's where we'll find our information." Tara said.

"Problem is," Natasha began, "getting in there." She looked back through the telescope. "You have Soulless everywhere. Soldiers and the creatures too."

"A powerful strike team could blast their way through to that tower," Jewls said. I shook my head.

"We don't have that kind of firepower at the moment. Even if we did, we'd both burn out long before we made it to the central chamber." I said, looking at her. Her cold eyes pierced my vision, but eventually, she relented, seeing the futility in it.

"You're right. Forgive me." She said. I was taken aback for a moment, but nodded.

"No need. I welcome the idea." I said. Arneli looked over the map with us.

"The Ikui tribe is being kept prisoner. We could always release them and fight along with them. It'd create enough of a reaction that people could get in." She said.

"No." Iraka stepped in. "I do not wish for anyone speaking on my people's behalf."

"Besides," Rex began, "they would see heavy casualties. Using them as a distraction would draw the strongest forces there. It would be a massacre." Olivia had been silent the entire time. I almost hadn't noticed it until I looked at her. I could see the cogs turning in her head. She snapped her fingers, eyes still focused on the map as she stepped forward.

"We'll have two teams." She said. "I'll lead one. William will lead the other." She drew the map to the ground, looking over the streets and layouts of patrols. "William, your team will be on drawing the attention of the soldiers. You don't want to make too much noise, you'd risk pulling too much." I nodded, and she returned the gesture, tracing a second line around the back of the city. "I'll take a group of scouts along the back edge of the city. We can release the Ikui. Those who wish may stay and fight, the rest will be brought to safety." She looked up at Iravek. "Does that work with you?" He thought it over and then bowed in acknowledgement.

"This arrangement works for me." He looked to me. "Respectfully, I would like to join William on this mission." Olivia looked at him, then at me. I nodded, and she turned back to Iravek.

"Granted." She stood up. "Any objections?"

"Just one." Natasha said, "How do you plan on reaching the tower?"

"One team will have to push to the tower, be it William or me." There was an uncertain quiet among the crew. Olivia sighed. "It's… a long shot, I admit. We're outnumbered by hundreds, but we *knew* what we were signing up for. The odds are, and will always be stacked against us." She looked at me, then to everyone else. "We *are* Celestials. We've taken the risks that the rest of the galaxy can't. Right now, the burden of a quintillion lives rests on our shoulders. No one else is coming to help us right now, and we know we are *out* of time." Her eyes scanned the crew with a seriousness and intensity I'd never seen. Behind it all, there was fear; fear that we wouldn't come back. I stepped forward, turning to the crew as I stood beside her.

"The Captain is correct." I said, "It's now or never. We make this run now, or we die trying. The fate of the galaxy is on us. The fate of people we care about is *on us*." I drew Isngr, thrusting its blade into the ground. "I may have come to you as someone without a clue about how the galaxy works, but I stand in front of you *now* as your First Mate to say that we *will* succeed. We *have* to… if we falter, we *all* fall, but that's why we have each other. When one of us falls, we *will* pick each other up. It doesn't matter if we've known each other for what feels like forever," I looked to Tara, then to Jewls, "or if we're bitter rivals." She gave me a nod, her arms folded over her chest. "We *will* do this together, or we won't do it at all." I drew Isngr from the ground, thrusting it skyward. "Now, are you with me?" I spoke those words in a hushed tone, letting the quiet set in. One by one, the crew silently agreed. Olivia nodded, stepping ahead of me as I let Isngr droop, sinking into the dirt once more.

"Then we move. Jewls, Tara, you're with William. Arneli, Natasha, you'll be helping me free the captives." She said. Lux chimed in.

"Er, Captain? What about the rest of us?"

"Stay with the ship." She said. "If things get too dicey, which they are liable to, we will need a quick exit. So you, Gatha, Iraka and Rex will all stay behind. Keep her warmed up and keep that med bay open. I'm sure we'll be needing it." Rex bowed, leading them up onto the ship. Olivia looked at all of us. "Now, let's get moving."

We broke up into our separate teams, beginning to walk out toward the forest. Tara began packing up ammunition and supplies as Jewls approached.

"You sure you're ready for this, Ortell?" She asked.

"Of course." I said, "Why do you ask?"

"I've seen you fight." She said. I stood with a sigh from where I was kneeling, meeting her gaze.

"If you have an issue, please make it known." I said.

"I think you do not understand." She said, "I do not doubt you, or dislike you. You annoy me, and get on my nerves, but I trust in your abilities now more than I ever have." She looked me up and down. "However, I can see the damage to your body. Your magic does not flow properly." She stepped closer, her arms tucked behind her back. "You're pushing yourself far beyond where you should. This is dangerous."

"I know." I said, "I am painfully aware of my state of being, but I'm not going to let it hamper the mission." She sighed.

"As long as you are aware." She nodded, looking out to the skies beyond the cavern, then to the supplies. "I need to prepare, and I suggest you do the same." I nodded, the two of us making our way to the piles by Tara. She looked at me as she slid a clip into a sidearm, placing it at her hip, tucking a few more along her belt.

"Been a while." She said.

"Been busy." I responded, rummaging through the crates.

"Feels a little more… dire this time, doesn't it?" She said, her gaze moving to the city. "I mean, compared to Furelle." I nodded.

"You could say that." I reached down inside, pulling out a small circular object, tossing one to each of them. We clipped them to our belts, shields whirring to life over us. A thin blue bubble meshed to our skins before fading into transparency. Olivia had shown them to us on the way here. Great against bullets and firearms, but it wouldn't protect from anything close quarters, or magic. Still, some protection was better than no protection. "I guess, this time, it just feels like there's a lot more at stake."

"Agreed." She said, fiddling with a shotgun, sliding a canister into it, clicking it in place. "To think we'd make it this far, though, from our little shack on Draenica."

"You miss it?" I asked. She gave me a toothy grin.

"Not one bit." She said. "Anyway, I think I'm getting used to life on the Sparrow. It feels like I'm finally *doing* something with my life besides running." She looked back at me, sliding the shotgun onto her back. "I can't exactly compare to you with your magic, but I've been learning a lot, too." She stood up. "Arneli and Nat have been teaching me a thing here and there along the way." She slipped something on her arm, flipping a few buttons on it. A small projection of the map she'd been working on appeared. "Here, everyone on the crew has their position synced up, with the exception of you." She tapped the side of the gauntlet to my shoulder. I felt a sharp sting stab into me as she pulled it away.

"Fuck!" I said, rubbing the sore part of my arm. "The hell was that?"

"Tracker." She said, pointing to a dot on the map. "There you are! It's short range, but it'll allow us to see where you are in a few kilometer radius." I squished my shoulder, seeing a slight bump under my skin.

"Alright, useful, I guess."

"It will be! We can all keep tabs on each other on the ground, and if one of us is separated, then we'll know where they are!" She said excitedly. I looked down at the map projected from her arm.

"Fair enough… So we're up here," I said, pointing to a section off the map, "and we're planning on hitting them over… here" I pointed to another section. It looked to be a central strip that ran its way down the center of the city. Jewls approached, looking down at the map with me.

"That would be correct, yes," Tara said. Jewls looked between her and me, and then spoke.

"We can set off a chain of explosives as we enter. It'll start by drawing the forces towards decoys, buying us more time." She said. I nodded.

"Smart, that should work."

"I can swipe a few charges from Arneli's arsenal." Tara responded.

"Good. Get those ready, and then we move." I said, looking out toward the city. Gods, I hoped we were ready.

Jewls and Tara flanked me as we made our way through the trees down the side of the mountain. Iravek stayed close behind. Over boulders and down cliffs, we slowly descended toward the base of the cavern. We made as little noise as possible, only the thin crinkle of leaves and snap of twigs underfoot. Light began to break through the cracks between the trees. Tara put a hand on my shoulder, stopping me. I paused, holding my breath. Through the line of trees, a set of Soulless guards made their rounds. Our eyes trailed them as they silently moved past us. Tara brought up her map, checking the layout of guards she'd observed, and nodded to us to move forward.

We ducked out from the treeline into the open stone of the city. We kept ourselves low to the ground as we snuck into a nearby alleyway. Tara kneeled down, pressing something into the groove of a wall. She pulled up a timer on her gauntlet.

"I did not think we would be destroying priceless ruins when I offered to join you." Iravek said.

"Don't worry. They're just sonic charges. They make a loud bang and send up a lot of smoke, but the buildings *should* stay intact. Got one charge that should deal some damage, but that's a last resort." Tara said. Iravek nodded, satisfied. Tara flipped down the timer, the charge beeping and flashing green. "Alright, good, let's keep moving." She looked to me, as if to take the lead, but I gently pushed her ahead.

"You know the deal here better than either of us. It's best if you take point. We'll follow." I saw a brief look of nerves in her eyes. She gulped and took a breath, pulling up her map.

"Right. Follow me then." She said, beginning to guide us through the maze-like roads of the city. Iravek was remarkably quiet for his size, more silent than any of us were. When I looked back at him, his eyes were ferocious and focused.

We pushed deeper and deeper into the labyrinth, setting up charges as we went. Behind us, as we walked, we heard a loud crack and boom as the first one went off. As soon as the smoke was rising, we heard guards moving quickly about the city. People were beginning to mobilize. In the shadows of the alleys, we could start to see soldiers moving past on the main roads. Tara checked her map again.

"The Captain's team is at the captives." She said. I could hear a sigh of relief from Iravek. "We just need to keep them off her long enough to get them out of there." I nodded.

"How many charges do we have left?" I asked. She checked her belt.

"One more. The dangerous one. We'll have to make it count." Jewls leaned forward.

"We'll use it to draw them into the central road, to us. It should give Sterling the time she needs to get to the chamber while we hold off the Soulless."

"Good plan." I said, "Tara, hold on to that charge. Once all the others go off, we'll pull them into the center. Hopefully, they'll be spread out enough by then that it shouldn't be an issue for us to hold them back." She gave me a thumbs up, patting the charge as we moved on.

Another charge went off as we pushed deeper in, then another. Four explosions would ring across the walls of the cavern as we made our way to the center. Tara's guidance kept us out of the eyes of the Soulless as we moved. So far, things seemed to be going according to plan. Soon, we found ourselves at the edge of the main strip. Trees lined the center of the brick-paved street. Iravek looked over my shoulder as we watched the Soulless. A number of the beasts patrolled the area, but not many of the soldiers themselves. I turned to the others.

"Alright, this is it. Is everyone ready?" I asked, pulling Isngr from my back. Jewls summoned her staff while the other two drew their arms, watching me expectantly. "Let's do this, then." I said, holding a hand out for the charge. Tara pulled it from her belt, placing it in the palm of my hand. I stood up, priming it as I walked out into the open air of the of the strip. The Soulless' heads snapped to me as Luccia formed beside me, the blue ribbon around her neck swirling in the wind that spun through the caverns. She turned her gaze to me, following my gate like a mirror.

“Lovely of you to join us.” I said, teasing her. She twirled her sword, the two of us watching the Soulless slowly encroaching upon us.

“What can I say?” She said, “You were looking a little tired, there, Hero. Thought you could use the backup.” I smiled as I reeled back, throwing the charge into the crowd. The Soulless began to zig and zag across the ground as the charge detonated. There was a bang, and then smoke obscuring the battlefield. The ones who’d moved first were momentarily thrown off-kilter, the zig in their dashes falling off balance. Jewls stepped from the shadows first, finding a perfect opening.

She dragged her staff across the tiles, a line of magic arching up from the ground, striking a hole into the crowd. Their bodies burst into ash as I stepped forward with Luccia. We brought our blades together, cutting swaths through the creatures. I had to keep my magic to a minimum. Martial work would have to suffice when possible.

I felt the wind shift by me and turned, bringing Isngr up. The blade of my sword collided with that of a Soulless. A series of bullets ripped through it as Tara and Iravek emerged to join us. Iravek cocked the bolt on his rifle back, firing shot after shot through the creatures, sending more flakes of ash into the air. I spun as Luccia took up my rear, bringing my sword across the chest of another Soulless. Jewls reached out as two ganglier ones lept at me. A barrier formed around me, the two crashing into it. Luccia twisted back, firing a barrage of bolts through it, obliterating them. I swapped with Luccia again as the Soulless surrounded us more and more.

I launched myself forward into the fray, slicing from side to side as I sidestepped one attack, blocked another, and returned the strikes. Sweat dripped down my brow as I jumped back from a set of claws, only to see them flash into ash. Tara stepped in beside me, raising the shotgun. She fired it once, then again, two more dropping. She looked up at me.

"Come a long way since Draenica!" She shouted, swiping her claws through one of the Soulless, knocking it off balance. She raised the shotgun, firing it through the Soulless and the one behind it.

"Tell me about it!" I said. I put a hand over her shoulder, blocking a slash with a barrier as I fended off another strike with Isngr. She ducked, blasting a hole through one, then the other. We flipped places. I shoved a hand forward, thrusting a set of darts through the Soulless ahead of me. My muscles were already straining, fighting back against me. I had to just push through it.

"To think-" she said, pulling her pistol, firing it into the crowd, "we'd make it this far!" I grinned for a moment, only barely catching the glimmer of scopes pointed in our direction from the alleyways and rooftops. She saw it too.

"Think we're running out of time here!" I said. I felt the first shots hit me immediately after. My shields flickered as the beams were absorbed. Iravek slid in, swinging at a Soulless with the back end of his rifle. He turned and snapped. A second thin barrier formed around each of us.

"I will assist as best I can," He said. "Continue fighting." Jewls swung her staff, a blade of magic cutting through the Soulless in front of her.

"Don't think we have much of a choice!" She said, shoving her staff into the ground. She pulled a hand back, throwing a set of orbs into the sky. They swirled through the air before zipping down, slamming into some of the soldiers. We had to hold on for just a little while longer so that Olivia and her team could get to the temple. I felt the blade of one of the Soulless strike my shoulder. I skidded back, seeing the barrier Iravek had formed crack under the power of it. He grunted as he clenched his fists. The cracks sealed again, but I could see he was tired already. He wasn't used to this type of combat. I kicked the Soulless back, thrusting my hands forward, sending wisps of the World Spirit careening into a group of them. They twisted and cracked, then burst.

"They have to be close-" I began, but another explosion cut me off. I thought it had to be one of Tara's charges that hadn't gone off, but then I was hit with the shockwaves. The sound of crumbling rocks echoed across the cavern walls now. I looked up, my heart dropping. The peak of the tower, our goal, crumbled, destroyed. I had to catch my breath, my mind racing.

"Fuck!" Jewls shouted, "What now?!" She turned, thrusting her staff into the Soulless across from me. "Without that information, we're screwed!" I looked back over again, seeing Koratha's ship beginning to rise from behind the tower, more and more dropships heading in toward our direction. Looking at everyone there, I could see the exhaustion setting in. Iravek could barely hold the barriers, Tara struggled to continue to fight, and even Jewls, I could see she was struggling to maintain her magic. It faltered as she cast, not at its full strength. They wouldn't survive if they stayed. I gritted my teeth, pushing Isngr into the ground. I drew the magic from the world in, pushing the tendrils into the ground. They snaked across the ground, clearing out a massive circle around us. I stood, feeling pain coursing through my body. There was a moment of quiet as I stepped forward, Luccia at my side.

"William..." Tara said, "What are you doing?"

"Get out of here." I said, pulling Isngr up. "I'll hold them off, make sure that you and the Ikui get to safety."

"William, don't be stupid." Jewls said. When she moved to grab my shoulder, she was met with a barrier blocking her path.

"I said to *get out*. That's an order." Tara's eyes were filled with concern and worry. She put a hand against the barrier.

"You made a promise..." she said.

"I'll keep it." I said, "I'll figure a way out." I looked back at them. "Now go. Please." Jewls lips pursed as she let go of the staff.

"Keep yourself safe." She said, tapping at the barrier. "We'll come for you." I nodded.

"I'll hold you to it." I said. Iravek stood, snapping a new barrier over me.

"I will join them in the search." He said. "Know that my people owe you their lives." He bowed to me. With a moment of hesitation, the three ran off, disappearing into the alleys of the city. I dropped the barrier, turning back to the army in front of me. Luccia looked to me with a worry strewn about her face.

"Is this it?" She asked. I cracked my neck, taking steps forward.

"Maybe," I said, "but we fight as hard as we can, got it?" She nodded, drawing her sword back. I formed an orb of magic into my hand, throwing it into the crowd. It erupted into a burst of energy, wiping out a patch of Soulless as more sped toward me. Luccia and I blocked and slashed, whipping magic through the crowds.

The Command Ship drew closer, beginning to cast a shadow over us as the darkness was lit up by flashes of blue and purple. Sparks flew as I blocked attacks from the bladed arms, as my shields and barriers deflected the shots fired from the soldiers. I ducked back, bringing up a wall to protect myself from the onslaught of claws heading my way. I pushed myself up, shoving the Soulless away.

Luccia stepped in front of me, fending off wave after wave of the creatures, blocking blaster bolts with barriers. I stepped up, only to see a blade pass through her form. She recoiled and stepped back, looking back at me. In pain, she coughed, her form starting to face.

"Sorry, Hero. Gotta step out of this one..." she said, dissipating. Her ribbon swirled back onto the end of the sword. I felt my heart sink, looking first from her now ripped ribbon, to the swarm in front of me. My grip on Isngr tightened. No. I had to hold the line.

I dug deep into that well of power within Isngr. I threw out bolt and beam, whipping the magic of the world around me through the Soulless. The strain of the magic tore my muscles apart as I held them back. I could feel it destroying me, but I *wouldn't* let them pass. They came at me from every angle. Through the pain, I swung Isngr, a wave of energy cutting out from me in all directions. I stood there, shaking. Blood, sweat and tears mixed together across my face as I stood back up. I felt a sudden pain in my leg as a bolt finally ripped through my shield. I cried out as I fell to my knees, holding my blade up to block another attack, thrusting my hands forward to send wisps through the dozens of Soulless in front of me. In the distance, I saw a faint glimmer of blue as the Sparrow took off, blasting away through one of the openings in the cavern. I laughed as my vision blurred.

A beam of purple and black shot down from the Command Ship. Through the mix of dirt and blood, I could barely make out the figure of Koratha approaching me. I couldn't move anymore. I was almost sure I'd shredded every muscle in my body. There was a coldness of the air as her boots clicked toward me. I could barely react, feeling a frigid steel rapier under my chin. I prepared for her to keep true to her threat, to feel my life leave me. Instead, I felt her lean forward and grab my jaw, dragging me to my knees, forcing me to look at her. There was something in her eyes. It looked like pity. She pursed her lips as I dropped Isngr, letting it clatter to the ground.

"We meet again, William." She said, "Feels like fate, doesn't it?" I could barely speak through the pain and exhaustion I felt.

"So… it would… seem." I said, blood dripping from my lips. She sighed, taking the cuff of her jacket, wiping my chin clean.

"Such a misguided virtuosity." She responded. "I will not kill you, William. Perhaps you were correct the last time we met. I believe you are far more valuable to us alive than you are dead." She looked at Isngr, gesturing to a soldier to retrieve it. They did, then looked behind me, seeing the dagger strapped to my belt.

"Ma'am, would you like us to take the knife as well?" She rose an eyebrow, looking behind me. When she saw it, a sickening grin crossed her face.

"No. Let him keep it." She said, returning her gaze to my eyes. "It will give him a… way out if he can't handle it." I glared at her as I felt my arms bound behind my back. She reached up, patting my cheek. "Now, now, William, don't be so glum. I do look forward to our time together." She stood up, turning. I prepared to be lifted, only to see her spin. In the blink of an eye, her boot cracked across my face, knocking me out cold.

Celestial Plains: The Dreamscape

Galactic Date 00:08:481 5028

There was an almost welcome cold when I found myself waking up. I had been slumped forward on a stone table, and wondered how long it had been, exactly, that I was in the Dreamscape. I groaned as I pushed myself into a sitting position. Across from me, as per usual, were Cleva and Luccia. All three of us were silent, and I could see in both of them the acknowledgement of the situation I'd found myself in. I noticed Luccia seemed more translucent than normal. I sighed, leaning forward on the table.

"I… fucked up, didn't I?" I asked. Cleva took in a deep breath, sliding me a glass of what I assumed was whisky. I looked to her first, and then grabbed it, swallowing it down, gasping and grimacing at the taste. I set the glass back down, sliding it back to her. She set it aside, shaking her head.

"You are… in a tight spot, I will admit." She said, "However, it is not an unexpected outcome." I watched them through tired eyes, waiting for her to continue. When it was clear she was waiting on me, I decided to ask.

"What exactly do you mean?" She and Luccia were quiet a moment longer until Cleva gestured for Luccia to explain.

"I've mentioned how much you reminded me… us, of Vale. Your sword's previous owner." She said, "There is… much we have neglected to tell you of your predecessor." I leaned on my forearm.

"What exactly is this all about?"

"It is about the path that he took, and the same path that you find yourself taking now." Cleva said, "Be it of your own volition and choices, or if it is bits and pieces of Vale shining through you." I nodded, allowing them to continue.

"Vale was…" Luccia paused to find the words, "he was… reckless, but kind and firm. He was often stubborn, took everything onto himself. Once he had an idea in his head, you could hardly sway him away from it."

"Sound familiar?" Cleva asked. I sighed. Unfortunately, it did. Luccia continued.

"Vale knew, as you do, that if this war was allowed to continue, all life in our galaxy could very well end with it. Complete and utter destruction is the only outcome that we find at the end of this tunnel. He wanted to change that, give us a fighting chance."

"Against my orders," Cleva began, "he and Luccia entered the Celestial Plains to put an end to Hilos and his war."

"I… did not survive." Luccia said. "I made a promise to him that I would be at his side, and that if I passed on, I would help who came next." She took in a deep breath, recalling the memories. "Vale knew he wouldn't be making it out alive, either. He was powerful, but the spell he had prepared would annihilate him." She turned, looking into my eyes, making sure I was watching her. "He knew, however, that it would buy you all time."

"The end of the First Soulless-Celestial War… that was…" She nodded.

"He fought Hilos and sealed him away for a time. In the process, though, it also would turn around on him. His body could not handle that much magic at once. As one last ditch effort, he bound his magic to Isngr, his sword. My spirit, with a promise unfulfilled, was also bound to the sword. As well, the shockwave of his spell found its way across the galaxy. As a side effect, many Celestials of the first war found their aging slowed. You may have noticed many in your journeys with memories of the first war." She said. I nodded, thinking back to Olivia's stories. She and others, such as the old Furin from Furelle, had mentioned it. I hadn't put much thought into it, but she was right. For that to be true, they would have needed to be over five hundred years old at least. Cleva cleared her throat.

"I… found the sword in the aftermath, and Luccia with it. For centuries, different carriers traveled the galaxy in search of Isngr's successor. I had not realized one had been found until you showed up at our doorstep." She said, "At the time, I figured there had to have been some mistake, that perhaps the wrong person had been chosen, or that you weren't truly its wielder and his successor." She looked down at a cold drink in her hands. "I only questioned my motives the second time I spoke to you." She laughed, tilting her head back. "Only *his* successor would be foolhardy enough to *steal* my best ship and challenge me." I could sense the sadness in her voice. There was so much nostalgia in it, memories that she'd held back for years. She tilted her head forward again. "You… are not him. There are times I see parts of him peek through, but I remind myself again and again that you are a different person, and one who makes his own choices." She smiled. "For one, he would *never* have found a crew to call his own."

"I was the closest anyone ever really got to him." Luccia explained, "He reminded me a lot of Jewls, actually… perhaps that was why he didn't pick her."

"Was she ever around the sword… before meeting me, I mean?"

"Of course. Many times, yet it never called out to her." Cleva responded. "I cannot begin to explain Vale's reasoning, or if he even exists within the sword, but I can say that you…" she stopped, trying to bring herself to speak. She cleared her throat again. "You, with how far you have come in so short a time, are beyond worthy of wielding that blade." I nodded as she stood up. "Forgive me. He was a dear friend to me, even if infuriating at times. While he was not one to reach out, he was protective of those he did care about." I nodded, silent. Hearing about him from these two, I wish I could just… meet him. The way they talked about him, he really did sound like me.

"So, what does this all mean for me?" I asked. Luccia cupped her hands together, leaning forward.

"The situation right now is that you stayed behind to protect your crew. Like we said, knowing you and Vale, it wasn't unexpected." I nodded again, quietly listening. "The facts are, Koratha took Isngr from you. You're in a holding cell on her ship, the Wingless Angel. You're… still within close enough proximity that you're still drawing on Isngr's magic and healing," her face lowered, "this is both a blessing and a curse."

"How so?" I asked.

"On the one hand," Cleva began, "it is a blessing to us, as you will still be able to tap into Isngr's strength in here. Not only that, but we will have an excess of time to train you. It will be intense, but in your current situation, it is beyond necessary."

"Alright. That all sounds good. How about the bad news?"

"The *bad* news is that you will likely not see Isngr for some time. You *may* be forced to leave it when you escape." She said, "We will address this issue at a later time. We do have a plan, but you must first train." I was quiet for a little, thinking it over. Without Isngr, I was without my major reservoir of magic, and without Luccia, as well. Looking between her and Cleva, I knew I had to trust them, that they *did* have a plan. I sighed.

"Okay." I said. "So what now?" Cleva ushered me to my feet. I stood by the table, tucking my hands behind my back.

"William Ortell," she began, "it has come to my attention that you have yet to formally be inducted as a Celestial." I cocked my head. She looked at me warmly. "It is tradition that every Celestial is taken under wing by either my or Solvemos, and made our disciples. Many who study under Solvemos learn the arts of war and martial prowess. I teach the other side. Under me, you would learn to *control* your magic." She looked off to the beacon in the distance. "Many of our troops now are simply gifted their magic and knowledge. Look at Jewls, for example. We simply do not have the time or numbers to train everyone individually. However, with you, I feel an exception need be made." She turned once more to look at me. "William," she put an upturned hand out to me, keeping her other hand behind her back, "would you do me the great honor of being my disciple and becoming, truly, a Celestial?"

I looked at her hand. I had already come so far. Already, there was no turning back. There was no hesitation as I reached forward, placing my hand on hers.

"Cleva, I would be *honored* to be your disciple. I will train under you to be the best caster I can." She let her head hang lower, dropping her hand.

"Then we shall begin immediately." She said, "You have much to learn. Hold your head high, William. The coming days will be the hardest of your life."

The Wingless Angel: Tanahen Orbit

Galactic Date 00:08:482 5028

A sharp intake of breath as a whip cracked against my bare back. I could barely feel it anymore it was so raw. It was just added heat to a fire that burned across my body. I gritted my teeth through the pain, letting my head hang down as I sat on my knees. I could feel the wetness of blood swelling down my back. My breaths shook as I sat there with bound hands. A masked man kneeled down in front of me, lifting my head up. The purple lights cast monstrous shadows across his hidden face as he looked into my eyes.

"We ask again, Celestial. What do you know of your base?" His voice was deep, like gravel against your ears. When I didn't respond, he brought a hand back, slapping me to my side. I grunted as I hit the steel of the floor, coughing. "Answer me!"

"I've told you, I don't know anything..." I groaned.

"You lie." He said. I *was* lying, not that I intended to tell him that. I felt the whip crack against me once again, screaming out in pain. "You will tell us the truth." My body shook, cold and hot all at the same time. I could only stare blankly at the wall. I wanted it to stop more than anything. We'd been in here for hours. My wounds from the battle had been slowly healing, but they opened fresh ones with every strike. I felt the man's hand around my throat, dragging me back up, setting me in place.

"Even if I did know, I wouldn't tell you shit." I spat blood at him. The red streaked the mask. He simply reached up, wiping it clean.

"A strong mouth on you." He said, placing a knife under my chin, drawing the tip to my throat. "I have been forbidden to kill you, but..." He traced the flat of the blade across my skin before swiftly slicing the side of my cheek. I winced. "I'm allowed to get you as close as I want." I glared up at him.

"Why does she want me alive so badly?" I asked between breaths. I felt the whip crack again.

"No questions." Another voice behind me said. The man grabbed my jaw. It was hard enough that I was afraid he'd break it as he pulled me in closer.

"You will answer our questions, not the other way around." He let me go. The whipping seemed to go on for hours upon hours. I prayed endlessly that they would finish, but there was no respite every time. Every time I refused to answer something, that whip came down, cutting a new line into my skin. I remember passing out a few times from the pain, only to be slapped awake by that man.

It felt like an eternity before the man finally put up a hand. He looked to the person behind me. I could hear the coiling of the whip and the click as it was clipped away.

"Bring him to his cell. We will continue this later." He said. They dragged me to my feet. I could barely feel my legs as they pulled me along. The hallways felt grim, black with the shadows of darkened steel, only single strips of light guiding our path. The person had their hands on my restraints, guiding me along down the narrow paths. Deeper and deeper we went, the bowels of the Wingless Angel confusing to my tired eyes.

We turned a corner, a number of empty cells waiting for me. The person turned me to one. They undid my restraints and shoved me inside. I fell to my side on the harsh steel floor. They looked down at me with disgust hidden under their helmet.

"So, this is the great 'Wielder of Isngr?' Hmm." They flipped on a purple force field between me and them. "Not so great after all, I suppose." I grimaced as I watched them leave. My eyes followed them as they stood outside the door to the holding cells. I was tired. The pain in my back was burning all over me as I sat cross-legged by my bed. I leaned forward, feeling my hair, the tips coated with sweat, blood and grime, hang down like a mess. I reached behind me to my belt, pulling the single knife I had been granted, looking at its gleam. As I examined its edges, I contemplated its use, but I stopped myself, and tucked it back in behind me, refusing to let myself give into darker thoughts. I took some deep breaths, placing my hands palm up on my knees, sitting up straight. I closed my eyes, breathing in slowly, holding, breathing out. Cleva had taught me that if I were to survive, I needed to keep myself calm.

I had another motive, though. In the short time I'd been here, I had noticed one peculiar detail. As I breathed, I listened, and through the cell, I could hear them. Guards passing by, talking. While they wouldn't get anything from me, I could still get something from them.

"We're leaving the system, did you hear?" One of them said to the other.

"Has the Commander said why?" the other asked.

"Not yet. We aren't returning to the Celestial Plains."

"What did she find in the temple?"

"She hasn't told anyone yet. I assume they're still analyzing things." They said. "I'm eager." So, no news yet. Figures as much. I'd just have to keep my ears open, hope that I could get some useful information before I made my escape. I had to know what they'd found on Tanahen. First, though, I let myself drift to sleep.

My eyes opened once more on the Celestial Plains. Cleva and Luccia stood there, waiting. Their eyes were serious, intense. I stood up from my cross-legged position, feeling at my back. No cuts, at least not here. Cleva looked at me with a sense of concern.

"Are you well, William?" She asked. I took in a deep breath of air, stretching my body. I was happy my injuries in my real body didn't also appear here.

"I will be." I said, "My body isn't in the best of condition, but I'll make the best of what I have." She nodded.

"You'll be out of there soon." She said. "Are you ready for your training?" I nodded, bending my knees, lowering myself. Luccia approached, nodding at my form.

"Let's get started." I said. Luccia moved across from me.

"Good. We'll be going in rapid succession over the next few days." I nodded as she stepped forward. I watched as she began to cast, copying her moves beside her. We started as simple as we could. I'd seen her creating pillars before. She pulled her hand to the air. I watched as she gathered her magic into a physical manifestation, dropping it to the ground, and followed suit. I reached up, drawing the magic out from within me. Rather than a pillar, however, it appeared as a ball, falling to the ground in a heap. She nodded, standing by me.

She would correct my form as Cleva watched. She lifted my arms, told me to focus on a shape. When I'd next cast, it was more correct, or at least she deemed it enough to move on.

"Why not have me master it like the other spells I learned?" I asked.

"We do not have the time for you to master every last technique I have." She said. "You need to have the tools first. Once you do, we will work on refinement." She turned back to me. "Now, prepare. We have a long way to go, and a lot to learn."

Over the next hours, she would work me to the bone. It seemed to come to me with a relative ease that I hadn't had at the start of it all. By the end of the first day, Luccia had me running through drills. I could feel my energy, even in here, waning, but I pushed myself on. Sweat dripped down my brow, and hers as well. Spells swirled around us in tight circles as Cleva finally approached me.

"Your control is getting better." She said. I almost forgot to respond as I focused all my attention on keeping a small glowing orb moving about me in intricate patterns.

"You really think so?" I asked. She nodded.

"I would say so. You have more, yet, to learn, but in one day already, you've grasped quite a number of techniques." Luccia looked up at Cleva.

"It's not unheard of." She said, "Once you know the fundamentals, the more advanced techniques are only a matter of practice and knowledge." Cleva nodded.

"I quite missed instructing students on the arts of magic." She swept her hand across, smoothly taking the orb I had been shifting about, cradling it gently in her own form. I took the moment to breathe and relax, only to have a moment of panic as Luccia passed me her orb. I clumsily integrated it into the same patterns I had been doing before as Cleva watched her orb with a calm tenderness.

"You used to personally teach your disciples?" I asked. She nodded.

"I did." She said, "The magic that flows through this galaxy is part of what allowed us to give it form. Hilos and I were the masters of its studies when we created what you call the Milky Way."

"Why does Hilos want to kill us all so badly?" I asked.

"It is… not entirely of his own volition." She said, holding out the orb. Its contents dispersed among the World Spirit, "We are commanded by a being even greater than ourselves. Told to make a perfect creation. Our galaxy was almost perfect."

"Almost?" I asked. She nodded.

"Life as you know it, sentient and flourishing, was never intended to exist. While my brother and I argued for us to keep it, my other brother, Hilos, had his reservations." She nodded to the orb I had been juggling, causing it to disperse as well. I took deep breaths as I leaned on my knees.

"Alright, but that doesn't sound like jumping to ending us all." She shook her head.

"No. He gave you a chance to defy his expectations. He let us know that if anything you did were to ruin our creation, he would not hesitate to wipe you out."

"So then, what did we do?" I asked, pushing myself back up.

“It was the creation of warp engines.” She said, tucking her hands behind her back. She stepped to the edge of the tower, looking out into the great beyond. Millions of tiny dots scattered the skies. “As you well know, when a warp core is pushed beyond the limits of space, a tear is opened. Rifts in the fabric of space-time.” I nodded. She looked down to me. “It was your race who discovered this, who pushed it too far. It was then that Hilos had had enough, and attacked.” She turned her gaze outward once more. “And we let him.” I furrowed my brow.

“Wait, but-”

“We had made an agreement. Terrans had shown themselves to be capable of ruining his creation. We agreed… at first.” I pursed my lips, shoving my hands in my pockets.

“So… what happened?”

“Earth was destroyed after a thousand year war. However, the Terrans had been assisted by many outside nations. The Furins most notably lent them their strength.” She looked down. “He turned his attention to them next. We had agreed that the Terrans had been in the wrong, but he had begun taking it too far. It was then that we stood against him.” I nodded.

“And now he continues to try to wipe out everything.” I said.

“That he does.” She responded, “I hoped for peace once, that we might get through to him.” She shook her head. “I have long since let go of that hope.” I reached up and hesitated before sighing, letting my hand fall on her shoulder.

“There’s… always a chance.” I said. Cleva laughed, reaching up, touching a warm gloved hand to mine.

“I am… grateful for your words.” She said, turning her head toward me. “I was always fond of many of you, much to my brothers’ dismay. It hurt me to see Earth destroyed, but I saw it as a necessary evil at the time.” I nodded.

"We all make choices we regret." I said, pulling my hand from her shoulder, sitting at the edge of the tower. Luccia joined me, the two of us looking up at her. "I know I can be… stubborn, and that I've made poor choices, but isn't that what life's all about? We learn and we grow from it. I think…" I looked down, "I think it's honestly our mistakes and how we handle them that make us who we are." Cleva chuckle, allowing herself to sit beside me.

"I have lived for many rotations of this galaxy, and yet-" She turned to the two of us, "mortals always manage to surprise me with their wisdom." Luccia stood up, moving to Cleva's opposite side.

"You were always good to me, to all of us. Even if you made mistakes before we met you." She leaned against Cleva's shoulder. "Just know that we always did appreciate you, every step of the way." I could sense the smile underneath her mask as she looked down at the disk of glowing stones below.

"Thank you. Both of you…"

On the Wingless Angel, I found myself over the next few days in the same habits of waking up from my training and waiting, just listening. Overnight, my wounds would heal, leaving behind deep scars along my skin. I'd spend my morning meditating, listening to the sounds of the guards talking back and forth, to the conversations of people passing about in the halls. Nothing new would come to light.

Yet each day, they took me out for yet another set of questions and pain. I can barely remember half of the days I spent on that ship now. I honestly think I don't want to remember, yet every day I'd come back with new wounds and marks. I remember the feeling of a brand pressed into my back, between my shoulders, leaving a burnt in scar to permanently mark me. I remember the feeling of wanting to give in then, to just shout out everything I knew.

But every time, they would pull the brand away, or for just a moment, the whipping would stop, and my head would fall. My vision would be a blur. Sometimes I couldn't see at all through the pain, but I'd grit my teeth through it all. I'd draw the memories of my crew to mind, of the promise I'd made to Tara, the memories of sitting on the edge of the tower with Cleva. No, I couldn't give in, and I knew it. So I'd keep quiet, and the pain would continue.

And at the end of it all, they'd pull me to my feet. Sometimes it was by the restraints that held me there, and on other days, when they were feeling particularly cruel, by my hair. They'd shove me back into my holding cell where I'd sit there, shaking, and listening. I'd fall asleep, and again, I would train.

The only thing that kept me sane was that training. I don't know how many days it went on, but Luccia and Cleva were what I looked forward to every single time they brought me back into that cell. Even on the toughest days of training, when Luccia would push me to my absolute limits, I found it as a comfort. On the days the torture hurt most were, I think, the days I worked the hardest.

Until one day, I found myself, toward the end of the day, sitting by the edge of my cell. I remember the restraints had been tight. They'd dug into my arm through the day, leaving them rashed and bleeding. I couldn't quite keep my focus on my meditations, but I could still hear the guards outside speaking back and forth.

"Did you hear they finally decrypted what we found on Tanahen?" My ears perked up as I silently listened in.

"It's about time." The other guard said.

"We're heading back to the Plains. The Commander is gathering a fleet to strike the Surillian system."

"You insane?!" the other guard said, smacking them. "He's right there!" I could tell they were gesturing to me. I stayed silent.

"Ah, don't worry about it!" They said. "He's always sitting there sleeping when we aren't laying into him. He's not going anywhere, anyway."

"I hope for your sake that you're right…" they said. I sighed. Good, finally something useful. I wasn't sure how much longer I would have had to wait. I breathed in, letting myself pass out for my training.

As per usual, Cleva and Luccia were waiting for me on the other side. As I stood, I nodded to the two of them, this almost becoming routine.

"Are you ready?" Cleva asked.

"One thing, quickly." I said, "I have information on where the Wingless Angel plans on striking." She gestured for me to continue. "I heard from the crew that the Surillian system is where the temple on Tanahen led." Cleva nodded, thinking.

"I see… We do not have much time." She said, looking to Luccia, "I think it's time we wrap this up." Luccia nodded, turning back to me.

"William." She said, a sharpness in her voice I'd never heard. I turned to look at her. "There is one last technique you have yet to learn. It may just be the most important one you come to know." She held out her hand, her blade appearing in it with a flash of light. "It has to do with what we call our Destiny Weapons." She held her sword out in front of her. "Any spellcasting Celestial is bonded to a weapon. I have Penumbra, you have Isngr. Normally, a Celestial can summon or send their Destiny Weapon off into a particular pocket of space for safekeeping. For some reason, unlike with these other techniques, this one has not come naturally to you."

"Does it normally?" I asked. She nodded.

"I do not know why. Maybe it's just because you have never had reason to send it away or to summon it, but it is necessary for you to learn it." She pursed her lips. "Without this technique, the minute you leave this ship, you will be without my help, or Isngr's, as you well know." I nodded. So this was their plan. I had to learn to summon Isngr. "Hold out your hand." I did so, following her instruction. "Good. Now, focus on the center of your weapon. Focus on the power it grants you, like it is a core of your being."

I took a deep breath in, trying to focus my mind. I remembered how Isngr felt. The weight of it, the strength of its magic flowing through me.

"When you have it, a clear image of it, pull it to you. Urge it to return to you." I nodded, trying to pull it in to me. I stood there, a silence between us all. Yet, try as I might, I couldn't bring it to me. We were quiet for some time, until I sighed, dropping my hand, shaking my head. There was a unanimous sigh of disappointment.

"I was… afraid this might happen." Cleva said. She approached me, placing a hand on your shoulder. "Do not despair. Celestial's Destiny Weapons would typically come to them at a time when they were most needed. The summoning comes naturally, as it has already happened once."

"So, since it never… chose to summon itself to me, I can't summon it?" I asked. Cleva shook her head.

"I… believe so." I looked at the ground. Luccia approached, a concerned look in her eyes.

"I'm sorry, William." She said, "However, even without Isngr, you are not without magic of your own." She had me look up at her. “Do not despair. We will find our way to each other once again.” I nodded.

“Alright… yeah. So I’m guessing it will be some time before I see you again, then?” I asked.

“Maybe. It could be as short as a day for all I know. Until then, though,” she reached forward and pulled me into a hug, “good luck out there, Hero.” She pushed back, clearing her throat, looking up to Cleva. “Alright. I think it’s time.” Cleva nodded.

“You are correct.” Cleva turned to me. “William Ortell. Next time that cell opens, you are to make your escape. You are ready.” I nodded.

“Understood.” I said. She reached a hand up, placing a gentle finger to my forehead, pushing me back to the waking world.

“Good luck.”

Deep Space: The Wingless Angel

Galactic Date 00:09:003 5028

I bided my time in the coming waking hours. If I were to make my escape, I would have to be quick and efficient in making my way through the ship. I pictured the route I'd taken through the many days I'd been here. It was muddled at best, but I knew we were *near* the escape pods. I'm sure that, with a touch of luck, I could get to them and get out. Gods, I was tired.

I rubbed my eyes, leaning my head back against the wall. Any minute now they'd be coming to take me to the interrogation rooms, I was sure of it. These guards ran like clockwork. Every day it was the same thing, same times. I tapped my fingers together, antsy, impatient. I was ready to be anywhere but here. My eyes blankly traced over the featureless walls. I turned my head, looking out the door to the two guards who stood watch over the cells. It felt like it was taking longer than normal.

I sat forward, reaching behind me, feeling the scars that adorned my back. Long strips stretched across it. On the one hand, I was grateful to Isngr for its healing, but at the same time, I wondered if they were only harsher with me for it. The skin on my back now was gnarled. I dropped my hand, closing my eyes. On the one hand, I wanted to just fall back asleep, but I knew it wouldn't help. It felt like I hadn't gotten any rest since I'd arrived. I suppose that, in a sense, that was true. Between the constant torture and the training on the Plains, I hadn't gotten any true respite from the moment I had been on board.

I heard a set of guards move in past the doorway and peeked up to look at them. Behind me, I prepared a spell as they approached. I watched as they typed in a code to the door, the barrier fading between us. One of the two of them looked down at me.

"The Commander wishes to have a word in her quarters." They said. My brow furrowed. The spell faded in my hand.

"No interrogation?" I asked.

"Not today, by her orders, though who *knows* what she has in store for you?" They said, a crooked look on their face. I narrowed my eyes. I knew I *should* make a break for it now, but… some part of me was curious. What in the Gods' names would she want to speak directly to me for? After all, she'd had them wailing at me for the past week. I… I had to know. The guard tossed a fresh shirt to me. "Put it on." I slipped into the shirt, eying the two of them as I rose to my feet.

"Follow us." The other ordered. I stepped out of my cell, for the first time not being led in restraints, as we moved through the ship once more. Rather than deeper down, the two of them loaded me into an elevator. I could feel my weight shift as it began shooting up. The two of them sulked behind me as I stood at the front, waiting. The door slid open to a short hallway. There was a hand on my back, shoving me off the lift. I glared back at them, stumbling forward.

Brushing myself off, I looked ahead at another set of doors, stopping in front of them. I turned back, seeing the guards motionless by the lift. I took a deep breath as I looked back at the doors, pushing them open. Golden light flooded the corridor as a lush set of quarters filled my view. Unlike what I'd seen from the rest of the ship, this room was filled with wooden, hand carved furniture. A red tablecloth sat across a dining table set with two large meals. Candles lit the table, and what appeared to be wine had been poured between two separate glasses. Koratha sat on one end as I stood there.

"Good. You're here. Take a seat, please." I frowned as she asked this of me. What the hell was this? Some kind of trick? I watched her eyes, but they looked back at me with the same intensity they always did.

"This is a… funny idea of a date." I joked, trying to break my own tension. Koratha looked at me with annoyance.

"William, I will not ask again." She said. I suppose I had come up here of my own volition, not that she knew that. Cautiously, I stepped forward, pulling out the chair to sit.

"What's all this about?" I asked.

"I can't ask to share a meal?" She asked, stabbing her fork into a piece of meat, neatly cutting it. She brought it up to her mouth to wait for a response.

"So what? This some kind of trick? The steak's poisoned? Or the wine, perhaps?" I had my arms folded over my chest. She groaned, standing up. She reached across the table, picking out a small cut of the meat, swallowing it, then sipping the wine. She sat down again, gesturing to my plate.

"Happy?" she asked. "If I wanted to kill you, I would not be so backhanded about it." I pursed my lips, but leaned forward, taking a sip of the wine. Despite its bitterness, I enjoyed the coolness of it sliding down my throat. It was the most taste of anything I'd had in the days I'd been here.

"So not poisoned. Why bring me here?" I asked.

"I wanted to speak with you alone. Away from prying ears if you would." She waved a hand aimlessly, leaning in over the table. She reached down, picking away at her food. "How long has it been?" She asked.

"Since what?" I took a bite of the steak. The tenderness of it was sublime. Maybe it was just that I hadn't had anything but tasteless mush, but gods was it good. Koratha sighed.

"Since you had to leave Furelle? Since you were forced into a world of running from a life of servitude?" Her eyes narrowed as she watched me, seeming to gauge my reaction.

"Ten years." I said, flipping the steak, looking over the char on its back. "My colony was attacked when I was fourteen." She nodded.

"I see."

"How did you know I grew up on Furelle?" I asked.

"You mumble in your sleep." She said, taking a sip of wine. "I stopped by your cell on occasion. I want to know what makes you tick, William."

"You keep tabs on your prisoners?" She shook her head.

"Just you." I frowned, sipping at my wine.

"Why such a vested interest in me?" I asked. She set her glass down, staring into the flame on the candles.

"I suppose one could call it… jealousy?"

"Jealousy?" She nodded. A faint smile touched her lips. It wasn't sinister like her others, but rather… melancholic.

"Yes." She turned to me. "I also grew up on Draenica." She said, pulling the collar of her shirt aside. On her shoulder over her breast was a burned in slave mark. "Not under the best conditions, though I guessed you would have pieced that together already." She picked at the food on her plate as she spoke, not looking up at me. "Orphaned as children, left to fend on our own. One of us watching as their loved ones died or were forced into slavery, the other had their wings taken." She turned her gaze upward, looking into my eyes. "Yet… here you are, and here I am." She sighed. "Putting you through all of that, I hoped you'd have broken, that you'd end up just like me, but looking at you now, it feels like I've only helped to strengthen your resolve."

For a moment, as our gazes connected, I felt almost a connection to her. I'd said it to Tara before, how I could have ended up like her. How without the people around me, I could have just as well given into my anger. When I looked into her, I saw past a layer of anger and vengeance and just saw… despair. I set down my utensils.

"I had a lot of friends I lost to slavers in my time on Draenica." I said. "I probably would have followed them too, if not for the people I surrounded myself with. For years, I tried to help whoever I could from that life. People who escaped slavery, people who were being hunted. I remember being so… angry at the world." I shook my head. "Even now…"

"Now?"

"How could I not?" I said, looking down at my palm. "I have every right and reason to be. They thrust me into this with little regard for what *I* wanted. There are days that I just wish this could all end, that things could go back to how they were before." I looked back up at her. "But I also know now that I can't just blame everyone. I know I can't turn that rage toward good people who did nothing to wrong me. Even the Celestials." Koratha sighed.

"I… wish I could distinguish those feelings anymore." She said. "For years, all I've known is hatred, rage. I've wished for nothing but vengeance on the universe that wronged me." She looked up at the lights along the ceiling. I could see a heavy weight over her. "I know there is good out there. You are a…" she groaned, "a shining beacon of it. One that, despite my efforts, never ceases to grow brighter." She stood up, snapping her finger. Out in the back of the room, a set of metal sheets pulled away, revealing the light of warp. She looked back, gesturing with her head for me to join her.

I stood, running my hand along the table as I approached.

"You talk a lot of feelings." I said, "Yet from my knowledge of Soulless, I was led to believe you lost all of them when stripped of your soul." She looked back to me with a smile as I walked beside her, leaning on the edge of the glass.

"Normally true." She said. "However, my situation was different."

"You were never turned, were you?" I asked. She nodded, turning back outside. She placed a relaxed hand on her hip as she watched the lights flicker by.

"An astute hypothesis." She said, "One that's correct." She gave me a smirk, glancing to the side at me. "Nice job, William." She turned to lean on the glass, folding her arms. "No, I did not lose my soul. My own anger drove me here, and I joined of my own volition." She searched my eyes, finding recognition in them.

"We… are a lot alike, aren't we?" I asked.

"More than you ever could realize." She approached me. She reached up, her hand moving to my cheek as she stared into my eyes. From her, now, I felt not that icy coldness from before, but dull heat, as if but barely warm embers of a fire still lingered in her. "About what you said earlier, when you walked in…" She stopped inches from me. "Maybe… in another life things may have been different…" She drew closer, her face almost touching mine. "I almost wish it could be…" I felt her hand draw back, reaching to her side. I regained control of my senses, hearing the thin hiss of metal being drawn from its scabbard.

Instinctually, I pulled an arm back, driving wisps of magic up into her chest. Koratha was launched back across the room. She tumbled and skidded, pulling her rapier out the rest of the way, her glare piercing through to me.

"And here I thought we might have been getting through to each other." I said, pulling my hands back, prepared for anything she could throw at me.

"We were," she began, standing, "which is why I have to kill you *now!*" She threw her hand forward, a series of beams arching toward me. I stepped aside, drawing her spell into the palms of my hands, launching it back in her direction. The spell split, threatening to encapsulate her. She phased out of the way, approaching me at blinding speeds. She brought her rapier forward, and I blocked it, parrying it to the side with a barrier.

"Then *why?!*" I reached around, sending a concussive blast across her back. She took the hit, rolling across the floor as we swapped places.

"You are a danger to *everything* I believe!" she shouted. She brought her hand forward. I did the same. Two beams of matching energy collided between us, igniting the room in brilliant blue and purple lights as we struggled against each other's power. "I am the Aegis of Vengeance! I cannot have you standing in my way any longer!"

"So what?!" I began, "You just kill me and act as if no one else will challenge this illusion you've made of the world?!"

"The only delusional one here is you, William!" She pushed forward, her beam breaking through mine. It sent me flying into the wall. I grunted at the impact before falling to the ground. In moments, she was upon me. I swept my leg to the side, catching hers. She tumbled down as I lifted myself to my feet. She kicked herself up, swinging her rapier at me once more. I ducked, finding my way behind her. She turned, and I grabbed at the rapier, catching her hand mid swing, locking her there.

"We *don't* have to do this."

"You know as well as I do that we damn well do, Ortell." She struggled, kicking me back off her. She drove her sword into the ground as I skidded along the carpet. I could feel the surge of energy under me beginning. I tried to move, but felt magical tendrils at my feet, locking me in place. An eruption of magic burst forth from under me. I could feel its claws digging into my very being. This would kill me if I didn't do something. I thought back to my lessons. Nothing had taught me how to deal with this. My mind raced as I felt my skin being cut and torn. I had an idea, but I didn't know if it would work.

I reached up as I'd seen Iravek do many times before, and let myself draw the magic around me in, then snapped. A thin veil of magic surrounded me as a shield. It took every ounce of my concentration to hold it up as I was battered by the onslaught of dark energy around me. At once, it ceased, and there I was, still standing. I turned my head, glaring at Koratha. She bared her teeth at me, rushing toward me, claws out. I stepped back from her swings as she swiped, cutting through the air like a furious animal.

"Why won't you just *die* already?!" she screamed. I ducked under a swipe and brought the magic in my body to focus in my fist, driving it into her. The single strike resounded around the room as she shot back, slamming into her bedside before falling to the ground. Her head hung loosely as she laid there, unconscious. I approached, pulling my fist back again. I could finish it right here… right now. I pursed my lips but… couldn't bring myself to. I let my arm hang low.

"Maybe… in another life, then." My head turned from her to the elevator. I could feel the latent power in me from Isngr still. I needed to escape while I had time. I pulled myself together and opened the door, seeing the two guards there, weapons drawn on me.

"You *will* cease!" One shouted. I glared at them, waving a hand in front of me as I walked forward. They began firing, the beams bouncing off a barrier into the ground. I reached back with my opposite hand, sending to bolts into them, knocking them into the wall. They groaned where they now sat, their weapons sparking and fizzing as I stepped into the elevator. I punched in the numbers I'd seen put in for the floor I'd started on.

The lift brought me down deeper into the ship, but before I could reach the lowest floors, it stopped. The power shutting off. I'd hoped that, if I were lucky, I'd just be able to walk out. I could already feel the strain on my body, but I wasn't about to let them take me again.

The door slid open to a whole platoon of Soulless soldiers and creatures, weapons pointed at me. I gritted my teeth. This was it. Now or never. I thrust my fist toward the ground. A shockwave of magic erupted out from me, knocking them back. I took the opening, sprinting forward. A few of them stood up, chasing after me. I turned, flinging a small orb at them. It cracked and blew, blasting open the floor and walls in front of them. The Soldiers couldn't follow, but a set of the clawed creatures, Stalkers Cleva had called them, darted along the unharmed ceiling, making chase.

One of them lept, hitting me along the chest. I rolled, flipping it onto its back, firing a blast of energy through its chest, letting it burst into ash as I continued on my way. The halls were labyrinthine at best, but floor by floor I fought my way down, tossing aside anyone and anything that dared get in my way. I zigged and zagged across decks, blasting holes through different sections of the ship.

As I sprinted away through an opening I'd made, I found myself greeted by the roar of the ship's engines and cores. As I dashed out onto the catwalks, I found myself in the rear cavity of the ship. Four massive engines were set in an array above and below me. I looked back, stepping out of the way as a soldier ran past me. They hit the railing of the catwalk, stopping to turn to me. I raised a foot, kicking them back into the wall, knocking them out. I breathed heavily, looking around me, the cogs in my head beginning to turn. If I left now, they'd get to the Plains and back long before we could get help. I had to slow them down. Time to do some damage.

I gripped the rail, vaulting over it, letting myself drop toward the engine below. Wind rushed past me as I fell. I reached out, gripping at the wisps of the World Spirit, slowing my fall to a halt, before landing on the top of the giant metal machine. The soldiers were pouring in from the hole I had just created, their footsteps echoing over the cavernous expanse of the engine room. I snapped a barrier around me, taking a deep breath as I pulled a hand back. Magic burst forth from me as I slammed my hand down. A beam burst through the engine. Its life hummed away as smoke rose, clouding the air. I heard rifles firing toward me as I gripped at more of the magic wisps, sliding down the edge of the engine to the paths below. The exit was just across the room. I wanted to completely immobilize the ship, but seeing the group of soldiers making their way down me, I figured quicker would be better. I took a deep breath as I ran to the center of the grates. Engineers scattered as I brought my hands up, focusing the energy in me.

Light gathered at my chest. I reached to it, drawing out long, snaking trails. They danced through the air around me, and I could feel my body beginning to break, only fueled by the adrenaline in me. I was running out of time, but I wasn't about to let them go without a fight. I brought the trails together in my hands, forming a spinning, tempestuous white-blue orb. I shoved it forward, letting it split into a hundred beams that arched across the cavernous room. I winced in pain as I watched them pulse through the air, connecting and colliding with the machines, tearing holes through their steel walls.

Cracks and booms echoed about as I walked toward the door. Explosions wracked the hull as the soldiers scrambled to get to me. Although I was sure the effort had cracked or broken most of the bones in my body, I took off in a limping run. I was almost there. Just one more level and I could get away from this burning hellhole. I stopped as I ran, seeing a force of soldiers waiting for me at the far end of the hall. I turned back, seeing the group that had followed me pouring in from behind. Both of my exits were blocked, and I knew I was too injured to fight all of them at this point. It felt like the room spun as I eyed them all, gazing down the barrels of their rifles. Yet somehow, despite this all, I did not feel fear of them. Not anymore.

"You don't have anywhere left to run, Celestial!" One of them shouted. I turned my gaze to them.

"I wouldn't be so sure." I said. My fingers curled, firing a beam below me. The floor opened, letting me drop down to the lower deck. I raised a hand above me, straining as I held a barrier up to block their entrance as I tumbled into the hangar below. I hit the ground with a thud, sweating, blood dripping from my lip as I forced my way to the edge of the wall where the escape pods waited. As they tried to break through my spell, I felt more and more pain in my body. I reached up, fighting through it all, opening the hatch.

Finally, I let my spell go. A few people fell through as I climbed into the pod, looking one last time. As the soldiers stood to pursue, I raised a hand, giving them a limp salute, before ducking into the pod, sealing the hatch behind me. I worked out the controls, smashing the launch button. The flaming heap of a ship that had once called me prisoner disappeared into space before me as I blasted off. I couldn't help but laugh as I laid back, the agony coursing through my body becoming all the more apparent as I closed my eyes, letting myself drift off to the nearest planet, free at last.

Unknown System: Unknown Planet

Galactic Date 00:09:003 5028

The escape pod rattled and rumbled as I tumbled downward from space. My breathing was thin. I don't entirely know how long I'd been in this thing, just waiting. I cradled my broken body, sucking in struggling breaths. I'd gone overboard, and I could feel the toll it had taken. My head tilted slowly down as my eyes drooped.

No. No, I had to stay awake. I shook my head. Gods, it was so hard to keep my eyes open. I could tell that I was far outside of Isngr's reach now. The pain was so great that I could not bring myself to speak, to scream, even to just cry. I rocked back and forth in my seat, looking out the porthole. Millions of stars passed me by in an instant as I fell. At least that's how it felt. I wasn't entirely sure of anything I was seeing at that point.

My head fell back, cradled by the cushioning seat of the escape pod. The more I breathed, the more it hurt to do so. Every breath I took, I thought, would be my last one. Everywhere I looked, it seemed the world left trails as if it were moving in slow motion. I had to just… calm myself down somehow. I closed my eyes, trying to keep myself awake as I focused on everything around me.

I breathed in, wheezing, as I pulled the air through my nose. The escape pod smelled musty, old, like it hadn't been cleaned or even used in years. There was this thin hum from the control panels around me, and a ringing from… somewhere. I couldn't tell if it was the pod or just in my head. The air was warm, and getting hotter by the minute it felt. I must have been getting closer to a planet, at least I hoped so. I licked at my lips, trying to keep them moist. A faint taste of metal was apparent in my mouth. I raised my hand to my lips, touching the tip of my tongue to it. When I pulled my hand back, I saw my finger now stained with my blood. I let my hand fall as I laid back, just staring out.

I knew I was in trouble, but I couldn't do anything about it, not here. All I could do was sit here and watch the stars as I felt my life slipping from my body piece by piece. I closed my eyes again, resigned to a fate not of my choosing, but one I knew was the cause of my own actions. Either I got lucky, or I'd die. My breath grew thinner and thinner by the second. Any minute and I'd be gone, I thought.

The sudden halt of the pod jolted me awake. It slammed into the ground of whatever planet I'd found myself on. I struggled to see straight as I unclasped myself from the seat. Tossing myself forward, I pressed the same red button as before, to no avail. I could barely think straight as I searched the pod for some way to open the hatch. At some point, I gave in, lying against the metal hatch, feeling its coolness on my skin.

I don't entirely remember what I did in the end, but I was awoken a second time by the hiss of the pod's hatch unsealing. I squinted as I looked up, a dim light peering in through clouds above. I reached up to it, my hand falling limply on the metal of the escape pod. I strained to pull myself out. I could barely make it to the top of the pod before I let gravity take me. I rolled over the edge of the pod and to the ground, splashing into a heap of mud. I gasped for breath as I laid there, feeling the cold muck on my back.

I… I had to keep going. I rolled over, forcing myself to stand up. Agony coursed throughout my body as I got to my feet. My legs felt so shaky and weak, but I forced them to push me forward. I limped, feeling like my boots were being dragged into the mud. As I moved, I realized that the pain was subsiding… as well as any other feeling in several places in my body. Adrenaline had taken over again as I held onto tree branches for balance.

Looking around me, I was unsure, but I thought I was in a swamp. There was a dense layer of fog across the ground, and while I don't remember much, the smell was enough to shock me awake. It was a vile scent that only sought to bring me further down. The leaves of the many trees around me hung low on thin branches, many of which dipped into the mud and water that I trudged through. It was in a brief moment of clarity that I looked up. The sky was clear. The Wingless Angel hadn't followed me here, though with the damage I did, I don't know if they were even capable of doing so.

I had to keep walking, though. It didn't matter the direction as long as I got *somewhere*. Already, I could feel the little bits of adrenaline left in me fading away, being replaced once more by the pain. It felt like someone had reached into me, crushing my bones, stabbing me thousands of times. It was so intense there was no way to describe it.

As I pushed along, I reached my hand forward. Maybe… just maybe this would be a time of need. Maybe I could pull Isngr from the air and everything would be okay. I tried to focus my mind, tried to bring it to me. I could feel the magic beginning to stir, but… nothing. I tried again, tears streaming down my face as I attempted in vain to bring the sword back to me again. It just wouldn't come, no matter how hard I tried.

I felt my foot catch a root, tripping forward into the mud. I slammed into it, coughing and hacking. As I tried to push myself up, I felt something in my throat. I heaved forward, a spew of vomit and blood gushing out over the ground. Not good. I grabbed a nearby hanging branch, pulling myself up. My arms shook as I could feel the cracked and broken bones in them struggle. Once on my feet, I leaned back against the trunk of the tree, raising my hand.

I wasn't going to survive if I didn't do anything. I could sense magic around me. Maybe I could tap into it. I closed my eyes, trying to remember Iravek's lessons, but in my state, I could barely remember anything. As I reached behind me, I grunted, drawing his dagger from my belt and holding it in front of me. I looked into its reflection, seeing my bloodshot eyes.

What was that thing Rex said? First, it was muscles that tore, bones that broke… then internal bleeding. I'd definitely pushed myself too far. I took the dagger, drawing it across my hand in some attempt to remember the spells Iravek had taught me. There was a moment as I stared at the blood dripping down my wrist where I almost couldn't remember, but I drew the memories out of me.

I put the dagger back as I raised my hand to it. My arms shook and shivered as I let myself fall back to the ground, sitting at the base of the tree.

I gritted my teeth as my breath shook. Faint light passed through the palm of my hand, sealing the cut I'd made. Now, to the hard parts. I shifted my hand over my body. My eyes lit up as I could almost see into myself. Punctured lung, injured stomach, other minor damage done across my internal organs. I took in a deep breath, moving my hand over my chest.

I could feel my breathing begin to clear, but already my body was straining from the magic. I remembered Iravek's words, that I couldn't heal too much or risk doing more damage. The worst damage was what I had to focus on. Already I could breathe better, so I moved to my heart, then to my stomach. The deadliest injuries healed, I let my arm fall limp at my side. I could still barely move. I was so weak, but at least I wasn't dying as quickly.

I had to keep going, though. In the distance, through the fog, I could make out faint lights flickering. Civilization. If I could make it there, maybe I could get help. I crawled forward, pulling myself up, beginning to trek toward the lights. All of my energy was being poured into just taking small steps forward. With each movement, it felt as if the mud slowed me further and further. I wasn't sure how long I would last, but I had to try.

I had to warn everyone. I had to get back to my crew. I shut my eyes, picturing them in my head. I wasn't about to die here, wasn't about to let Jewls show me up, or break my promise to Tara. I'd show Arneli and Natasha what I was made of. I couldn't wait to hear Iraka and Rex chew me out. I *had* to make it.

I stumbled again, feeling the strain in my body as it barely held itself together. I couldn't make out what was ahead of me through the fog in my mind, let alone the one all around me. I leaned against another trunk as I stood, limping forward toward the lights.

Each step shot waves of pain through me. I could barely think straight, barely could keep myself awake through it all. The lights were getting closer now. I could make out the faint outlines of people in the distance. With a hand, I reached out, trying to speak, but no words could escape my mouth, no matter how hard I tried.

The last of my energy gave out, and I fell to my side, crashing into the mud. My vision was too hazy to make anything out. I couldn't bring myself to move anymore. I just lay there, straining to stay awake, but my eyelids were so heavy. Slowly, they fluttered closed as I relinquished myself to fate. I'm dying, I thought. I knew I was. I tried to hold out, but with no energy left, I couldn't. I just let go, allowing myself to fade away.

Nufaro System:
Rishik
Galactic Date 00:09:015 5028

The next time my eyes opened, I found myself not in the mud I had fallen in, but rather laid out in a bed made up of thick, padded leaves. I had to push myself to even sit up, the blankets that had been placed over me drooping to reveal several bandages wrapped around my body. A fire crackled in the room I was in, the windows drawn shut to keep the heat in. I was alone, at least for the time being.

I sat up at the edge of the bed, listening to the crackles as I stood. The shirt I'd been given to wear on the Wingless Angel hung from a rack on the wall. It was freshly cleaned and stitched up, to at least look a little nicer. I lifted it, inspecting the hems and seams. Whoever had brought me in had taken incredible care with the embroidery on it. It felt newer, fresher than what it had symbolized before. I slipped it on gingerly over the bandages. It was warm but breathed nicely. The fabric gave off a faint scent, almost akin to lavender. I brushed it out, looking at a nearby nightstand. My belt rested on it, Iravek's dagger neatly placed by its side.

As I moved to grab it, I became acutely aware of the state of my body. I felt… fine. The agony I'd been in when I'd passed out had all but washed away. As I rolled my shoulder, I could still feel a few twinges in my muscles, but I felt like I'd been brought to full health. I took another look at my surroundings again. Between my escape and getting here, I barely remembered anything. I couldn't say if this place was the source of the lights I had seen, but it seemed more than likely.

I picked up my belt, looping it through my pants, and made sure it was snug tight before picking up the dagger. It had been polished to a sheen. I could see my face in its short, curved blade. I narrowed my eyes as I looked myself over. Gods, I looked scruffy, but I also felt like I looked… different in another way? It wasn't necessarily physical, just something in my eyes. As I tucked the dagger back into my belt, I sighed. I couldn't quite place what it was. I tucked my chin into my fingers. Ah, there was little point on dawdling on the topic. I looked up at the door at the far end of the room. The most important thing on my mind was finding a way to get ahold of my crew.

I made my way out, pushing open the door with an almost comical creak. More lights lit up the next room as a set of two Olari sat speaking quietly over a meal. The blinds were pulled up in this room. It was dark outside now. I could make out more glows of light from other houses nearby. The pair turned to me. The one on the right, a man, spoke first.

"You've finally awoken." He said bluntly. I reached up, feeling my head as I responded.

"Yeah." I said, "H… how long was I out?" The other Olari, a young girl, spoke up.

"It's been almost a week!" She said. "A few of the others found you in the mud and brought you to us for healing." She had a bright and sunny disposition when she spoke, cupping her hands together on a cup as she brought it to her lips. The other, I assumed her father, spoke again.

"You were in awful shape. That you weren't dead by the time we got you is a miracle in its own right." He said, a gruff and glum tone about his voice. The green in his scales had begun to fade from age. I could tell he'd been doing this for some time. "You're welcome, by the way."

"You healed me?" I asked.

"Don't know who else you expected." He said back, stabbing a fork into a set of greens, tossing them into his mouth to chew. "You should rest still. Even though you're stable, you'll need time before you're fully capable. Magic injuries do a number on you." He side eyed me. "Speaking of, how exactly do you let it get that bad? You a novice or something?"

"Uh… a touch of one, yeah." I said. Not entirely a lie, just not the full truth.

"Well, you should at least study up on what that shit does to you if you aren't careful." He said, stuffing another fork-full of greens into his mouth.

"Yeah, believe me I've uh… been warned… a lot." The Olari man raised an eyebrow at me before gesturing with his head to join them. I made my way to the table, pulling out a chair to sit. The man looked to the young woman.

"Hinima, would you please bring our guest some food?" She nodded, hopping up from the table and into the kitchen. He turned his attention to me. "I could see you managed to patch yourself up a touch before you got here. Probably saved your life, even if the work was amateurish." I shrugged.

"Lifeweaving isn't exactly my specialty. Did the best I could." He pointed a fork at me.

"Well, 'the best you could' was damn well good enough." He leaned over on the table. "I've never seen that severity before, though. You may be new, but that's a lot of power that had to be flowing through you to break you that bad."

"How exactly can you tell?" I asked, "Couldn't I have been hurt that badly just cause my body wasn't used to it?" He chuckled.

"Son, I've been a Lifeweaver for a hundred-thirty years. I think I can tell that your body should be able to handle most magic pushed through it." I folded my arms, sitting back.

"Fair enough." Jeez, how old *was* this guy?

"So…" he touched at his food aimlessly, "not that it's any of my business, but how does someone like you end up in a situation like that?" His daughter, Hinima, returned with a plate of food for me. It looked like fish with a side of salad. It wasn't anything particularly special, but after the food I'd been eating, it seemed like practically a five star meal. The man raised a hand. "Ah, you know what? You can tell me later. Eat up, get your strength back." I nodded, beginning to bite into the fish, enjoying having something other than mush. I looked back up at him.

"I never caught your name." I said.

"You never asked." He said with a hint of a smile. "Just call me Doc."

"Alright then, Doc," I said, "if I were looking for someone who could get me access to a radio I could use to call a ship, who would I talk to?"

"Specific question. Well, if I were, hypothetically, looking for that, I'd tell you that the only person with a communication relay would be the village chief."

"Thank you." I said, biting in again, grimacing as I pulled out a bone, setting it aside. "I'll head out and talk to them afterwards, then."

"Hmm."

"Hmm?" I raised an eyebrow.

"I'd toss you a warning that our chief can be a touch… prickly. Especially to people not from around here." I pursed my lips as Doc said this.

"Alright, then, what would you suggest?" I asked.

"Well, I'd suggest you talk to her."

"But you just said-"

"I know what I just said." He responded. "Some problems you can't just hit with a spell to make go away. Have to face them head on. You want a radio, go through her. Sure, she's not the nicest fellow, but you aren't going to get a radio without her." He waved a hand at me, "Oh, but of course, do what you will."

"I… alright." I looked down at the fish again, quickly finishing up what was on my plate. I set my utensils down, pushing the plate back. "I thank you, Doc, for your help. I really should be trying to contact my crew, though." He raised an eyebrow at me once again.

"A crew, eh? I suppose I should have guessed something like that." He waved a hand at me again. "Yes, you should be on your way, I suppose. Feel free to stay with us while you wait." I nodded, standing from the table. Hinima waved to me quietly as I made my way to the door. I waved back, giving her as much of a sunshine-filled smile as I could. She giggled as I pushed open the door, stepping outside.

The air was cool, but not cold like Furelle. The village seemed to be built on top of a small, grassy mound in the middle of the swamp that I'd been wandering through… what was it? I think they said about a week before. Gods, I'd been gone a long time. As I started wandering through the clearing at the center of the village, I thought back. Hell, it had been at least two weeks since I'd seen anyone, longer yet since I'd even set foot on the Sparrow.

A few Olari moved past me as I wandered in my thoughts, many of them giving me weary looks. I guessed they saw little in terms of outsiders. Not to mention that I showed up in a ball of fire from the sky and then wandered into their camp, mortally wounded. For a village that appeared to be so isolated, it wasn't exactly a dreamy first impression, that much was for certain. Still, despite the uncertain looks I received, there was a certain peacefulness about the place.

It reminded me a lot of the slums back home. That wasn't to say they had run-down shacks barely considerable as homes, just that there looked like there was a sense of community among everyone there. As I looked around, I could see people trading materials with each other, sharing food and drink together. It was something I missed from the slums. I don't know if it would convince me to return anymore, but there was a sort of togetherness there… not unlike that between me and my crew, I supposed.

At the opposite end of the village was a house more elaborately decorated than the rest. I could only assume that this would be where I would find the chieftain. I began making my way over, taking in the air. It had a certain mustiness to it. I don't entirely know what I expected from a swamp. It was, however, dulled by the smells of the many campfires burning around the edges of the village. Perhaps it was to keep the smell out, or to add light for people out hunting. I couldn't say for sure, but it helped either way.

I approached the chieftain's cabin, making my way up its steps. The wooden railing was smooth to the touch, cool in the swamp air as I looked ahead of me at the door leading inside. I raised a hand and knocked. A grizzled old woman's voice responded.

"Please enter." They said. I looked down, reaching to the knob, twisting it open before stepping inside. I was immediately hit with the scent of incense wafting through the air. My face contorted as I stepped into the smokey, half-lit room. A frail-looking Olari woman looked up at me from the far end, draped in black and red robes, a pipe tipped from her lips. "Oh. It's you…" I shut the door behind me, waving the incense from in front of me.

"You don't have to sound so disappointed." I said.

"Unfortunately, I am," she responded, blowing a puff of smoke at me. "I see you're finally able to stand."

"I am, thanks to Doc." I said, "I heard they found me outside of the town was brought in to be healed."

"You were. We've been watching the skies since."

"Watching the skies?"

"For *Soulless.* Wounds like yours don't just appear from nowhere." She set down the pipe. "What do you want?" She asked.

"I'm looking for a radio. I just need to contact my crew."

"And why would I give you that?" She raised an eyebrow.

"I'd be out of your hair-er… scales faster." She looked to the side, thinking for a moment, before shrugging.

"You make a good argument. Can't say no to a deal like that." She said, pulling herself to her feet. She sighed as her joints creaked and moaned. “Alright, outsider, come with me.” She began a slow trudge toward a set of blankets hanging between rooms.

“You really don’t like outsiders, do you?” I asked.

“Nope.”

“Can I ask… why?”

“Cause it usually means trouble.” She craned her old neck to look back at me. “Someone with power like yours doesn’t come naturally.” She opened an eye slightly wider. “I’m assuming you’re a Celestial, then?”

“Quite the guess to make.” I said.

“Eh, not entirely.” She pushed the fabric aside, leading me into another room. “They’re the only ones with power like that. Unnatural it is. They don’t know how to control it, burn themselves through.”

“In my case, I don’t think I had much of a choice.” I said.

“That *is* what many people say.”

“Listen, I’ve worked my ass off to get here.” I retorted pointedly.

“Oh, did you now?” She asked. She paused, turning to a table. In the middle was the radio. “Alright then. Before I let you use it, tell me about how hard you’ve worked, then.” She sat opposite of me, gesturing to the chair across from her. I pulled it out, eying her. “Start from the beginning.”

I began to explain everything, beginning with Furelle. The chieftain was argumentative much of the way, but as I explained the pieces of my story, I could see her beginning to understand. I realized as I spoke how lucky I’d been to find the people I had. Without any of them, I don’t think I would have made it this far. I owed everyone my life. Tara, Olivia, Jewls, Gatha, I’d risk everything for them. I… already had. I began to slow down as I spoke of our time on Tanahen, of my capture.

"Yeah, that was… our last mission together." I looked up at her. "The Soulless found something on Tanahen, coordinates for a weapon they think they can use to kill a god." Her expression turned sour.

"Can it?"

"I don't particularly want to find out." I said. "My crew was cornered, so I gave them a chance to escape, and gave myself up to the Soulless. I spent a week in captivity." I narrowed my eyes. "I'm sure you saw the scars." She said nothing for a moment, but then looked up at me.

"I see. So you expounded every ounce of your energy to make your escape."

"And in making sure I could delay them as long as possible. Their ship was badly damaged by the time I escaped, but… I don't know how much time we have." She nodded, sighing.

"Alright, Celestial. You've convinced me a second time. Perhaps you're more tolerable than I anticipated." She gestured to the device between us. "The radio's yours to use." She stood up to leave. Before she walked out, she turned to me, giving me a lighthearted smile. "Oh, and welcome to Rishik, by the way."

I nodded back to her as she dipped through the doorway. Before calling them, I picked out the radio's galaxy map, finding where I was. Rishik, a planet of the Nufaro system. Alright. I typed in the ship's signal, pressing a key to hail them. The radio crackled for a few seconds as I waited in anticipation. My heart pounded in my chest as I watched the signal. Finally, the projection steadied out, and my heart filled with elation as I saw Olivia on the other side. She had her hands tucked behind her back as she began to speak.

"This is the Blue Sparrow, who is-" She looked up and her words caught in her chest as a beaming smile poured onto her face, tears beginning to well in her eyes. "William!" I gave her a wave, smiling back at her as I saw the rest of the crew trying to squeeze into the frame. "I-I thought you were dead!" She stuttered, trying to stifle sobs of joy. I quickly saw the joy leave her face as she looked up at me. "I let you down. We ran without looking back, thought there wasn't a chance-" I put up a hand.

"Come on now, Captain. You really think a small army's gonna slow me down?" I joked. A small start of a smile reappeared as she stepped back, sinking into the crowd. Jewls leaned forward, looking up at me.

"I'm genuinely impressed you *aren't* dead." She said, folding her arms over her chest. I shrugged.

"I had a touch of luck here and there."

"Seems to be your specialty, Ortell." She responded. Iraka looked in after her.

"Aye, on that, we can agree. How are you faring? Anything broken?" He said.

"More importantly, your body, is it fully intact? Rested?" Rex asked.

"Yes yes, I'm fine. I had to go a little overboard when I escaped the Command ship, but I got some help." I looked out the windows to the village outside.

"Hey now-" Gatha's voice cut through as she wiped a tear from her eye, "cabin boy!" She fluttered up. "Just you remember that you have a *lot* of cleanin' to do when you get back, you hear me?" She lowered herself down, "Gods, I'm just happy you're okay. Stay safe, okay kiddo?" I chuckled.

"Hey, I'll be back before you know it and we'll get that engine room clean as a whistle."

"You better!" Arneli said. "It's been too quiet here without you around." Lux jumped in with her.

"Aye! Whatever happened to drinking and making stories together?" He asked, "I may just be your pilot, but we missed you, mate." I smiled, looking to Tara. She gave me a knowing nod.

"I *did* make a promise, after all. Don't worry about me."

"Where are you, anyway?" Natasha asked, "And why did it take so long for you to get ahold of us?"

"I've honestly been out cold most of that time." I said. "As for where I am, I'll forward you my coordinates. I'm in the Nufaro system, Rishik." I swiped the map to them. Lux looked over the coordinates with Tara.

"We're only a touch over a day away." He said, "We'll make it to you in *no* time, just you wait!" I gave him a small salute.

"I look forward to it. I'll be waiting." We waved as I reached forward, cutting the transmission. I'd be home soon. As I got to my feet, I took a deep breath, pushing in my chair. I ducked out through the open doorway back into the main room. The chieftain looked up at me, puffing her smoke.

"It sounds like they really care about you." she tucked her head down, "and that you care about them." I nodded.

"I do."

"Good, good. You have room and board. You may take your leave." She said. I looked out to the door, making my way back outside. Night was falling. The first stars were visible in the sky, but there were still touches of light on the horizon. I pulled out that dagger again as I took in the cool breeze, listened to the fires and the rustling feathers. I closed my eyes, taking it all in, before opening them once more to look at myself in that dagger's reflection.

I think I'd figured it out. It *was* something in my eyes, a certain gleam and look in them. I wasn't the same person who'd left Draenica, or the same kid who'd been driven from Furelle. I tilted the dagger, seeing the reflection of my ponytail in it. As I looked up at the sky, I sighed, gripping the ponytail in one hand, raising my dagger underneath it. I drew it to the side, chopping away at my hair in a single slice. I let my hand open, dropping the clump of hair, letting it float away in the wind as I basked in the starlight. I'd be back home soon.

Rishik:
Tuvan Village
Galactic Date 00:09:017 5028

"You need help with that, Doc?" I asked. He had a log of lumber balanced over his shoulder. He looked from it to me and gestured with his head for me to come over. As I moved beside him, he passed the log over to me. I grunted under the weight, but it wasn't anything I wasn't used to. He put a hand above his eyes like a visor, looking at the now empty space where a pillar had once stood at the front of his house.

"You think you could get this one standing in the old one's place? It's a bit much for my old bones." He asked, rolling out his arm.

"Of course, it's no problem at all." I said. I took a few deep breaths, trudging toward the house. The thing felt like it weighed half a ton. I'd have to be careful getting it set in place. I reached up with my free hand, focusing my energy. The faintest wisps of magic pushed at the roof, giving me just enough space to set the pillar into a freshly made hole. I slid it off my shoulder and set it upright before lowering the roof back down. I let out a breath, wiping my forehead.

I'd been practicing, trying to build up my own magic. Without Isngr, it felt like I barely had the energy in me to do even the simplest spells. Still, as I took a few steps back, looking at my handiwork, I had to admit, *some* magic was better than none. Doc clapped me on the shoulder.

"Not bad." He said. "Make yourself any more useful and I might just need to keep you." I chuckled, putting a hand on my waist.

"Well, you'll just have to wait. I already told your neighbor I'd help fix up some of their floorboards." He hummed at me.

"Ah, then you should be on that. Take Hinima with you. She's a good helper. Plus, she had a few questions she wanted to ask you. Figure it'd be as good a time as ever."

"Sure thing. I'll be heading over soon. Just send her along." I gave a wave as I began to walk through the village toward the next house. I kept myself busy and moving. It kept my mind off of other things. I honestly didn't want to think of what could be happening out there while I was down here. As I walked, I heard a small patter by my side, seeing Hinima joining me.

"Hello!" she cheered. I smiled down at her.

"And *hello* to you." I responded.

"Whatcha doing?" She asked.

"I'm going to be fixing up some of the houses while I'm here." I said. She pouted, but I gave her a small wink. "Though I *do* hear you have a few questions for me." She lit up again.

"Oh! I do! But so do some of my friends!"

"Well then, it sounds like you should go get them then!" I waved her off as I entered the house I was to be working on, beginning to pull up the old boards to reset them and replace them. No sooner than I'd started was I surrounded by a group of kids, bombarding me with questions.

"So do you fight pirates?"

"Have you kissed someone?"

"How big is your ship?" I put up a hand.

"Alright, alright. One at a time, yeah?" I pointed to the first kid. "Alright, I'll start with your question." I ducked back down to the floor, sanding some of the planks. "We don't normally fight pirates, no. However," I popped back up, "we fight against some even *nastier* people. We call them the Soulless."

"Oh! The chieftain told us about them!" Hinima said. "She says that they don't attack us because we're such a small village."

"She's probably right about that." I said. "Oh, but you should see them. They're big and mean and *love* to hurt people. So we make sure they don't *get* to do that." I kneeled back down, beginning to hammer a floorboard back into place.

"What about the other questions?" Another asked.

"Hmm? Oh right." I began. "I've kissed a few people. Not since I joined the Celestials, though." I said. There was a collective 'aw' among them. I rolled my eyes, looking back. "Well, when I'm out there kickin' butt for all of you, when would I have the time?"

"Okay, but the heroes in the flicks always kiss someone by the end!" One of the other girls said. "You have to!" I laughed.

"Alright, listen. My story ain't over yet. Maybe I'll kiss someone by the end of it. Sound good?" The girl gave me a delighted nod. I stood up, dusting myself off as I looked at the floor. "Alright, that's that done. Come on, let's go, still got a few stops to make." As we walked out, I could see a few more curious ears beginning to follow behind.

"And what about your ship?"

"Oh, the Sparrow? Well, you'll see her when she gets here. I wouldn't want to spoil the surprise for you." I said, helping one of the villagers carry a sled of fresh supplies up their front steps. They gave me a grateful wave as I set it down for them. The kid pouted, and I shrugged. Another young man, this one older than the kids who had been following, joined in.

"I heard from Doc that you could use some powerful magic. Could you show us?" He asked. I smiled, but shook my head.

"Unfortunately not." I said, "When I was taken prisoner by the Soulless, they took my sword, which gave me the magic to cast those spells." They looked disappointed. I held out a hand, creating a small orb of light, holding it there. "Ah, but as soon as I get that sword back, you'd best know I'll put on the biggest light show this side of the galaxy. You keep your eyes on the news channels and you might just see me up there." I turned, beginning to fix up a set of walls on one of the houses, nailing on a piece of boarding over one of the holes in its side.

The day slowly began turning to night as I moved from house to house around the edge of the village. The group following me seemed to grow larger and larger by the hour as I was asked about where I'd come from, how old I was, and just about any other question you could think of. At some point, it began to get harder and harder to remember who exactly had asked what. Before I knew it, the sun's light had faded from the sky, replaced by the pitch black of night. Fires roared at the edges of town as they prepped communal dinners among the village.

I sat at the outskirts, enjoying a brief moment of reprieve from the onslaught of questions. On the menu, it seemed, was a fishy chowder. As I watched from the shadows outside the circle, chowing down into the food, a voice snuck in behind me, catching me off guard.

"Quite the crowd you had today." The chieftain said, making me jump.

"Gods' sake, going to give me a heart attack." I said, settling down, taking a big bite from a spoon. She gave me a wrinkly smile as she looked at the village people gathered around the flames.

"Almost two hundred years I've looked after these folks." She looked up at me. "We've had Soulless patrol these areas before. It's near enough to their home that they've considered outposts. You can forgive me for being weary of your presence."

"It seems reasonable, given the circumstance." I looked down at her. "You obviously care a lot for these people. I'd probably be just as cautious if I were in your place."

"You place caution for others, but not yourself." She said.

"I've heard that a thousand times." I said dismissively. She whacked my shin with her cane. "Ow! What was-" She pointed it up at me.

"You'll hear it a thousand more times, then!" She bonked the end of the cane on my forehead a few times. "Maybe it will get through your thick skull!" I rubbed my head, backing away.

"Hold on, fuck. One moment, you want me out of your hair, now you're lecturing me on taking care of myself?"

"You have a good heart in you, that much is obvious." She planted her cane back into the dirt. "From how they look at you and how you talk to them, I can see you aren't someone I should worry about. Time and time again, you tell stories of injuring *yourself* in combat. You have an entire crew who can help lift the burden *with* you. Look at our village." She pointed out to the circle. "Take Sulu. He is our carpenter. He works on the houses and makes furniture. Filki is our metalworker. He provides tools to Sulu. You don't see Sulu trying to make every tool he needs, nor do you see Filki trying to make his own furniture." She turned back to me. "You *can* be strong, but you should not take all the burden." Her eyes softened. "I can see in you someone with the potential to burn bright as the cosmos itself, or someone destined to fizzle out into a ball of embers. Make your choice, Celestial, or the world will make it for you, and the world is *not* kind." She tapped her cane against my shoulder. "Get some rest. Your crew should be here tomorrow. You will need your strength." She began to walk past me when, once again, she stopped. "Oh, and on behalf of me and the village, thank you for your work today." I nodded.

"Thank you for the wise words." I said in response. She waved a hand at me.

"Eh, they are of little meaning to me. They're a gift for you to take and do with what you will." She kept walking. "Now go. Sleep." I slurped down the rest of my food, setting it aside. I turned, stepping up into Doc's cabin. The swell of warm air as I stepped inside was already enough to nearly put me to sleep. My muscles were all sore and tired from the day, but in a familiar way, not like the shorn and torn muscles I'd get after practicing with magic. In a way, it felt comforting. As I flopped down onto my bed, I listened to the crackle of the embers of flames at the far end of the room, it felt like the first bit of true, calm rest I'd gotten in a long time. Tomorrow, I'd see everyone again. Gods, I looked forward to it.

Rishik:
Tuvan Village
Galactic Date 00:09:020 5028

There was a raucous commotion outside the house. It drew me from a cold nightmare. I shot up, my hand to my head as I heard the voices. I could barely remember what I'd seen in my dream. There were just brief flashes of feelings, helplessness mostly. I was in a cold sweat, catching my breath from whatever I'd been running from. I swallowed and wiped my brow, sliding up out of bed, slinking into my clothes. The noise from outside only grew louder. What in the gods' names was going on out there?

I strapped the dagger to my belt, beginning to make my way out the doors. Doc and Hinima were nowhere to be found inside. It looked like some food had been left simmering. It was unlike them to just leave food unattended. Nervously, I reached back to fiddle with my ponytail, only to remember its absence. It had taken time to get used to the feeling of air on my neck, but it was welcome. Yet, despite my habits, I feel like I didn't miss it. It didn't *feel* like me anymore. I let my hand drop as I stepped past the table, pushing open the door.

The entire village was abuzz, people talking and muttering, grouping up around the edges of the town. I furrowed my brow as I walked forward, looking for Doc to ask him what was going on. I hopped my way down the steps, looking around at all the people gathered outside. In the distance, over the commotion of voices, I could hear a faint growl in the sky. I turned to look up. As soon as I did, I was knocked off my feet by a rush of wind. A streak of blue crested over the treeline, its engines roaring as it looped back around. It peaked back over the edge of the swamp trees, its engines kicking up leaves and dirt. The fires at the edge of the village rippled in the gusts as it lowered itself into the clearing at the edge of town. I couldn't begin to describe the elation I felt seeing the Sparrow again. How long had it been since I'd last been on her? Been in my own room? I laughed in pure joy as I made my way to her.

There was a hand on my shoulder as I walked, urging me to turn around. I looked, seeing Doc there. It seemed half the village was with him.

"Hey, William." I smiled.

"Hey, Doc." He cleared his throat and scratched at his neck.

"Listen, I'm not really one for big goodbyes or anything. Hell, I didn't even think I'd like ya when we first met." I gave him a chuckle.

"Reassuring, Doc."

"Hey now, let me finish." He said. He reached back to another villager who held a small crate. "It's not much, but we put together a care package for you, for the journey." He held it out to me and I lifted it from them. It was quite hefty. I cracked open the top, looking inside.

"Hey, you guys didn't have to do this."

"Well, we felt like we wanted to do something for you after all your hard work." I smiled at him.

"You saved my life. Isn't that enough?" The chieftain popped out from the crowd, looking up at me.

"At least he's humble." She reached up, tapping the crate with her cane. "There's some food in there. It's dried. Should keep." Doc reached forward, sorting through the crate in an almost anxious way.

"I've also supplied you with a few supplements, a couple ointments. I don't know how dry your skin gets in space, so I tossed in a few of my moisturizers. Oh, and these vitamins should help with getting your magic back into shape. I also-" He stopped, setting down the small jars of medicine he'd put in there, sighing. He looked up at me again, putting a hand on my shoulder. "You know what? You'll figure it out. I'll be missing you, kid. You're a good one." I returned the gesture.

"I'll be thinking of all of you the rest of the way. Thank you for *everything*." I felt a small tug at my shirt, seeing Hinima at my side. She looked up at me with a determined stare.

"You'll come back sometimes, right?" I chuckled.

"I'll try," I said, "but I have a whole galaxy out there. A lot of it is in trouble. I'll tell you what, though," I looked to the Chieftan, "if trouble ever comes knocking, call us and we'll swoop right back in to save the day." The Chieftan nodded. Hinima swung her arms around my waist.

"I suppose that's okay…" she said, her face squished into my side.

"Maybe when you grow up, you can join us out there." I said.

"Oh now, don't be going and filling her head with ideas." Doc said, but sighed, looking at her. "Ah… it's not as if she hasn't had the idea in her head since she was a little lass." He pursed his lips, giving me a faint smile and a wave. "We'll be seeing you, William." I waved back, adjusting my hold on the crate, now under one arm.

"Be seeing you, Doc." I nodded to everyone, waving as I began to make my way for the Sparrow. The cargo bay doors lowered for me as I took in one final breath of the swamp air. I'd almost become accustomed to it. It felt a shame to leave it behind. Looking at the crate in my hands, though, I knew I still had a little piece of it to take with me. How many homes had I been adopted into now? It felt like everywhere I went, I had a new ones.

Still, I knew my time here had come to an end. I stepped up onto the ship, waving back at everyone as I disappeared into the shade of the cargo hold. As I smiled, watching them, I felt a pair of arms swing around my chest, dragging me into a tight hug.

"There you are!" Gatha was the first to greet me. I put my arm back around her as she squeezed.

"Hey, hey, I missed y'all too!" She pulled back as I looked up to see the rest of the crew beginning to pour in from the upper decks. They crowded around me, ecstatic at my return.

"You seem well." Rex said, "You do not seem to be suffering any ill effects."

"Nah, I owe that mostly to the village." I said.

"Hell, I'd say you came out looking stronger than ever, kid!" Arneli exclaimed, punching at my shoulder. I laughed, boxing back at her.

"I'm feeling it too!" I said. Arneli looked up at the back of my head.

"And where did that ratty little ponytail go exactly?" She asked, waving her hand up where it used to be. I raised the dagger, flipping it in my hand before tucking it back away.

"Cut it off. Didn't need it anymore."

"Well, it looks a lot better, I'll give you that!" she said. Jewls pursed her lips as she looked at me.

"Where is Isngr?" She asked. I stopped, frowning as I glanced to her.

"Koratha took it from me when I was captured. I could not retrieve it." She nodded, taking in a deep breath. I prepared myself for the onslaught of insults, but she just tapped the knuckle of her index to her chin and looked back up to me.

"It will come to you when you are ready." She said, before sulking into a corner. I was… surprised, though it was pleasant. Through the small group, I saw a small pair of glowing eyes peaking through. I furrowed my brow.

"Iravek?" I asked. The figure stood more upright, revealing his height as he bowed to me.

"I said I would assist in finding you." He said.

"What about your whole idea of not flying?"

"I made… a compromise. My tribe owes you its lives tenfold. For me to forsake such an ancient rule was hardly an issue." I smiled, returning his bow.

"Well then, I'm happy to have you on board with us." I said, before looking around. One figure in particular was missing from the crowd. "Where's the Captain?" I asked. There was a deafening silence in the air, as it seemed no one wanted to respond. Finally, Iraka cleared his throat.

"She… locked herself in her quarters when she found out you were alive." His tone was dark, concerned in a fashion I hadn't heard from him. "She already didn't take your disappearance well. Fought to the last to try to rescue you. I don't think she really forgave herself for leaving you behind." I nodded.

"I… I see." I took in a deep breath, closing my eyes. "Alright, everyone," I snapped my eyes open, looking around to the crew, "I understand that we all want to have our time to relish the moment." I smiled at them, feeling the warmth emanating from them all. "However, I need us in the air and in orbit. We have a lot to discuss and our next moves to plan. With Olivia out of commission, I will act as captain for the time being." They nodded, standing at attention. "Good. Let's get this bird flying, then." I could see the reluctance in the crew. There was an excitement in knowing their crewmate was safe, but they understood that time was of the essence. They turned, running off to their stations.

I sighed, looking back one more time, before making my way up the stairs. I turned, making a brief stop in my room. Already, I was surrounded by the quiet hum of the ship's engines. It felt like my room hadn't changed a lick since I'd left. Gods, I was just happy to see it all again. I dragged my shirt off, looking at its clean, intricate designs. I tucked in the sleeves and folded it, laying the shirt at the end of my bed, turning to the lockers. My clothes were all there, neatly preserved as if I'd never left. I pulled one down from the rack and slipped it on. *Now* it felt like I was really back.

I spun on my heels, heading once more down the hall. The Sparrow had a familiar smell to it as I closed my eyes. It felt clean. At least that was the word I could best think of to describe it. I pressed my hand to the white walls as I strode over the deck, taking in the familiar senses. As I moved, I stopped, seeing Olivia's closed door. I took a deep breath, walking to it, raising a hand. I hesitated, unsure at first if I should give her space, but decided to knock anyway. There was no response. I sighed and leaned up against the door.

"Hey. It's me." I said. Still no response. I continued. "Listen, I... can't imagine what you're going through in there. Just... understand that I don't blame you for anything that happened. I made my own choice to stay behind. It wasn't yours, or anyone else's fault." I lowered my head, folding my arms over my chest. "With how things are going here, and how they'll be going in the future, we all could use a captain. A *real* captain like you. We all need you. *I* need you." I was, once again, met only with silence. I sighed, standing up, tapping at her door softly. "Alright. We're heading into orbit. We have a lot of things we need to plan and prepare for. Whenever you're ready, just... we'd be happy to see you and have you back." I nodded to no one in particular, stepping away, making my way forward again.

As I approached the helm, I tucked my hands behind my back, looking at everyone hard at work at their stations. Iraka and Rex stood to either side of the doorway, overseeing as I moved past them to the podium at the center of the upper deck. I had those flutters in my chest again, same as I had the first time I'd stood up here giving commands. Still hard to imagine that I'd come so far since then. We all had, really.

Yet, I saw a look in their eyes as they turned their gazes to me, awaiting my direction. It was an almost unanimous trust and respect. It was a look I hadn't expected, yet here they were, waiting on me to give the orders. I settled my nerves, closing my eyes to regain my focus. I leaned forward, turning back to Gatha.

"Engine status?"

"Online." She said. "Still all warmed up from our descent. Ready to go!" I nodded, turning to Natasha.

"Ship systems all operational?" She nodded, silent as she looked back to me. I nodded back, looking to Lux next. "Alright, Lux, bring us out. Steady orbit at thirty-six thousand kilometers."

"Aye aye." He said, pulling us up. I gripped the rail tightly as we took off, the blue skies and swampy trees disappearing from around us as we soared high past the clouds. Within minutes, we were steady in high orbit. I loosened my grip on the rails. It felt like riding a bike. Never really forgot how to do it. I looked around at the crew again.

"Alright. Good job everyone. Now, we have new information to parse and a lot of planning to do. I want to see everyone in the war room, stat. Dismissed." I watched as they all stood from their stations, beginning to pass me by as they left for the room. I was about to follow when I felt a hand grab at the back of my shirt. There was a gentle quiet as I turned around, seeing Tara. Her head hung down. She took a deep breath, looking up at me.

"I never stopped training, you know." She said. I looked at her hands, where bandages were wrapped around her knuckles. She sucked back tears as she tucked back her lips, closing her eyes. "You *ever* pull a stunt like that again, I *refuse* to stand by and let you just take it." She put her hands up on my chest before fully wrapping them around me. I could feel her fingers digging into my shirt.

"Tara, you-"

"No." She said. "I was barely strong enough to escape from slavery. I was terrified of coming out on this journey, even if I didn't want to admit it to you. I wasn't even strong enough to help my best friend when he needed me." She pushed herself off of me. There was a defiant spark in her eye as she caught her breath, wiping her eyes. "You made a promise to me, yeah?" I nodded. "Well, here I am, now, making one to you, Ortell. I came on this ship to get away from slavery, but I *told* you I'd protect you." She pursed her lips, looking up at me. "You may not *need* it anymore, but I'm promising here and now that if you ever go into some crazy shit, you'd damned well believe I'll be coming with you." She tapped a fist to my chest, holding it there. "There's no Ortell without Verikov from now on. You get that?" I picked her hand up from my chest.

"You were never weak." I said. "Your brilliance has saved my life more times than I can count. You saved my life on Draenica over and over again. You helped me outsmart that thief on Xenova, hell even now you're practically unrivaled in navigation." I clasped her hand in mine. "I know you won't let anything happen to me, just as much as you know I'd die before letting anything happen to you." She nodded before dropping her hand, taking a step back.

"Heh… do you ever just wish things could go back to how they were? On Draenica, when life was simple, and we could just take days to sit in the shack, cook up some grub and watch the holo for hours?" I thought about it, leaning against the door frame.

"Some days," I said, "but more and more I think of this place as home." I looked down the hall. "When I was gone, you all were what filled my mind the most." I felt her hand reach up, tugging at the back of my collar as I was turned, revealing the burned in mark from my time aboard the Soulless ship. She chuckled a little as her finger drew over it. "I'm sorry, is my *scar* funny to you?" I asked. She broke down, tears streaming down her cheeks as she laughed.

"I'm sorry it's not funny, it's just…" she pulled down the back of her collar, showing off her slave marking. "We match." A smile spread across my face as I felt the mark between my shoulders, before joining in her laughter. It was such a simple thing, but it had me curled over in laughter. To think such a small gesture could turn that scar into something positive. She wiped the tears from her eyes as she flipped the hair from my face. "Come on. We can't keep them waiting long." She said, before taking off down the hall.

I watched after her, before turning to look back out into space again. I sighed, reaching forward, closing my eyes in an attempt to bring Isngr to me once again. I was, of course, met with disappointment. I shook my head, but turned my hand over, focusing my strength into it. Again, a small orb of light floated up from my palm, swirling with a pale blue glow. I sighed, closing my fingers in over it, drawing some comfort from the fact that I wasn't completely without magic.

I spun around, making my way down the hall. There was an almost expecting, anxious silence that tore through the halls as I strode around the corner into the war room. The crew was sat there, circled around the projector table, looking up to me. Silently, I leaned over the table, bringing up the galaxy map.

"You have new information?" Jewls asked pointedly.

"I do." I said. "While I was on board the Wingless Angel, I was able to figure out the information they'd recovered from Tanahen, and what their next move will be." I spun the galaxy map around, halting my finger on one of its furthest edges. "Here. The Surillian system." I said. "As far as I could tell, this seems to be the next point. It could be the location of this weapon we've been searching for, or just another stepping stone. However," I zoomed out, showing our current location, "last I was there, Koratha was making her way for the Plains to garner a fleet to take with her there." Tara spoke up next.

"So we aren't sure of exactly what we'll find there?"

"Other than an army of Soulless waiting for us? No, we aren't." I tucked my hands behind my back once again, scanning their faces. "However, if they're intent on taking this planet, I can assume this won't be a simple mission. I'm open to suggestions from the crew on how to proceed." Lux was quick to speak up, appearing to have already been deep in thought.

"I've flown through my fair share of war zones, but if they're bringing a whole fleet for a blockade…" He looked up at me. "I'm good, but I'm not *that* good. To break through a line like that, I'd need a distraction, and a damn good one."

"Not to mention," Arneli began, "even though we're all pretty tough, they'd be bringing their best to fight out there. Breaking through their lines on foot would be a nightmare of a task." Natasha leaned forward, croaking her words.

"If we can get Lux a distraction, we could slip past a lot of those defenses while cloaked." She leaned back, turning her attention to me. "I've seen the types of bases they set up, though. They'll be heavily fortified. Inside and out." I shook my head as I pursed my lips.

"I believe you, but I wouldn't be so sure about that this time." I said. "Koratha seems to have it personal with me now. After our last match, I'm almost *certain* she'll want a second go. My guess is a more heavily fortified frontline unit, with weaker units closer in to bait us into a false sense of security." Jewls folded her arms over her chest.

"How can you be so sure of that?" She asked.

"I'm not." I said, "But it's what I'd do if I were in her position." I stood to my full height, steadying my thoughts again. "Nothing is certain at this point." Rex cleared his throat to speak.

"We can all agree, a distraction is needed. Certainty or not, we must keep the Soulless occupied on something other than us." He paused, crossing his fingers together. "However, if we do not wish for mass casualties in the case of us or our distraction, it must be a sizeable one."

"What do you suggest?" I asked.

"From my experiences in war, this is not a mission to be taken lightly, or done alone. To take on this fleet, we will need one of our own to combat it."

"We could request the aid of the Federation." Iraka said, continuing to jot down notes in his holopad.

"It's… possible." Arneli said. "You would need someone on the inside to petition for a War Summit, though." Tara looked up at me knowingly. I knew who I'd have to call, though after the amount of time away I'd spent, I felt almost hesitant.

"I have a… connection in the Federation that I can contact. They'll be able to help us get a foot in at the least." I leaned forward against the war table. "Alright. I'll make the call, get us that summit. Unless there are further suggestions, everyone is to return to normal duties." Everyone agreed, people beginning to stand and pour out. Lux stopped as he passed me, though.

"I have a few friends among some of the other Celestial crews. I'll make a few calls, see who I can get." I nodded to him.

"Do that. Let me know our numbers as soon as you can." He returned my nod, disappearing down the hall. I stood there for a moment before shutting the door to the war room behind me. I stepped forward, creating a secure channel between us and the Supernova, hailing them. I stepped back, waiting. It rung only a few seconds before being picked up. A tall Furin woman stood in the projection, looking down on me. There was little emotion I could gleam from her face as she eyed me. She eventually spoke.

"This is Captain Nauav of the SFS Supernova. CNS Blue Sparrow, what business do you have with us? We read your position being halfway across the galaxy." I put my hand over my chest, nodding my head to her.

"Forgive me, Captain. I am acting Captain William Ortell of the Blue Sparrow. I have urgent business with one of your crewmates, Maurel Illani." I said. The captain watched me, unsure. "If you so wish, you would be free to join in on this conversation. The things to be discussed could very well affect you as well." The captain narrowed her eyes, but turned her head, quietly giving an order to find Maurel. I had to be honest, I was… unsure of this. The last time we'd spoken, I'd been a wreck on Draenica. Still, I needed her help, now more than ever.

We were silent as we waited. The captain seemed to respect the quiet, something I greatly appreciated. I closed my eyes, waiting with my arms folded. My foot tapped impatiently at the carpeted floors as we stood there in anticipation of Maurel's arrival. Soon, I heard footsteps from their side of the channel. I popped up to my feet as Maurel strode into the frame, saluting the captain.

"Captain, you wished to speak with me?" The captain only thrust her head to the projection at her side. Maurel turned to face me, her brow furrowing. "Wait… William?" She asked. With one hand tucked behind my back, I raised a hand to her, a thin smile on my face.

"Hey Maurel." She looked confused as she looked at me, then angry.

"I've been trying to contact you for *weeks*! I thought something had happened to you, that slavers had gotten to you! Where are you? Are you okay?" She asked in rapid succession.

"Right. Sorry about that. I haven't been able to get into contact with anyone for some time now." I pursed my lips, watching as she did the same.

"This is the one from Draenica?" The captain asked. "I thought you said he refused to join the military." Maurel narrowed her eyes as she looked at me.

"What do you mean?" She looked more closely at what I was wearing, seeing the patches across my shirt. Her face softened. "Oh, William… what have you gotten yourself into?" I gave her a smile as I raised my arms, weakly showing off the uniform.

"Well, I joined the Celestials." I dropped my arms. "Wasn't fully my choice, but I'm here, and I'm doing what I can to keep the galaxy safe." She nodded.

"Gods, you look so…" She smiled, a hand on her hip. "I'm proud." I nodded back.

"We'll have time to talk more soon and catch up, I hope." My smile dropped, turning more serious as I looked between the two of them. "However, I brought you here for a reason." I said. "The Soulless are in search of a weapon to bring down the Gods. They're amassing a fleet to hit the Surillian system in search of it. I need the help of the Federation so we can get in and make sure they *don't* get this weapon."

"The Supernova would not be able to move from its position at this time." The captain said, but looked to Maurel. "However, I am assuming you wish to call a War Summit?" I nodded.

"I do."

"I see. I could spare Maurel to act on my behalf." She handed something to Maurel. "You may act as my representative during this summit." The captain turned back to me. "I will warn you, while I am in favor of this directive, I can not be so certain the rest of the Summit will be. You are about to attempt an assault in Hunter Collective space. There is much danger involved with bringing an armada through there."

"Understood. Thank you, Captain." She nodded to me.

"Just know that I do this only because Maurel trusts you. I would not take someone's word so lightly from anyone else. I will have Maurel rendezvous with you at Solar Station for the Summit, and have the station's current coordinates sent to you directly." A notification popped up on my holopad as she sent them over. I picked it up, familiarizing myself with the new information.

"Got it." I nodded to her before looking to Maurel. "Look forward to seeing you again in person. Been a long time." She smiled knowingly at me.

"You better have a full story prepared for me. I thought I told you to stay out of trouble, didn't I?" I shrugged.

"You'll just have to find out when you get there." I said, reaching forward. "See you soon." The call cut out as I turned, making my way to the helm. People were quiet at work as I strode up to the podium. Lux hung up on a call, looking back to me.

"Seven crews will be joining us on both air and ground forces, William." He said.

"Good to know. Thank you Lux." I said. I leaned over the rail. "Alright, the summit is on. We rendezvous with Solar Station. Tara, set a course for the Warus System." She nodded, getting on it. I closed my eyes, looking down. I could only hope they'd listen.

The Blue Sparrow: Transit to Solar Station

Galactic Date 00:09:023 5028

The trip to Solar Station was short. In the time, I managed to catch most of the crew up to speed with everything I'd gone through. What free time I had, I often spent training. Tara and I sparred below decks, studying hand-to-hand skills as Arneli or Jewls watched over us.

For all the grief I give to Jewls, I had to complement her training when it came to martial arts. I remember standing across from Tara, sweat dripping down our bodies, bruises covering our torsos. Jewls stepped in, putting hands between us to break us both apart.

"Good. Tara, chin tucked *down,* not up. You've got foam on. Don't be afraid to use your claws. They won't actually *hurt* him."

She said. "Remember to use what you have at your disposal. You haven't studied in magic, so you'll need whatever you can to get an edge above your enemy." Tara wiped the sweat from her head, standing up straighter as Jewls turned to me.

"Good work so far. I can tell you're holding back with those magic infusions. You should be for a fight like this. However, I want to see full force on the dummies when we practice on them. You need to build up your magic until you have Isngr again, and even then." I nodded, rolling out my arms. "How's that going, by the way?"

"It's going alright. I'm starting to be able to cast some of the old spells, if weaker than before." I said, stretching my wrists. My knuckles and forearms were sore. Tara was damn strong. You wouldn't expect it from her size, but, despite what Jewls was saying, every time she struck, I could feel the air being knocked from me. Jewls threw towels over the two of us unceremoniously.

"Alright. Enough for today. Hit the showers, both of you." She said as I dragged the towel down from on top of me, Tara doing the same. Jewls and I shared a knowing and respectful look with each other as Tara gestured for me to come along. The two of us began walking up the steps to the upper deck as she wrapped the towel around her neck.

"Not bad, Ortell." She said with a smirk. "Though it does seem that magic is a bit more your strong suit." I laughed, but winced.

"Ah, yeah, you could definitely say that." I felt the bruises over. "You certainly gave me a thrashing in there."

"Well, you didn't do *too* bad. You keep sparring with me and you'll maybe even *learn* a thing or two." She gave me a wink, nudging me with her wing. As she did, she looked down at my exposed back, frowning. "They... really did a number on you, didn't they?" I tried brushing it off.

"Nah, it's fine. It healed over within the day." She stood in front of me, stopping me.

"Nuh uh, mister!" She shoved a finger toward me. "You aren't going to just deflect like that." I flinched back as she looked up at me with those unwavering green eyes. They had the same intensity in them as the day I'd gotten Isngr, when she'd gone off on Xervan in my defense. "I can tell how much it hurt you. I can see it when you sleep." She moved behind me, running her fingers along the lengths of scarred skin on my back. "Did you ever feel like giving up?"

"I'm here aren't I?" I said.

"That's not what I asked." She said, moving ahead of me again, looking up into my eyes. "It's okay. You don't have to answer. Just…" she pursed her lips, "you've been there for me for so long. Let me be here for you, okay Ortell?" I didn't really know what to say. I just froze up. She smiled, closing her eyes. "I'll take that as a yes." She spun around, leading the way to our room. The two of us stopped at the door.

"You can hit the shower first. I've got a quick thing I need to do anyway, and I'll hop in after you." I said. She gave me a thumbs up, slipping on into the room. I sighed as the door shut behind me. I closed my eyes as I leaned against the wall for just a moment.

Tara always had a way with words, yet lately more than ever. I took a deep breath, looking back at the door. I did care for her, but I always worried now that she would get hurt if she tried to protect me. Seeing how hard she worked at me, I couldn't help but feel like my worry was misplaced. I rubbed my forehead and sore body, turning to move further down the hall.

Olivia's door rested just a few rooms over, waiting for me. I sat down beside it as I'd done many times over the past day. The last 24 hours felt… long. I folded my arms over my knees, taking in a long, deep breath.

"Hey, Captain." I said. No response. "I know what you're going through is tough. Just… listen. I know I've said before, but I'm not mad or angry about anything. Hell, not even disappointed." I let my head hang low. "Honestly, I'm not even sure what I'm doing walking into all of this. This whole galaxy is new to me. So many things I don't know or don't understand." I said. "I could really use you, you know? Just… when you're ready, okay?" I sat in silence, never hearing a response. For a few minutes more, I waited, before giving up, getting to my feet, beginning to return to my room. Once at the door, I listened in, heard no water running, and decided to knock.

"Come in!" Tara called, the door sliding open. She was back in uniform, using a hairdryer on the ruff of feathers around her neck, moving it up to her wings. "Damn, things take forever to dry." She muttered. "Almost prefer molting season." I furrowed my brow as I undid the wraps on my hands.

"You molt?" I asked, stepping into the head, closing the door behind me. Through the thin walls, she responded.

"You lived with Draens for how long again?" She asked as I stepped into the shower. The hot water soaked over my skin, bringing a calming warmth as I tilted my head back, letting it rush through my hair.

"Nearly a decade."

"And you had no idea that we molted?"

"Guess I never really paid attention to it." I said. I heard her laughs from behind the door.

"Man, you really *are* oblivious sometimes."

"Hey, we both know you're the observant one." I rinsed my hair. I heard a ping from outside.

"Oh! Looks like we're coming up on Solar Station. Better hurry up and be out there, *Acting Captain.*"

"Shit, I'll be out in just a minute!" I said, shutting off the water, drying myself off, pulling my pants up. I stepped out, seeing Tara waiting with a fresh shirt, her arm folded over her chest. She handed it to me. "Thanks."

"Don't mention it." She said as I pulled it on. "Come on, let's get up to the helm." She ran out the door, dragging me in tow. Up the familiar corridors and out into the open helm we went. Iravek stood by the railing, looking out in amazement at the show of lights flowing around the edge of the ship. Tara let me go, moving to her post as I moved to the center of the room, looking over at Iravek.

"Though I have seen them many times since joining your crew, they always amaze me." He said, the mandibles across his face shifting and clicking together as he spoke. My attention turned back out to the flow of Warp Space.

"I can agree with that. I've been out here a month and a half, and I'm still getting used to it." I looked back at him, leaning back against the rail. "Never had a chance to thank you." I said.

"What do you have to thank me for?" He asked.

"The magic you showed me saved my life." I said. "When I crashed on the planet you found me on, had I not known that little bit you taught me, I don't think I'd be standing here today. At least, that's what the doctor told me." I could see his attempted smile as he bowed to me.

"Well, then I am grateful to know I have made some impact." He said before turning back to the space beyond. "I could not have dreamed I would find myself here. Very few of us find our way to the stars. Fewer still choose to embroil themselves into war. Still, though I miss much of my tribe, I do not think I would rather be anywhere else but by your side." I smiled as he opened his arms. "I have been informed that outworlders call this a hug. It can show platonic affection and comfort. Would you like one?" I chuckled a little, but didn't want to be rude. I stood and walked to him as he wrapped his arms around me in an almost crushing manner.

"Oh, uh, buddy, a little tight."

"Ah forgive me." He loosened up before letting me go. "I am unfamiliar." I rubbed my arms where he'd held me.

"Do Ikui not, like, hug each other?"

"It would be considered rude." He said. "You must understand, if something is grasping you, it often means it is a predator. It can cause great distress."

"So how do you show affection, then?"

"Pheromones!" He stood there silently as I watched him.

"That… makes sense, I suppose."

"I do not expect you to fully comprehend. We are from different species and cultures. Though I appreciate your effort to understand." I nodded.

"And it's good you're learning some off-world customs. Keep working at it."

"I shall." He said, bowing his head as he backed away. Tara turned to look up at me.

"Approaching Solar Station. Dropping out of warp in one minute." She said. I leaned forward, gripping tight to the rails as we began to slow. Finally, there was a thud as we halted.

Solar Station was unlike anything I'd seen. The size of it was incredible. Lights flickered across the city sized structure as it slowly rotated. Federation ships of all sizes moved in and out of the various docks across the station's edges. Between sections, you could see trams passing back and forth. As we drew closer, the flagships of the Federation fleet grew into view, docked in the station's largest ports. They were the size of a small town themselves, and next to this thing, they were dwarfed. Millions of people had to live here. It was incredible. Natasha looked out to the station, the faintest hint of a smile touching her tired eyes, before she looked over to me.

"William, we're being hailed by Traffic Control."

"Push them through." A Terran man stood on the other end, sifting through holographic files.

"Blue Sparrow. Welcome to Solar Station. We have you slated for arrival at the request of Captain Nauav. Is that correct?"

"Yes, that's right." He sifted through a few more things.

"Ah, yes I see. You're here for the War Summit. Big hearing that's going to be," He said.

"You heard?" I asked.

"Me and half the galaxy. A summit like this is big news. Broadcast galaxy wide." He looked up at me. "Your crew was the ones who called it, weren't they?"

"Yeah, that was us alright." I said, getting nervous. He threw up his eyebrows.

"Fair enough. Well, good luck to you. It's not going to be easy to get the leaders to agree on everything. Especially Xenova."

"What's wrong with Xenova?" I asked.

"If you don't know, then you might not be prepped enough." He said. "Xenova's notorious for their debates. It's a bureaucratic nightmare trying to get anything done with their government. Trust me, enough of them come through these gates trying to argue that I'd know. The most recent counselor is the worst." He stacked the files together, clearing his throat. "Well, I wish you luck. There's an open space at Port 7, Docking Bay 53." He gave me a salute before disconnecting. I took a deep breath, looking down at Lux.

"You heard the man. Port 7, Dock 53."

"On it." He said, pushing forward. Jewls walked up beside me. She gazed over the station's lights, her hands tucked behind her back.

"You look nervous." She commented. Before I could speak again, she interrupted me. "Don't be." She said. "If there's one thing I know you're good at, it's running that mouth of yours until people have no choice but to listen."

"No words of wisdom or advice, then?" I asked. She grinned as she kept her gaze forward, arms folded over her chest. She stood stoic as ever as she turned her head to me.

"Not this time." She narrowed her eyes, looking back outside as we pulled into dock. "I thought for sure you wouldn't have made it off Koratha's ship. You proved me wrong. If you can get through that, I don't think a few politicians are going to stand much of a chance, do you?" I chuckled.

"Really think that low of me, did you?" I asked.

"I did." She said bluntly. Yeah, I don't know what I expected. The Sparrow settled down cozily into the dock, the hum of its engines quieting down as Gatha let out a breath.

"Alright. Generators online, engines and core powered down. We're all set to go!" she said to me.

"Good." I said, looking outside. "Okay, here's the deal. Summit won't be for a few more days so that we have time to get everyone we need here. Until then, I'm authorizing ship-wide shore leave." There was a unanimous sigh of relief. It felt like most of us hadn't stopped working a second in the past couple months. Natasha leaned back in her chair, looking out at everyone.

"Hey, I know a bar around these parts we could hit up. Give us all a bit of time to wind down. Relax. That okay with you, William?" she asked.

"Sounds good. I honestly think I might join you for that. Gods knows I could use a drink after the week I've had." She smiled a touch again. It was good to see her hopefully warming up to all of us.

"Hell yeah!" Arneli cheered. "We goin' drinking tonight!" She hopped up from her station, strutting past me as a worried Rex followed behind her.

"I must advise *caution!* We don't want a repeat of last time!" He called, following her out.

"What the hell happened last time?" I muttered under my breath as they walked out. Iraka overheard me as he patted my shoulder.

"I don't know, but I'm hoping I get to find out." He whispered as he passed me by. The rest of the crew funneled out, leaving me behind for just a moment as I watched them, my arms folded over my chest. A few minutes had passed before I finally decided to push myself up to follow after them, though I had one stop to make first. As I moved down the hall, I stopped in front of Olivia's door. I raised a hand up and knocked.

"Hey." I said, "If you're feeling it. We're all going out for drinks. Don't feel pressured to come, but we'd love to see you there." I didn't hear any response still. I sighed, beginning to walk away, but I was no more than a few steps down the hall when I heard the door open behind me. I turned, seeing Olivia standing there. There were bags under bloodshot eyes. She looked like she'd gone through hell and back. In her hands, I saw the finished patches and smiled. I held out a hand to her. "Let's go, Cap'." She smiled as she joined by my side, the two of us beginning to walk together. She wiped her eyes as we began to make our way out of the cargo hold.

"I'm sorry." She said.

“You have nothing to be sorry for.” I responded.

“No, I mean for everything.” I didn’t speak, deciding to let her continue. “I was never a great captain. I sat on the sidelines, made everyone do my work for me. Then I had *you* as a first mate and saw you doing so well. I thought I’d just hide in the shadows and let you take over.”

“Olivia…”

“Then I thought I was doing so well. I’d turned around, was helping everyone, but then… on Tanahen…” she sniffed. “I didn’t know what to do.”

“You did what you thought was best.” I said.

“I did, but it turned out you were alive and…” I stopped in front of her.

“And I made my own choice there. You made the right choice, and I’m here now.” She nodded, wiping the tears from her eyes.

“Gods. William, I look to you every day I’ve been on this ship and asked myself how you did it.”

“Did what?”

“So damn well where I didn’t. I could see clear as day on Tanahen how much the crew trusted you. They trusted your words and your comforts far more than I could ever offer them. You gave them hope to move forward and you still do that even now. I can’t see myself doing that.” She said.

“But you did.” She shook her head.

“I led them, sure, but they trusted you and your judgement. You’ve listened to them. The people you’ve brought on board, and even the people *I* recruited, look to your guidance more than my own.” She sighed as we continued to walk. “Truth of the matter is, I was never a good leader. I always did better when I followed, and… I think that’s okay, and I’m realizing that.”

“What do you mean?” I asked. She bit her lip.

"I… don't think I should captain the Blue Sparrow anymore." She said, holding out the patch to me. I froze again, looking at her.

"Captain-"

"Olivia." She corrected. "It's just Olivia."

"I-I can't take this." I said, trying to push it back to her. "I'm your number one, your first mate." She shook her head.

"William. You've already been captaining her, even if it wasn't formally. This was meant to be on your arm from the moment we met, not mine."

"But-"

"No buts." She said before sighing. "I have… something to admit."

"What is it?" I asked.

"The… crew already knew that I had planned on doing this. I wasn't in any mental state to lead once we found out you were alive. We agreed it would be best if I stood down from my position."

"They… knew?"

"They did." She said. "They didn't lie, though. I never formally stood down, and I couldn't face you when you came on board… but they did know." That explains why everything wasn't a mess the moment I got on board.

"They really trust me that much?" I asked. She nodded.

"We've already agreed on it. All you have to do is accept, if that's what you want." She said, holding the patch up to me once more. From a simple scrapper, to crewmate, and a first mate, and now here. She looked up at me expectantly. I took the patch from her, but held onto her hand before she could let go.

"Just so you know, I couldn't be where I am without you as my captain. I don't care what you say, you will *always* be at the top for me." She smiled up at me with those tired eyes.

"You do not know how much that means to me." She said, letting go of the patch. "You've grown so much from the young man I met on Draenica. I cannot begin to say how proud of you I am." She reached up, adjusting my collar. "You're going to bring this galaxy to its knees. I just *know it.*" I could feel that tightness tugging at my chest again, as all I could do was smile and cry with her as she held me. Gods, it felt like it'd been so long. I swallowed my emotions as I leaned back, looking down at her. She smiled, saluting me. "Shall we go then, Captain?"

"Aye we shall." I said, the two of us making way for the bar. It was a loud place, and not hard to find. When I walked in, the crew saw Olivia with me, cheers ringing out across them.

"The captain's finally here!" Arneli shouted, raising a drink. Olivia gave a glance up to me without a word. They caught her meaning almost immediately, seeing the new patch pinched between my fingers. Arneli slammed her glass down, jumping up. "And my bet was that you wouldn't take it!" I recoiled a moment as we approached.

"Hold on now, you all had *bets?*" I asked, sitting in at the table by them.

"Just to see if you'd take it." Iraka said. "I was against you, too. Thought you'd be too enamored to let her relinquish command." I contorted my face.

"Come on, really? *Me*, enamored?"

"I figured you'd take it." Jewls said, a wing half stuffed in her face. It was the only time I hadn't seen her sitting or standing all prim and proper. She pointed the wing at me, the flush in her face clearly visible, as well as the slurring in her voice. Ah, of course, she was drunk. "Had my bets on you all the way… at least after you came back. Hated your guts-" Lux cut her off.

"Alright, socially responsible Irishman here to tell you you've had enough." He said, sliding the drink from her. I laughed as she eyed him before slinking back into her chair. "For the record, I had my bets on you, so you'd better be paying up, Arneli!" She flipped him off.

"Sorry for not telling you the full truth of the matter." Gatha said. "We wanted you to get used to the role first before springing anything on you."

"No offense taken." I said. "Honestly, had you not, I don't know if I *would* have accepted it."

"Well, *Captain*," Tara said, "I think, before we go any further, you two both need some drinks and food." She slid us both mugs of beer before swigging hers down. I took a large gulp of mine, feeling the bitter broth wash down my throat, a light warmth filling me.

The lot of us sat there the rest of the night, telling stories into the wee hours of the evening. Honestly, after a few drinks, I don't wholly remember much other than Rex desperately attempting to get us to slow down a little. Either way, we somehow made it back to the Sparrow at the end of our evening out, laying ourselves out in our bunks, or in the case of a few of us, wherever we could comfortably lie down.

The last thing I remember of that night was Olivia looking relieved for once, and having fun. I'm glad she could finally enjoy her life on the crew, and I'd do my best to uphold my new position. For her, and for everyone else. If I didn't, who knows what would become of the galaxy? Gods, I wasn't looking forward to facing the summit, but looking at everyone else there, I felt like I could take it. I was still scared, sure, but I knew they at least had my back.

Warus System:

Solar Station

Galactic Date 00:09:038 5028

The day of the Summit had come at last. Council Ships from around the Federation had been pouring in for days, the station feeling fuller and fuller by the hour. I was beyond anxious as we waited, unsure what exactly to expect in there. Each passing day only made my anxiety grow, as I anticipated the worst. What if they didn't listen, or they weren't willing to send help? Even with the Celestial crews Lux called, we'd be in a lot of trouble.

Still, there was one good thing coming. Maurel was finally coming back. Gods, I hadn't seen her in person in… years; I think. She'd left with the Federation as soon as she could enlist. I respected her choice, but I remember feeling bitter about it for a while. Now, it almost feels sensible, and silly that I'd have so many reservations about it.

I thought about that as I sat by the waiting rooms at the docks, a spare captain's patch turning over in my hand. Most of them had already been sewn into my uniforms, with help from Olivia. It felt odd, having to get used to not calling her my captain anymore. I don't know if I'd ever get used to it. To me, I think, she always would be a leader to me, or at the very least, a source of counsel. It was hard to imagine that I'd be here without her.

I thought back to when I first saw her on Draenica. I'd written her off as nothing but another Celestial drawing people to their dooms. It was hard to believe how wrong I'd been about her. I remember when she first gave me the position of First Mate; it felt like such a jump in responsibility. I'd barely been there a couple weeks and there I was, set to be a point of guidance for the crew when I barely knew a thing myself. I'd learned a lot from them all already, and I knew I had so much more to figure out as I went.

Some days, I really *did* feel like the captain of the Sparrow, but there were other days when I was that same unsure person who left Draenica. I could only hold out longer. Fake it till you make it, they say. I sighed, looking up at the arrivals. Maurel's ship should be pulling into dock any second now. I almost felt more nervous about meeting her again than I did about the Summit. I flipped the patch repeatedly in my hands, bent it between my fingers, tapping my foot impatiently.

"Waiting for someone?" A voice broke through the wall of my thoughts. I looked up, Maurel standing over where I sat. I grinned, hopping up to my feet.

"No one in particular. Just felt like sitting around the docks, as one does." I responded jokingly. She smiled before pulling me into a hug, squeezing me tight.

"Ah, I missed you!" She exclaimed, before pulling back, looking me up and down. "Gods, have you gotten taller?"

"Probably. It's been around six years since you saw me." I said. She looked more toned than the last I'd seen her, though I suppose that came to no surprise, given her circumstances. She put her hands on her hips, taking me in.

"You cut your hair?" She asked, noticing the lack of ponytail.

"Yeah, felt like it was time for a new look." I showed off the back of my head. I'd gotten it freshly cut up with our spare time. She pursed her lips and furrowed her brow as she looked closer at me.

"So… how did all this happen? Last I talk to you, you're vehemently denouncing the Federation and Celestials, and next thing I know, you're in charge of a front-line ship." I nodded, gesturing with my head for her to follow along with me.

"It's a long story, but we've got time." I said. As we began our walk, I went through everything, from Xenrus crashing on Draenica, through to my capture on Tanahen, to where we were now. I could see her face turn from interest, to worry, to horror at the things I'd experienced over my time in the Celestials. Finally, I finished my recapping of the events of the past couple of months.

"William…" she began, "I'm… This is a lot to wrap my head around." She said.

"It's… certainly a lot." I admitted.

"Okay, but you were *tortured.*" She stopped me, turning to face me in the hall. "William, *none* of this is normal." She paused before continuing. "Are you sure you aren't in over your head?" I frowned, looking at her.

"I'm fine." I said. "I have people around me who help and that I can rely on." She sighed.

"Yeah... yeah. Just... No, you're right." She looked at the scarring that had crept up my neck. It was barely visible above my collar, but you could still see it. "You're sure this is what you want?" She asked.

"I am." I said. "I feel good here. I'm doing good things, and I care for the people I serve with." She nodded.

"I'm sorry. It's hard for me not to be concerned. You've always been a little brother to me." She glanced back at the scars. "I just wish I could have been there, or that you'd at least have sent something to let me know."

"Yeah, it... would have made it easier, for sure. I would have contacted you sooner, but by the time you were available, I was..."

"Locked in a Soulless ship..." she shook her head, "and now you're running head first, right back in."

"It's not like we have much of a choice." I said, my brow furrowed. "I'm not about to sit by as the Soulless look for a weapon that would win them the war."

"I know, I know. I'm just..."

"Concerned, I know."

"Guilty, actually." She sighed, looking up at the ceiling as we walked. "Like I said, we still got the news. I saw the Blue Sparrow more than a few times popping up, but... I had no idea that you were there with them." She looked down. "I don't know. It's going to take me some time to really take this all in."

"Take your time." I said. "I'm still working on accepting it all myself. The past couple of months feel like they've gone by so fast." I sighed, looking down to check the time. "Come on, the Summit's starting soon. We should hurry." She nodded, the two of us picking up the pace. As we made our way through the halls, a few people passed us by, also seeming to head in our direction. One person, though, tapped my shoulder. I turned, seeing a taller woman. She was Terran, with short, thin black hair and wrinkled skin. She watched me with emerald eyes and thin pursed lips as she reached out a hand to me.

"William Ortell, right?" she asked. I took her hand, shaking it.

"That's me." She smiled.

"Good to meet you. LeeAnne Mitchell. Captain of the Darkstar." I nodded to her. "We've heard a lot about you through Lux. Looking forward to working with you."

"Can't say I've heard of your crew, though I'm still new to all of this." I said. She shrugged.

"Wouldn't expect you to. Our crew focuses on reconnaissance and sabotage. I'd be more concerned if you *had* heard of us." She punched my shoulder. Despite her clearly holding back, it had a surprising amount of strength behind it, despite her more frail frame. "You're a new captain, right? Lux mentioned it last we called."

"You got that right." I said, "He calls you often?"

"Oh yeah, he and I go way back. His dad and I were seeing each other for a while and-" I put up a hand.

"Out of respect for him, I think that's all I need to know." She shrugged.

"Fair enough. Oh, right, just wanted to reach out. I know what it's like being thrust into all of this without experience. You need any advice. Just call me up and I'll do what I can to help!" She gave me a wink, throwing another surprisingly powerful punch on my shoulder, before walking off. "Oh, and good luck in there!" She jogged down a separate hall as I rubbed my shoulder. Maurel looked at me as if I were a stranger.

"Something wrong?" I asked.

"No, just… I feel like I've missed a lot more of your life than I'd thought." She shook her head. "Gods. Alright, come on, let's just… get to the Summit." We kept moving until the groups of people thinned out. As we walked, I saw Olivia pacing back and forth in front of a large set of double wooden doors. She looked up at me, striding over to where I was walking.

"There you are!" she said. "Gods, I was afraid you'd be late."

"What's the status in there?" I asked.

"The Council Members are waiting for you. They're ready whenever you are to begin the hearing." She looked over at Maurel, holding out a hand. "Olivia Sterling, by the way." Maurel took her hand, shaking it firmly.

"Maurel Illani." She said. "You used to be the captain, correct?" She nodded.

"I was. Handed it off to our boy here recently." Maurel looked between her and me, before back to Olivia.

"Thanks for taking care of him." Olivia waved a hand at her.

"Oh, he doesn't need me to take care of him. Though he can never get his collar right. I just keep him going in a straight line."

"Don't sell yourself short." I said, moving toward the doors. "You did plenty before you passed the ship onto me." I said, putting my hands on the handles of the doors. "You both ready for this?" They nodded. I took a deep breath and pushed. The doors swung open to a giant gray and white room. Thousands of people filled the stands around the edge of the room. There were civilians, soldiers, press workers flashing us with the lights of their cameras. Blinding white spotlights shone down on the room as five people sat high above us. One of each of the Federation races made up the Council. A Terran woman sat on the far left, then a Furin, a Xenovan, a Dervan man and finally, an Olari man. As I stood beneath them, it felt more like I was on trial than being at a war meeting. The three of us strode in, finding ourselves at the center of a stage in front of the five.

I took the lead, standing at the head of a podium, as I looked up and around at the people surrounding us. This was so much worse than I could have imagined. My heart pounded in my chest as I sweat, anxiety filling me from head to toe. The crowd quieted down as the Xenovan Councilor put up a hand. The room was, at once, silent.

"William Ortell. Celestial, Captain of the Blue Sparrow. You have called upon the Solar Federation to offer a fleet of ships to attack the Surillian System." The Xenovan's voice rang across the hall of the hearing. His turtle-like neck craned to look down at me, the ridges of their environmental suit creaking with age as their gaze met mine. Their voice boomed as they spoke again. "Having read your report, you claim your information was based off of what you personally heard while being kept prisoner aboard the Soulless Command Ship, the Wingless Angel, is that correct?" I cleared my throat, stepping up to the microphone.

"That is correct, sir." There were murmurs among the crowd as the Councilor put up their hand, silencing the room again.

"We have read your reports on your request. Unless there is anything further you can add, I unfortunately do not find reasonable evidence to lend an army to your cause." He said. The Furin nodded.

"We do not doubt what you heard aboard the Wingless Angel, we must emphasize. However, the Furins are also choosing to withhold without further evidence. There are simply too many unknowns. This could be bait to focus your attention elsewhere, lure us away as they attack our planets and colonies." My heart dropped as I looked to the other councilors. The Olari spoke next.

"The Olari differ in opinion." He said, looking down at me. "We have decided to offer our army, so long as other races are persuaded to join you. Having consulted with our arcane advisors, they have informed us that great disturbances have been made in the World Spirit. If what you say rings true, its effect would be scarily similar to what they are describing." The councilor sat back. "However, we cannot leave our homeland undefended without knowing that our efforts will not be for naught. If you have anything to convince the rest of this council to join, we would be happy to be by your side." Okay, so that's one army. It wouldn't be enough, but it was a start... if we could get more on board. The Terran leaned forward next.

"We heed our Olari brethren's advice," they began. "however, Terra Nova lies on the border between Federation and Hunter Territory. This assault could easily be seen as an attack on the Hunter Collective. It's well known that the Collective's very heart rests near the Surillian system. We cannot afford to risk a war against the Hunters *as well* as the Soulless. Terra Nova would be devastated on both sides if that happens. If you can give us reassurance that this can be avoided, we would be happy to join you as well." Olivia looked to me as if to ask permission to speak. I nodded, allowing her to step forward. She stood up by the podium, adjusting the microphone down to her.

"I have a history with the Athena's Eclipse and the Hunter's Collective, and many connections within. I can reach out and ensure that the leaders of the Collective understand the situation. I will inform you on the resolution of these conversations once they happen." She said. The Terran leader nodded, thinking.

"I understand. If you give us that reassurance we need, we will join you." The Terran Councilor looked last to the Dervan man at the opposite end.

"I, unfortunately, agree with the Xenovans and Furins. The Soulless are at our doorstep consistently. Leaving ourselves open to an assault when we have so little information is not something that I can reasonably risk. Unless you can provide us with something more, we will have to turn down your request." I sighed, frustrated, looking to Maurel. We didn't have anything else yet, and she could see that. She stepped forward, turning the microphone up to her.

"Thank you Councilors. We appreciate your insights into our situation. In light of your concerns, we would like to request a recess as we regather our information." Again, there were murmurs among the crowds around us. The Council didn't seem too pleased with us, yet the Xenovan Councilor raised their hand, settling the room down.

"Very well. We will have a brief recess. Everyone may exit the room, and we will return in two hours for you to make a case for your side." He waited for any objections. When none arose, he nodded. "Adjourned."

We stepped back outside into the hallway. I honestly should have expected that kind of response. They were correct. We didn't have any other proof than my word. I ran my hand up through my hair as I looked out the windows at the exterior of the space station.

"So what's the plan?" Maurel asked. "That couldn't have been all you had." I wracked my brain, thinking.

"It was." I said, pacing back and forth. "Well, we know we can at least get two of them on our side. Olivia, head back to the Sparrow. See if you can't get a written statement from the Collective on getting us some diplomatic protection while we're out there. We don't want any incidents." She nodded.

"Got it. Do you have a plan for the others?" She asked. I stared intently into the ground, trying to think of something, anything.

"Come on, you have to have something." Maurel said. "You always have backups upon backups when it comes to plans." She thought along with me. "Gods, if only we could show them the Soulless moving there." I looked up at her.

"Gods… yeah. Yeah, I think we might be able to do just that." I said. "I've got a call to make myself. Olivia, do your thing. Maurel uh…" She put up a hand.

"I'll uh, just wait. I trust you'll get what you need." I nodded.

"Right. Reconvene here when the recess comes to a close."

Our two hours came to an end much faster than we'd initially anticipated. It felt like barely minutes had passed since we'd left the Summit. Without any idea of what we were walking into, we were wholly unprepared for what we'd been asked and challenged with. I now walked, a data pad in tow as I strode back to the Summit. Olivia and Maurel were both waiting. Maurel tapped her foot impatiently as she looked up at me.

"About time." She said. "They were getting impatient."

"Well, it's a good thing I'm here then." I said.

"I really hope you have something for them." She replied, turning back to the doors.

"I do, don't worry. Olivia, do you have what you need?" I asked.

"I do. We'll have the Terrans at our backs for sure." She said.

"Good. We need all the help we can get." The three of us pushed open the doors again, the noises of the crowd around us turning into an uproar as we approached the podium at the center of the room. The Councilors looked down upon us still, waiting patiently. Both Olivia and I set down a datapad upon the podium as we awaited for them to speak. The Xenovan raised his hand, the room silencing.

"The recess has concluded. This War Summit is now back in session." He craned his head down at me. "William Ortell, do you have any additional evidence or information to inform us of?" He asked.

"I do." I said. "If I may invite someone to speak with us remotely?" I asked. The Xenovan gestured with his hand for me to continue. I slid my finger on the datapad, bringing up a call with the person I'd been in contact with. A projection of Cardenian Hal flickered above the pad. I swiped it forward, bringing it up to size. Hal put a hand to his chest, bowing to the council courteously.

"Introduce your guest." The Xenovan Ordered.

"This is Cardenian Hal. Head Quartermaster and Lead Informations Specialist of the Celestials." Hal nodded as I introduced him, stepping forward.

"My job is to track the movements of fleets and their actions across the galaxy. This includes the Federation, Republic, Celestial, Soulless and Hunter fleets." He leaned forward, sweeping out a series of galaxy maps that filled the room. "Recently, around the same time as William's reports, a single command ship returned to the Celestial Plains." One purple dot moved inward toward the center of the Milky Way. "Not long after, large fleets of Soulless ships began exiting the Celestial Plains, heading for the Hunter's Collective."

"So? they could be preparing for a trap." The Xenovan said.

"Which is what my initial thoughts were as well," he said, "but then they began to pull out from major battlegrounds across the Galaxy. Monteria, Furelle, and the Actillion Colonies, all heading for the same place. This was before the War Summit was announced publicly. We can only speculate they want desperately to defend something there." Olivia stepped forward beside me.

"If I may?" she asked. Hal nodded to her, moving aside. "Loh Amidani, leader of the Athena's Eclipse in the Hunter's Collective, corroborated on these details when we contacted her during the recess. The Surillian System is very close to where they keep their base of operations. She's expressed concerns of the Soulless activity there." She swiped something up, a ping coming from the Councilors' data pads. "A written and signed letter granting us immunity in their systems, as well as a pledge to assist us if we choose to attack." The Terran looked over to the Olari, both of them nodding with each other. The Terran looked up at us.

"We'll take this new information and join you." She said.

"And with the Terran and Hunter assistance, we grant you our fleets as well." The Olari said. The Dervan scratched their chin.

"Hmm… This is evidence enough that I can believe your claims to have merit. However, we still cannot offer much of our fleet, as the war on Furelle holds our attention." He glanced up at us. "This said, I will see what I can do in rallying the Bandit Clans to assist." I nodded. It was something, at least. The Furin spoke next.

"We share similar sentiments to our Dervan brethren. There is a lot to be said and done in retaking Furelle, especially while the Soulless, as you have said, have pulled away. However, we can spare a few fleets to help you push against them in the Surillian system." The Furin looked to the Dervan. "It may also buy us some more time if we keep them occupied there."

"Agreed." The Dervan said. "You'll have the fleets you need." I sighed, relieved, and looked to the Xenovan. They still seemed weary. They sat back in their chair and intertwined their fingers over their chest.

"Do you have a plan of attack, then? What reassurances can we be offered that we will not be heading into a deathtrap?" He asked. I was caught in my words. I didn't really… have a plan to attack. There was a flap from behind me and a gasp as someone flew in down from the rafters behind us. Tara swooped in, dropping Jewls and Rex behind us before fluttering down beside me. "What is this? Who are these-" Tara saluted the Xenovan.

"Forgive us. Tara Verikov of the Blue Sparrow." She said, stepping forward. "Since I've joined, I've been studying the Soulless' Tactics."

"And I have firsthand experience with how they like to attack and defend their positions." Jewls was beside her. "Jewls Reynar of the Blue Sparrow."

"Jewls?" The Furin Councilor asked. "I know you. You've been on Furelle for the past few months coordinating our troops' movements." She nodded. "With her knowledge we were able to push the Soulless back to Surillia Coast from the Midland." The Xenovan Councilor hummed. Rex finally moved forward as well.

"I too have experience in dealing with Soulless inflicted wounds. They require special treatment. I would be happy to work with your ship wide practitioners to train them in these types of injuries." The Xenovan nodded cautiously.

"Despite the unorthodox interruptions, I have… no further objections." He turned his head to Tara and Jewls. "When a ground plan is formulated, forward it to us so we may know your movements. Elsewise…" he sighed, "our fleets are yours." There was a cheer among the crowds, as we could only sigh in relief. We had the backup we needed. I straightened myself out as cameras flashed behind me, looking to everyone.

"Maurel, will you be joining us?" I asked. She almost looked surprised.

"Of *course* I'm joining you. You say the word and I'll be there to help." I smiled, patting her shoulder, before turning my attention to the rest of my crew standing there.

"Alright, to the Sparrow everyone. Make preparations to leave immediately. We're setting a course for the Surillian System." They saluted before running off down the hall. Maurel stayed behind, looking me up and down one more time.

"I still worry about you," she said, "but… you're right. It suits you." She sighed as she turned, beginning to walk out the door.

"Well, if this is the weapon we're looking for, maybe you won't have to worry for much longer."

"Optimistic as always." She said. "I'm glad at least that's still the same." The doors shut behind us. I smiled, nudging her shoulder. She nudged me back as we walked. I could only hope for a quick conclusion to this war.

Deep Space: The Blue Sparrow

Galactic Date 00:09:051 5028

I sat in the Galley alone. Everyone else was off on duty, either helping the other fleets with preparations and planning, or running the ship. I felt like I'd barely sat down at all over the past few days since the summit. Between preparing plans for the battle, to training to get my magic up, there was little time to rest. Lux had mixed me a nice drink before heading off for his watch, and now I sat there, slowly swirling the glass he'd made it in, listening to the ice clink against the sides. I heard a set of footsteps approaching me, but didn't look up. Someone sat across from me, leaning on the blue plastic of the table.

"You know, I don't think it's going to get any more mixed." Olivia said. I finally looked up, shrugging.

"I suppose not." I said, taking a sip. The drink was sickeningly sweet. I grimaced a bit. She saw the face I made, holding her hand out for me to slide it to her. I shifted my wrist, the glass skidding across the table into her palm. She took a sip and grimaced as well.

"Fuck. For such a good cook that kid *cannot* mix a drink." She slid the drink back to me. "How you holding up?" She asked.

"Nervous." I said. "We're running headfirst into the biggest battle I've seen." Olivia pursed her lips, looking up at me.

"I get that." She said. "It's not going to be easy, I'll be fully honest with you... but you're a good leader. You have a good crew and a lot of people who are here for you." She stared down into the table. "It's a good thing you're here, truly. You could honestly use the rest."

"Yeah, it's been a tiring week." I said. "Hell, it's been a tiring month."

"I can imagine!" She said, leaning forward. "Swept from your home into a grand adventure across the galaxy with your best friend and a-" she put a hand over her chest dramatically, "dashing captain to usher you along on your journey to taking charge of the ship. Saving the galaxy in its time of greatest need!" She leaned back, throwing a hand up over her forehead, turning up the theatrics. "Oh *swoon*!" She said. I laughed as she melted backward over the table. She opened her eyes, looking up at me. I lifted her back up into her seat, sitting her down.

"Of course, they would be *swooning* for his former captain more than him, dashing as she is." I teased. She smirked.

"Oh well, of course!" She said with a laugh. "Who *wouldn't* fall for this woman?" She posed. I smiled, leaning forward over the table.

"It's good seeing you like this," I said.

"Like what?"

"Loose, carefree. You've been so stuck in your head since I came onboard. It's good to see you finally able to relax." She chuckled, swiping the drink from me.

"I suppose so. It's... nice not having that pressure on my shoulders anymore... *not* that I meant to just dump it on you-" I cut her off.

"I accepted the position, didn't I? I'm happy to be where I am, and I'm happy you are where you are." She nodded, leaning forward, taking a sip. She grimaced again. "I don't know what you expecte-"

"Shup-up-up!" She put up a finger, taking another grimacing sip. "I'm hoping that the more I drink, the better it'll taste."

"Somehow, I don't think that that's how it works." I said.

"Well, how would *you* know?" She was about to take another sip when I took the drink, sliding it back toward me.

"Alright, no more." She pouted at me, but let me keep the drink. I sighed, tapping my fingers against the table. Olivia watched my fingers tip and tap against the plastic, creating a soft drum on the table.

"Any luck with Isngr?" She asked.

"Not yet." I said. "I'm not sure what I'm going to do if I can't summon it before we face Koratha." I said. "I was barely able to take her on *with* its power. Without it, I've just felt..."

"Weak?" she asked.

"Yeah." I said, going quiet. Olivia waited for me to talk, but when I stayed quiet, she shifted.

"There's... something else, isn't there?" I looked up from where I stared.

"Hmm?"

"Something else you're not mentioning. I can see there's more troubling you than just Isngr." I sighed, clenching a fist on the table.

"It's… Koratha." I said. "When I was on the Wingless Angel, she and I talked. She was actually… calm for a while." I looked into Olivia's eyes. "She's… not Soulless. Not truly. She joined them willingly, out of a want for vengeance." Olivia's lips stretched as she looked at me, letting me continue to speak. "When we fought on the Wingless Angel, I had a chance to end things then and there but… I couldn't. I looked at her and saw someone like who I was. Someone who, despite everything, deserved better than what she got."

"Tara mentioned Koratha had been a slave." She said. She was quiet a moment as we both sat, thinking intently about the situation. "Do you wish for her death?"

"Not particularly as odd as it sounds." I said. Olivia's gaze was soft as she stood up, moving to my side at the table.

"Then don't kill her." She said. She put her hand over mine, squeezing it. "You have an incredible heart in you. You're my captain now, and I believe that your judgement is far more sound than any I could make."

"Well, what *do* you think?" I asked.

"Does it matter? It's been clear from the moment you two met that this battle was between the two of you. Follow true to your heart. Don't taint that judgement of yours. You said yourself. She was driven by vengeance and anger. If you give into those same emotions, you could be just like her. Be the better person." She nodded up at me. "You got that?" I nodded.

"I… I do." As we sat there, I was silent. She let my hand go, looking out at the walls.

"Can I come with you?" She asked.

"To the planet?" I asked back.

"Yes." She said. "You'll need a team to have your back. As you are, you won't be able to take on Koratha on your own." I nodded.

"You're right." I said. I thought back to the words of the chieftain on Rishik. Even if I had Isngr, getting to Koratha alone would wear me out, and I wasn't even sure of what her full strength looked like. I sighed. "Alright. You can come with me. I'll bring you and Tara with me." She nodded.

"I see. Is there any particular reason you chose her?"

"Yeah." I said. "I've made a few promises to her that I plan on keeping."

"You two are close." She said. "You've known each other… how long again?" I thought back.

"Nearly a year now, I think." I said. "It's certainly had its ups and downs, but I've always been sure she had my back." Olivia gave me a knowing smile.

"You have feelings for her?" She asked.

"I-wha," I stuttered. Olivia chuckled, leaning in closer.

"Oh, touched a nerve there?" She asked.

"I, uh, don't think of her like that." I said. "Listen, she's one of my closest friends, sure, but we've always kept things between us professional." Olivia smiled as she looked up at me.

"I see. Well, you two make a good team." She said. "Saw it from the day I met you. Try to keep her close." I nodded, cupping my hands together. I'd never really thought of Tara in that way before. Sure, she was my best friend, but she didn't see me as anything more and neither did I… right? Oh, gods, this was *not* the time to be putting ideas in my head. "Try not to break yourself thinking there, Ortell." She nudged me. "Just, for once, let things flow." She took another sip of the drink, her face contorting as she pushed it back. "Alright, I suppose you were right about this thing." I gave her a weak smile as I nudged her back, sliding the glass away from us with a finger.

The two of us sat in the galley for hours, just talking and conversing over our times together. It felt nice to have a moment with just the two of us like this again. A moment where we could just laugh and talk, and where we weren't consoling each other. By the time it was time for watch, the drink Lux had made was sucked down. It… never tasted good. She left to rest, as I headed up to the helm to oversee the work done. As I leaned against the rail, I felt a tap at my shoulder, seeing Tara there.

"Hey. Cap-erm… Olivia mentioned you wanted to bring me with you to the field when we get to the planet."

"Ah, she already told you, huh?" I asked. Tara smiled.

"Thank you," she said, "and don't you dare make any more dumb self-sacrificing choices while we're there or I'll personally find you and drag you back here myself this time." I put my hands up as I backed into the railing.

"I will try my best to stay in one piece." She put her arms around me.

"Good." She felt warm, pressing her face into the collar of my shoulder. She cleared her throat, taking a step back to look at me. "Started this together, and ending it together. Let's show these Soulless what we're made of."

Surillian System: The Battle for Nashu

Galactic Date 00:09:066 5028

The Sparrow sped through the corridors of warp space. Its blue and purple walls flashed as they passed by us at lightning speed. Flanking us were the hundreds of ships from all races across the Federation. It was time. We were moments away from dropping into the battlefield. The air around us was filled with a righteous energy as I stood, my arms folded behind my back, at the podium of the helm. Olivia stood nearby as everyone sat ready at their stations. My gaze was forward, fierce as I looked toward the end of the tunnel ahead of us. The fleets were ready. They had to be. Only a few moments more. Tara looked up at me from her station.

"Captain. Dropping warp in 10." I nodded as she began to count down the seconds. Ten, nine, eight. My heart pounded as I gripped the rail, waiting for that light to envelop us. Seven, six, five. I wanted to close my eyes, to shut it out, but I kept my sight forward. Four, three, two. I braced myself as finally she hit one.

The Sparrow slammed to a stop, followed in quick succession by the sounds of the rest of the fleet halting behind it. The blue light of Surillia, a star sharing a name with my home, glowed. I looked to its light in the distance. Surillia, the Furin word for life. Odd that a weapon would be found in a place like this.

Ahead of us, a wall of black and purple clouded the stars as the Soulless surrounded the planet of Nashu. We had our target. I turned to Natasha, beginning to bark orders.

"Natasha, open fleet-wide channels. Gatha, activate cloaking. Lux, evasive maneuvers, Tara, get us a route through their line." There was a unanimous 'Aye' from them as they spun to work. Lux shoved the throttles forward as the Soulless opened fire on the fleet. The channels opened as we ducked and dodged through the lines of fire, a few hits grazing our shields, but the fleet was keeping much of their attention.

"Blue Sparrow." The Olari Councilor called in. "We have scans of the planet, sending them to you now."

"We'll keep you covered while you approach." The Furin said. "Gods speed to you." More and more ships dropped in from warp. The Terrans, the Xenovans. With each ship added to the fray, it became more and more difficult to weave between the fire of either side. I looked to Tara as her console pinged.

"Just got the data from the Olari fleet. Plotting a course through their lines now." She looked up at me. "It looks like most of their forces are focused on a single temple. That's probably our target." The ship rocked as we were hit with cannon fire from a passing fighter. Lux swore.

"Try to hurry it up if possible! We're caught between both sides right now. This isn't looking good for us!" He gritted his teeth, working furiously at the Sparrow's controls. Gatha was quick to redirect some of our shields.

"Try to get us out of the Soulless' line of fire!" She called to Lux. "With our cloaking up, we're sucking a lot of power with these hits!" Lux circled back around as Tara worked on a navigation solution to get us to the ground. A series of carriers disengaged in front of us. Arneli was quick to aim, sending a barrage of shots toward them. The carriers erupted in flame as we sped through the fire, the ship creaking as bits of metal bounced off its hull. I grunted as we moved between the Soulless ships, inching closer to the planet by the second.

"Any time, Tara!" I said.

"Just give me a sec! It isn't exactly easy when we're moving so much!" She shouted back over the roar of the engines and explosions around us. On either side, ships were cracked into pieces, cannon fire shredding and sheering off sections of ships. Pieces of steel floated through the empty space between the two fleets as each ship's shields struggled to hold the air within their hulls, flickering as they fired back. Tara slid her hand over, throwing a holographic screen to Lux. "Got it! There's your solution!" Lux nodded, plotting it in. He jerked the controls, the Sparrow arching through the air, dodging and weaving between the Soulless fleet. We narrowly avoided fighters and boarding ships as they rushed toward the Federation fleets.

We made it past the Soulless barricade, the planet Nashu awaiting us. Lux pushed us forward, beginning to tip us toward the clouded skies below us. I squinted, seeing something faint coming from the planet's surface.

"What the hell is-" A bright light erupted from the planet's surface, streaking its way into the sky toward us.

Lux was quick to bring the Sparrow out of danger in the nick of time. A brilliant purple and black beam shot out from the planet's surface. It fired just under our wing, connecting with Nashu's moon far, far behind us. A shockwave sent our ship reeling. We gripped on for dear life as we spun off our trajectory. For a brief moment, the lights and power flickered out before slowly coming back online. I breathed heavily, looking out into the battlefield. We'd slowed, peering out to the ships behind us. It seemed both sides had a momentary loss of power as this beam broke a line between the two. One by one, the ships regained power, beginning to fire.

"What the hells was that?" Gatha asked.

"Could that have been the weapon?" Maurel asked, walking up beside me. "If there was something powerful enough to kill a god, that looks like it'd be it." Natasha shook her head.

"I don't know about that, but I'm picking up some odd readings from the scanners." She said, looking back at us.

"Go ahead. What are you seeing?"

"It looks like, whatever that thing is, it's dampening the power output of the Federation fleets, and nearly doubling the power capacity of the Soulless!" I looked from her back out to the battle. Oh gods.

The Federation was getting torn to shreds. They were managing to hold the Soulless at bay, but their weapons were now barely making a dent against the Soulless' shields. I nodded slowly, looking to the crew.

"I don't know what that *thing* is. If it's our weapon or something else deployed by the Soulless, but that doesn't matter. We can be almost certain that that's where we find Koratha." I looked at Sterling and Tara. "Our current priority is to find whatever it is and shut it off."

"Or reverse it." Jewls said. "If you can turn its power against the Soulless, that'd be even better." I nodded.

"Agreed. Lux, get us to the ground. Nearest landing zone to whatever's generating that beam!"

"On it, Captain!" He said, pulling us around, and down toward the planet.

Tints of flame began to spark around the edge of the Sparrow's hull as we broke in through the atmosphere. Lux's face contorted. He dragged the throttle back, tweaking and swiftly shifting through one set of controls after the other. The Sparrow flashed down into the lower atmosphere, passing through thick black storm clouds.

Lightning cracked, striking trees and lightning rods around us, fires quickly smothered by the torrents of rain pouring from the storms brewing above us. Ahead of us, in the distance, a Faraxian temple laid, awoken, flowing with shadowy power. It looked the same as the magic Koratha had used against me. I was certain that that was where I'd find her.

Lux set us down on a clear patch of ground. The Sparrow rocked briefly before settling. Rain pelted the edges of the hull with a chorus of small thuds.

"Alright," Gatha started, "engines are powered down. Keeping the core online and cloaking active in case you need our support out there." I nodded.

"Good idea. We very well might." I said. Natasha pulled up on her screen, leaning her chair back to look up at me.

"Got confirmation from the other Celestial groups. They've made it to the ground and are preparing to hit them from all sides. Just waiting on us." I nodded, looking out over the crew.

"Alright, here's the deal. It's going to be just like Tanahen, only a hell of a lot more dangerous. We'll be splitting into three groups. Ship crew is going to be Rex, Iraka, Gatha, Lux and Arneli." I looked to Arneli as I said her name. "I need you here on Gunnery. If we need air support, you provide it, got it?" She saluted me from her chair.

"Aye, Sir."

"Good."

"What about me?" Natasha asked.

"You fought the Soulless when they first broke free, didn't you?" I asked. She slowly nodded. "You good with a gun, then?" She sighed.

"It's been… a long time, but you get me a hill and something with range and I can help." She said.

"Then you'll be on the first ground team. It'll be led by Jewls. Maurel, Iravek, you're with them." Maurel tilted her head.

"Not with you?" She asked.

"I need some of my most skilled people there. The first ground team is going to be working with the other Celestial crews to draw the majority of the Soulless away so that my team, Olivia and Tara, can slip past." They nodded to me. "We'll likely still encounter resistance along the way, but we should be able to manage. Us three will get into the temple and shut off the weapon. Any objections?" There was nothing said in response. As I looked over everyone's faces, they only seemed ready for what was ahead. "I trust everyone here to come back in one piece. Hold back the Soulless, trust your fellow Celestials, and we'll all come out of this alive. Let's move out!"

We took off down the halls of the ship, gearing ourselves up in the hangar. I strapped on a shield, hearing it spin to life at my waist, grabbing a pistol from the weapons locker. Without Isngr still, I'd be a sitting duck most of the time, and I didn't want to waste too much magic just getting to the temple. It would have to do. Olivia tossed a rubbery poncho to me as I inspected the weapon.

"Do you even know how to use that thing?" She asked as I slid a holster onto my belt. I made sure the dagger Iravek gave me was secure at my waist as well, before looking at her.

"I mean, it can't be hard, right? Just point and shoot, just like magic." Her face contorted as she reached up.

"That's the safety. At least know that you need it turned *off* to shoot." I looked at the switch she was pointing at, flipping it off and on.

"Huh. Yeah, I guess that's good to know." Tara walked past me, slipping a poncho on over her clothes.

"Oh, moving up to guns now?" She asked, beginning to outfit herself with several weapons. I gave her a look. "I suppose it's fair, given the circumstances." She inspected a rifle before slinging it over her shoulder. I slipped my poncho on, looking out into the rain.

"Can't be taking any chances out there." I said. Olivia took a deep breath as she pulled out a pistol and a shotgun, feeling the heft of them in her hands.

"Been a while." She said. "I was admittedly a little rusty back on Tanahen, but I think I've gotten the hang of it."

"Just be careful, both of you." I said. "I'm not about to lose anyone on my watch." With everything clipped into place, I straightened myself back out, looking outside once more. "We all ready?" I asked.

"Good here." Tara said.

"My gear's set." Olivia replied. I gave them both a nod, gesturing for us to move out. I felt a hand on my shoulder, seeing Jewls with her crew.

"Hey." She said. "You keep yourself alive too." I looked from her to Maurel and the others behind her. They gave nods, sharing in her sentiments as they grabbed their gear. I gave her a brief, affirming nod.

"Don't worry. I'll be doing my best." I said. She gave me a firm slap on the shoulder, gesturing for me to head out. I ushered Tara and Olivia forward as we stepped off the Sparrow. Mud squished and squelched under our boots. We left deep impressions with each step we took forward. The wind roared and bellowed around us as the torrents of rain crashed into the ground. We had to shout just to be heard over the sounds of the storm.

"I say we try to stay close together in the trees!" Tara said, squinting.

"I think that may be our best bet. We'll get as close as we can and fight our way in! Olivia, what say you?" She put a hand above her eyes like a visor.

"I agree! It'll give Jewls and her team time to move into position so that we can strike." She gave me a thumbs up. "You lead, I'll follow!" I nodded, beginning to trudge forward through the mud. Gods, when was the last time I'd even seen or felt mud? I closed my eyes as I pushed forward, beginning to push branches out of my way. I think it had to have been Furelle. The day I'd left. It had rained the night before, and the streets were still wet. It seemed only fitting I'd be fighting Soulless on a day like this.

Thunder crashed through the air as blinding lights filled the sky. The sounds of fighting far in the distance had become apparent. Natasha must have informed them that we'd begun to move. I picked up my pace, Tara and Olivia keeping up with me as we marched forward over the uneven terrain. I could see my breath in front of me as icy cold water dribbled down from the leaves above us, soaking our hair and rolling off our ponchos. We pushed aside the last of the branches, coming to a stop on a short hill. I put up a hand for us to stop, the three of us kneeling down.

Half a mile of a ruined city looked to separate us from the main temple at its center. Little was left of the houses that once likely stood tall and proud here. That beam from the temple cast an eerie purple glow across the open pathways that led to its center. Tara tapped my shoulder, handing me a set of binoculars, pointing out to our left. I put the binoculars up, peering out into the distance. It looked like the Celestial crews were certainly helping. A lot of the Soulless forces were being drawn to the far side of the camp. I turned, looking out to the temple, nearly recoiling.

Koratha stood at the edge of the doorway, her hands tucked behind her back as she stared directly toward us. Yeah, she definitely knew we were here. She glanced down. I followed her line of sight, seeing lines of Soulless soldiers and beasts making rounds in the direction we were heading. It wasn't enough to be concerned, but it felt more like she was baiting us in to her. I handed Tara her binoculars back, standing up again.

"How's our way in look?" Olivia asked.

"We've got our work cut out for us," I said, "but I'm confident. If we keep to cover, we should be able to make our way in without much issue." I drew my pistol, beginning to slide down the side of the hill. "We take it slow, and we hit them hard." My boots hit the ground by the edge of the buildings. We ducked behind the walls, feeling them crumble at our backs as we looked out into the muddy streets.

I looked up into the sky, seeing flashes of blue and purple from the heavens as the fleets fired on each other. We had to be quick if we didn't want more casualties. I nodded to the other two, beginning to rush forward. A small platoon of soldiers and beasts guarded the first ring of the city streets. I think I'd seen three rings on our way in. We'd have to break past each line to get in. The soldiers shouted, raising their weapons toward us. I braced with my shoulder as the first shots hit our shields, then raised my pistol, beginning to fire.

I hit a Stalker first, bursting it as I slid through the mud into cover. Tara ducked beside me, firing into the crowd. Her rifle shredded through the shields of one man, bringing them down as Olivia weaved through the gunfire. She ducked as one man brought out a blade, swiping her claws through his throat before turning, blasting a hole through another soldier. A blinding blur darted across the pathways as more of the beasts hopped from wall to wall. I ducked back as a set of claws grabbed at me. In the brief moment the Stalker stopped, a single *bang* rang across the clearing. A sniper bolt shredded through its body, bursting it. Our coms crackled to life.

"I've got you covered up here!" Natasha called as we heard her vent the heat from her rifle. "Keep moving forward before- shit!" We heard the sounds of faint engines through the sky. Purple streaks soared under the clouds as Soulless fighters joined the fray, beginning to lay down fire across the battlefield. A set of bolts hit where Natasha had been, sending up a blast of black and orange as smoke rose in its place. My heart dropped for a moment, until I was hit with a sense of relief, my coms crackling on once more.

"I'm alright," she called, "but I'm not going to be getting any clear shots with those things aiming for us!" I tapped my earpiece.

"Alright, Sparrow Team, you're up! Nat and the rest of the Celestials are in desperate need of air support. Let's show them our teeth!" A low roar echoed through the air as the Sparrow uncloaked, rising into the sky like the shadow of a predator rising from the grass. It blasted forward, sending shockwaves through the air as it fired off volley after volley toward the fighters. I looked to Nat's position. "That should keep them occupied for a while!"

"Sound's good, Cap!" I could make out the faint glint of her scope as she settled back in. Olivia looked at the two of us, anxious.

"That last fight is sure to draw more of the Soulless to us." She said. "We need to be moving." I nodded, ushering us forward across the battlefield. Overhead, the fighters struggled to keep up with the Sparrow as it effortlessly zigged and zagged through the skies. Still, with the power of the beam, the constant fire from the Sparrow did little, it seemed, to deter them. We had to keep pushing.

Tara pulled me out of the way, pressing me to the wall as a bolt of magic passed by me. I regained my balance, seeing a faint shape dart behind cover. I ducked around, my gun drawn, only to be met with the barrel of another team of soldiers. Their weapons lit up, shredding through my shields before I could pull back. I took a hit to my arm, wincing in pain as I pressed myself against the stone. Tara and Olivia quickly moved ahead of me, flanking the soldiers as I focused healing magic into my wound, taking deep breaths as I felt it seal. As soon as I saw the skin reconnect, I grabbed my pistol, turning the corner, only to find the entire team laid out, the two's guns smoking. They looked back at me with nods. I stood up fully, looking out to the temple.

"William." Natasha called in. "Looks like you've got two small armies heading your way. Broke off from the main group. I've been whittling them down, but I'm not sure how long I can manage to keep myself moving and hidden here."

"Got it." I said. "We'll get to the temple as fast as we can. Sparrow, see if you can't block their route somehow. Buy us time to get in there and get this thing shut off!"

"On it Captain!" Lux responded. We broke off in a sprint down the alleyways as the Sparrow dipped and turned. We were struck with a gust of wind that plastered us to the walls as the Sparrow dove in close. A round of blasts echoed off into the distance, followed by the sounds of crashing stone and pillars.

"That did it!" Nat called. "They're going to have to spend a lot of time finding a way around that!"

"Good work, Sparrow crew! Keep up with those fighters, and do what you can to support the other crews." I looked up, seeing even more Celestial ships in the air now, all in a swirling dance to the death with the Soulless pilots. "Nat, keep them covered as best you can and give call-outs. Use your best judgement. You've got eyes on the whole field from where you're at."

"Will do." She said. "Looks like your path is clear from there on out. Get on in there and give her an ass kicking, won't you?"

"I can definitely do that!" I said, motioning for us to move forward. The three of us tucked our weapons away, running through the rest of the ruined city. As war waged in the skies and in the ruins around us, we clambered up the rain slicked steps toward the temple. We burst through the entrance, our weapons drawn.

In the center of the room, Koratha stood, her hand rested lightly on a console. The beam that fired heavenward erupted with deep groans and hums as she turned back to look at us. There was a vitriol as she looked at me. She turned her view from me, looking over the walls.

"Your weapon isn't here." She said. "They built this in its stead; however," she began, "the weapon we're looking for… everything we could ever want to know is written on these walls."

"It isn't too late for you to stop this." I said. She laughed and shook her head, turning back to me.

"You really don't get it, do you, William?" she asked. "Why would you leave me alive on the Wingless Angel? You had me right where you wanted me. You could have finished it, lived like a hero to the people… yet here we both are." Tara glanced between the two of us. Koratha looked to her next. "You, I've seen you a few times yourself. Don't think I haven't caught a look at that mark on your back, too." Tara squared up.

"And here *I* am." She said.

"You still have your wings." Koratha said. "Come back when they've been docked and see where you are, then." Her eyes narrowed, looking between us all. "The short of it is that only one of us is leaving alive. You, or me."

"Why?!" I yelled. "Why insist on this *vendetta* of yours? Why make the choice that all life has to die? To be wiped out? You could have done something good and turned the world into a better place so people *wouldn't* have to suffer like you!"

"Because it was easier!" She screamed, drawing her blade, pointing it toward me. "Because it's all I've known! Everything else was *taken from me*!" With that, she lashed out at us, swinging her rapier with wild abandon. We split as a slash of purple magic cut through the air at us. I pulled up a barrier as she rushed in close, slamming her body against the thin wall. "Because I *won't* let anyone else take anything from me ever again!" I shoved her back. She flipped through the air, cutting an X with her blade, sending it flying it at me. I dodged to the side as it hit the ground.

"You don't *have* to lose anything!" I shouted back. She dodged and weaved through Sterling and Tara's attacks like a blur as she shifted across the ground. Tara pulled herself just far enough back to avoid Koratha's swipes as Olivia rushed in behind, firing her shotgun. Koratha's shields absorbed the attack. I sprinted to them, gripping Koratha's wrist, disengaging her from Tara. "You could *leave.* You don't have to live with that rage!" she growled, twisting my arm, raising her foot. Her boot collided with my face, sending me backwards into Tara. The two of us tumbled over each other as I rolled to my feet. Koratha was quickly upon us, dragging the tip of her blade over the ground, creating sparks as it struck the stone floors. I halted her with another barrier. As we struggled against each other, I could see the struggle and pain in her eyes. Even now, she seemed to be overexerting herself. Yet, how? I looked to the console. That magic… it was her's, wasn't it? So all this time…

"Finally getting it, aren't you?" She asked. She drew herself back, throwing her magic fueled body into my barrier. I winced as I felt it shatter under her strength. I stumbled back, but was helped to my feet by Olivia.

"Koratha, if you keep going, you'll rip yourself apart!"

"Already have been! If I have to die to make sure you don't get out alive, then I *will*!" Olivia gritted her teeth, drawing her pistol.

"This isn't good, William. Even now we're barely touching her."

"Then… show no quarter." I said regretfully. We wouldn't win by pulling punches. She grinned as I flicked my fingers forward, beginning to throw out volleys of bolts. Koratha brought her own barrier up, taking the hit with ease as Olivia blindsided her. One blast to one side. She winced as her shields barely held on, only to be hit from the opposite side by Tara. Koratha tumbled across the floor, struggling to her feet. She zipped forward toward Olivia. She attempted to block the quick swipe of Koratha's blade with her shotgun, but it sliced clean through it. Koratha drew her blade back as Olivia stumbled off balance, but felt a pair of claws dug into her back as Tara struck again.

She tossed Tara off of her, throwing her to the side as I swung wisps of magic. One to catch Tara, and another striking Koratha, slamming her into the console. She winced as she was struck, but pushed herself back to her feet, swinging her arm behind her. A banshee-like shriek echoed through the temple as a wave of black erupted from her, knocking us to our backs, soaking into our bodies. I felt like I could barely move as she weakly grabbed her rapier, beginning to walk toward me. She wiped blue tinted blood from her lip as she approached. I could feel myself pinned in place by whatever spell she'd cast, and despite my struggle, I couldn't break free.

She walked to me, standing a few feet back, flicking her wrist to lift me into the air, binding my arms to my sides. I could see her heaving for breath, having used up so much of her energy already. She pulled her blade back, glaring into my eyes.

"Finally…" she muttered. I closed my eyes as she shoved the blade forward, waiting for an impact. Instead, I heard a gut wrenching lurch as the blade hit another body. I opened my eyes, seeing horror. Olivia had jumped between us, using her body as a barrier, now impaled on Koratha's bloodied blade. We both stood there in shock, Koratha taking a step back as she withdrew her blade, her breath shaking as I dropped to the floor. Olivia stumbled to turn to look at me, as I could only watch in shock. Dark magics had been pumped into her, spreading through the hole in her chest as she tumbled onto me.

"Olivia!" I cried as she laid in my arms, looking up at me with a motherly love. She smiled as she gasped through the pain.

"Sorry, Ortell." She said. "Couldn't let you go down just yet."

"Come on, you have to-" She stopped me, reaching up to adjust my collar. She shook her head as black veins spread across her body, patting my cheek.

"Don't let her win, you got that? You're better than her… remember what you said to me…" She was slipping. I tried to move my hand to heal her, but she pushed it away. "You know you'd die if you tried…" I shook as her hand limply fell against her chest. "Sorry I couldn't help more…" she said, as her head fell lifelessly limp. A pain in my chest, and rage building in my throat, I set down Olivia's lifeless body, pursing my lips, closing my eyes.

"You did so much more than enough…" I whispered, taking in a deep, shaking, anger filled breath. My eyes snapped open as I glared at Koratha. She watched me with the same rage I now felt. I took a step over Olivia's body, feeling a static shiver running up my spine, into the hairs on my neck and arm as I held my hand out to my side. There was a bright, brilliant flash of light.

Isngr found itself into my hands again, called to me once more. At once, I felt its power fill my body, rushing through my veins, an overwhelming tempest of magic erupting throughout my very being. Koratha smiled as she looked at me.

"I will *end* you." I growled. "I will shred your limbs from your body. I will *cut you down* till there's nothing *left* of you!"

"It's about time." She said, drawing her hand back. The beam that soared into the sky halted as she drew it into her body, gasping as it enveloped her. She rose into the air as if possessed. The shadows of black and purple swirled around her in a frenzy, exploding into a pair of smoking wings. Tara joined me at my side, looking up first at Olivia, then to me with concern. I rushed forward, Tara following behind.

Koratha dove into the ground, unleashing a frenzy of shockwaves across the temple. My form lightened, shifting into swirling tracks of light as I blinked from place to place across the floor, dodging and weaving through the attacks to get closer to her. Koratha swatted me away with a wing, knocking me back to the wall with Tara alongside me. I saw her bring her arm back, a streak of black reaching across the floor. Tara stepped in front of me before I could stop her. My heart stopped, thinking in a brief moment that I'd lose her, too.

There was another flash of light moments before impact. A glistening kite shield formed from the light into Tara's hands as she took the brunt of the impact. She grunted, holding firm against the attack. She pushed with her shoulder, deflecting the beam into the ground with a burst of dust and smoke. As the cloud settled, she looked to the shield in surprise, then up to me.

"Calm yourself down, Ortell! You're going to get yourself killed!" Without question, she brought the shield up. Pushing away another attack. She had a Destiny weapon too? My eyes shifted from her to Koratha. If there ever was a time of need, this was it. She looked up at me with gentle, tear-filled eyes. I could see the pain burning in her mind as she defended me. "Keep *yourself* alive, at least." Tara was right. I pursed my lips and focused. Olivia was gone. Even as the sounds of combat rang about me, I knew I would have time to mourn later. Right now, I needed to stay alive. I needed to make sure her sacrifice wasn't in vain. My eyes slowly opened, renewed with focus.

"Cover me!" I shouted.

"Right!" She loosened herself up, the two of us charging forward, screaming as Koratha rose up, diving toward us. Tara blocked with the shield as Koratha drove her blade forward. It skidded to the side as Koratha landed, flipping around to attack us. Her blade would collide with mine, sending waves of raw magic reverberating across the temple. She rose a hand, firing a bolt toward me, but I was ready.

I shifted my shoulder to the side, avoiding the bolt, before droving a beam up into her stomach. It shot her back off me, but she caught herself in the air. I could see the veins in her skin popping out, a deep purple. Her body was literally shredding itself apart with every attack, yet she didn't care. Tara rushed ahead of me, waving off spell after spell slung at her, flapping her wings to launch herself up.

Koratha wasn't able to avoid Tara as her shield struck her from the sky. I ran under them, jumping up, unleashing a barrage of beams and bolts into Koratha. She let out a scream as she fell to the ground. She flipped to her feet as she fell, throwing her sword at me. I blinked to the side, narrowly avoiding her strike. As it hit the ground, she landed, flinging hundreds of small black tendrils at us. I brought a barrier up around me, feeling them strike in against me, struggling to hold them all back. Tara was thrown from the air, crashing into the ground as her shield was pummeled. She rolled away, throwing her shield. It hit Koratha, knocking her from her attack, giving us an opening.

I dropped my barriers, blinking forward to her. She brought her rapier up, our swords locking in a flash of purple and blue. I could see her struggling. This was it. I disengaged as she brought up a barrier, slashing at it. The barrier shattered, knocking her back before I raised my hand, sending a barrage of strands from the World Spirit into her. She slammed into the wall, the last of her magic dissipating. Threads of black and purple peeled from her, eventually leaving only her broken form. She struggled to breathe through gritted teeth. I strode to her, pulling my blade back to finish her. She looked up at me, a softness in her.

"Well then? What are you waiting for?" She asked. "You want me dead, don't you?" She winced, barely able to sit up. "Finish me! Let me *die!*" She shouted, before coughing and hacking up blood to the floor. I shook, trying to hold on to that anger, but as I looked at Olivia's lifeless body, all I could hear were her own words to me, and the words I'd left her with on the Sparrow. I pursed my lips, before thrusting Isngr into the ground, leaning down by Koratha's side and placing a hand over her. Through closed eyes, I looked to see where the magic had done the most of its damage to her. I took a deep breath, beginning to draw the World Spirit through me to heal her. It was stinging a little, but my body had grown strong to the amounts of magic I'd put through it. Koratha looked up at me in at first disappointment, then disgust, but then, sadness.

"No... why?" She asked, trying to reach up to stop me. I pushed her hand away as Tara walked over to me.

"You're... healing her?" She asked.

"I'm not letting her die." I said.

"But why?!" Koratha winced as she tried to speak. "I tortured you. I killed someone you loved. I've done unspeakable-"

"Enough!" I shouted, pushing more magic into her, sealing the wounds on her internal organs. "You said that in another life, things could be *different.* Then make that *this life.*" I said. "You are more than your rage and anger. You *can* be more than those things. Just let go of it, get help, get *out of here* and make something of yourself that isn't *THIS!*" I drew my hand back, standing up.

"William, you're letting her go? Are you crazy? After everything she's done, she..." Tara paused, looking from me to Koratha. She saw a look in my eyes, one of recognition as I looked down at Koratha. "I… I see." She took a step back. "You're sure she won't just go back to doing this again?" She asked. I pointed my sword at Koratha's throat as she laid there.

"Don't get me wrong, I don't forgive you. I don't believe I can. I *hate* you with my whole being." I unsummoned Isngr, reaching out to her. "But I know you can be better than this." She glared at me.

"So I'm just supposed to what, *trust you*?"

"I'm giving you a second chance at life. Giving you a chance to not just be a Soulless Commander, to live a life that isn't fueled by anger and rage." She pursed her lips and closed her eyes.

"I don't deserve it." She said.

"You don't," I said, "but I'm giving it to you anyway." Tears formed in her eyes as she gritted her teeth. She finally took my hand, letting me help her to her feet. She stumbled back against the wall as Tara cautiously kept her weapon pointed at her. I could see the anger washing away from her face as looked into my eyes.

"You won't mention this to anyone?" She asked.

"To everyone else, you'll be dead. Koratha will be gone. You can live your life as whoever you want." She nodded.

"I…" She looked at her hands in shock. "I don't know what to…"

"Just go." I said. "I won't follow, but if you stray, I'll make sure the last thing you see is my blade."

"I understand." She said. She looked at the console. "It's yours. Fair and square." We turned to the console, nodding as she leaned back. Taking a deep breath, I put my hand on it. I began to push my magic into it, the beam from before restoring itself, now with a pure blue. I grimaced as I felt it pull at my body. Even as strong as I'd gotten, it still took a lot of my energy. Finally, I pulled away, feeling drained, but it was active again, and on our side. Tara pulled my arm around her as I stumbled back. I looked up to the edge of the room. Koratha was gone, likely having slipped out unnoticed. Good riddance.

"Come on, big guy. You did good." She said as we stumbled toward the exit. Above us, we could see the Federation ships bolstered with this weapon's energy. The Soulless fleets were being shredded. The Wingless Angel was the first to fall, bursting into flames, before being snuffed out by the vacuum of space. More followed. Soon, knowing they had lost, the Soulless ships began pulling into warp, escaping while they had a chance. Tara just leaned her head on my shoulder as we watched. I looked to Olivia, holding back a well of sadness as I sunk to my knees, Tara following as all we could to was wait and watch.

"We did it." I said. She nodded.

"We did." She looked back at Olivia. "Even if… some of us couldn't make it." I lowered my head.

"We'll make sure they know that without her, we wouldn't be here. Any of us." We stood up, beginning to limp away, wanting to put as much space between ourselves and this place as we could. We may have won, but the victory only felt hollow.

Sol System: Titan

Galactic Date 00:09:096 5028

I let my head hang low as I stood in front of the funeral pyre. I squeezed my fingers together, hearing the rustle of flowers in my hands. Looking up, I took in a long deep breath, watching as the remaining pieces of Olivia burned away, returning to the World Spirit. I let the flowers tip forward before tossing them into the flames as I watched her go.

"So long." I said. "You taught me so many things, gave me so many chances and opportunities. If I could bring you back to say goodbye for real, I would, but," I looked up into the sky past the hangar in front of us. "somehow I feel like you're happier where you are now. Maybe even back with your old crew now." I took a few steps back, feeling Cleva's hands on my shoulders. The rest of the crew, Cleva, Solvemos, even other crews, had all come and joined in for her cremation. We'd made it through the ordeal with almost no casualties but, looking at the three pyres in front of us, I understood that, in war, it would be inevitable. Cleva sighed, looking at the three, before stepping in front of me, turning to face the crews.

"Thank you, everyone, for joining in. May our friends, our brothers and sisters, find their way to peace in lives beyond." She bowed her head. "Now, while we mourn, we must also celebrate their passing as they reunite with the world, and with us as well. Please, partake in food and drink, share their stories. It is our memories of them that keep them alive." As she took steps toward me. The room became abuzz with conversation, the different people and crews beginning to mingle as they moved toward buffet tables set toward the rear of the hangar. Cleva looked down at me, placing a hand on my back to guide me.

"You wanted to talk?" I asked.

"I did. You're the hero of the Battle of Nashu, Soulless Slayer they're calling you."

"I've heard. It's been a lot of attention, honestly." I said. Cleva nodded.

"It is. Not all of it positive either. Don't let these titles get to your head. You have a lot of training left, and now a target on your back with the Soulless." She paused. "Has she appeared yet?"

"Luccia?" I summoned Isngr, feeling her energy stirring within. "She has, a few times, though it took a bit for me to connect with her again." Cleva nodded.

"Good. You'll need her for everything to come. I assume you haven't had time to translate everything from Nashu yet, have you?" She asked.

"Actually," I said, pulling out a data pad, "I sent it off to a contact of mine. They managed to get me everything I needed." Cleva tilted her head.

"A contact? Someone within the Celestials?" I shook my head.

"No. Someone outside. They can be trusted, I promise."

"Do I get to know the identity of this mysterious contact of yours, then?" She asked in a teasing tone.

"Ah, perhaps one day. They aren't too fond of many people knowing about them." I said, scrolling through the images. "However, they got us a lot of good information." I said, showing them to Cleva. "The weapon the Soulless was after wasn't there, nor is it something that can actually kill gods."

"Then what is it?" She asked. I scrolled to what looked like a set of three mirrors being held by the Faraxians.

"These. The Mirrors of Mortality, they called them. They appeared to have been built on Nashu, but moved elsewhere around the galaxy. Apparently, they need stronger magic to function properly."

"Any idea what they do?" She asked. I nodded.

"They can't kill gods, but they do have an effect on them. It seems that they send out a galaxy wide shockwave of sorts, rendering anything within it mortal." I said.

"That is…" Cleva began, but was cut off. Solvemos stormed in, looking at the images.

"Dangerous." He said. "A weapon like that cannot be allowed to exist."

"It's not like we have another choice." I said, looking up at him. "Nothing else we do is going to have any effect on Hilos." Solvemos glanced at Cleva, then to me.

"I dislike the idea of making ourselves as vulnerable to him as he will be to us. This is a bad idea." I narrowed my eyes.

"Thousands of people, no probably millions, have died in your name. They've risked death for you. Be clear with me if you're saying you would not do the same for us." The slits in his helmet seemed to narrow as he turned his gaze toward me.

"You may be a Celestial now, boy, but that does not allow you to speak to me in such a way. You out of line!" He drew his sword on me once again, yet this time, I stood unflinching.

"Is that your answer, then?" I asked. Cleva stepped in between us, lowering her brother's blade.

"William is correct. It is a sacrifice, but it's one we must make. What other choice do we have? Hilos cannot be harmed, much as we cannot right now." She froze, keeping her gaze locked to his. He eventually withdrew his blade, shaking Cleva's hand from his shoulder.

"You *would* take the mortal's side." He glared down at me. "Do what you wish. I will have no part in a suicide mission." He turned, beginning to storm away. "If this galaxy burns, let it be on your shoulders, William Ortell." I watched after him as he left.

"Is this going to be an issue?" I asked.

"I sincerely hope not." Cleva said. "My brother and I have our differences and do not always agree, but it rarely progresses far. I can only hope he isn't blinded by fear enough to see logic." She turned to face me again. "Was that all, William?"

"Not quite. There was one other thing. A mural here." I showed her an image of a picture that portrayed sets of Faraxians worshipping what appeared to be an orange and black globe.

"What is it?"

"We aren't sure yet. Our informant let us know that an artifact looking similar to that was shipped off before our arrival. Whatever it is, it's in the hands of the Soulless now." As I paused, I looked down at that orb. Something about how it was described sent a shiver down my spine. The writing around it described it as giving the power of a god to mortals. I didn't dare tell Cleva this, though. She had enough to worry about for now. She sighed, rubbing the chin of her mask.

"Alright. We will keep an eye out for more information on this artifact. For now, though, your objective is to follow these leads. Scour the galaxy in search for these mirrors and find a way to turn it on the Soulless." I nodded.

"Yes, ma'am." I said, tucking the pad away. I strode away, taking one last look back at Olivia's pyre, giving it a two-finger salute, before gathering everyone back up to meet me on the Sparrow.

With the funeral coming to a close, we had our next mission in hand. Crew had their orders to get the ship ready for launch, and after I'd said my goodbyes to the other crews, I made my way up through the cargo bay; the doors shutting behind me. Up the stairs I went, double timing it down the hall and into the helm. Jewls saluted me from beside the podium, a fresh set of First-Mate patches sewn to her clothes. I saluted her back as I strode forward.

I picked up my newly tailored captain's jacket, sewn with its deep navy blue cloth, swinging it on over my uniform. It was the same as the one Olivia had worn. It fit like a glove. I straightened it out and adjusted my collar as Tara looked up at me.

"Captain, do we have our heading?" I looked out to the galaxy map projected in front of me, scanning over the entirety of it. We had so much left to explore. They could be anywhere in that expanse of stars. Hundreds of thousands of planets that could house the machines. We would need to narrow it down, starting with-

"Set a course for Xenova." I said, tucking my hands behind my back as she began to set in a course. Lux brought us out of the hangars and up into the blackness of space. Tara gave him a thumbs up, and he put his hand on the warp throttle, counting us in.

I had no idea what was in store for us, what the future holds. Yet, as those stars stretched, and we were sent flying through space, all I could say for sure was that, looking at everyone around me, I was hopeful. I had a crew I could trust, and one who looked to me with much of the same sentiment. For what was to come, though, I knew we'd need more people. Our skeleton of a crew was good, but we'd need to fill out our ranks. I sighed, satisfied with all we'd accomplished so far, even with just us. One league of this journey was over, but we had so much left to do, and so, with light in my heart, I welcomed whatever came next.

5028

Journey: Part 1

Nashu: The Viridian Frontier

Galactic Date 00:09:066 5028

To have been a Commander, and to have let this happen to me. To have experienced power unrivaled by anything, and yet still be beaten to submission. I could not help but be riddled with my own rage as I limped away from that temple. That I was alive was, alone, a miracle. I hacked and coughed as I stumbled through the loose silt, dragging myself away from this accursed place.

Blue light pulsed into the sky behind me as I gripped my side. I pushed myself against one of the broken walls as a shockwave hit me, knocking my weakened body into the stone. It appeared William had managed to turn the machine against us. Against the Soulless. I shifted my gaze toward the skies. Was there an "us" anymore, even? I'd failed. My conviction had faltered. There was no way I could return now, I reckoned, as I watched the fleet I had once led broken now under the combined force of the Federation.

I felt broken over their downfall. I, at once, knew that the Soulless' death meant little, yet I feared for my own life. Hilos would not often spare those who failed, especially on tasks as important as this. Even if I were to return now, I knew that would spell disaster for me. William's sparing of my life was now my blessing and my curse.

I thought of his words to me, to the pain and anger that filled his face, and at once I saw a mirror of myself. I saw the hate controlled creature I'd become. Yet still. Even with a sword to my throat, he refused to end my suffering. He begged me to escape and find some sort of forgiveness that he could not give me. How, though, did he expect me to do that? I was a murderer. I'd committed atrocities. I did not deserve even the smallest amount of forgiveness.

A jolt of magic surged from within my body, creating arcs of black and purple that wrapped around me. Pain seared my very being. My breathing caught, and I dropped to the floor, curled up as it wracked me with agonizing shocks. It felt as if it went on for an eternity, paralyzing me outside the temple grounds, before finally passing. I gasped for breath as my body was returned to me. I reached up to the wall, pulling myself to my feet. The pains still ached through my body. What in the hells was that? That magic I had used before, that had taken me over, that had… broken me… It must have had something to do with that.

I had to find help. William had healed me, sure, but I knew that his magic would only go so far. Who, though, would help? Perhaps somewhere I wouldn't be known, where my face would be blank to all that were there. A colony. Yes. Yes, that would have to work for now. I'd take a shuttle to the nearest colony and have them heal me.

I began to move through the grounds of the temple again. Each step hurt now. Whatever that shock was had shaken me to the very core. Maybe it was something William had done to me? Gods, I couldn't be sure of anything now.

No, I had to stay focused. Getting away from here was my priority. If the Soulless found me, I'd be dead, and that went doubly so for any of the Celestials. I glanced into the distance, seeing the group that had been fighting what had once been my crew. They still patrolled the area. I lowered myself below the edge of the broken wall, peaking out at them periodically. None had seemed to notice me. I would be swift and quiet. The shuttle I'd used to get down here would be just beyond the edge of the woods.

Dirt crumbled in my palms as I pushed myself along the edge of the walls. Thunder and lightning crackled through the clouds overhead, while rain drenched my clothes, soaking deep into the fabric. I lowered my head as the sting of the cold water wrapped itself around me, digging into my skin like the icy claws of some unseen beast.

The trees at the edge of the temple grounds met me, finally, with cover from the storms that tormented this place. I looked back at the temple again, leaning against a tree to catch my breath. Another surge of magic wracked my body. I fell against the tree to my side, my arms wrapped over my chest as I struggled against the pain, as I tried not to scream out.

It subsided. I reached up to my collar, ripping away the excess cloth, tossing it to the mud as I chugged breaths of air. It took all I had to not collapse there yet again. I gritted my teeth, sinking my claws into the bark of the tree at my side, forcing myself upright. Water dribbled down past the leaves above me, the droplets almost feeling warm compared to the harsh cold of the wind that blew over my damp clothes. I glanced back again one more time.

I could have won. William had grown… incredibly strong, but he had a lot to learn. The two of them, though? They would be a force to be reckoned with, for sure. I groaned, slamming my fist into a tree, snapping my stride back in the direction of my ship. I never should have let him live, but even when I had all the chances in the world, when I had him trapped in a room, broken at my heels… I couldn't. It was a difficult feeling to explain, but seeing his determination… it gave me almost a sense of hope. Even for a moment, it pushed away my anger.

Then there was everything here. Even when I'd taken someone important from him, he sees it fit to spare my life. I'd turned my back on everything, on everyone, yet in him I'd found an unlikely kinship. I didn't know what I could do now. Still, anger and vengeance burned through me. It had all but consumed me in our battle, but now I was alive… and once again on my own. The Soulless would never take me. Any Celestial who knew my face would kill me on sight. Gods, who knew if *anyone* would really want me now?

I let my head sink forward as fatigue grew in my body. The lasting effects of our battle had worn me thin. I could tell I wouldn't last too long out here if I didn't hurry up. I kicked myself into a jog, a pounding growing in my head with each step into the thick, wet mulch. Through the edge of the forest's end, I could see the starts of my ship, hidden with moss and leaves. I squeezed my way through to the open clearing on the other side, keeling over into the mud, feeling it coat my palms and pants.

Gods, I was so tired.

I mustered up all my strength and gripped the edge of my ship, hauling myself up. Dirt stuck to my muddied palms as I attempted to brush it and the leaves away before quickly giving up. It'd come off in flight, and I didn't have the energy to clear it all myself. So I slowly trudged into the rear entrance to the shuttle.

As I dragged myself down into the pilot's seat, I wiped the mud and dirt off on my pants before leaning down over the console. I had to go somewhere, do something, but I didn't know what. At this point, there was only one thing I *could* do. I needed a healer. Like I'd thought before, a nearby colony would do. I'd go there, wait for the dust to settle. I spun up the galaxy map and plotted a course, giving little thought and care about where I'd end up, and laid back, letting myself sink into the chair.

To go where the world would take me, I suppose that's what I'd do now. It wasn't like I had anywhere else, or anyone else, to turn to. Gods, what had I become?

HAWKING: TANIS COLONY

GALACTIC DATE 00:09:087 5028

I sat at the table of people I didn't know. People I didn't care about. The Actillion family that had taken me in after my escape from Nashu lived in nothing but a rickety shack on this wasteland of a world. My fork poked away at the gruel that passed as an excuse for food on the plate in front of me before stabbing through the thin slab of meat. I think it was supposed to be a steak of some sort, but there was no way to be sure.

Slowly, I raised the food to my lips, sticking it into my mouth. Gods, it was vile. The meat was chewy, laden with grizzle, and over-spiced. My sharp teeth dug and ripped at the chunk of flesh, to no avail. Probably would have been rancid without the abundance of seasoning. I choked down the food as the man, the eldest of the family, looked up at me, his tendrils sucking the food from his fork.

"So, Willow, you've been with us for a week," the man started, "how are you feeling? The wounds from the Soulless seem mostly healed." His name was Jani, a healer of sorts. He was unlike the lifeweavers we'd seen in our ranks and on many of the colony worlds. It was his work that had saved me.

"I'll be fine." I stabbed my fork in for another bite, forcing it down. "Just need my ship repaired and I'll be out of your hair." The woman to his side, Raxis, cocked her head to the side, tucking her hands together.

"So soon? You only just arrived, and those attacks you've been suffering haven't gone away." She said. I sighed, rubbing my eyes.

"I have places I need to be." I set my fork down, pushing the plate back from me, having lost my appetite. "Thank you for bringing me in, but it's going to take a much more powerful healer to stop whatever… the Soulless did to me." Jani shook his head, holding back his offense. You could see it in the way his carapace contorted, wrinkled even.

"I suppose there isn't anything I can do to convince you of more bedrest, is there?" I cupped my hands as he spoke, tucking my nose in between my fingers.

"I don't mean to offend, but I'd rather be anywhere but here." The room was silent, and I shook my head. "Again, I'm grateful for your help, but…" I stood up, pushing my chair in, "I'm not doing any good being out here." Raxis spoke up as I turned toward the door.

"Willow, dear?" My head turned to look back at her.

"Hmm?"

"You're always welcome to come back. I know we haven't known you long, but we always have an open bed for a stranger, or a guest." I nodded, beginning to walk toward the door, when I was once again interrupted.

"Be careful if you're leaving." Jani said. "We heard news of a few Soulless ships that were approaching the system over the past few days. Given how your last run-in ended-"

"I'll be alright… but thank you for the heads up." I finally was allowed to step outside, pushing the door open into the glaring sun of the wasteland, letting the door swing shut behind me. Why anyone would want to live out here was beyond me. All that was on this planet was dirt, sand, and brown.

Then again, Tanahen felt just like this when I was there. Nothing for miles in sight except a stray tribe, or in this case, village. I was lucky to have even found this place. My ship was clipped on its way out of the system and struggled to make the journey. Guess that's what you get when you drive a Soulless ship through a Federation fleet. I doubted there was much that could be done to repair it, but that didn't stop the mechanic from insisting on taking it.

A swift whoosh blew overhead. I looked up, backing into the shadows of the house I'd just left. Two small purple streaks shot across the clear blue sky, unmistakable in their tone. Soulless. I groaned, pursing my lips. Probably here from the battle like I was, but I'd be willing to bet anything they wouldn't be nearly as nice. Wasn't my problem. As soon as I had a ship, I'd be along on my way.

Then again, I wasn't exactly sure on where I'd go. I supposed I could join the coming Soulless. I might even be lucky enough to survive returning to the Plains. On the other hand, I wasn't a fan of the thought of William's sword at my throat. If I knew anything about him now, he wasn't exactly one to go back on his word. So joining them was out of the question, but that left the question on where I'd go next.

I wracked my brain, going over my viable options, walking off toward the mechanic's shop. As far as I could think, there weren't many places I could go. Most people would, thankfully, not know my face, and the new name I'd chosen, Willow, would hopefully put them off my trail further. I could go to Xenova, I'd at least be safe there. I could also just lie low in one of these colonies until the war passed.

On second thought, I'd rather take my chances with the Soulless than to sit aimlessly on my ass waiting for the fighting to blow over. Still, I wasn't exactly left with a lot of options. With a hollow wind passing through the gaps between the houses, I could only tuck my head down and just let my mind wander. Maybe I'd think of something, even if I knew that I'd have to make a choice of my very limited opportunities.

Not paying attention, I smacked into the door of the mechanic's shack, hearing it creak and wobble as I held my nose, feeling a heat and sting emanate from it. I winced and swore, kicking the thin wood with indignation before looking up at the shop. It towered over most of the other small buildings that surrounded it, yet still seemed to fit in just fine. The wind tugged at the hinges on its flapping gates, a metallic rattle and squeak echoing across the emptiness. I wiped my nose and reached forward to the gate, pulling it aside to step in. The heat was no better in here, nor the wind. You could hear it cry as it passed between thin gaps in the walls, pulling and tugging at tools that hung from posts. In the center, my ship hung, suspended from the rafters by a series of pulleys and chains. It looked as if it had been half torn apart.

Just glancing at it, I could see why. I was no engineer, but even I could tell that it was totalled. Warp core was ruptured, main engine looked burnt out. It didn't look good. Someone popped up from within the cockpit, lifting a set of goggles to look at me. The mechanic. I'd met them when I first limped into town. At the time, they were not a friendly sight.

Like me, Khurad was a Draen, but unlike me, he was Oc'r, a white feathered bastard. Just seeing him the first time made my blood boil, but despite my delirious, blood loss induced rants, he was the one to bring me and my ship to the village. As Khurad saw me, he gave me a nod in greeting, sliding off the side of the ship, landing with a *thud* and a cloud of dust. As he brushed himself off, he tossed his goggles aside.

"Willow! Here to check up on your ship?" He asked.

"I'm going to assume that the news isn't good." He shrugged.

"Can't say it is. She's shot, and I don't really have the parts to fix her." He moved to the side of my ship, patting her side. "Whatever you hit, she's beyond my capabilities to repair. Even requesting parts from the Collective would take a while. We only ever get shipments… maybe once a month."

"So I'm out of luck then?" I asked, leaning against the bow of the ship.

"I wouldn't say entirely." He turned, placing his back against the warm metal, aimlessly tapping his fist against the hull. "You could always take a shuttle out of here. The port's a town over, but it's not a long journey. It'd take a day or so by foot, a little less if you could get your hands on a speeder." I raised an eyebrow.

"Do you have one?"

"Of course I do, but it's not something I'm just going to part with." I rolled my eyes. He sighed, looking up at the old ship. "Listen, we take what we can out here. I can, at the very least, offer you a sum of credits to scrap your ship for you. Won't be enough to get you a new one, at least not of this caliber, but it'll get you off planet."

"How much are we talking?" He gave it a moment to think over an offer, stepping back to look at the ship.

"Given what you're handing me, I could easily part with 5k."

"You could easily go higher." He shrugged.

"Sorry, not much market for broken ships." I shook my head, rubbing at the bridge of my nose. "If you don't mind my asking, why are you in such a hurry to get out of here, anyway?" I glanced up at him.

"Just trying to… get out of dodge."

"From the Soulless?" He asked. I hesitated to respond, but eventually nodded. "Hmm." He turned around, rifling through his toolset. "You have any idea where you're going?"

"I was planning on going wherever the ships took me. Not much of a plan from there." Khurad folded his arms over his chest, leaning his head down.

"I see, a wanderer then. This war's created a lot of those, especially of our kind."

"Our kind?"

"Draens. Me included." He said, tipping his head up, pulling down the front of his collar. He was branded, but it wasn't a slave mark like the one I had.

"What's that supposed to mean?" I asked. Khurad chuckled, pulling a cigarette from his rear pocket, tucking it between his lips. He lit it with the flick of a lighter, keeping his eyes closed. Then he took a long deep draw in before letting out a puff of smoke.

"Surprised you don't know. Traitor brand. I used to be a slave runner. Slipped people out of shitty situations, and into better ones." He looked to my lack of wings. "I assume you were a slave, since you're docked." I pursed my lips as I thought on how to respond. Never heard of a slave runner before, let alone of a traitor brand.

"I was, but I'm not familiar with you or your people."

"Then you got out before we started our whole operation." He sighed, tapping a curled fist against the wooden support he leaned on. "I saw enough hell when I was there. After being caught and branded, I was practically run off planet." I glanced outside to the empty wastes.

"And so you ran. Got as far as you could from the people who saw you as a traitor."

"You speak from experience."

"I can empathize. I'll say that much." The two of us sat in silence as he puffed at his cigarette. Eventually, he spoke again.

"You look like the type of person who knows their way around a fight. At the very least, you managed to get off of Draenica, and if your story's true, you were out there fighting Soulless."

"I guess you could say I know my way around a gun and a blade." He hummed at me as I said this, tapping his hand to his chin. "Something interesting about that to you?"

"Well, it's up to you, but if you're lacking direction, I might have a solution for you." I raised an eyebrow, keeping my arms folded over my chest.

"Consider my interest piqued."

"Alright, I'll consider it." He pushed himself up from the pillar. "It's not exactly the best solution, but take this." He leaned behind him, pulling open a rusty old drawer from his workbench. From within, he dragged a dusted up piece of paper, handing it to me. I cocked my head to the side curiously as I took it over.

"The… Draenitian rebellion?" I looked up at him, pursing my lips. "You can't seriously be suggesting I go back, are you?!" I shoved the paper back into his chest, my face contorted in disgust. "After I did all I could to get the hell off of that planet, you seriously expect me to just turn around and go back?"

"People are fighting for their right as living creatures over there. You should understand that." He said. I rolled my eyes, beginning to storm out. He groaned. "Fine, it's your choice, but before you go," he tossed me a card. I caught it, "the money for the ship." I didn't say anything as I pocketed the chip, ready to leave for the town he spoke of.

As I pushed open the gate, however, my eyes widened. Crunching footsteps echoed across the town as three Soulless soldiers stalked the main road. I gasped, pulling the door back. Khurad was at my side at a moment's notice, peaking out of the cracks in his shack.

"Damnit! What the hell are the Soulless doing here?" He whispered. My brow furrowed, but I didn't answer his question. They patrolled with weapons drawn, but not a soul was in sight. I could only hope that they would give up and search somewhere else. I wasn't expecting them to get here so quickly.

"Alright! This is going to be how it works!" One of them shouted from beneath their helmet. "You're going to give us your food, your water, and your credits! If none of you are out in the next minute, we'll just have to resort to some… less savory methods!" I gritted my teeth. They were being damned unprofessional. We trained them better than to stoop to the level of common bandits and thieves, even I knew that.

"What's the plan, Willow?" Khurad asked.

"You're looking at me?" I put a hand over my chest as I looked back and up at him.

"You're the one here with combat experience. You wanna run, you say the word, and we're out of here."

"Possibly. There's only three of them, though..." I narrowed my eyes as I turned to look back out. They were already approaching one of the houses. It'd barely been a few seconds, and already they were trying to break down the doors. I pursed my lips as the hinges fell off with ease, the soldier marching in. Gunfire rang through the empty village, and screaming filled our ears.

"Fucking hells, they'll slaughter everyone..." Khurad said. "You have to do something!" My eyes glared back up at him.

"And why do I need to be the one to? They should have brought out what was asked of them!" Khurad looked at me with disbelief.

"You're really going to just let these people die? Sitting on the sidelines of Draenica, I understand, but here? You said there were *only* three, as if you knew you could take them."

"I could." I said.

"Then why not?!" His voice was barely above a whisper, but I stood, clapping my hand over his mouth.

"Because it's not my fight!" I slowly lowered my hand. "If I get involved, then I put a label on my head that I don't need." I took a step back as he looked at me with the same disgust that I had given him moments before.

"Fine. Just sit on the sidelines and be a nobody, then! Rot in hell like the coward you are!" He shooed me with an open hand before peering outside. He was reaching around behind him to a primitive looking pistol. Gods, if he went out there, he'd get himself killed. My eyes burnt as I glared at him. But realization dawned on me as his words stung me.

A coward? Is that what I'd become? All I'd done was run. The Soulless wouldn't take me, the Celestials would kill me on the spot, and yet here I was trying to find some way out of all that. He was right. I'd grown lazy and cowardly. So what, I was beaten by

William? He wanted me to live and be more than I was? Then I would. I took a few strides forward to Khurad with a groan.

"I'm going to need a gun." I held out a hand expectantly. He narrowed his eyes, but reached to the holster at his back, slapping a pistol and shield generator into my palm. I examined them carefully. I wanted to avoid using my magic as much as possible. Between whatever curse was affecting me, and the people here seeing me for what I really was, it would be best to keep it as a last resort.

Satisfied with the weapon, I held it loosely at my side, activated the shield, and drew my rapier. I turned to the door, taking a few strides toward it before stopping.

"Keep the door closed. Don't come outside till they're taken care of, no matter what happens." I said. He nodded, and I pulled the gate open, letting it swing closed behind me. All was silent but the rattle of the wooden blinds on their rusted hinges, and that hollow wind that separated me from the lot of them. As their gazes slowly turned up toward me, I knew it was my last chance to back down. I could still join them and attempt to get my old life back.

There are few words that rang true more than Khurad's, though. I was a coward if I went back now. I'd be running from everything that made me who I was, just as I had been before. It'd been made sure I knew that.

"Well, well! Looks like someone's finally come out to greet us!" One of them said.

"I thought Soulless were supposed to act with a little more professionalism!" I called back, standing my ground at the far end of the street, a dozen meters between us. The three looked between each other, before looking back at me.

"Oh? And what do you know about being a Soulless then?" Another called. I took a deep breath, eying each of them. They must have been vets to be acting like this. The oldest ones were always the cockiest. Even with their personality wiped at conversion, it didn't stop them from developing into this. I'd seen it too many times to count, often from my fellow officers. Being vets, though, I'd have to be a lot more careful.

"I think she's itching for a fight. She don't got any food on her to hand to us!" The third finally spoke up, their voice heavy with a Terra Novan accent. I tightened my jaw, adjusting my grip on the gun.

"Consider this your one and only warning to leave this place! If I need to put you in the dust, I'll do so!" The men scoffed at me, nudging each other. One of them raised their rifle, pointing it in my direction as if I were some creature to be hunted for sport. I guess that was their answer then.

I dove behind the stone bricks of a nearby well, hearing blaster bolts strike behind and beside me. Pieces of rock burst upward, raining dust on me. I gritted my teeth as I stood from my cover, firing on them. The bullets from my gun struck their shields, bouncing clean off. The men laughed as I ducked back behind another building, quickly spilling out empty casings and reloading.

"Really think that's going to do anything to us?!" One of them called out. "We have military grade weapons. Your little pistol's useless!" My eyes narrowed as I listened from my hiding spot. They were approaching me. I tucked the pistol into my belt, prepping my rapier. I felt so powerless without my magic. Maybe I didn't need to be, though. I knew those shields inside and out, knew what made them tick, knew what would likely get through them.

I peaked out to get a good glimpse at them. Two of them were in light uniforms, and one in heavier armor. If I infused the bullets with magic, they'd be able to pass through the shield. The two without armor would be easy to bring down, but the last one… he'd be an issue. I'd have to think about that when the time came.

I thrust my rapier into the dirt, grabbing the pistol again. With a single deft move, I moved back into the street. My hand shifted over the side of the pistol as I pushed magic from within me, charging up the weapon. I winced, feeling the pulses of that accursed affliction baring its fangs against me, but I kept myself strong. Dust rose from the ground as I skidded out of my hiding place, blurring their visions. I could taste the grit of dirt on my lips as time seemed to slow. I brought the gun up, then fired.

One, two, six shots loosed. Black streaks of magic soared through the air, too thin for normal eyes to see, striking my targets. The two Soulless flanking the armored man felt the sting of my shots as the magic-infused bullets ripped straight through their shields. They stumbled back before falling to the ground. I dumped the bullets to the ground, reloading as I eyed the last of them.

The final soldier halted as the dust cleared, looking back at his two fallen allies as I stood up straight. Still, I could feel that magic backfiring across my body. Even such a small cast was triggering it, and just looking at this man, I doubted I'd be able to pierce his armor with just a few bullets and a sword. The soldier removed his helmet, revealing a heavyset Terran man with gangly brown hair and bushy eyebrows.

"Nifty trick you have there…" he said, turning his gaze back to me, "Turncoat." My eyes went wide. Turncoat? Shit. He must have seen the magic. "What are you going to do when these people find out who you really are?" He asked, ensuring he was loud enough for half the town to hear. "What do you plan on doing? Where do you plan on going?!" I could feel the anger boiling up in my chest, the magic within me wanting to bubble over. Then it hit me. Another wave of that magical backlash, this one worse than the last.

I keeled over, the sparks and arcs of magic coursing through my body again. There wasn't anything I could do as the man waltzed over to me, bringing his foot up and across my face. I flew back, rolling across the dirt. The wind was knocked from me, and the waves of pain hadn't yet ceased.

"I left that life behind me!" I tried to yell through gritted teeth. The man could only laugh.

"Left it behind? You know we can't do that! We're Soulless! There's no running from what you or any of us have done!" The pain was subsiding, and I could see people beginning to exit their homes, watching the ensuing battle. The man picked me up, gripping my collar, and threw me back into the well. The stone cracked as I slammed into it, my shield fizzling, trying to keep itself up.

Slowly, I pushed myself to my feet, fighting through the pain that filled my body. That had to have cracked at least a few bones. I could feel myself heaving with my breaths. I glanced around at the people around the town. They looked at us both with fearful eyes. He grinned, putting his hands up in a taunt.

"Well? What're you going to do, then?" He called. "Backed into a corner with no way out. They know your secret now! I *know* you have more fight in you than that!" Something in me slipped as he eagerly pushed me on. Silence enveloped the air as my hairs stood on end. A cold, empty chill seeped from the ground. I glared through lowered eyes, thrusting my hand out to my side. Magic coursed through the air, dragging my rapier to me as rage overwhelmed me. My shadow appeared to stretch as I approached him. His grin faded quickly as realization dawned on his face.

"Wait a minute. It's you." He took a step away from me. "Y-you're dead. We were all told that they killed you."

"Clearly they were wrong." Within the blink of an eye, I had teleported within range of him, drawing the tip of my rapier to his throat. His body lifted from the ground as black tendrils of magic constricted him, squeezing him tight. My lips twitched into an angry grimace as I looked up into him, a primal rage coursing through me. "I wanted nothing but to be left alone! Wished to make a new life!" I squeezed him tighter, his face growing red. "Then you *had* to come." I drew my fingers back. "I warned you what would come if you did not leave." He shook his head frantically, begging till the very moment I brought my fingers together. Black spikes drove their way through his body from all sides. His head fell limp as blood pooled across the desert sands, seeping into the dirt. Yet despite the power that filled me, his death brought no pleasure.

I withdrew my hand, letting his body fall to the ground, his skin and blood blackened. Another wave of agony forced me to my knees, and I could feel the warmth of blue blood dripping from my nose, pooling at my lips. There was silence from the village as I kneeled there, letting the waves of pain wash over me. White hot searing heat burned at my skin, at my muscles, down through every fiber of my body. I could hear ringing, taste metal in my mouth as I lay there, curled over.

A divine punishment. That's the only thing I could describe it as. That was the only thing it could be. Any time I used my magic, I would be struck by this… *thing.* This was the worst I'd felt it, worse even than the first times. I struggled to even breathe as I sat there on my hands and knees.

Eventually, as with always, the pain passed, and I stood up, leaning back against the well, my hand over my chest. I looked out over the run down town that had taken me in. Three corpses lie in the street, and every face that watched from their homes looked on at me in abject horror. I didn't know who that soldier was, but they were right. There was no running from who I was or what I did. It would stick with me till the day I died.

My face softened as the magic faded from me, and I pushed myself up. I didn't know where I planned on going, without a ship and without anyone who trusted me, but I began to walk. My plan was to just leave town and go wherever my feet would take me.

"Willow!" Khurad called, appearing from behind the gates of his home. I barely gave him a second glance, continuing to walk. He put a hand on my shoulder. The two of us stopped, yet I didn't turn to face him.

"What?"

"That was… incredible! I've rightly never seen anything like it!" He patted my back. I looked up at him with confusion and tiredness.

"It was a form of dark magic gifted to me by the god Hilos. There's little 'incredible' about it." He pursed his lips.

"Listen, Soulless or not, you saved our hides." He looked out at the people of the town. "Even if they're afraid of you, *I'm* grateful." I didn't respond, and he sighed. "Listen, it doesn't take much to see that you aren't one of them. I don't care who you were then, and I don't think I particularly want to. I'm a man who cares about who and what you do now."

"Sincerely?" I asked.

"Absolutely." He told me with a nod. "Your past is yours to know, and if it's not something you want to talk about, then it's a skeleton in the closet. We all have 'em." I looked out at the sunset as he put a hand on my shoulder. "I can tell you're going through some shit, trying to better yourself."

“Something like that…”

“We all falter and fall. Some longer than others, and some harder. I respect you giving this path a chance.” He turned to look out at the empty wastes ahead of us. “Any idea where you’re going next?” I thought it over and then nodded.

“I do.”

“Hmm?” He raised an eyebrow as I reached to his shirt pocket, pulling the paper he’d tried handing me before, waving it in his face.

“I’m going back to Draenica.”

Draenica:
Hope
Galactic Date 00:09:120 5028

The shuttles from Tanis Colony to Draenica took days. I was used to sleeping aboard the Wingless Angel in the utmost of comfort. In the cheap cotts of these small ships, it felt like I was sleeping on a rock most of the way. Anxiety poked and prodded at my mind, anyway. I hadn't been back since I'd escaped my slavery. Every time I closed my eyes, I got flashes of the life I'd left behind.

The battle between William and me weighed on me the most. The woman I'd accidentally killed, his face so filled with anger and hatred for me. I was still that person now, a killer fueled by an unjust vengeance against a galaxy that wronged her. It only seemed right to send William the information I'd collected on

Nashu. It wouldn't fix all the wrong I had done, but I could only hope that it would be a start. One thing rested uncomfortably in the back of my mind, though. That artifact I'd sent back to the Soulless… Something was off about it. It almost… shivered against my touch, as if it wanted to reach into me. I could only hope it would amount to little more than another curiosity.

Unconsciously, the closer we got, the more my hands would stray toward my shoulders, feeling at the remnants of my wings. I could only wish that I could feel them there again. Yet I knew that this was the whole reason I had to come back. There was no way I could truly redeem myself, but I could make sure no one else ended up how I had.

And so when the shuttle began to pull into Draenica's atmosphere, I rose to my feet, one of only a few people stuffed into the cramped ship. Through the windows, I watched as clouds passed us by, making way to the volcanic blackness of my homeworld. I can't say I missed it.

Gold tinted buildings rose from the planet's capitol, Hope, as we descended toward it. I braced myself mentally as I gripped the railing at the ship's ceiling, waiting as we pulled into port. The doors slid open, making my way to the hot, sulphurous air. I breathed in my first breaths of my old home.

Already, before I could leave, I could see the contact Khurad had informed me of before I left. They were going to get me into the Resistance. To think I'd left one war only to throw myself into another. At least this time, I hoped I was on the right side. Our eyes met, and they waved at me, beckoning me to them. I smiled for the first time in what seemed like an eternity.

I took my first steps off that ship, leaving my old name, my old life, everything that I was behind me. In that moment, I took my first steps onto Draenica and into my new life.

Appendix:

Species Database: Draens

Home Planet: Draenica

Star System: Blackwater

Sector: Syrius Supercluster

Supporting Governments: Universal Republic,

Appearance and Biology

Draen biology is most similar to that of birds. They have a four-chamber heart, like most mammals, with light, hollow bones with small strut like pieces crisscrossing within the bones to reduce the weight of their bodies. They have long feathered wings that stretch from their backs, the typical wingspan usually equaling twice their height. Their eyes are either solid green or a dark orange and have a membrane called a tapetum lucidum. This membrane reflects a lot of the light back toward their iris to improve their night vision. During the day, this membrane pulls back like an eyelid.

Draens are found in usually either black or white, and are heavily feathered, with rough skin. The black toned Draens are known as the Frev'n, while the white Draens are known as the Oc'r. Biologically, there is almost no difference, the only one being in the color of feathers and skin. The only fundamental difference is that the Oc'r were adapted to snowy climates in the Northern sections of Draenica, and blended into the thick powder while hunting prey, while the Frev'n were nocturnal hunters in the forests below. The black skin and feathers allowed them to camouflage into the darkness of the giant mushroom forests of the lowlands. Being aerial predators, typically, they would hide in trees, or on top of mushrooms, hanging onto branches with their tails, and swooping down and snatching their prey.

In gender, you will find a mix between male and female throughout the planet, though, similar to humans, the percentage of females over males is slightly higher.

CULTURE

For Draens, music and writing are sacred. To an outsider, the common music for Draens is often described off-putting, made primarily of polyrhythmic percussion and microtonal melodies. They used mainly wind instruments made from a form of purple heart wood indigenous to their planet, while in their most common musical form, Darmshi, three pitched drums play conflicting rhythms over each other. The wood of the flutes is primarily purple, laced with thin stripes of red throughout. This wood had a very hearty and deep, resonant tone. The craftspeople who made these instruments were highly revered, and each one usually was unique with depictions of mythical events.

They are extremely poetic in writing, but most of their pieces retain a sad and hopeful undertone. It must be understood that the Frev'n are often enslaved by Oc'r and, as such, the only way for them to escape from that world is through writing and music. Dance, as such, is another form that you find most Frev'n very fluent in. Traditional dances were done as if chained to one another, and are fairly simple, yet very expressive.

On the topic, culture between Frev'n and Oc'r Draens varies drastically due to their circumstances. Frev'n are typically distrusting of most people, though will latch to people who can earn their trust. This is especially true of those who have been released from, or who have escaped slavery under the Oc'r. It is important to note that they rarely find company with other Draens, but rather to people of other races. A notable example in history is Verabille Tor, a noted assassin, finding close kinship to Natasha Krugov, a Furin thief, a race thought to be mortal enemies with Draens due to strained pasts. It should also be noted that, because of their troublesome past, most Frev'n that escape slavery turn to crime of other sorts. Most of them find themselves especially well suited as assassins, or stealth reconnaissance experts, for those who join the military.

For some very unlucky Frev'n who attempt to escape, a few Oc'r Masters turn to amputating their wings in a process known as docking to prevent them from flying away or attempting to escape again. Because of some incidents with Frev'n slaughtering their masters after such events, it has become less commonplace, though the practice still exists. It is important to understand that a Draen's wings are a strong part of their identity, and thus removing them is, in a way, removing their right to their identity.

Oc'r culture is split between those defending the slavery of Frev'n and those who stand against it. By the current day, the amount of Oc'r who actively keep and trade slaves is much fewer, but it is still a common problem. More so now, you will see Oc'r attacking slave trade caravans to free slaves before they can reach new masters. This is considered illegal by Draen governments, and can be punished by life in prison, and prison in Draenica is the last place you want to be.

Draenica is one of the harshest homeworld environments in the known galaxy. While Ordelia has its vast deserts, Draenica is ravaged by volcanic activity, and animals that have adapted themselves to deal with the constant fall of ash and dust on the lower plains. The planetside is cracked and split apart by fissures. The prisons themselves are placed above these fissures, held up by large steel struts. The only way in or out is through the front or down into the crevice below. Heat from within the surface of the planet makes these prisons unbearably hot and humid. The overly humid environment prevents most Draens from flying. If they fall, they die.

The harsh environments, which have prevailed since as long as any species have known the Draens, forced Oc'r into tighter knit communities. Cities that existed closer to the ground were walled off and maintained environmental shields that protected them from the constant ash. The homes and buildings in these cities range in material from shotty wood structures in smaller shanty towns, to tall steel structures in the largest of cities. The environmental shields were adapted from the technology Xenovan's used to reroute their moon's constant acid rain around the city and into the ocean below. While the Xenovan's environmental shields spanned across their entire moon, the Draen's smaller shields were designed to only protect the small area of a village. For larger cities, special manufacturers created taller towers that could span the diameter of the city.

On the higher plains of Draenica, safe from the volcanic lowlands, lies a much different story. Draenica's capital, Hope, remains a major trade connection for all races. Despite the outward appearance of the city, of which reflects a general calmness and grandiosity, the underbelly still hides a lot of the problems that exist on the lower plains. Slave trade is still a major issue, despite its practice being outlawed in the capital. Rings are brought down daily, though most slaves are just sent out to the lower plains. Due to this, and many other transgressions and disagreements, Draenica is fractured among its people, and has yet to show an ability to unite under singular ideals. At the time of the second Soulless Celestial War, an underground Civil War is ongoing on Draenica, in the attempt to oppose the slave trade, and unless it is settled, unity looks to be an impossibility.

PRONUNCIATIONS

Furelle: Fyur-el

Isngr: Iss-ing-ur

Luccia: Loo-shah

Koratha: Kor-ah-thah

Iraka: Ee-rah-kah

Gatha: Gah-thah

Arneli: Ar-ne-lee

Maurel: Mow-rel

Cleva: Klay-vah

Solvemos: Sohl-vay-moes

Hilos: Heye-lohs

Art

WILLIAM ORTELL

Tara Verikov

OLIVIA STERLING

KORATHA WILLOW

Cleva

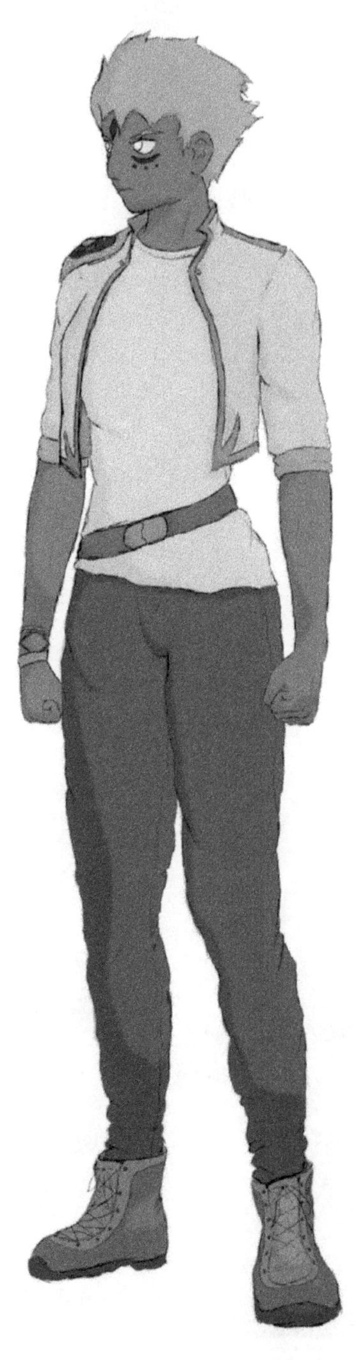

Jewls Reynar

Draens

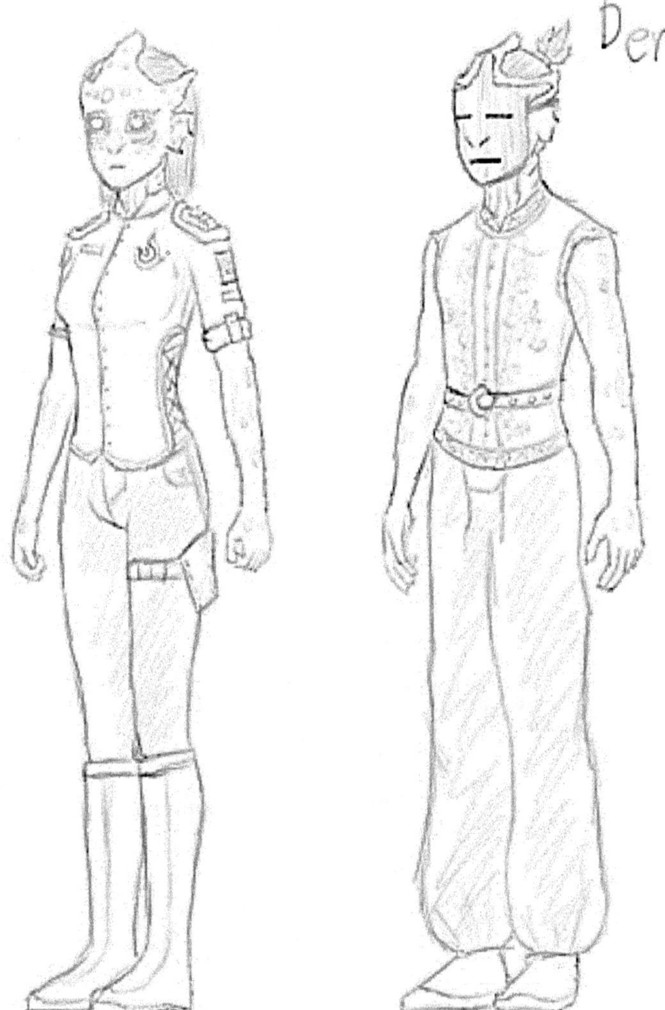
Dervans

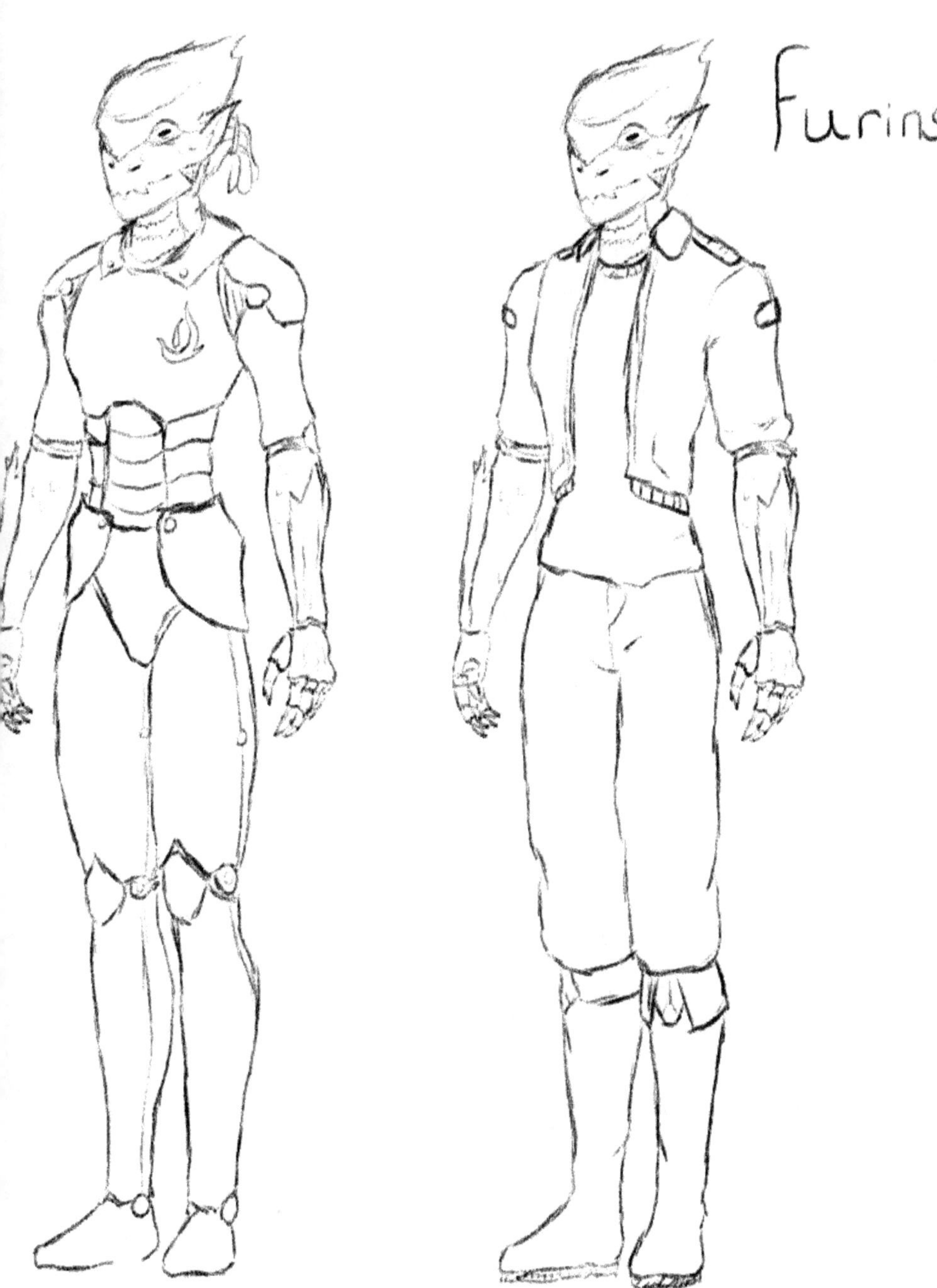
Furins

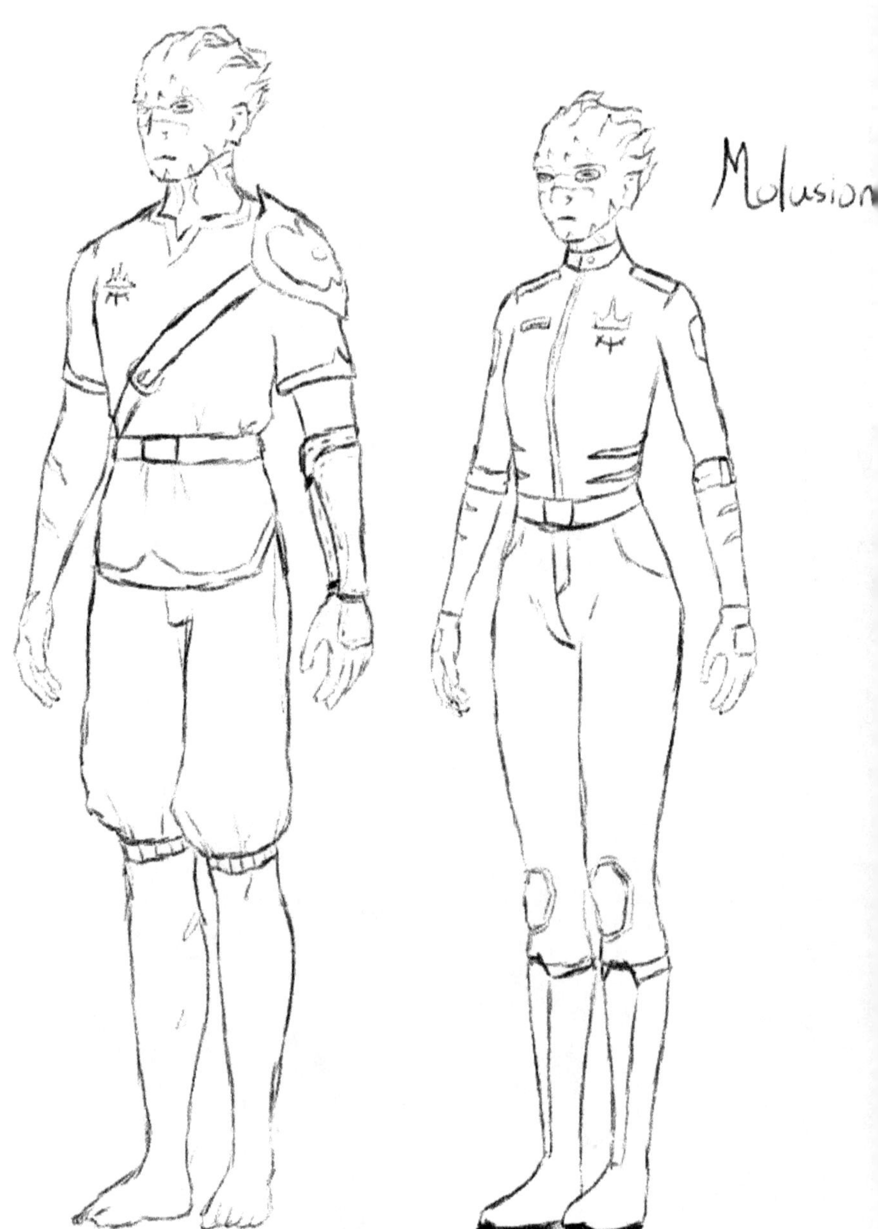
Molusion

Olari

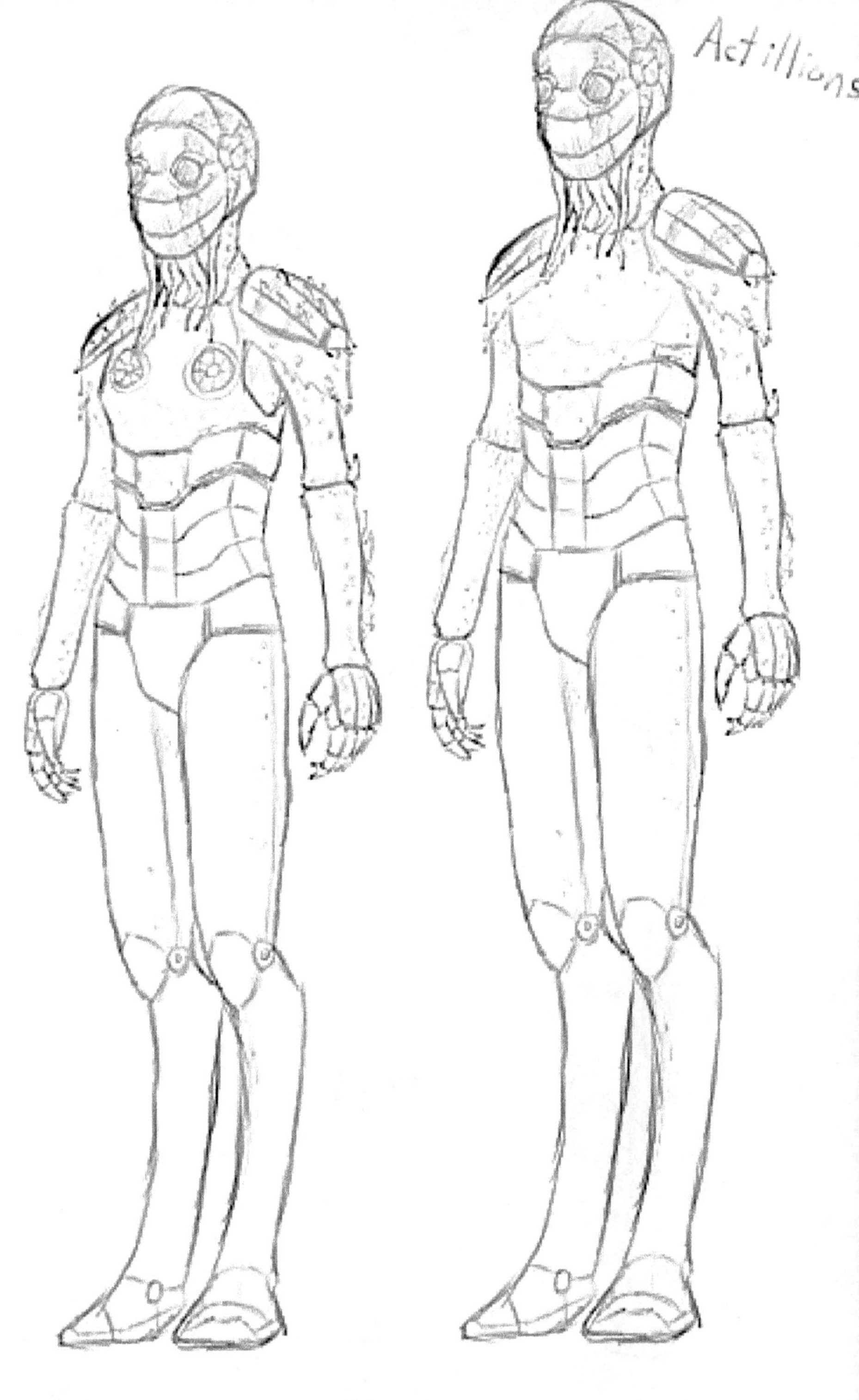
Actillions

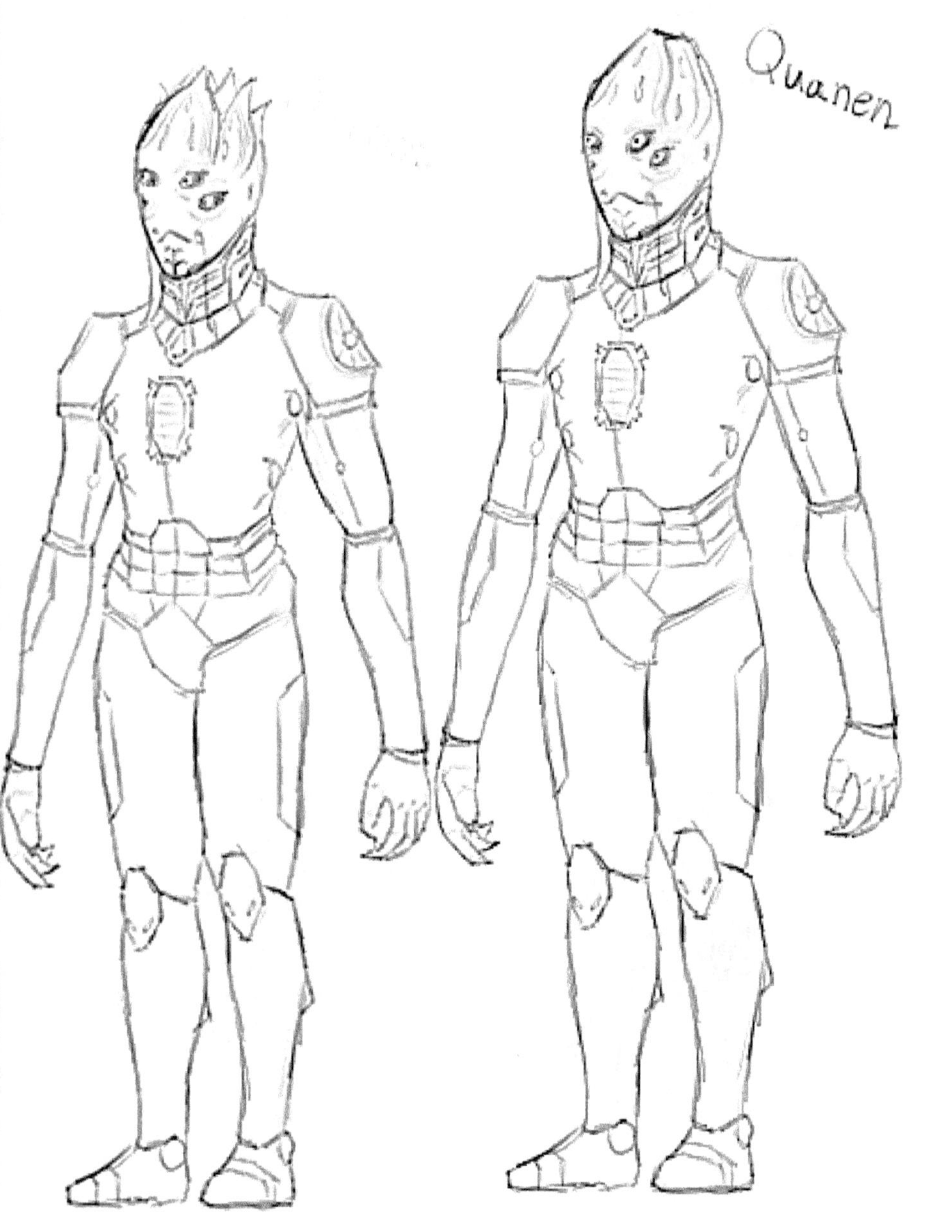
Quanen

Iku

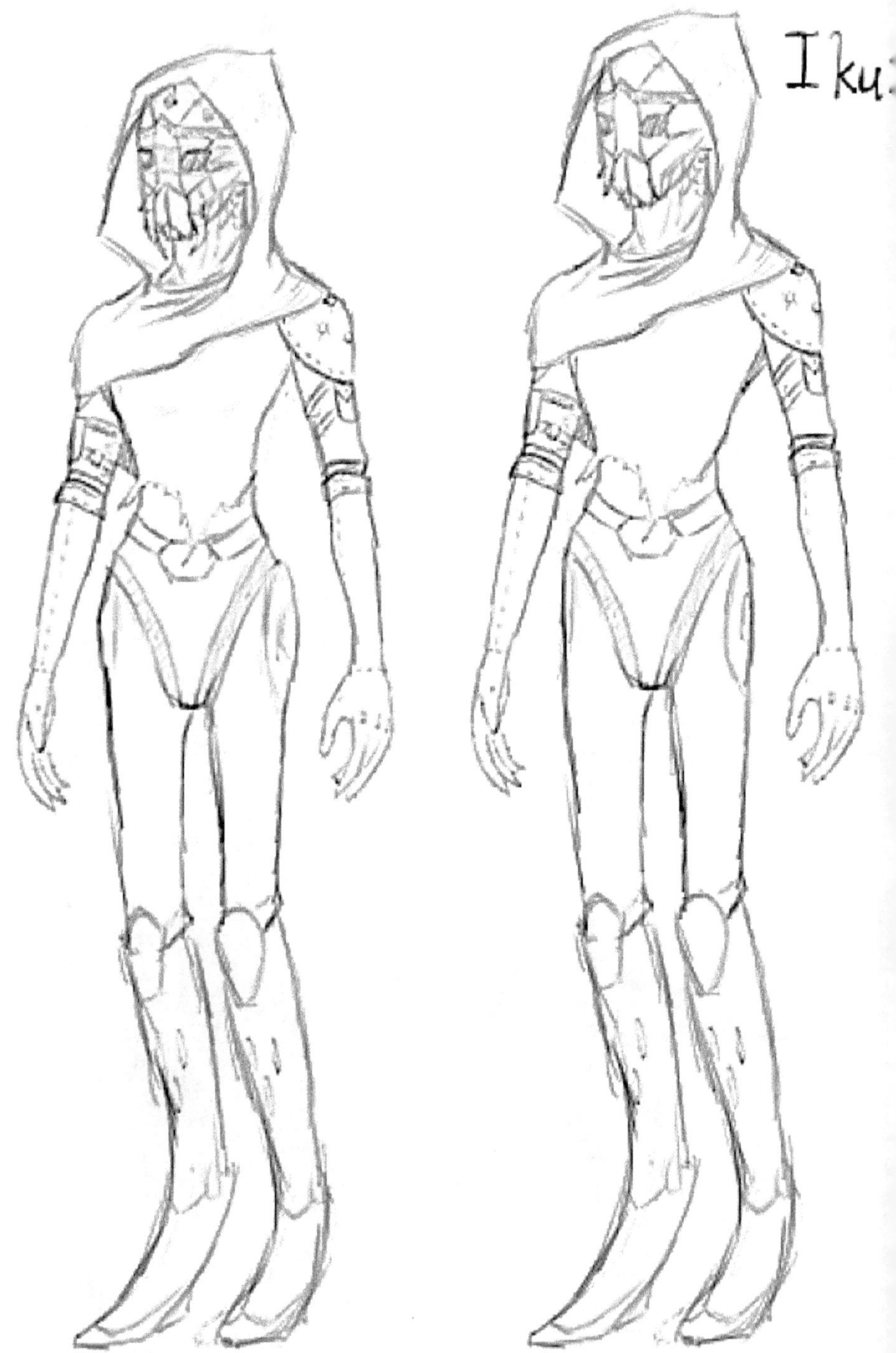

Kinth

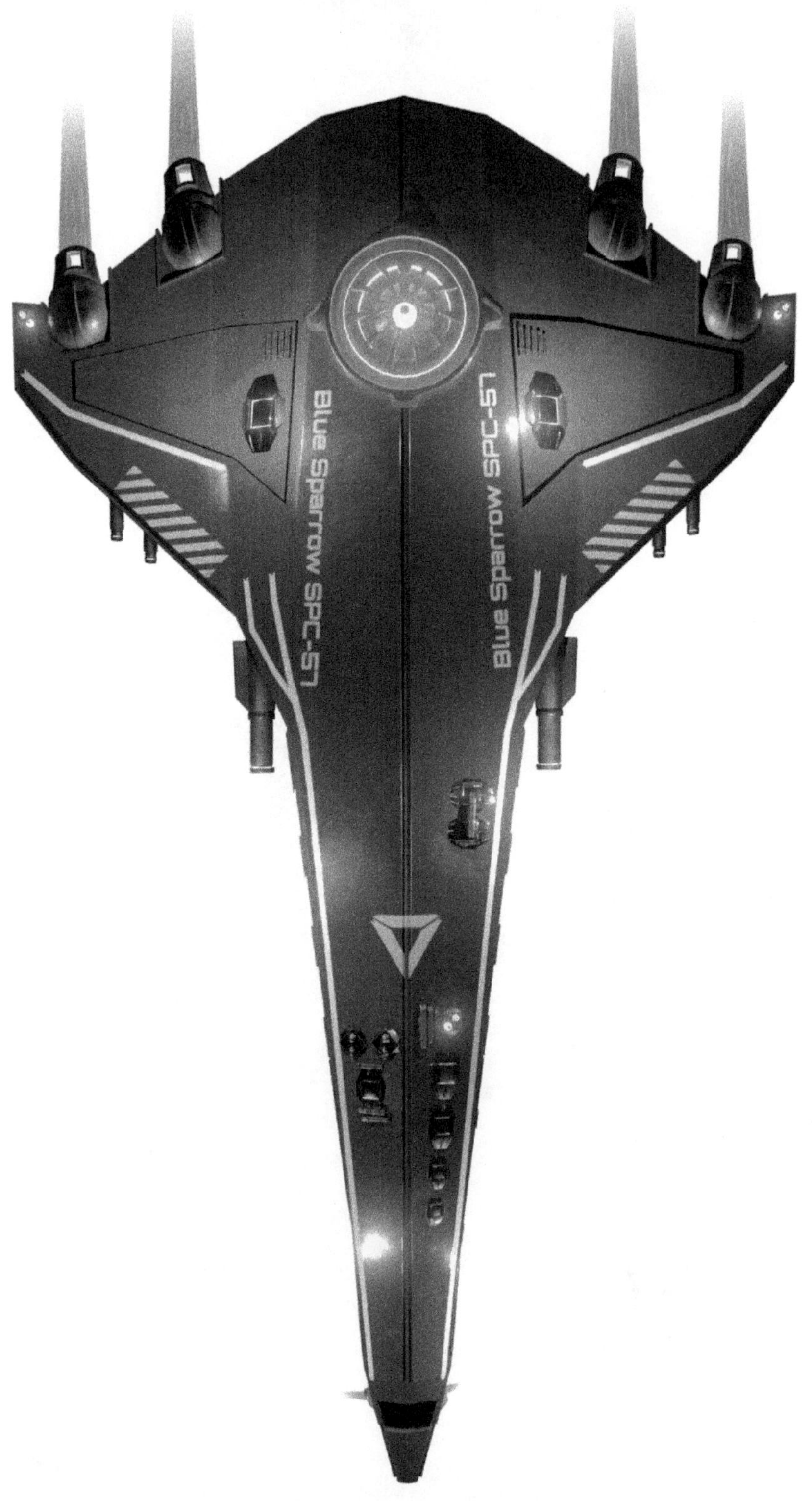
Blue Sparrow SPC-57
Blue Sparrow SPC-57